RED HORIZON

A PROSECUTION FORCE THRILLER

LOGAN RYLES

SEVERN RIVER
PUBLISHING

Severn River Publishing
SevernRiverBooks.com

ISBN: 978-1-64875-722-8 (Paperback)

ALSO BY LOGAN RYLES

The Prosecution Force Series

Brink of War

First Strike

Election Day

Failed State

Firestorm

White Alert

Nuclear Nation

Fallout

Full Dark

Red Horizon

The Reed Montgomery Series

The Ian Hale Series

Line of Fire

Path of Terror

Price of Allegiance

Dogs of War

To find out more about Logan Ryles and his books, visit

severnriverbooks.com

1

Narva, Estonia

Death rained from the eastern horizon.

It began two hours before sunrise, with incoming Kh-101 cruise missiles appearing as orange streaks, flying only fifty to a hundred meters off the ground as they circumvented ground radar and zipped toward their targets.

A soft scream. A flash of exhaust. A moment of perfect silence as a city of fifty-three thousand civilians and some thirty-four thousand ground troops held their breath.

Then thunder detonated on the Estonian-Russian border, plumes of fire ripping toward the sky as buildings exploded. Cars flipped. Homes and roadways collapsed. Schools and hospitals caved in.

And still, the missiles just kept falling. Hundreds of them, slicing toward predestined targets and unleashing four-hundred-kilogram payloads of high explosives that hurled shrapnel like shotgun blasts. So many buildings burned that many streets appeared as bright as day. The shudders of detonating warheads were so persistent that the ground trembled—a perpetual, man-made earthquake of destruction that began and would not stop.

And that was just the first wave. Seated in a concrete bunker at the emergency defense base established just half a mile north of Narva, Korporel Jaan Saar of the Estonian Defense Force monitored a sweeping radar screen and could actually *see* the Russian military as it mobilized. Gathered just across the border, the swarm of hostile ground troops, armor, and attack helicopters had gathered for weeks, swelling to a force nearly a quarter the size of the entire population of Estonia. While NATO command scrambled and Estonian generals rushed to bolster domestic defenses, the dread that consumed the tiny Baltic nation grew palpable.

Like a cloud. Like a toxic fog that swarmed Saar's hometown of Tartu and left his aging mother wringing her hands. His young wife clinging to their newborn son, eyes wide with fright as she watched the twenty-four-hour news stream reporting Russian incursions of Georgia, Azerbaijan, and then Armenia. Russian threats pouring west out of Moscow.

Into a Western-allied Europe that was left desperate, helpless to answer.

As a *Seireoperaator*, or surveillance specialist, Saar could have been sent anywhere. His wife, a devout Lutheran, prayed for him to be deployed someplace in the west, hundreds of kilometers from the swell of Russian aggression. Maybe even out of Estonia altogether, lent to a NATO ally who needed a radar operator.

But Saar wouldn't have accepted an international transfer even if one had been offered. He'd seen what the Russians had done in Crimea, Ukraine, and then the Caucasus. Once Moscow obtained a footing, there was no reversing the tidal wave.

The Russians had to be stopped at the threshold—at the very first inch of sovereign Estonian soil. That effort might well be a fool's errand, but Jaan Saar had seen the future in his eight-month-old son's eyes. The hope of a life free from tyrannical threats and military terror. A dream worth dying for—worth running to the front lines.

So when the orders came, even when his wife broke down into sobs, Saar didn't hesitate. He reported to Narva, ranks of Estonian soldiers already outnumbered nearly ten-to-one. He strapped on a bulletproof vest and a Kevlar helmet. He clutched the cross necklace his wife had given him and prayed for her. For his son. For his country.

Not for himself—Jaan Saar never prayed for himself. He took his post behind the radar equipment as the cruise missiles reduced a proud Baltic city to chaos. Bodies stacked, and frantic radio chatter poured from the ground units scattered around the city. In vain the anti-aircraft divisions turned 23mm Soviet-era guns on the whining missiles, hoping to knock them out of the sky before they could land. But with the enemy ordnance flying at speeds of nearly nine hundred kilometers per hour, hitting them midair was like trying to hit a mosquito with a spit wad.

It was over before it began. Saar watched as one Estonian position after another was overcome by wilting fire, the semicircle of destruction bending ever outward of downtown. Turning northward.

Turning toward him.

Every man in the radar post knew what was about to happen before it did. A sudden calm fell over the room as the latest wave of missiles fell within two hundred meters of the bunker, decimating an aircraft hangar. In unison each soldier looked up from their screen, turning their gaze toward the concrete ceiling above—poured only two weeks prior, not yet fully cured. An imperfect defense against absolute wrath.

The world stood still. Saar blinked, and a single tear slipped from his eye.

When the next wave fell, the Estonian radar position was blown into eternity.

2

The White House
Washington, DC

President Maggie Trousdale was wide awake when the phone next to her bed rang. The room was dark and she'd lain alone for nearly an hour, staring at the ceiling as trickles of sweat dripped from her forehead and onto her pillow.

It wasn't hot in the White House. In fact, it was almost chilly. With the climate control pumping, Maggie's body alternated between washes of heat and shivers that reached from her scalp to her toes. Impulsive, irresistible, and painful. She swallowed and closed her eyes, steeling her mind with words she had memorized as a small child.

The Rosary. A prayer her Catholic mother had taught her but Maggie had long neglected to practice. She fumbled through the Apostle's Creed, the Lord's Prayer, the trio of Hail Marys. Rosary beads would have helped, but if Maggie owned any, she had left them somewhere in Louisiana. It had been years since she'd attempted to pray like this, years since she'd attended mass or paused amid the chaos of a rocketing political career to look farther ahead than the next election.

Maybe, if she'd invested in her claimed faith, or had prayed harder, she could have held the world back from the brink of Armageddon. Maybe she would have made better choices—confronted a boiling Russian threat earlier, and with more aggression.

Maybe she wouldn't even have been shot. Would never have needed a liver transplant. Would never have been consumed by pain.

Would never have become addicted to opioids.

The fifty-five thousand square feet of the White House weren't sufficient to house all of Maggie's what-ifs. She prayed with regret now. She prayed with passion, confusion, some desperation.

But what bothered her most was *why* she prayed. Not for a world standing on the edge of the abyss, or for a country facing a collapsing economy and the prospect of the most horrific war mankind had ever experienced. Not even for her own administration, her own good judgment, and the protection of American armed forces standing at the gate.

What drove Maggie to prayer was so much more primitive, so much more selfish. She prayed because she was breaking. Because the withdrawals hadn't lessened, or even stabilized, but were growing worse. Because her body was falling apart...right when the world needed her the most.

The phone rang and Maggie opened her eyes, caught between a hot flash and a shiver, fingers clutching the sheets. She stared at the ceiling, shadows playing across the sheetrock as faint beams of light cut between the blinds.

Her vision wavered. She blinked again and her eyes stung with sweat.

And still, the phone rang.

Maggie sat up. She drained the water glass from her nightstand. She wiped her lips and finally lifted the receiver.

"Yes?"

"Madam President, it's John."

Maggie wasn't sure when General John David Yellin, chairman of the Joint Chiefs, had begun identifying himself by his first name. Sometime after the dozenth crisis—so many emergency Situation Room meetings that Yellin seemed to spend more time in the White House than the Pentagon.

It was just another symptom of an administration caught between an anvil and a sledgehammer.

"Yes?" Maggie said again. She already knew what Yellin would say—why he was calling. Her stomach twisted with fresh nausea.

"It's begun, ma'am," Yellin said. "The Russians are assaulting Estonia, and the Belarusians are rolling over the Latvian border. NATO is under attack."

Maggie expected to feel something at the announcement. A jolt of physiological lightning, perhaps. A tidal wave of dread. A rush of anger.

She felt nothing. Maybe because she was so exhausted, but probably because this moment had been anticipated for weeks, so discussed and deliberated that the reality of a war with Russia felt inevitable. Like the next sunrise.

It was coming—that was all.

"Okay," Maggie said. "Initiate with Operation United Resolve. We'll meet in the Situation Room at eight a.m."

"Very good, ma'am. I'll see you then."

Yellin hung up. Maggie replaced the receiver and sat with her hands wrapped into fists, pressed into the mattress. Head bowed as she closed her eyes and breathed.

She fought off the call of small white pills by focusing on the domino chain even now toppling from Washington to London, from Paris to Berlin, and straight to the Baltic.

Operation United Resolve.

NATO's response to Russia.

3

Moscow, Russia

Disgraced and hunted former SVR officer Ivan Sidorov hid from his enemies in plain sight.

Deep inside the Russian capital, occupying a hostel under the name László Varga, a retired Hungarian oil merchant, Ivan was surrounded on all sides by men who wanted to kill him. His saving grace, for the moment, was the fact that those men were preoccupied with their much greater desire to kill the rest of humanity.

It was no surprise when Russia stormed across the border into NATO, and no secret as to why. President Makar Nikitin had been spewing nationalist, survivalist rhetoric for months, priming an economically challenged and restless Russian populace for an expansionist movement that mirrored those of Imperial Japan and Nazi Germany.

The message was simple: *We are dying. We are throttled on every side by the West. Our very way of life, our entire identity, is at stake. If we do not fight, we will be exterminated.*

So let's kick down the door of Eastern Europe and touch off a war that might leave all of humanity rotting in a nuclear wasteland.

Of course, Nikitin never actually *said* the last part, but Ivan saw right through the madness of his rhetoric, easily identifying the power-lust that motivated Russian aggression. Ivan suspected—or maybe he only hoped—that much of ordinary Russia saw through it also. That they opposed a presidential regime that had developed into something much closer to a dictatorship. That there was still hope of turning back the clock on this insanity.

But with every hour that slipped past, with every shot fired against the nuclear-armed West, that hope felt fainter. The shouts of celebrating Russians that churned through the streets, pumping their fists and cheering the passage of military convoys, were no encouragement. Some of those revelers swarmed the sidewalks simply for an opportunity to blow off work and chug vodka with the government's hearty blessing.

But how many actually *believed* the lies Nikitin peddled? How many stood behind this agenda of death?

Ivan was an old man. He'd survived the fall of the Soviet Union and the tumultuous years of reformation that followed. He'd served his country—a country he truly loved—in ways that sometimes left him awake late at night, sweating and enduring the screams. The memories of merciless bloodshed and the dry mouth it left him with.

He'd done it all because he believed—beyond reasonable argument and sometimes even beyond sanity—that Russia could be something great. A beacon of leadership and stability for a chaotic world. A bastion of economic, technological, and social progress. A superpower in all the best ways, a servant of her own people.

Well. So much for that.

Ivan rose from the outdoor café table where he'd taken his breakfast, tossing inflated ruble notes next to his plate for payment. He stepped to the sidewalk, sparking up a cigarette and watching another tidal wave of revelers headed toward the Moskva River and Red Square. Many were kids—all were drunk.

None had any *clue* what evil they celebrated, like fools cheering the groan of hell's opening gates. Ivan had seen those gates himself, in a hundred little holes across a planet scorched by the depravity of man. He knew the curse of war better than most—and that was *conventional war.* Bullets and land mines and child soldiers and famine.

Blips on the radar compared to the absolute destruction of a widespread nuclear conflict.

Starting down the street, Ivan joined the tidal wave with his head lowered, a cap pulled down low, his collar turned up. Shuffling, just one of the mob. If identified, he'd be lucky to be shot in the face. A worse fate awaited him in one of the Federal Security Service's torture dungeons, kept alive for miserable months as the FSB worked to extract every ounce of punishment they could imagine for his betrayal.

Treason against the state? Only if you considered *the state* as a synonym for *Makar Nikitin*.

The tidal wave surged northward along the sidewalks of Yakimanskiy Proyezd, a six-lane thoroughfare that crossed the Moskva and led straight into the heart of Russian governmental power, where the *real* party began.

Tens of thousands of revelers. None protesting. All cheering. Culminating at Red Square and directing their attention toward the Kremlin. Some shouting Nikitin's name like that of a superhero, others screaming "*Russkiye idut!*"—the Russians are coming.

Or, still more ominously: "*Net granits dlya russkikh!*"

No borders for Russia.

Ivan stood amid the throng, ignored by the drunks as he overlooked the multicolored onion domes that topped the Kremlin towers. Striped and gleaming in the sunrise, a reflection of art and culture and heritage.

But not to this crowd. To them, that building represented *power*. Overwhelming and crushing and indiscriminatory. The kind only a young man finds attractive and only a very great fool thinks he can control. Ivan had seen it before, and if he hadn't lived so long and experienced so much, he might have been defeated by the euphoria surrounding him. He might have already lost hope, believing that the very spirit of the Motherland stood behind Nikitin, ready to follow him straight into the chasm.

But even though ten thousand simpletons choked this square, screaming their drunken lungs out, Ivan hadn't yet lost hope for two reasons. The first was a simple matter of percentages. Russia was a nation of 143 million people—ten thousand was a drop in the bucket. Not everyone could be this foolish. Maybe the rest only needed a leader, a man who could defy Nikitin and bring sanity to Moscow before it was too late.

That brought Ivan to the second reason he felt justified to hope. Not a population of people, but one specific person—a man who just *might* still possess both the will and the means to stand in Nikitin's way.

His name was Maxim Romanov—and he was the man Ivan Sidorov had returned to Moscow to meet.

4

The Naval Observatory
Washington, DC

The vice president of the United States had been exiled.

Ejected from the West Wing after a Situation Room confrontation with his boss, Jordan Stratton didn't regret his defiance of Maggie Trousdale. It may have cost him his office, his influence, and even jeopardized his career.

But what was the point of any of those things as compared with the very survival of Stratton's homeland? He'd confronted Maggie for one simple reason—she was wrong. From the start of their partnership in the White House, Maggie had made it clear that she wasn't looking for a silent lackey or a simple vote-winner. She wanted a partner, an advisor—a warrior able to corral Congress and assist with her agenda. A true right-hand man.

Stratton had taken that job description literally, and in his heart he still believed that Maggie was sincere when she outlined the arrangement.

Before she was shot.

Before America shuddered under repeated terrorist attacks.

Before the planet itself careened toward a conflict that would make the last World War seem like a dress rehearsal.

Nobody could have predicted such a sequence of disasters. Much of the news media blamed Trousdale. The nation was so intoxicated by fear that schools stood half empty and ballparks were closing down altogether.

But despite the defeat, despite the exile, despite the blows that rained like artillery shells, Jordan Stratton hadn't given up, and he hadn't quit. Because his oath as vice president wasn't sworn to Maggie Trousdale, it was sworn to the United States and to its people.

Those people needed him now more than ever.

Seated behind a sprawling mahogany desk in the office of his private residence, Stratton ignored the squeal of his twin daughters playing in the yard outside as he slurped coffee and scrolled through his daily briefing. Assembled under the supervision of his chief of staff and delivered each morning on an iPad, the report was like a summary of international headlines...and was, in fact, mostly sourced from mass media.

Stratton still maintained a top-tier security clearance, but he'd been cut off from the White House Situation Room. From the CIA. From all the usual sources of minute-by-minute intel that fed the Trousdale Administration. Certainly, he still had *some* sources—those were incorporated alongside updates from friendly reporters who fed Stratton's office news stories before they broke.

Enough to lead a nation? Not hardly. But enough to keep Stratton apprised of the global situation, like a backup quarterback studying enemy tape, just in case. And the tape, both this day and every day prior for two weeks, was terrifying.

The very fabric of a global order, so long spoiled by relative peace, was coming apart at its very seams. Moving at lightning speed with new developments by the hour, Stratton traced conflict to every corner of the planet.

The Middle East, where terror strikes had birthed a full-fledged war between Israel and Hamas in the Gaza Strip, and Israel and Hezbollah in Lebanon. Tel Aviv launched invasions of both regions with full US support, announcing their intentions to erase both terror groups from the face of the map.

And that was the *smaller* of the two Mideast conflicts. The real war lay some five hundred miles to the east, where a full-fledged Iranian invasion of Iraq had penetrated all the way to Baghdad, threatening to engulf the Iraqi capital within weeks. As Iraqi troops initially offered staunch resistance, the government in Baghdad had refused to request Western aid—perhaps jaded by memories of the last time Western troops deployed into the Cradle of Civilization. It was a brave choice, and a foolish one.

Iraq was outmatched. As their ground forces amassed casualties, they finally requested international assistance, but too late. The US and Europe were in no position to supply troops, not only because US Marines had already deployed into Beirut, but because a far larger, far deadlier threat to Western survival was already kicking down NATO's door.

Russia was on the move. Penetrating Estonian borders and sidestepping NATO strongholds, they were driving straight toward the Estonian capital of Tallinn even as their Belarussian allies marched on neighboring Latvia—another former member of the Soviet Union that the regime in Moscow had long coveted. And even as NATO scrambled to respond, a third and final dragon reared its head from the Far East. A literal dragon.

China had deployed into the South Pacific—the full might of her Navy, swarming shipping lanes and defying US regional control. While one US warship already rested at the bottom of the Taiwan Strait and an air battle between Chinese and American fighter pilots had left dead on both sides, that flash of heat had quickly frozen over into something much colder and somehow much more terrifying.

No further attacks from the Chinese, just massive mobilization. Troops assembling on the Asian mainland. Airwings running sorties right up to the edge of Taiwanese airspace, so close to American fighters that rival pilots could flip each other off. It felt like a sealed boiler, just shuddering as the pressure increased, the Chinese taking their time, waiting for the perfect moment.

A moment when America was stretched too thin. When crises in the Middle East and Europe offered the perfect opportunity.

And then...it would be total war.

Stratton finished the report just as he finished his coffee, and he set the iPad down to look out his office window over a rolling lawn planted thick with the multicolored flowers that his wife loved so much. The family dog barking. Louise and Lindy chasing him, and in turn being chased by him.

A scene of serenity. Of the ordinary. But Stratton barely noticed. Seated in his chair, overlooking the lawn, he reflected on the briefing and filled in the gaps between what the *New York Times* and CNN claimed to know... and what they didn't know but was probably still true. The backside of this disaster. The nightmare that now confronted Maggie Trousdale's White House.

All the phone calls pouring in from allies overseas. The race against time to move troops, to initiate pre-planned battle strategies...and then to modify those strategies the moment the gunfire started and everything changed. The competing emergencies, the limitation of resources. The last desperate efforts of the State Department to forestall open war and obtain a cease-fire.

Chaos, yes. And that wasn't even the problem that kept Stratton up at night. What he worried about most was so much simpler, and yet so much more terrifying. It was the question of whether or not Maggie Trousdale, a woman shot through the gut and struggling to survive on a liver transplant, known by Stratton to be addicted to painkillers and so recently reflecting so much irrational behavior, could save America...or was even now being pushed over the edge.

In short: Was Maggie Trousdale the answer, or the poison pill?

As Stratton stared into space and let the facts tumble in his mind, the door opened behind him. The soft footsteps of his secretary padded on the carpet. She cleared her throat.

"Mr. Vice President? They're here."

Stratton didn't look back. He told her to show them in. Continued to gaze over the lawn as two persons entered and stood awkwardly around the coffee table, waiting for him. Waiting to discuss a nuclear solution that Stratton couldn't *imagine* using.

And yet...

He stood. He smoothed his jacket and took an armchair in the sitting area without a word. The two others took a seat also. A woman and a man.

The woman was his chief of staff. The man was chief legal counsel to the vice president of the United States. Both were stone-faced and silent.

"What happens in this room," Stratton began, very slowly, "*never* leaves this room. Not under any circumstance."

He looked them each in the eye. Without blinking, they both nodded. Stratton inhaled. He flexed each one of his fingers until the knuckles popped. He looked to the attorney.

"You have it?"

"Yes, sir."

"I want to read it."

A hesitation. "You don't have to, sir. I've prepared a full briefing—"

"Davis," Stratton cut him off. He didn't say another word.

The attorney reached into his briefcase. He produced a printed document and extended it to the vice president.

Stratton took it without a word. He returned to the window where he could listen to the children play. Listen to the dog bark. Feel the sunshine on his face.

Remember every reason he loved his country.

Then, slowly, he began reading.

The Twenty-Fifth Amendment of the United States Constitution.

Concerning Article Four—Procedure for the Vice President to Remove the President from Office.

5

The White House

From halfway down the twenty-three-foot length of the Cabinet Room conference table, Maggie sat twisted in her chair, her attention directed to a projector screen. The chair to Maggie's left, usually occupied by Vice President Jordan Stratton, was conspicuously empty.

Every other chair around the table was full, as were many chairs that lined the wall. Additional staffers, aides, and advisors stood in the background.

But only one person spoke. Secretary of Defense Steven Kline addressed the room in a controlled monotone while an aide operated the slideshow, projecting a map of northeastern Europe that looked like something out of a war film—a spiderweb of borders dotted by cities, all overlaid by bold red lines progressing west out of Russia.

Progressing *rapidly* west.

"The Russian incursion of Estonia has now penetrated nearly half the width of the country," Kline said. "Overwhelming ground force supported by light armor circumvented NATO defenses at Tapa Army Base and as of noon local time today are driving straight for Tallinn. Assuming no change in present course or speed, they will be within striking distance of the

Estonian capital by midday Friday, at the latest. Aerial bombardment may begin well before then."

The map displayed the Russian warpath in vivid detail. Slicing across the Russian-Estonian border at the town of Narva, Russian ground troops had proceeded west across the Narva Isthmus and split their forces in two prior to reaching the Tapa Army Base, where Estonian forces were stationed alongside NATO troops. The two Russian arms had swung wide before pinching inward toward the base, mounting what *appeared* to be a flanking attack.

NATO command had responded accordingly. NATO troops were withdrawn into the base—defensive measures were taken. A European Alamo was established.

And then? Russia turned on a dime. They ignored Tapa altogether. They broke toward Tallinn with only scant Estonian resistance standing in their way. They left the NATO troops to huddle in their emergency fortress while the Russian's took the real prize—strategic control of an entire nation.

All within seventy-two hours.

"This isn't Ukraine," Kline said. "Nikitin has been planning this incursion for months and he played us like a violin. By strategically sidestepping direct NATO engagement, he's left us in the awkward position of drawing first blood."

"First blood?" That was General John David Yellin, chairman of the Joint Chiefs. Yellin had finished his coffee—he'd probably drank a few coffees. He was bristling for a fight. "Eight thousand Estonians are already dead, and four cities are burning. I'd say Russia has drawn first blood."

Maggie shot Yellin a look—enough to silence him. Kline continued.

"Be that as it may, no Americans or non-Estonians have died under Russian fire. Nikitin is recycling the usual justification for his attack—that ethnic-Russians living in the Baltic are being oppressed and must be defended. It's just like Crimea in 2014."

"He's testing us," Secretary of State Lisa Gorman said. "He's stalling for time, peddling nonsense. Just like Hitler in Poland."

"Exactly like Hitler in Poland," Kline said. "And just like Hitler, Nikitin has an ally. Belarussian ground forces are also on the move, deploying against the Latvian border and drawing both Latvian and NATO forces away from the action in Estonia. Belarus has yet to fire a shot, but that could change in a heartbeat. President Zhukov has issued demands for NATO forces to vacate Ādaži Military Base—of course we are refusing. Nikitin has echoed the demands."

Kline lowered his laser pointer, pivoting to Maggie. For a moment, nobody spoke.

Then Kline said: "They're moving at lightning speed, Madam President. Much more aggressively than we could have anticipated. Barring a miracle, Estonia will fall by the weekend. After that, there will be nothing to prevent Russian forces from wheeling southeast to converge with Belarussian forces and swarm Latvia. We're talking days—a few weeks, at most. A modern-day blitzkrieg."

Maggie's jaw tightened, but she still didn't answer. She was fixated on that map, arms folded to steady her quaking body. Blinking irregularly to clear burning eyes. Monitoring her breathing and trying *so hard* not to tremble.

It was the withdrawals again. Another wave of brutal physiological cravings spilled through her body at the worst possible moment. Claws reaching out of the mire to drag her in.

Focus, Maggie. Do your job.

"What forces do we have available in Latvia?" Maggie said.

Yellin stepped to the plate with a nod from Kline. "Our forces in Latvia are largely concentrated at the Ādaži Military Base just northeast of Riga. It's the headquarters for NATO's Enhanced Forward Presence battle group, and usually houses about fifteen hundred troops. That number has been inflated to nearly six thousand over the past weeks. Most of those troops are Canadian, with detachments of Spanish and Polish infantry to support. They're good soldiers, ma'am, but dramatically outnumbered."

"And our troops?" Maggie pressed.

"Barely represented. Our largest European military force is concentrated at US Army Garrison Bavaria, in Germany. Currently that detachment includes eighteen thousand ground troops with supporting armor and air cavalry. Per my recommendations, an additional twenty-six thousand troops are assembled on standby here in the States and could be shifted to Europe within ninety-six hours."

More silence. Maggie was watching. She understood.

The implications were still difficult to swallow.

"We're behind the eight ball, ma'am," Kline said. "Operation United Resolve never allowed for a Russian assault this aggressive. It'll take weeks for us to close the gap, by which time..."

He trailed off. Maggie turned.

"What, Secretary?"

Kline shifted. He looked to Yellin.

Yellin didn't hesitate.

"By which time the Baltic will be lost, ma'am. Estonia, Latvia, possibly Lithuania."

"*What?*" That was Gorman. "You can't be serious."

"The general is right," Kline said, his voice turning cold. "We simply don't have the troops in position—and that's our own fault. I've advised this cabinet for weeks that a war in the Baltic wouldn't look like the war in Ukraine. Russia could blitz, and that's exactly what they've done. NATO has their pants down—Europe has slow-walked our reinforcement agenda. I've been ringing phones off the hook and nobody is answering. I guess I called during nap hour—another climate change rally. You know what changes the climate, secretary? *War*."

As Kline spoke, another wave of chills ran down Maggie's spine, accompanied almost immediately by sweat. A hot flash. Shortness of breath. She smacked her hand on the table—everyone spun her way.

"That's enough, Steven," Maggie said. "You made your point, the world is on fire. You don't think we all know that?"

No answer. Maggie guzzled water to buy time. She was lightheaded and wanted to wipe her face but couldn't afford to displace her makeup. She'd layered it on thick that morning to hide the flushed skin...or the pale skin. Whatever her body decided to throw at her that day. It could change at the drop of a hat.

"I don't want excuses. I don't want accusations," Maggie said. "I want a revised plan. *Now*."

She turned to Kline. He was still flushed, jaw tight. Maybe embarrassed. He deserved to be.

"More troops in Europe," Kline said. "That's the plan. We send the twenty-six thousand now and we gear up another fifty as quickly as possible. Then we get Brussels on the phone and we decide how NATO is going to handle this. Better yet, we decide ahead of time and then issue marching orders."

Maggie cocked an eyebrow, resisting a shiver. A headache was coming on—she blocked the pain out.

"And how is it going to be, Steven?"

"It's going to be war, ma'am. Full-fledged and savage. If we're lucky, it stops there. But if we don't confront Russia now, Nikitin will *never* stop. Not until he dominates the planet."

Maggie waited, but Kline said nothing more. She looked to her right, down the table toward Gorman. The secretary of state, a reliable voice of *diplomacy, diplomacy, diplomacy*, said nothing. She stared back and didn't object. Didn't argue.

How could she? Everyone in the room knew Kline was right. Maybe they had known it for months, even as Russia stormed the Caucasus. Even as Russian ground forces amassed just east of the Estonian border. As Iranian troops stormed Iraq, and Iranian-backed Hamas and Hezbollah militants assaulted Israel on two sides. As China deployed into the South China Sea and sank a US warship.

As the radioactive dust of two nuclear explosions, one of which had decimated the Panama Canal, seasoned the earth's very atmosphere with the flavor of dread. Of misery. Of so much *death*.

Much of it yet to come. Maggie thought of the twenty-two thousand Marines she had already deployed to Beirut, engaged in a no-holds-barred death struggle alongside their Israeli allies. Of the airstrikes she'd authorized over Gaza, and the dead fighter pilots still lost in the Taiwan Strait. Of all the bloodshed, all the chaos.

How had she let this happen?

"Move the troops," Maggie said. "Move as much conventional force as you can to our forward NATO bases. Lisa, I want you in constant communication with our European allies. Arrange a joint phone call with as many as you can for tomorrow afternoon—I'll speak with them myself. Barring any American deaths, we'll stick with Operation United Resolve and bolster our positions across Poland and Germany. Call for a cease-fire for Russia, and give them one final chance to turn back."

Kline snorted. Maggie's gaze snapped toward him.

"You have something to say, Steven?"

"They're not turning back," he said, very calm.

"I know. So we're going to hit them, but like you said yourself, they've planned for this for months. I want to make sure that when we hit them, it's over and done. No mistakes. *No more nukes*. Understood?"

"Perfectly, ma'am."

Maggie nodded. "Okay, then. You all know what to do. Get it done."

Everyone stood in unison. Maggie remained seated. As the aides and cabinet members filed out, Maggie shuffled with her notes and pretended to be reading. Pretended not to be consumed by her own lightheadedness. The pulsing pain in her abdomen. The shivers.

When was this going to get better? When would she be able to breathe, to focus? She'd cut herself off from the medication nearly two weeks prior. Shouldn't the withdrawals have been relaxing?

"Ma'am?"

Maggie looked up to find the room nearly empty. Only one person remained—Jill Easterling, her White House chief of staff. A tiny woman with a cloud of light blond hair and a squeaky voice that disguised her wolverine temperament, Easterling looked as tired as Maggie felt.

But she stood straighter. She didn't shiver or sweat. She gently closed the door.

"What is it?" Maggie said, her gut tensing. If anyone had detected signs of the withdrawals racking her system—if anyone had noticed and hung back to say something—it would be Easterling.

But when Easterling spoke, it wasn't about Maggie's condition.

"You asked me to check up on James." Easterling's voice was tentative. Maggie squinted.

"What?"

"Mr. O'Dell."

Maggie knew who Easterling referred to—it simply took a moment for her to wade through the muck in her brain and place the memory. Yes, she had asked Easterling to find O'Dell. A longtime bodyguard from her days as governor of Louisiana, James O'Dell was a Cajun from the swamps outside of New Orleans, every bit as savage as Maggie could be. He'd come to the White House to assist in her security—a needless measure, but Maggie liked him. She trusted him. She felt good with him around.

And then...

Well, he became something more. Something so complicated, confusing, infuriating.

Enthralling.

Until he disappeared, anyway, two weeks prior. Maggie had called. She couldn't find him. Nobody knew where he was. She thought he might have gone back to Louisiana, and she understood. She might have left him in peace there.

But she couldn't help herself. It was the vice she couldn't relinquish. So she'd asked Easterling to check around, and now...

"New Orleans?" Maggie said.

Easterling said nothing. There was a glint in her eye that Maggie didn't like.

"Jill?" Maggie pressed.

"Central Detention Facility," Easterling said. "District of Columbia Department of Corrections."

Maggie blinked. The words landed meaningless in her mind, at first.

And then: "*What?*"

Easterling took a half step closer. Her voice lowered to barely above a whisper.

"He was arrested by the FBI. They're holding him on charges of capital murder."

6

Al Udeid Air Base
Near Doha, Qatar

A cloud of American nicotine hung in a haze around Reed Montgomery's head as the jet touched down. A scream of tires, a plume of similar gray smoke, and the C-130 Hercules ripped down the airstrip, all four turboprops howling as the brakes fought forward momentum.

It was thunder and it was fury. The tarmac shuddered under Reed's boots and the scream of the engines pounded through his head, but he didn't so much as flinch. He didn't look away or shield his unprotected ears.

He simply lifted the Marlboro cigarette and took a long drag, watching as the Hercules ground to a gradual stop, turned in place, and entered a taxiway. The airplane was running light—Reed could tell by the way it bounced on its landing gear, heavy suspension designed to support as much as forty-two thousand pounds of cargo now carrying considerably less. Maybe it was nearly empty.

The one item of cargo Reed cared about weighed barely ninety-five pounds, dripping wet. And yet the US Air Force had deployed the Hercules to India to collect that cargo. They had flown straight across an

Arabian Sea infested with US naval activity, turning north and skirting well beyond Iranian airspace before landing on this tiny peninsula of land parked in the middle of a developing regional conflict.

One passenger on the manifest. Two tiny feet, one shaken body. Reed lifted the smoke and inhaled, a tremor rippling down his arm as he blinked and saw black walls. Iron bars. Blood draining from his own forehead and stinging his eyes.

And screams. So many screams.

The Hercules stopped, and Reed started forward. He finished the smoke and dispensed the cigarette butt to the tarmac before lighting up a second. There were NO SMOKING signs displayed on a nearby chain link fence, and Air Force MPs posted in a shack not far beyond, but nobody challenged Reed. Nobody so much as acknowledged him as he neared the lowering tailgate of the C-130, engines finally winding down, Reed's ears still ringing.

He inhaled another drag, looking past strands of shoulder-length hair that fell into his eyes. He hadn't cut his hair or so much as shaved in weeks. He couldn't remember the last time he had showered. The clothes he wore were Air Force–issue PT gear. The boots were lifted from a Marine Corps supply depot on the far side of the base.

Nothing quite fit. Reed barely noticed. He bought Marlboros—the most popular cigarette in Qatar—from a twenty-four-hour convenience store, paying a one hundred percent excise tax without complaint. Lighting up and smoking. And smoking.

And wishing he was someplace else—anywhere where hard liquor was available.

The tailgate struck the ground, and the Air Force crew chief hit the tarmac. He nodded at Reed but didn't comment about the cigarette or Reed's generally homeless appearance. There were many such ragtag personnel on this base, dressed in mismatched clothing and coming and going without any declared rhyme or reason. Most of them carried advanced security clearances and sidearms locked and loaded even in restricted areas.

Nobody challenged them. Nobody wanted to talk to them, either. Everyone knew what they were.

Everyone wisely gave them space.

Looking into the tail of the Hercules, Reed's suspicions were confirmed by a nearly empty cargo bay. Maybe half a dozen airmen, two pallets of nondescript supplies...and one undersized figure walking slowly toward the tailgate. Limping a little. Dressed in baggy off-brand clothes with auburn hair pulled back into a ponytail. A brass cross dangling from a chain around her neck. A small backpack slung over one shoulder.

She reached the top of the tailgate and stopped. She blinked in the Qatari glare. Reed lowered the cigarette, noting the marks on her neck. The strain in her eyes. The bruising still visible on her arms.

It was enough to turn Reed's stomach. To tighten his chest and spark a different kind of ember someplace deep in his guts. A murderous, angry flame.

But Lucy Byrne didn't look angry. She didn't look sad. She offered a very small smile, reached the bottom of the ramp, and threw both arms around Reed. She pulled him close.

"Good to see you, Prosecutor. I'm glad you're okay."

Reed and Lucy rode in an electric UTV through a morass of military facilities.

Consuming twenty-five square kilometers of desert space, Al Udeied was closer to a city than a traditional military base, with a standing force of some ten thousand United States military personnel calling it home. In the past ten days, that force had multiplied nearly three times over as one screaming military cargo jet after another touched down, unloading hundreds of American soldiers armed to the teeth.

Ready for war.

Now the streets of "Log Town"—the logistical core of the base where temporary personnel lived—were reduced to a mire more resembling a major US city at rush hour than an instillation of war. Reed could have borrowed any number of Air Force Humvees from the motor pool near the barracks where he had lived since transferring off the USS *Makin Island* the previous week, but he preferred the UTV for its maneuverability. Little larger than a golf cart, it was capable of off-roading or even plowing along sidewalks in pursuit of his destination.

Soldiers cursed and flicked their middle fingers. Officers shouted and threatened to call the MPs. Reed ignored them all, weaving his way into the furthest recesses of Log Town, past a hospital and fields of desert-tan Army tents erected for temporary housing, a garage where military mechanics serviced Humvees, and the DEFAC—the dining facility, where flavor went to die and nutrition was a matter of opinion.

The air tasted of exhaust and heat, even in December. Dust coated every vehicle, every sign and sidewalk. Passing soldiers sweated. Every polished surface reflected a glare so sharp Reed kept his eyes squinted even behind Army-issue safety sunglasses.

He smoked. Lucy clung to her seat next to him. And he drove.

Standing near the edge of Log Town, a row of two-story brick buildings looked older than much of the local construction. Blasted by sandstorms with paint peeling from their walls and windows coated in heat-reflective tint, the exterior AC units chugged, but Reed knew it would be hot inside. He cut the UTV off and stamped out his smoke, then held the building's door open for Lucy. She proceeded without comment, and the MP riding a stool behind a desk buzzed them through a secure-access barrier without so much as a blink.

Reed was a known quantity. Lucy was an expected addition. Reed led the way down a tile hallway lined by metal doors painted in utilitarian tan. The stairwell standing at the end smelled like urine, and at the second floor the temperature spiked. Reed sweated as he turned another corner and selected a blank door with no window. It opened with the swipe of a key card, and Reed pushed inside.

The rich odor of fresh coffee flooded a darkened interior—not because Reed or anyone else in this room wanted coffee but because coffee was the only form of air freshener the Air Force could provide.

The room was small. Two tables, three cots, a sagging recliner, and a TV on the wall. Piles of clothes spilling out of military duffel bags. Rifle cases stacked along one wall.

And one man waiting in the shadows, propped up in the recliner with one arm in a sling and his right thigh wrapped in bulky bandages. He wore the same Air Force PT gear as Reed, but the clothes fit him even worse. He was unshaven with a flat-top haircut so grown out he was starting to develop bangs. Bare feet the size of clothes irons jutted out over the recliner's extended footrest, green socks stained with sweat.

But when Rufus Turkman saw Lucy, he smiled. He clenched his teeth as he reached for the footrest's lever. Lucy hurried toward him, beckoning for him to stay still.

"Relax, Turk! Don't get up."

She wrapped him in a hug every bit as tight as the one she'd given Reed, and Turk patted her back with his good arm while Reed closed the door and reached for a bottle of water.

It was warm like everything else. But it was wet.

"Good grief, Turk. Did you get shot *again*?"

A little good-natured disbelief entered Lucy's tone. Turk snorted.

"Didn't you hear? That's how this works. Reed takes the glory, I take the bullets."

Lucy laughed. It was a soft sound. Not all that hearty, but at least genuine. She squeezed his good arm.

"I'm glad you're okay."

"Yeah," Turk said. "You too, Lucy."

The room fell quiet as Lucy glanced back to Reed. The resulting stillness felt awkward. Reed's fingers crinkled around the bottle and he swallowed, realizing Turk and Lucy were waiting on him.

Again.

"I guess...I guess we should call them," Reed said.

Lucy took a seat, and Reed opened a laptop. He input a series of passcodes to access a secure military satellite internet link. More passwords to access a video conferencing system—not usually available to non-uniform nobodies with dried blood under their fingernails and stories they couldn't tell, but Reed had pulled strings. Better put, the CIA had pulled strings on his behalf.

The contact he wanted was pre-loaded. He selected it and slapped the Return key. He slid a chair next to Turk's recliner, and the computer beeped.

Then connected.

7

Ministry of Defense Headquarters
Moscow, Russia

Never in his greatest fantasies had Makar Nikitin envisioned the Russian invasion of Estonia proceeding so perfectly according to plan—and, as president of the Russian Federation and supreme commander in chief of her armed forces, he had fantasized a *lot*.

Storming over the border at Narva under the muscled umbrella of mechanized armor and strategic bombers, tens of thousands of Russian soldiers had penetrated as far as Jõhvi on the very first day, fully forty-five kilometers inside NATO territory. On the second day, those soldiers were reinforced and split into an apparent pincer approach against Tapa Army Base, the primary NATO stronghold in the region.

As Nikitin's military advisors predicted, NATO's reaction was both instantaneous and defensive. Instead of meeting Russia on the open field of battle, they withdrew into Tapa, leaving key roads and bridges unprotected while taking cover in preparation for a full-frontal assault.

But that assault never came. Why should it? Nikitin didn't care about Tapa. The NATO soldiers could rot there and it wouldn't matter to him. His soldiers blazed right past, continuing to route vastly outgunned

Estonian resistance on their way north toward Tallinn—the capital of Estonia, and the real prize.

Now Russian ground troops were almost within striking distance of the city, and NATO was *still* scrambling. Airlifting troops and supplies to forward bases across Poland, activating reserves and calling for emergency United Nations summits. Condemning Russian aggression and begging for the rest of the world to condemn it with them.

Like that mattered. Like *anything* would stall Russia's advance. Nikitin had planned for this moment his entire career. His military advisors had correctly theorized that despite the seizure of Crimea and the war in Ukraine, despite the Russian occupation of Georgia and the military incursions into Azerbaijan and Armenia—despite all the warning signs of Nikitin's ultimate objectives...nobody *actually* believed that Russia would challenge NATO. Nobody could fathom that Nikitin was bold enough to go toe-to-toe with multiple nuclear-armed nations—the United States being chief amongst them.

But he was. He'd salivated over this move for so, *so* long. Now it was here, and save for one tiny, aggravating little detail, the results couldn't be better.

Yet that one detail threatened to undermine the entire war effort.

"Why aren't they moving?" Nikitin barked the question the moment he exploded through the double doors of the National Defense Management Center. A rough equivalent of the Situation Room built beneath the West Wing of the American White House, but optimized for military control, the sprawling conference room could easily serve as the central nervous system for the entire Russian war machine.

Monitors and digital maps to track all troop movements—both Russian and the enemy's. Direct communications with the front lines. Links to the SVR and the Ministry of Foreign Affairs. Seating for the full assembly of both Nikitin's cabinet and all his top generals.

Even three kilometers removed from his usual executive offices at the Kremlin, Nikitin felt more comfortable in the NDMC than anywhere else in Moscow. It was the power room, the heart of his war effort. But for the moment, it wasn't Russia's war effort that bothered him—it was China's.

Displayed across a bank of flat-screen monitors mounted across one entire wall, a sweeping picture of the South Pacific displayed every known location of both Chinese and American warships. Clustered around Japan for the Americans and across the South China Sea for the Chinese, the two fleets converged and faced off near Taiwan—the real battle line of a war that was somehow *still* cold.

Because despite sunk American warships and downed Chinese fighter planes, neither side of this confrontation had crossed the threshold into total conflict with the other. Facing each other off, waiting for the other to blink, they stood at general quarters with their fingers on the triggers of the most deadly floating machines known to history...

And yet nobody fired. *Why* had nobody fired?

"What are they doing, Anton?"

Nikitin addressed the only other man overlooking the map—Anton Golubev, a face and a name without any official title, and yet anyone who understood Nikitin's regime could tell you that Golubev, the so-called "Ghost of the Kremlin," might just be the second-most powerful man in all of Russia. He was Nikitin's "fixer." His right-hand man. His emissary to those who needed to be motivated—frequently off the books.

He was also the man responsible for liaising with the Chinese regarding what was *supposed* to be a three-pronged military assault of the West—Russia in Europe, Iran in the Middle East, China in the Pacific. Yet China had stalled.

"Preparations for advanced military action," Golubev said. "Every time I ask, it's all they will say."

Nikitin had heard it before. He had a pretty good idea what it meant. As he stood in front of the map overlooking the battle lines of blue and red warships, he couldn't help but notice just how many of those blue warships had re-routed away from the South Pacific and into the Arabian Sea, there to confront a vastly inferior Iranian Navy and to launch missile attacks in support of Israel. Dozens more of Americas proudest warships sailed the Mediterranean and the North Atlantic, direct threats to Russia's European ambitions.

All of those ships should be distracted by open naval warfare in the Pacific. By the threat of an imminent invasion of Taiwan. The Americans should be stretched thin around the globe, fighting on every side. That was the entire *point* of the three-pronged strategy. It simply wouldn't work with only two prongs.

Cowards, Nikitin thought. *Sniveling rice rats.*

"They don't believe we can do it," Golubev said. "They don't believe we can defeat NATO. They're stalling to see how the dice land before they commit to a full war."

Stalling. Indeed they were. Nikitin should have seen this coming. From the start, his "allies" in Beijing were by far the most flaky of the three-legged Eastern alliance known to Western media as the Trident Powers. Iran couldn't go to war quickly enough. Certainly, the Russian generals were ready.

But China just needed more and more coaxing.

As Nikitin pondered, the double doors behind him opened again. He could tell without looking who had entered. The heavy footsteps and slight wheezing were a dead giveaway. Maxim Romanov, prime minister of the Russian Federation, was a hundred pounds overweight and looked fifteen years older than he actually was. A long-standing Russian politician with family roots that dated back to the Bolshevik Revolution, Romanov was a passive sort of character with a disdain for personal conflict.

That suited Nikitin just fine. He enjoyed a prime minister who could be easily bullied. But lately...something was different. Romanov appeared more agitated, became more vocal in frequent war-planning meetings. He was concerned about overreach—he thought Russia's war plan was too aggressive, too greedy. He favored diplomacy and dialog with the West.

Nikitin had heard it all before. If he had the power, he would have neutralized the prime minister's office altogether—erased it. As it was, he was forced to tolerate Romanov for a while longer.

"Good morning, Mr. President," Romanov huffed as he neared the map. Nikitin noted Golubev stiffening next to him, his lip curling.

It was a physiological reaction Nikitin was tempted to mirror.

"All is well in Estonia?" Romanov asked.

Nikitin simply grunted. He wasn't thinking about Estonia, or even Europe. He was thinking about how he could push China over the edge.

"If you have a moment, Mr. President, I have a diplomatic proposal prepared for your consideration. A method for early termination of hostilities in Europe."

Nikitin blinked, his focus finally faltering. He turned.

"What?"

Romanov wiped sweat from his forehead—the pig was always sweating.

"It's something the Parliament put together. Only a recommendation, of course. With the seizure of certain strategic objectives across the Baltic, we believe NATO could be convinced to cede that territory altogether in exchange for a cease-fire. They're nervous about Poland."

Romanov forced a laugh. Nikitin didn't smile. He stared with his jaw locked, waiting until Romanov's smile faded and the prime minister swallowed.

"You recommend a cessation of hostilities, Mr. Prime Minister?" Nikitin's voice was barely above a snarl.

"Well...ideally, yes. Of course. In the interest of preserving Russian blood."

"Russian blood concerns you?"

This time it was Romanov's turn to stiffen. Indignation flashed behind his eyes.

"Absolutely, Mr. President. As it should concern any true patriot."

Nikitin smiled. It was exactly the response he wanted.

"I couldn't agree more, Mr. Prime Minister." Nikitin said it, then without breaking eye contact with Romanov, he addressed Golubev. "Anton, we have attack submarines in the South Pacific, do we not?"

Golubev grunted. "Da. The *Krasnoyarsk* and the *Novosibirsk*. Nuclear-powered Yasen-class boats."

Nikitin smiled, just a little. "Ah. Yasen-class. Our latest in attack technology. They're very quiet, aren't they, Anton?"

Even though he was still staring at Romanov, Nikitin could hear the smile in Golubev's response.

"Indeed, Mr. President. Very quiet."

"Excellent. So perhaps the *Krasnoyarsk* and the *Novosibirsk* can arrange a little escalation, for us. Something to *motivate* our friends in Beijing."

Romanov's mouth opened, his eyes growing wide, but Golubev spoke first.

"I'll see to it personally, Mr. President."

The Ghost of the Kremlin departed, and still Nikitin didn't look away from Romanov. The prime minister's face had drained of color. Something like genuine fear clouded his eyes.

"What are you doing, Makar?" Romanov said, his voice lowered to a hiss.

Nikitin drew close. He lowered his head until he settled at eye level with the shorter Russian politician. He spoke through his teeth.

"What any true patriot should, Maxim. *Preserving Russian blood.*"

8

RAF Akrotiri
Akrotiri, Cyprus

Almost nobody on this corner of the airbase sounded like Wolfgang—they sounded much more like Kirstin Corbyn, the only British member of the Prosecution Force. As an overseas military installation held and maintained by the United Kingdom since 1955, that made perfect sense. The Royal Air Force maintained both fixed and rotary winged aircraft at the base. Corbyn had once been stationed there, back when she was a helicopter pilot for the RAF working search and rescue operations over the eastern Mediterranean.

Back in the day, Corbyn had said. But that day was long past, and RAF Akrotiri was no longer a search and rescue base, it was a full-fledged war outpost. While almost everyone in this particular corner of the facility spoke with a British or Scottish accent, Wolfgang knew that on the far side of the island, thousands of American expeditionary troops gathered in preparation to reinforce the ongoing Marine assault of Lebanon and the Hezbollah militants who operated there.

Real war.

"I've got Reed on video," Corbyn called from across the tent barracks, distracting Wolfgang from his overwatch of a nearby airstrip. All morning long, flights of Typhoon FGR4 multirole fighters had exploded off the tarmac, banking eastward toward the exploding conflict in Israel and returning hours later with empty weapons hard points.

Another brutal air strike. Another step closer to the end...one way or the other.

Wolfgang dropped the tent flap and grimaced a little as he advanced to the table where Corbyn waited. Even weeks removed from Azerbaijan and the nightmarish days he'd spent inside a dungeon there, every part of his body ached. It hurt to walk. It was still difficult to sleep.

Sometimes, maybe that was a blessing. At least when he was awake, Wolfgang couldn't suffer the nightmares. One glance into Corbyn's flashing dark eyes, laced with bloodthirsty rage, and Wolfgang knew she was suffering also. She was back on her feet, much the same as him. Hopped up on pain meds and fueled by a thirst for vengeance, the soldier in her refused to quit.

Wolfgang had never been a soldier, at least not in any official capacity, but he thought he understood. Settling into a chair next to her, he rocked back a canned Coca-Cola and enjoyed the burn on his throat. Then he looked to the screen...and there he was.

Reed Montgomery, "the Prosecutor." Rufus Turkman was there with him, as was a third face—smaller and somehow brighter than the first two, with flashing green eyes and a warm smile.

"Lucy," Wolfgang said. "You're back!"

Lucy simply nodded. She didn't elaborate, and somehow Wolfgang knew not to press her. The details of her own torment in a different dungeon in a different nation had never been disclosed, but Wolfgang could see in her face that the horrors were real.

For that matter, he could see it in everyone's faces. Every surviving member of the Prosecution Force, now pared down to five people. Weathered. Wounded. Beaten.

The video call fell silent, and Wolfgang fiddled with his Coke. Corbyn was the first to break the silence.

"So? What next?"

There was an edge to her voice that cut like a scalpel. That anger flaring up. That warfighter spirit. It didn't bother Wolfgang...maybe it just made him tired.

"I spoke with the CIA this morning," Reed said. He sounded even more tired than Wolfgang felt. More...dead, somehow. "They're going to arrange air transport back to the States for all of you. It may take a few days...logistics are stretched. Kirstin, if you'd rather go to England, we can make that happen."

Dead silence. Wolfgang felt Corbyn stiffen next to him. She blinked.

"What?"

The tension was palpable for the other side of the screen, too. Turk was sitting up. Lucy looked toward Reed.

"*All* of us?" Lucy said.

Reed didn't answer.

"Am I hearing you correctly, or have I gone daft?" Corbyn said. "Did you just say you're sending us *home*?"

Reed simply nodded. "That's right. Effective immediately, we're disbanding the Prosecution Force. The CIA has promised payouts to all of you for your work in Azerbaijan. Turk and Lucy will get something for India. I'm fighting for medical care, also. We'll have to see about that."

More silence. Corbyn quivered next to Wolfgang, feeling like a boiler threatening to explode. She blinked hard. Her fists tightened.

But it wasn't Corbyn who spoke first—it was Turk.

"Are you serious?"

Reed turned glassy eyes toward Turk, unblinking and a little hazy. As though he wasn't really there—as though his mind were a thousand miles away. Wolfgang had never known the Prosecutor to use mind-altering substances—at least, nothing worse than liquor—but Reed almost looked high.

"That's the order," Reed said.

"And *you*?" It was Turk again. He sounded angry—more than angry, he sounded betrayed. It was possibly the most emotion Wolfgang had ever heard in the steady Tennessean's tone. It caught him off guard.

It bounced right off Reed.

"Don't worry about me," Reed said. "Just do what I tell you."

That was too much. Corbyn broke first, unleashing a string of curses so interwoven with British slang and her street-London accent that Wolfgang barely understood half of it. More than cursing, Corbyn was crying—she was shaking, hands clasped on the table's edge. She shouted at the computer screen.

"You scum-sucking, bottom-dwelling *ponce*!" The table trembled as her arms shook it. Wolfgang reached a hand toward her shoulder and Corbyn jerked away. She was still glaring at Reed. "Strickland *died* in that dungeon. They filleted him one strip at a time, and he's just shouting and laughing and egging them on—to keep *me* alive. You think I've forgotten that? You think a soft bed and a strong drink will wash it all away? I'll burn in *hell* before I go home."

Corbyn's voice was so loud that Wolfgang knew somebody in the next tent probably overheard—but what did it matter? He was listening. He was controlling his own breathing and the boiling fire in his gut the best he could.

But he *felt it*. Everything Corbyn said. Every curse, every trembling shout. Wolfgang didn't join her, but he could have. He could have put his fist through the screen and choked Reed's life out—squeezed until Reed's eyes popped out of their sockets.

What was he *saying*? That all of this was pointless?

Corbyn finally drew breath, and Lucy filled the gap. Her voice was gentle—as controlled as Wolfgang's breathing—but there was an edge barely concealed beneath.

"Kirstin, we hear you. Nobody has forgotten Kyle."

Corbyn turned away. She was sobbing. Large, hot tears rolled down her cheeks. She scrubbed but barely seemed to care. Wolfgang turned his glare on Reed.

"So what, Reed? Is this how it ends? We followed you into hell because you said it mattered. Now it doesn't?"

Long pause. Reed stared blankly into the screen. He blinked. Wolfgang again wondered if he was high—if he was doped in some way.

But no, it was deeper than that. It wasn't physiological. This was psychological. A full break? A final collapse?

If anyone had earned one, it was Reed Montgomery. Wolfgang had felt the warning tremors and watched the spiderweb cracks for as long as he'd known Reed. The inevitable was just that. The earthquake had to come.

But not now. Not this way. Not after this team—a ragtag band of misfits with no place to call home and psychological trauma of their own fit to fill a dump truck—had followed him straight to the edge of a cliff and jumped over without a second thought.

Because they believed. And right now, when all was lost...they were *begging* to still believe.

"We lost," Reed said, his voice suddenly very soft. "The world is going to war. We couldn't stop that."

"We *know* about the war," Wolfgang snarled. "That's what we came here to fight."

Reed nodded. Then, perfectly monotone, he said: "And we failed."

"*Like hell we did!*"

Turk took over. He exploded out of the chair. In a split second, half his body rose out of view of the camera. The table shook and Lucy startled. Wolfgang had never heard Turk shout like this before—he was screaming, like he was on fire. He was shoving past Lucy and bearing down on Reed.

Like a Marine drill instructor. Like a rabid dog off his chain.

"These people—your *team*—followed you around the planet to stop this war. We've lost blood. We've suffered more than most soldiers could ever imagine. But we're still *here*. Are you listening? We're still here, and if we ever had a job to do, that job matters more than ever. I left my wife, my child, my whole *life* behind because you are my brother. Because you had a mission to complete. Because you convinced me that that mission *mattered*. Did you lie?"

A long pause. Reed didn't answer. When Turk next spoke, he roared so loud that the cheap computer speakers buzzed on Wolfgang's end.

"*Did you lie?*"

Reed stared, glassy eyes tilted upward toward Turk's invisible face. In the background Lucy stood motionless, still calm but very attentive. She didn't intervene—she didn't attempt to calm Turk.

Nobody did. Everyone wanted to hear the answer. Moments trickled by, and still Reed remained silent.

Then, very slowly, Wolfgang detected the change. Not really a softening, but a shudder. A loosening of Reed's jaw. A flicker in his eyes. Some kind of life, or fighting spirit, or maybe just more anger.

"I have never lied to you," Reed said, his voice calm but no longer monotone. It rang true. It rang deep.

Like it used to.

Another lengthy pause. Turk breathed hard. His hand lifted, and Wolfgang thought he might be wiping his lips. Then the hand dropped. Turk's body language loosened, if only a little.

"Okay," he said. "Then you get the CIA on the phone. You tell them we're coming home when the job is done...and not five seconds sooner."

"The...job?" Lucy's voice was tentative. Turk didn't hesitate.

"*End the war.*"

Then, without another word, Turk staggered out of the camera view. Wolfgang glanced left and found Corbyn staring. Across the video feed, Lucy stared back. Reed watched Turk go.

Then Corbyn extended a hand and ended the call.

There was nothing more to say.

9

The George Bush Center for Intelligence
Langley, Virginia

The Sensitive Compartmented Information Facility, or SCIF, lay buried deep within CIA headquarters. Built inside a barricade of soundproof walls, with secure communication feeds and access only by biometric approval for Agency officers with a very high level of security clearance *and* an express need to know, the SCIF was designed as a place to assemble, review, and discuss the most sensitive forms of intelligence in the most secure way possible.

The design wasn't unique to the CIA. The Pentagon and various other federal agencies possessed similar builds. The military even maintained a selection of mobile SCIFs. But Deputy Director of Operations Silas Rigby doubted very seriously that any of those units rivaled the CIA's collection of SCIFs. This one in particular, constructed underground with armed security to reinforce the biometric door locks, was a place only a handful of Agency personnel could access. Rigby himself had seldom set foot in this room, not because it was off limits but because he'd never had a need. The use case of SCIF 10-ALPHA was unique. It wasn't a place for monitoring overseas operations or dissecting tens of thousands of hours of collected video feeds. It wasn't a place for meetings or analysis.

It was a place for games. Specifically, computer games, and even more specifically, the kind of computer games that just might predict the end of the world.

Standing at the back of the room with his arms crossed, Rigby was silent as a team of fifteen specialists operated multi-screen workstations linked to supercomputers so powerful that their exact capabilities were only theoretical. Heavily equipped with advanced artificial intelligence that was always self-developing from every data point it consumed, the invisible weapon concealed within armored computer cages was perhaps the most advanced intelligence tool the world had ever encountered. A marvel that rivaled the power of a nuclear weapon.

Only, instead of destroying lives, this weapon's job was to save them. To run endless calculations and hypothetical war scenarios, adjusting for tens of thousands of micro-variables that ranged from logistical logjams to unexpected severe weather, defecting conscript troops, war machine malfunctions, and political indecision on the home front.

In a game as complex—and lethal—as global war, *every* hypothetical mattered. The smallest detail could be the difference between decisive victory and slow, grinding defeat. Across Virginia at the Pentagon, the Department of Defense ran these simulations using their own supercomputers, but their chief focus was on the actual combat element of war.

The CIA's interest was much broader. Every analyst in this room was fed an endless stream of intel updates from all around the world. Not just Russian troop movements and Iranian fuel reserve values, but whispers on the streets of Bangkok and in the ports of South America. Rumors of third-world militant involvement, European separatist agitation, infrastructure sabotage in Africa that might threaten the supply of essential natural resources to China, and all the other minuscule items that meant so, *so* much in the big picture.

Because bullets alone don't win a war. Soldiers can't fight on an empty stomach, and they can't fight without gasoline, either. Without the support of their citizenry back home. Without communications and geographic access and assistance from the right locals at the right place and time. War had always been and would always be *so much* more than a matter of brute force. It was chess on its most advanced, deadly level.

Silas Rigby's job was to play that game over and over again. Adjusting for all variables and searching for the best possible solution, the most likely strategy to win.

Three weeks in, and the supercomputers had not shut down. Rigby's staff had barely shut down. But the answers…

Rigby chewed gum and slurped coffee—a bad combination, but his ADHD demanded movement and his exhaustion demanded caffeine. He scanned the wall-mounted display screens, tracking yet another simulation of mass European war. The belligerents were assumed—NATO versus Russia and Belarus. In this particular hypothetical, Russia had already seized control of the Baltic and was sweeping into Poland. Belarus circled to join the assault. Conventional missile strikes harassed NATO bases across Eastern Europe while American, British, and German fighter pilots fought their Russian counterparts high overhead.

Weeks spun like the second meter on a stopwatch as the simulation progressed. Hundreds of thousands of Allied troops stormed the continent. Battle lines bent and shifted—sometimes in favor of NATO, sometimes against it. The civilian populations of Poland, Slovakia, Hungary, and Romania all suffered horrific casualties. Mass electrical failures swept the continent. Food shortages led to famine across Eastern Europe. Russian troop deaths compiled as computerized Moscow conscripted replacements from Russia's peasant population. Negotiations for peace or even a ceasefire fell dead on the floor of the United Nations. Rigby watched it all, chewing ever faster as months stacked into years.

One. Two. Three.

And then it happened. His stomach fell. The coffee mug hit the desk as he watched the map. The computer zoomed out, and a collective silence fell across the room as every analyst looked up.

Fingers off their keyboards. Eyes blinking behind smudged glasses as one hot flash after another blinked across Europe—small, at first. Then quickly growing larger and reaching farther. Another two weeks, and intercontinental ballistic missiles—*nuclear* missiles—rained over mainland North America.

And that was that.

Rigby spat his gum into the trash and extended a hand without comment. The analyst nearest him printed the report and handed it off. Rigby folded it, still staring at the map screen as the flashes grew less and less frequent...but the causality estimator ran off the charts.

"Run the next," he said simply.

Then he left the room. He rode a secure elevator, poking another stick of gum into his mouth and wishing he had a blunt instead—not that a decorated, security-cleared CIA official like himself knew *anything* about recreational marijuana use.

At Langley's executive floor, Rigby cleared more security. He passed deputies of his own, secretaries and analysts. Some acknowledged him with a subdued "good morning" but Rigby said nothing. He marched right to the end of the room where a wall of glass panels stood obscured by electric blinds. Reaching for the door, Rigby found it unlocked, and he entered without knocking.

CIA Director Dr. Sarah Aimes sat behind a desk laden with computer monitors, just concluding a phone call as the door closed. She didn't even glance Rigby's way. She just sat, staring at the phone, the gray streaks running through her dark hair fifty percent bolder than they'd been only a short time prior when Aimes had first ascended to the director's position and Rigby had been appointed as her DDO.

She looked as tired as Rigby felt. Beaten, also. But not down. She was fixated on the phone, chewing her bottom lip. Thinking about something.

Rigby gave her the time, taking a seat in front of his boss's desk without comment or permission. Things worked a lot differently in Aimes's CIA than they had during the reign of her predecessor. With a zero-tolerance policy for bureaucratic nonsense or pretentious formalities, if Aimes's door wasn't locked, you were free to enter. If you thought she was wrong, you were expected to say so. If you had a concern, you were expected to voice it.

And if you failed at your job, you could expect to be fired. Very quickly. Because too many lives depended on the Agency. Rigby and Aimes had both witnessed firsthand the impact of the old guard and their ecosystems of self-preservation.

Things had to be different. But was it already too late?

"That was Montgomery," Aimes said, almost absentmindedly. "The Prosecution Force is refusing to come home. They..." She shook her head, snorting softly. "They want another job."

Rigby said nothing. He was well familiar with Reed Montgomery and his crew of off-the-books problem solvers. In very recent memory, against the direction of his boss and perhaps against his own better judgment, Rigby had worked with Montgomery directly on a mission that just might have kept India from sliding into alliance with China.

Montgomery was impressive in that mission. He'd been impressive in every mission he'd executed on behalf of the CIA...or sometimes in *spite* of the CIA. But what Rigby now held in that folded report was bigger than any maniac with a backpack full of hand grenades and a death wish.

It might be bigger than the whole human race.

"You have something?" Aimes said, finally shaking herself free of an exhausted daze and looking up.

Rigby passed her the print-off without comment. Aimes donned reading glasses and leaned back. She flipped through each of five pages, her brow knitting a little deeper with each one.

"I directed my team to focus on a non-nuclear military victory," Rigby said. "We've run those simulations all of last week, then we moved to a non-nuclear military cease-fire. A long-term armistice. A non-nuclear semi-surrender of Eastern Europe..."

Rigby trailed off. Aimes looked up. She removed her glasses.

"What are you telling me, Silas?"

Rigby breathed deep. He shook his head.

"I'm telling you we've got the tiger by the tail. I'm telling you...we're going to lose."

10

Moscow, Russia

Night fell over the Russian capital and the swarms of pro-war demonstrators gathered in Red Square morphed into something much closer to a drunken hive of revelers. With liquor flowing, drugs openly dispensed from one winter-gloved hand to another, and audible cries of ecstasy leaking out of the camping tents that sprang up all along the sidewalks, everything about this assembly was the kind of thing Makar Nikitin should have—and typically *would have*—quashed.

Quickly. With force and a nationalistic appeal to traditional moral virtues and the self-respect of the state—things that heartland Russians believed in. Things that kept Nikitin in power.

But Ivan Sidorov didn't think for a *moment* that Russia's president actually shared any of those values. That he actually cared about traditional moral virtue or the fundamentals of a conservative Russian society. More than anything, Nikitin cared about power. Quashing demonstrations had kept him in power—now, indulging demonstrations would fuel his war. With Russian TV cameras on every corner, a carefully curated broadcast bereft of the drugs and sex might just convince the nation that all of Russia stood behind Nikitin's invasion of Estonia—that all of Russia would follow him straight into Western Europe.

It was a lie. But a lie told long enough, told loud enough...

Ivan threaded his way through the revelers, skirting swishing tents and stepping over a kid barely old enough to drive who already lay passed out next to a broken vodka bottle. From not far away a radio station van projected Russian rock music with a decidedly nationalistic flare, while a food truck dispensed hot *chebureki*—fried meat pies served with cheese and mushrooms, a dream combination for the drunk and hungry.

Ivan couldn't help but notice that nobody paid for the food. Prices weren't even listed. In place of a menu was a poster, gaudily printed with a comic-book-style image of Nikitin in full military uniform. The caption read: *Россия не начинает войны — она их заканчивает.*

Russia doesn't start wars—it ends them.

It turned Ivan's stomach, all of it. In the faces of the next generation he saw anger, indignation. An outrage misdirected at vague overseas monsters instead of at the corrupt government that lay barely a stone's throw to every side of them. The *real* perpetrators for Russia's ongoing economic and infrastructural nightmares. The heart that pumped poisoned blood from St. Petersburg to Vladivostok.

And wouldn't stop pumping until the whole nation quaked in nuclear death throws.

Ivan turned away from the food truck despite his hunger. He'd worked the crowds well over the course of the afternoon, using the swarm for effective cover as he navigated right under the noses of the Russian security agencies who wanted his head on a platter. He bought a hoodie, blood-red with the phrase *Берём своё*—we take what is ours—printed across the chest. He wore a Russian flag print hat and pretended to drink beer. He blended in well, because Ivan Sidorov had spent the better part of his long and chaotic life learning to blend in well. To hide in plain sight, to work the angles and exploit people's assumptions and slip like a knife right to the most vulnerable core of his target.

Now that darkness had consumed Moscow and the Russian security officers monitoring Red Square were accustomed to the gathered revelers, Ivan could afford to be a little more direct. He departed the thickest swarms of demonstrators and edged closer to Lenin's mausoleum and the outer walls of the Kremlin complex. There were sixty or eighty cars gathered there—mostly belonging to the revelers, and mostly illegally parked.

The Moscow police, it seemed, didn't care about the violation. Ivan would have bet money that Nikitin himself had personally ordered them off, eager to indulge his most ardent supporters in their wholesale exhibitions of brainwashed allegiance. Whatever the case, the cluster of vehicles had remained all day and was now an known quantity to the security personnel that surveyed Red Square. Their license plates would have already been run, checked against databases of known domestic threats to ensure that enemies of the state—persons such as Ivan Sidorov, for example—had not mingled with Nikitin's throng of true believers.

No threat found, no threat assumed. The carnival at Ivan's back must have been an engaging spectacle for bored FSB agents manning remote cameras all day long. Certainly more interesting than one old man stumbling back to his car.

Ivan thumbed the key fob he'd lifted from a drunk college kid and rolled it in his hand. On the back side of it's plastic case, it featured the silver Lada logo...but that wasn't particularly helpful. As Russia's primary automotive brand, there must have been a few hundred thousand Ladas scattered around metro Moscow alone, and at least thirty of those were present in the knot of beater economy cars gathered near the Kremlin wall. Old man or otherwise, checking one door handle at a time would arouse suspicion.

So Ivan began clicking the lock button as he approached the makeshift parking lot, and by the time he'd closed to within fifty yards of the nearest vehicle, taillights flashed in blazing crimson. It was a Lada Kalina, a subcompact hatchback that made Ivan sore just looking at it. He routed easily toward the car as though he'd known where it lay all along, and subtly rolled the driver's seat back as he slid inside.

Cramped. Dirty. Smelling of body odor and sour fast food trash. A real pit, but the engine started and the fuel gauge displayed half a tank.

More than enough.

Ivan took his time backing onto the street. With his head rising high into the Lada's sloping ceiling, he enjoyed the benefit of concealing his face from the majority of nearby cameras—like an oversized hat. He shifted into drive and rolled as slowly as he dared toward the outer edge of Red Square...and then turned toward the Kremlin's main entrance.

It was all a guessing game at this point. Ivan Sidorov had been inside the Kremlin a few thousand times. At different stages in his career, he'd even worked there. He knew his mark personally—had shaken his hand, in fact. Prior memory of the target's patterns informed Ivan that even though this man usually worked in the Russian White House, he visited the Kremlin for meetings every Wednesday, and usually departed about this time. Eager to get home to his rosy wife, a hearty dinner and a horde of French bulldogs. The man was obsessed with them—rumor had it, he even shared his bed with them. He enjoyed his domestic routines.

But that was during *normal* times. Pre-war, pre-international crisis. Now, the target might stay late. Meetings could run to midnight, or even later. This scheme might not work at all.

But Ivan was ready to roll the dice. He slid the Lada onto a public parking lane just west of St. Basil's Cathedral and killed his lights but left the engine running. Under the illumination of streetlamps, the breadth of Red Square was fully illuminated all the way to the hulking face of Spasskaya Tower, the Kremlin's main entrance. Ivan could actually see the security staff stationed just inside. He watched via his side-view mirror as a trio of Mercedes-Benz sedans entered, and one van departed.

But the car Ivan was looking for, while black, would be considerably longer and more striking than even an S-Class Mercedes. Weighed down with armor and featuring a Russian national flag, the Aurus Senat was an absolute monster of a limousine, hulking and bold and very similar to the car that Nikitin himself used.

But Nikitin wouldn't be in this car. Nikitin preferred to fly if he left the Kremlin—which he seldom did, these days. Why bother? His grip on Russian power was near absolute.

Near.

Ivan adjusted the seat back. He tapped one finger on his thigh. He watched the tower and his stomach growled, but he ignored it. He checked his wristwatch every few minutes, conscious that every ticking second increased his personal risk and decreased his prospect of success.

He might have arrived too soon. Maybe he should have waited it out in the crowd a little longer. He didn't want to be late...

Ivan's thoughts trailed off as headlights flashed from inside the tower. Bright and bold and quite similar to the headlights of Nikitin's car, but this wasn't Nikitin's car. The Aurus passed through the gate and dipped into Red Square with a flutter of the Russian flag. Even from two hundred yards away, Ivan could hear the surge of its twin-turbo motor. He traced the monster as it turned, rolling south toward the Kremlin Embankment.

And after that?

Ivan couldn't be sure. The location of Prime Minister Maxim Romanov's private residence was an obscured secret that Ivan could have easily uncovered during his days as a senior SVR agent, but he hadn't needed to know then.

Now there was no option left except for Ivan to do things the dirty, old-fashioned way. The way that could very easily leave him rotting in a ditch...

Or might just save Russia from imminent destruction.

Sliding into reverse, Ivan backed the Lada away from the cathedral. He gave the Aurus time to turn west along the Kremlin Embankment.

Then Ivan Sidorov followed.

11

Wells Fargo Center
Philadelphia, Pennsylvania

The stands were packed—twenty-three thousand sweaty bodies that overwhelmed the AC systems, every one of them on their feet. Every one of them roaring back at the six-piece band and the lone singer standing beneath glaring lights behind the mic.

It was an encore performance of Banks Montgomery's most popular original song, a war-spirit ballad called "Home Front." Laced with military imagery and heavy with undertones of threat, loss, and resurgence, the song was sad and angry all at once. Less about the war, more about the fight. More about the *need*.

And the relentless will to overcome.

It was brash bravado at its best, poured like jet fuel on a fire. Banks's co-writers had expressed concern about some of the more traditional sentiments, worrying about signals of blind nationalism. Banks knew better. She'd walked the streets of her new home in Nashville and watched as packed sidewalks slowly emptied. As a once-crowded hockey arena struggled to sell tickets and the local minor league baseball team canceled games for nonattendance.

Not because people no longer cared, but because they were *scared.* Terrified to leave their homes after repeated terrorist attacks, a shuddering economy, and two nuclear blasts overseas. Crushing miles in her tour bus, Banks had crossed from sea to shining sea, and in every corner of America the story was the same.

Whites and minorities. Conservatives and liberals. War hawks and isolationists. *Everyone* was scared, uncertain where to turn, teetering on the edge of a societal collapse that would drag the entire Western world with it.

They *needed* the blind war spirit—that same cocktail of relentless belief and absolute commitment that had conquered the Great Depression, won back-to-back World Wars, and stared down the Soviets. Even more than dollars or bullets or hope itself, America needed belief. She *needed* bravado. She needed to not be afraid.

And thus was born Banks's tour—the *Not Afraid* tour, because why make it complicated? It began in DC, where Banks performed swelling outdoor concerts for free until her manager insisted that she hit the road. The amphitheaters were no longer larger enough—hockey and basketball arenas were next. From Los Angeles to Denver, New Orleans, Chicago, and now Philly, every stop included multiple shows—every show was sold out.

And now Banks wasn't the only one. Other artists were launching similar campaigns, playing shows aggressively seasoned with patriotic anthems and guest appearances by senators and military personnel. Those shows weren't as popular as Banks's, but they still had no trouble selling tickets. Many of the proceeds were donated directly to organizations dedicated to supporting the creature comforts of frontline troops.

Slowly, but surely, Banks could feel the tempo changing. She could feel the fear subsiding into something closer to anger—indignation. A revulsion to cowering in the shadows. A desire to rise up and strike back.

America was coming off her leash, and it was the most beautiful thing Banks had ever seen.

"Home Front" concluded for the second time and Banks stood with her head rocked back, clinging to the mic stand in mock paralysis. It was a performance technique, but also an opportunity to catch her breath. Drenched from head to toe in sweat, panting with her heart hammering,

Banks had consumed nearly three liters of water prior to taking the stage and hadn't needed to pee once.

They didn't warn you about this sort of thing when you turned up on Music Row with empty pockets and a head full of dreams. They didn't tell you about the extreme physical toll, the exhaustion, the stop after stop after stop with only a couple of hours each night for Banks to spend with her toddler son, Davy. In some ways, it was a war of her own, with its own tremendous cost.

But Banks would pay it without a second thought. Not for the fame or the money, neither of which were as glamorous in reality as in her imagination, but because somewhere on the far side of the planet, a man she couldn't help but love would give his very life for her and Davy. Hundreds of thousands of men and women like him were lined up to do the same.

This was the home front battle.

Banks leaned forward, bangs sticking to her forehead as a wash of dizziness cascaded over her. The band was silent and the crowd thundered for minute after punishing minute. Cheers blended with claps and chants of "*Not afraid. Not afraid.*"

Banks smiled. The crowd roared louder. She released the mic and drank water. She looked up into the furthest reaches of the arena, way up into the nosebleeds where only the glimmer of cell phone lights marked the individual dots of so many thousands of people. Americans of every stripe and creed—*her* people.

She blew a kiss. They blew the roof off. Her smile stretched to a grin, and she caught the guitarist smirking and rolling his eyes at her.

Let him. Banks was made for this moment. She'd waited her whole life for it.

Back at the mic. The crowd slowly calmed. The band remained silent. When Banks hit the first note of her closer, hers was the only voice in the arena. Every breath held, every eye fixated on her. She sang the national anthem without any effort to add her own flare or flash—she sang it straight up, just the way it was written, as sweet and slow and somber as it should be sung.

And when she reached the crescendo, the crowd joined in. The building shook. The band played. Banks hit the high note and held it until her lungs felt ready to burst. The mic left the stand and the stand hit the ground and she shoved a fist into the sky.

It hurt. The noise actually hurt. Banks's head pounded and her hand shook, but she let them have that moment. She wanted them to bask in it, to bring it home with them. To spread it like a virus at work and at school and across the whole northeast.

"I love you Philadelphia!" Banks shouted. "You are *not afraid*!"

The best part about touring as a star was all the *help*. After years of packing her own instruments and gear from one barroom set to another, Banks couldn't deny the luxury of walking right off stage and straight into her bus.

Soaked in sweat. Breathless and ready to drop. Still riding the high of the performance while her mind surged ahead to the next set or the next city. In this case, New York. Madison Square Garden. *Three* sold out shows.

Absolutely unbelievable.

The Prevost tour bus pumped a rush of icy cool rush AC as Banks passed a sitting area equipped with couches, a full dining set, two guitars held on racks, and a kitchenette large enough to cook Thanksgiving dinner in. Her road manager sat at the table behind a computer with a phone held to his ear. He caught her eye and gave her a big thumbs-up as she hurried past, eager not to be ensnared in conversation. Davy slept in the back of the bus in her private room, which was also where the shower was. With any luck, she could be undisturbed for at least a few hours.

"Hey, Banks!"

Banks's gut tightened. She stopped inches from the door to her room and glanced back.

"Yeah?"

"*Phone call.*" The manager mouthed the word—he was still on the phone himself. He pointed to Banks's cell phone resting on the kitchen counter.

"Thanks." Banks took the phone and hurried through the door before the manager could say anything more. On the sheltered side she leaned against the wall and exhaled, suddenly overcome by exhaustion. In the dark with only the chug of the bus's diesel to break the stillness, her ears rang. Her body ached. She couldn't decide if she wanted to shower first or see Davy or just pass out right in bed.

She lifted the phone instead, more curious about the time than the missed call. Then she saw the number—an international call with a sat phone code. In an instant the exhaustion and the headache and the ringing ears were all forgotten. She was already unlocking the phone, breathing fast and redialing.

Please pickup. Please pickup.

In more ways than one, Banks hated herself for the longing. Not only because it was painful but because a smarter girl might have jettisoned the feelings long ago. Might have wised up, learned her lesson, not been so foolishly attached to—

"Banks?"

Reed's voice crackled from the far side of the globe. Banks didn't know exactly where—she'd talked to him twice in the past week and all he would say is "Middle East," which concerned her much more than she admitted. As with every time before, Reed sounded tired. He sounded beat, even broken. He sounded lost beyond some untouchable void that she couldn't quite reach through...

Why did she love him this way?

"It's me," Banks said, smiling softly.

"I, uh...I tried to call earlier," Reed said.

"I was in concert."

"Oh?"

"Philadelphia. You know that arena where the Flyers play? We sold it out...twice."

Pause. Banks wasn't sure if Reed heard her. When he finally responded, she realized she was holding her breath.

"*Twice*?"

Banks grinned. She didn't say anything more. A single tear leaked out of her eye and she scrubbed it away. She could hear his breathing, soft but a little raspy. He just...he didn't quite sound like himself.

"I miss you, Reed," Banks whispered.

Silence. It was the usual response to her expressions of affection, and that hurt worse than a punch to the gut. For months Banks doubted whether the feelings were reciprocated at all. Whether Reed had fallen out of love with her long ago, wanted nothing more to do with her...

But no. She knew better. She'd seen his desperation when she awoke in a hospital, the victim of a terrorist's bomb. Reed Montgomery was a very, *very* damaged man. He'd never been good at processing emotions, and that was before the trauma of nearly losing his wife...and their unborn child.

Banks pushed the thought away. She couldn't think about that. It hurt too much. She thought of Davy, and how he'd sang with her prior to the show, dancing on the bus bed. She wanted to tell Reed the story.

But Reed spoke first. "I miss you so much."

Banks's breath froze. Her mouth hung open. The tears bubbled in her eyes and she didn't know what to say. Forgot how to move. Outside, her road manager knocked on the door, but she tuned him out.

She was lost in that phone call. Everything else simply faded from existence.

"I'm sorry," Reed said. "I'm sorry for...everything. You never deserved this life. I never deserved you."

Banks blinked. A lump rose into her throat. The tears came a little faster, but she didn't wipe them away. The manager gave up and finally left.

And then, Banks laughed. Just a short, breathy sound, come and gone.

"You know...you may be right."

She couldn't tell if Reed took the joke. If he laughed or smiled or responded at all. She thought of him in some barracks on the far side of the planet, all alone...and she just wanted to hold him. To be held by him. To break through this fog of terror and come out on the other side whole.

"I *love you*, Reed Montgomery. Your son loves you. And we're waiting for you to come home a hero."

12

The White House
Washington, DC

"Everything, everywhere, all at once. That's our problem."

The voice of CIA Deputy Director of Operations Silas Rigby remained calm as he stood at the head of the conference table, clicking through a slideshow prepared by the Agency. This was only the second, maybe the third time that Aimes had passed presentation duties to her second-in-command, but Rigby took to the responsibility like a fish to water. With natural poise and a talent for remaining on target that Maggie prized like pure gold, Rigby guided the crowded room through maps of Europe, the Middle East, and the South Pacific.

Tracing battle lines. Strategic targets. Supply routes and logistical chokepoints. Not just military concerns but civilian and political factors also. All the tens of thousands of micro-ingredients that the CIA had fed into their supercomputers to predict each move of the enemy, every possible response by the West, every subsequent response by Russia, Iran, and China...and so on. Cycle after cycle, playing chess eight and ten moves ahead. Getting inside the heads of the enemy.

Searching for that one path to victory that avoided both surrender and nuclear war. Two unacceptable options.

"The Agency has analyzed the political and military posturing of every belligerent," Rigby said. "In thousands of case studies involving superpowers and their relationships to smaller allies, we've identified core personality types which reappear in nearly every global conflict. These profiles are similar to character sketches in a movie—the archetypes of a villain and their supporting cast. In this case, the Agency is confident in stating that Russia is both the instigator and the ringleader. Iran's roll is closer to that of the disinhibited follower, otherwise known as the 'secondary psychopath.'"

Rigby made air quotes. Somebody tapped a pencil. Rigby continued.

"Traditionally this player can be highly destructive in their own right but may rely on encouragement or agitation from the ringleader. However, in my personal opinion, that understanding of Iran lacks the context of radical Islamic influence, which has motivated the government in Tehran to act of their own accord—they simply lacked the opportunity to do so. In this way, if you'll pardon the political incorrectness, I prefer to think of Iran as a vicious dog on a chain. Russia let them off the chain."

Rigby paused there, glancing down the table as though ready for some pushback. None was offered—maybe because Iran was rolling into Baghdad as Rigby spoke. The metaphor of a monster let off its chain rang true.

"Continue," Maggie said simply.

Rigby returned to his presentation with another press of the slide remote.

"The real question mark in our analysis is China. While at times demonstrating characteristics of a primary accomplice or even a co-conspirator, China's lack of open military aggression following the skirmish over the Taiwan Strait is both puzzling and counterintuitive. As Russia storms the Baltic and Iran overwhelms Iraq, Beijing's opportunity to exploit American distraction has never been greater. Their own military readiness is unparalleled in recent history. And yet...they aren't moving. They're just waiting."

"Scared?" It was Yellin who spoke, and there was no bravado in his voice. It was an honest question.

"Possibly," Rigby said. "But we don't think so. Our intelligence mapping indicates a hole—a missing piece in our understanding of Chinese war doctrine. It's as though...they're waiting for something. That's the best way I know to put it."

"Well, that's a little unsettling," Yellin said.

Unsettling was the right word. Over the past week, Maggie's meetings with war planners and diplomats had universally orbited around a single problem: Russia's invasion of Eastern Europe, and the NATO security crisis it unleased.

What little oxygen remained after discussions of confronting a belligerent nuclear super power was directed at the crisis in the Middle East. Specifically, at the tens of thousands of US Marines landing in Lebanon, and the specter of Iran looming over Israel.

Nobody talked about China. There wasn't any *time* to talk about China. America was indeed distracted. So...why wasn't Beijing exploiting the opportunity?

Maggie wondered, and Rigby resumed his presentation.

"The Chinese puzzle notwithstanding, the Agency continues to evaluate simulations of a widespread European conflict. As directed by the president, our objective is to halt Russia's incursion while preventing nuclear war. War games conducted over the past two weeks have been nearly exhaustive. Calculating for the escalation of ground hostilities in Europe, the parameters under which Russia would be expected to use nuclear force, the limitations of current NATO war doctrine, expected resource shortages and—"

"Deputy." Maggie's voice cut a little deeper than she intended, but she didn't regret it. The suspended tension in the room was palpable—it was time to land this plane.

"We all know the problems," she said. "Tell us if you found a solution."

Long pause. Rigby glanced once to his boss, but Director Aimes made no effort to intercede. She simply nodded. Rigby faced the president.

"If we engage Russia in an open European war, and are successful in repelling their advance, our analysts believe that President Nikitin will use nuclear force in the name of national defense. Every simulation we ran concludes with that result. The only scenarios we identified which avoid nuclear conflict all involve a gradual loss of territory and eventual surrender of Eastern Europe. In some cases...Western Europe was even threatened, in which case our simulations included the potential for France or even Britain to implement their own nuclear defenses."

Silence again. This time it was Yellin who broke it. He leaned forward.

"Are you telling me...we've already lost?"

"With respect, General, it's not my place to say. I'm only here to say that the Agency was tasked with identifying a path to victory barring the use of nuclear force...and no path has been found."

The meeting ran for another three straight hours.

Seated at the middle of the table with every part of her body aching, a pulsating fire radiating out of her abdomen and right to her fingertips, all Maggie could do was focus on the problem at hand.

Listen to her generals. Listen to her State Department. Listen to her advisors.

And then, eventually, make a decision. To escalate or not to escalate? Except it was really no choice at all, because Russia had invaded NATO, and if the US didn't respond now, the game was already over.

The US must escalate. Maggie would authorize phase two of Operation United Resolve—the deployment of more troops, the initiation of air strikes, and the declaration of an immediate naval blockade of the Baltic Sea. All the initial setup for what already appeared to be a long, catastrophic conflict.

As the cabinet room slowly emptied, Maggie remained behind, drinking water and sweating. Conscious of the fact that she looked terrible, and unable to be concerned about it. For months she had calibrated and polished her appearance in the desperate effort to quench media rumors of her physical decay...and really, where had all that effort gotten her? The media rumors ran rampant anyway, and Maggie couldn't be concerned about them, either.

She could only think about her next round of meetings with Congressional leadership—the first opening discussion of the unthinkable. A possible declaration of war against Russia.

"A moment, ma'am?"

Maggie looked away from the project screen, which still displayed high-resolution maps of Europe with Russia's battle lines drawn in classic red—the bad guy color. The voice that addressed her was that of Director Aimes. She and Rigby had remained behind—along with a trio of aides packing up equipment, they were the last in the room.

"Clear the room, please." Maggie addressed the aides. They departed without hesitation. The doors closed and Aimes drew back a chair. Rigby sat next to her.

"You're not very good at your job, Deputy."

Maggie meant it as a soft joke. Nobody laughed or even so much as smiled.

"They're only simulations," Aimes said. "Ten thousand variables could occur at any moment. As new data is fed into the computers, there's always the hope that we'll identify a window of opportunity. It's an ongoing process."

Maggie nodded. She felt sweat sliding down her forehead, despite the bitter chill of the room.

Why was she *always* sweating?

"You had something to add?" Maggie said, suddenly eager for a moment alone.

Rigby glanced sideways at his boss. Aimes simply nodded as before.

"Ma'am..." Rigby began, then stopped. He cleared his throat. "There was one anomaly to our simulations. One possible...uh...*scenario* which prevented nuclear war while halting or even reversing the Russian advance. I avoided presenting it in the meeting because it's...well. It's volatile, and extremely controversial. But I wanted to make you aware."

Maggie waited. She lifted her eyebrows.

Aimes stepped in, dropping the words like hot rocks.

"Regime change, ma'am. A complete replacement of the Nikitin administration from the inside out. A coup d'état, in other words."

Maggie blinked. It wasn't what she expected. Looking at Aimes, she could hardly believe what the director was saying. Rigby must have sensed the disbelief, because he rushed to fill the silence.

"Our intel indicates that the vast majority of the Russian populace, and potentially even core segments of the Russian government, don't support Nikitin's war. There are concerns of nuclear holocaust, or at the least, unchecked demographic collapse as hundreds of thousands of Russia's young men are killed. Given Nikitin's crackdown on free speech, it's logical to assume that sentiments such as these could be even stronger than they appear. Under the right catalyst, our simulations indicate that an uprising could be triggered, and if Nikitin were somehow replaced...the entire Russian war machine could implode overnight."

Rigby never broke eye contact as he delivered the spiel, and when he concluded, Aimes jumped right in.

"There's something else, ma'am, regarding what we discussed about the Chinese. It could be that the hesitation we sense from Beijing is linked to their uncertainty about stability in Moscow. In other words, China is aware that Nikitin may be suppressing internal opposition, and they want to wait and see if he can maintain a war in Europe before they risk their own open confrontation with America. They're playing it safe, in other words—waiting to see how the dice will fall."

"And waiting to see if Nikitin can survive his own war," Rigby added.

Silence. Maggie processed the information with ease. The mental fog was gone—she saw the picture in perfect detail. She also understood why Aimes and Rigby hadn't presented this scenario in the meeting. The chaos and debate it would have unleashed would have been overwhelming.

But Maggie didn't care about that. She'd held discussions like this with the CIA before—many times since assuming office. Already her mind was spinning ahead, careening down a road of possibilities. Of angles.

Maggie leaned forward. Even though they were alone in the room, her voice dropped to just above a whisper.

"Are you suggesting that we *prompt* regime change in Russia?"

No immediate answer. Rigby looked to his boss, and Aimes interlaced her fingers over the polished surface of the table.

At last Aimes said: "We're suggesting that America is between a rock and a very hard place...and that all available options should be on the table."

13

Department of Corrections Central Detention Facility
Washington, DC

They cuffed him hand and foot even before they guided him out of the windowless concrete box where he'd spent most of the last three weeks.

Walking with the swish of a generic white prison jumpsuit hanging loose around his legs, James O'Dell said nothing to the guards who escorted him. He said nothing to the correctional officers who buzzed him through multiple solid steel doors with security glass inserts. He walked with his head up, jaw closed, not making a sound as he was guided to a small concrete room only a little bigger than his cell.

There was no bed, no sink, no toilet. Just a metal table bolted to the floor with metal benches likewise bolted on either side. A bright light hung overhead, and a two-foot-square window mounted high in the wall allowed views of thunderstorm clouds outside.

One man waited. He wore a black suit and a striped red-and-gray tie. He rose as O'Dell entered but didn't offer his hand. The guards guided O'Dell to the far bench and instructed him to sit. They didn't unshackle him, and the man in the striped tie didn't complain about it.

The guards departed the room and locked the door behind them, leaving O'Dell alone...with his lawyer.

The attorney settled back onto his bench, dispensing a legal pad already covered in notes from his briefcase. It landed with a smack. The attorney clicked open a pen and stared at O'Dell—a long, exhausted look.

Then he sighed.

"Okay, look. I don't have long, so I'll cut right to the chase. Since our last visit, I received the discovery file from the prosecution—this is all the evidence they plan to use as proof of your guilt."

O'Dell knew what it was. Before serving as special advisor to the president—before even serving as her security guard way back in Baton Rouge—he'd been a Louisiana state cop. He knew all about evidence and the right of discovery. The fact that the prosecution had thrown their cards on the table so soon was not a good sign.

"I'm not going to lie to you, James," the attorney said. "The government's case is...it's a slam dunk. Okay? I mean they have you on camera. They have you blocks from Jacob Grover's house. They have you leaving not long after a neighbor reported a gunshot. They searched your house and they found a pair of socks with blood spatter on them. They're running DNA now but...come on, man. What are they going to find?"

O'Dell clenched his teeth. He couldn't help it. He *knew* he forgot something—why did it have to be socks? He'd come home so late that night. So tired, so distracted by concerns for Maggie. She was literally dying, desperate for a liver transplant and wasting away while awaiting a suitable donor organ.

He'd trashed his clothes. Actually, he'd burned them on his barbecue grill. How had he forgotten the socks?

Maybe they weren't the same socks. Maybe the blood was his own—the result of a scratch. But even as he hoped, O'Dell knew better.

When Jacob Grover had pressed that revolver against his head, sobbing and begging, he'd refused to pull the trigger. O'Dell had to help him.

It got messy.

"That wasn't a rhetorical question." The attorney sounded irritated. Probably, he was. He hadn't been hired by O'Dell, he'd been *assigned* to

O'Dell. A public defender with too much on his plate and not enough compensation to motivate him. It was a raw deal for both parties. O'Dell should make it easy on the guy—help himself out.

But he didn't answer. He didn't say a thing. The attorney cursed.

"Okay, fine. You want to play it that way? Perfect. Let me tell you how this will go. They're going to convict you—that's going to happen. First degree murder. That's murder with intent, life in prison with no possibility of parole. You *die* in a concrete closet. Okay? A young man like you, healthy and fit, you're looking at *decades*. Bad food and cellmates who want to shank you in your sleep. A slow, miserable death."

The mental image was clear, but O'Dell didn't need to be told. Not because he'd ever served time himself but because, as a former cop, he was familiar with the inside of detention facilities. The last three weeks had refreshed his memory. He knew *exactly* what lay ahead of him...

But how could he turn back? What options did he really have?

He did this for *her*.

"If it's over and done, why are you here?" O'Dell spoke for the first time, his voice flat and cold. Despite the tone, the attorney seemed to brighten.

"*There*. Now you're thinking rationally. I'm here because there *might* be an opportunity to cut a deal. It's a microscopic chance—no guarantees. But apparently, the prosecution thinks you know things. I have no idea what, but they hinted, and if you talk—freely and on the record—I *might* be able to get the charges reduced to second degree murder. You're looking at fifteen years and then some parole. Could be less, if you really keep your nose clean. It all depends on what you know and how honest you're willing to be."

How honest you're willing to be.

The words echoed in O'Dell's mind, and his chest tightened again. He'd expected this, of course. He knew it was coming.

And he knew it was no option at all.

"James?" the attorney prompted. "You start with me. I can't represent you if I don't know what you know."

O'Dell still didn't answer. His mind had already left the room, winding backward. Across the past three...no, four years. Was it five?

It was all a blur. All those long days and late nights, carrying a gun, ready to jump in front of a bullet. Eventually *failing* to jump in front of a bullet. Watching Maggie Trousdale, his charge, his focus, maybe his obsession, topple to the ground. Struggle for long months after. Nearly die multiple times.

All because *he* failed to save her. Because he failed to wrap her in an invisible shield the way she so deserved. Maggie—*his* Maggie. Muddy and beautiful and amazing.

"*James*."

The attorney's voice turned hard. O'Dell's mind ratcheted back to the present. His dark eyes snapped toward the lawyer's. He swallowed once.

"Get Maggie on the phone," he said.

The attorney blinked. His face screwed into a frown. "Who?"

"Maggie Trousdale."

"The *president*?"

"Get her on the phone," O'Dell repeated. "I'll only talk to her."

14

The Naval Observatory
Washington, DC

Stratton smoked Cubans.

Not because they were better—these days, a solid Nicaraguan or Honduran cigar could be just as excellent. Stratton didn't smoke the Cubans because they were illegal, either. For a man with means and connections such as him, petty matters such as trade embargos were as minor an annoyance as a parking ticket, and just as easily dismissed. There was no thrill to be found in bucking a system so weak.

Jordan Stratton smoked Cuban cigars because that's what Strattons *did*. His father smoked them, his grandfather smoked them. His great-grandfather was rumored to have lit up a Toro while standing over the smoldering battlefield of San Juan Hill, a lever gun resting on one shoulder.

It was almost definitely a myth, but still the most badass story Stratton's family could claim. Sometimes he thought of his great-grandfather, surrounded by a cloud of smoke, overlooking so much carnage, and the mental image added a little piss and vinegar to Stratton's blood. A little savage resolve.

He needed savage resolve now. Maybe more than ever in his life, the circumstances around him felt like a battlefield...and the battle wasn't over. It was only getting started.

Alone in his study, Stratton dropped the stub of a Cohiba into his ashtray and immediately lit up a second, savoring that first perfect draw as he dialed his desk phone.

It rang. And rang. And rang.

He was just about to hang up when someone finally answered. A soft voice spoken in barely above a whisper. Focused, and tense.

"Sorry, I needed to clear my office."

Stratton settled into his desk chair, his body relaxed even as his mind raced, just as it had for days. Keeping him awake. Turning his stomach. Adding layers to the field of gray that spread across his scalp like a different kind of invading army.

War.

"What's the update?" Stratton said simply.

"We held a cabinet meeting this morning," the speaker said. "The CIA presented findings from war game simulations—the president tasked them with identifying a strategy that avoided both defeat and nuclear escalation."

"And?"

"And...they failed. So far."

Stratton puffed. He rolled the cigar and looked out the window—over the lawn, toward the eastern horizon.

"What's the status in Europe?"

Stratton already thought he knew. CNN's reports at this point would be nearly as good as the Pentagon's. But there might be nuance. There might be subtext.

"Estonia will fall. It's already too late. Latvia is putting up a good fight against the Belarussians, but as soon as Russia pivots to hit them from the east...it'll be over just as quick. Lithuania will be next. Maybe as soon as next month."

Next month. Unbelievable.

"Where the hell is the NATO response?" It was the only question that mattered.

"It's building," the speaker said. "US and European troops are gathering in Germany, Romania, Poland. The president has authorized a full naval blockade of the Baltic Sea."

"A *what*?"

"It's part of her war strategy, Operation United Resolve. She wants to choke Russian naval activity."

Stratton swore. He smacked the cigar against the ashtray, dispensing ash. It was terrible cigar etiquette—he didn't even care.

"This isn't a *naval war*," Stratton snapped. "They're *invading* NATO."

"I know."

The answer was subdued. Strained. As stressed as Stratton felt.

He took a breath and replaced the cigar in his mouth. For a long moment he didn't move, didn't speak. Just refocused his mind.

Think, Jordan. Be rational.

"Does Operation United Resolve involve fighting back?"

The question was seasoned with a little bitter sarcasm—Stratton couldn't help himself.

"It does," the voice answered. "But I think the speed of Russia's attack has taken everyone off guard. The cabinet is scrambling. There's a lot of concern over China, also, and we're still landing Marines in Lebanon. It's too much at once."

"Chaos?" Stratton prompted.

No answer. He didn't really need one.

"Listen to me." Stratton's tone lowered a notch. "This isn't personal. This isn't opportunistic. This is about the fate of the Western world—okay? Maybe the entire human race. Nikitin is running wild, and nobody is standing in his way. The bolder he feels, the more likely he is to do something drastic. You are my eyes and ears inside the administration. I *need to know* if and when I need to act. Do you understand? I don't *want* to do this. But if she can't get the job done...I will."

Long pause. Stratton waited.

Then the speaker said: "I understand. I'll keep you posted."

"That's all I need."

Stratton moved to hang up. The speaker caught him before he could.

"There was...one other thing."

"What?"

"A meeting. Between the president, Aimes, and her deputy. Silas Rigby. It occurred after the cabinet was dismissed."

"What about?"

"I don't know—I'd already left the room. She dismissed everyone but them."

Stratton considered, pinching the cigar between his teeth as he once again stared out the window. He looked generally toward the White House, and he imagined he could see it. He imagined he could penetrate those high walls and find Maggie in the Oval, or in a cabinet room. Maybe in her residence.

What was she doing? More importantly still, what was she thinking?

"Keep me posted," Stratton said. "Try to find out what was discussed in that meeting, and get me an update on Chinese activity if you can."

No answer. Stratton sat up.

"This is the fate of the country," he said. "You understand that? Three hundred sixty million people. Their lives are on the line."

"I understand."

"So call me back."

Stratton hung up. He sucked on the Cuban, allowing smoke to boil into his sinuses and roll out through his nose. He accessed a secure web-messaging software on his computer and scrolled through a list of contacts before selecting one labeled simply as "Bob."

Stratton messaged.

Update?

Long pause. Stratton puffed smoke and spaced out in front of a hazy screen. Thinking...wondering. Agonizing.

Then "Bob" messaged back.

He still won't talk, still won't cut a deal. He's demanding to speak with the president.

Stratton's brow furrowed. He hesitated over the keys. Then he typed back:

Is she taking his calls?

The response was immediate.

I don't know.

Stratton sank his teeth into the cigar. He jabbed out a final message.

Find out.

Then he logged out of the computer.

15

Rublyovka, Russia

The dacha was a big one—Ivan knew that even without actually seeing the house. Removed from a winding asphalt street and surrounded by a cover of Norway spruce trees, the entrance of the property was guarded by a one-piece iron gate and an accompanying security shack. Lights marked the drive, and in the distance beyond the trees, additional lights twinkled from the property itself.

A *large* dacha, yes. An exclusive, rural escape for the prime minister of the Russian Federation, dually protected by a full detail of the Federal Protective Service. No doubt there were cameras at the gate, perhaps dogs and heavily armed security agents patrolling the property. Sneaking past the fence and closing to within view of the house without being shot through the head would be like winning the lottery for an average operative.

But nothing about Ivan Sidorov was average, and he knew the Federal Protective Service's playbook better than they knew it themselves. These guys weren't trained in countersurveillance or even close quarters combat. They were trained to establish a perimeter and let absolutely nothing get past them—to face outward and dump bullets like rain if threatened. In this most basic strategy they excelled.

But if Ivan got in their blind spot, if he somehow slipped *inside* their perimeter...well. He liked his odds better than theirs.

Ivan drove past the property only once after trailing Maxim Romanov's Aurus out of Moscow. A second pass would have been helpful, but it would also almost certainly alert the FSO agents at the gate, so he parked the Lada at a petrol station two kilometers down the road.

Now on foot, dressed in all black and fading between the trees like a ghost, Ivan leveraged satellite imagery on his phone to scope out the terrain. It wasn't a perfect strategy—on this street alone half a dozen elite dachas sat buried in the forest, the thick cover of evergreen trees obscuring the satellite's view. Ivan hadn't actually *seen* which driveway the Aurus turned down. He couldn't risk following that close.

Yet he felt good about his choice in address. Of the six houses depicted on the satellite screen, all were large with sprawling wings and covered pool houses. All six consumed sizeable chunks of cleared land surrounded by trees, and all six were likely the vacation estates of mega-wealthy Russian businessmen and political power players who spent their weekdays in Moscow. People like Romanov.

But only *one* of those six properties had been blurred out of focus by the satellite mapping software—no doubt the result of a direct government order, something that even the oligarchs couldn't always obtain.

It was as good as a mailbox printed with Romanov's last name.

Ivan found the gate first, clearly visible from his position of concealment a hundred meters away across the street. He located one guard in the security shack, visible under glaring security lights, and two more working the outside perimeter of an iron fence either side of the drive. All dressed in black, all heavily armed. All oblivious to his presence.

For the moment, anyway. This was the outside of the box—the hardened edge of defense. They wouldn't hesitate to open fire if unauthorized movement was detected. It was Ivan's job to never give them the chance.

Rising from the forest floor, Ivan moved light on his feet as he tacked right, up the length of the road for one klick before darting across and passing to the dacha's south side. He was unarmed, which wasn't ideal, but gunfire would blow his cover anyway, and he didn't need a gun to face the first gauntlet.

He only needed the leather belt secured around his waist.

Ivan passed the outer ring of defense with ease—it consisted of the same iron fence that connected with the gate at the driveway. Eight feet high with pointed metal teeth affixed to each picket, Ivan knew the fence wasn't electrified because it was buried straight into the ground without any insulation barrier. After waiting ten minutes to identify the route of the nearest passing guard—fifty meters to his left, at the closest—he unzipped his jacket and flipped it over the top of the fence to cover the metal spikes. Then he grabbed the horizontal bar that ran just above eye level and hoisted himself up like a gymnast.

Sixty-three years old. A bulky two hundred pounds stripped naked. And yet Ivan Sidorov *still had it.*

He landed on the far side of the fence like a cat, collecting his jacket and sweeping it back on before passing into the trees. The guard completed another mechanical loop of his walking circuit, passing right by Ivan before turning toward the driveway some half a kilometer away—well out of view. Well out of hearing range of anything short of a full scream.

He would never get the chance to scream. Ivan swept the belt off and crossed behind the guard without a sound. All the leaves were already crushed—the sticks kicked aside. The Federal Security Service had done Ivan's work for him, just as he knew they would.

He reached the guard. He dropped the belt and yanked and drove one knee into the guy's spine. The guard turned rigid and jerked, one hand snatching at the belt while the other flailed for the submachine gun strapped against his chest. The weapon was suspended on a two-point harness and secured tight against his body for comfortable carry while not in use.

A rookie mistake.

Ivan drove the guy straight into the trunk of a waiting spruce tree before he could reach the sub gun's grip. His unprotected face met the bark hard enough to bust his nose, and still Ivan yanked backward on the belt, sealing off airflow. The guy couldn't so much as choke, let alone scream. In a last desperate attempt of self-preservation, he flailed for his sidearm, maybe thinking of squeezing off an unsuppressed shot to draw the attention of his comrades.

Ivan expected the move, and released pressure on the guy's spine at the last minute. He drove his booted foot into an unprotected right knee, hard enough to bust the joint. The guy turned rigid, instantly forgetting the pistol. He twisted and fell, consumed by pain. Thrashing once more, still unable to scream.

And then he was out of air. The game was up. Ivan squeezed a little harder and pushed him all the way to the ground. As the body turned limp, Ivan released the belt and drove his boot straight into the back of an unprotected neck, smashing vertebrae and severing the spinal cord.

Lights out. No chance to wake up and be a problem. Silenced the Russian way.

Ivan mashed the stopwatch function on his wristwatch before tugging the body into the trees. He had it concealed amid a thicket of brush and stripped down to flannel underwear inside of sixty seconds. He knew how all the gear worked—where all the fastening buckles and adjustment straps were located. He could manipulate everything from the clothes to the plate carrier in the dark—and he did, jamming his large feet into boots that were just a little too small and zipping up a jacket whose arms were just a little too short. The plate carrier landed over his chest, and Ivan loosened the submachine gun's two-point sling, freeing it for use. He took the sidearm, also—an MP-443 Grach chambered in 9mm, with accompanying spare magazines and a razor-sharp NR-40 combat knife.

More than enough.

Back into the trees, Ivan monitored radio chatter through a captured earpiece and moved along the dead guard's path. He completed the circuit, passing within distant view of the driveway and the security shack and making sure the guard who was posted there saw him—more time bought.

Then he turned toward the inside of the box and accelerated between the trees. Following the driveway and looking out for cameras, for infrared monitors. He couldn't map them all—eventually he would be spotted. That was okay. Ivan was already inside the Federal Security Service's blind spot, already closing on the dacha that sat atop a low rise with a jet-black

Aurus limousine parked under an adjacent carport. By the time they identified him—*if* they identified him—it would be too late.

Ivan would be inside the dacha. He would be having a man-to-man chat with the occupant. And if things went sideways...well. There was still the captured submachine gun hanging around his neck.

Two minutes to target. Ivan Sidorov accelerated up the hill.

16

The South China Sea
258 Nautical Miles Southwest of Taiwan

It was four a.m. The crew aboard the RFS *Krasnoyarsk* had run their boat at ultra-quiet for nearly sixteen hours. Stalking in tandem with the RFS *Novosibirsk*, a matching Yasen-class attack submarine, they had slipped west out of the Philippine Sea and glided right past a pair of American destroyers without detection.

Running deep, running slow, the two Russian submarines followed orders from the Ministry of Defense to a T. Parting ways with the *Novosibirsk* just thirty-five miles outside the knot of American warships gathered at China's doorstep, the *Krasnoyarsk* circled south while the *Novosibirsk* circled north. Both attack boats swung wide of the American task force, reducing their speed to barely a creep as they turned nose to nose, fifty miles apart.

Then they proceeded right down the middle of the no-man's-land between American and Chinese warships.

There were thirty-nine contacts in total—fourteen American, twenty-five Chinese. On the Dragon's side of the standoff a cluster of heavily armed Luyang III destroyers were surrounded by twice as many Jiankai II frigates, with three corvettes and two submerged attack submarines patrolling the outer edges. Notably missing amid the Chinese naval firepower was the People's Republic's only operational domestic carrier, the *Shangdong*. That vessel, the Russians knew, lay sheltered much closer to the Chinese shore under cover of land-based air power.

The American fleet, in contrast to the Chinese force, almost appeared diminutive. Eight Arleigh Burke–class missile destroyers were joined by three Ticonderoga-class missile cruisers, all deployed in a rough circle formation around the three-vessel core of the American task force—two amphibious assault ships and one Nimitz-class supercarrier.

Yes, the American force *appeared* outgunned, at least based on sheer numbers. But the crew aboard the RFS *Krasnoyarsk* were students of history, and they understood the difference between quantity and quality. The Americans were unmatched masters of quality, and there were only fourteen American warships confronting the Chinese because there only *needed* to be fourteen. In truth, half as many might have been enough, and the Chinese knew it, also.

Maybe that was why they were stalling. Hissing at the United States and baring their teeth...but not daring to pull the trigger. Waiting, hoping for somebody else to do the dirty work for them.

Well. If that was what they wanted, the crew of the RFS *Krasnoyarsk* were up for the job.

At twenty miles out, Captain Pelkov selected his target. She was the USS *Gettysburg*, a 9,600 ton, 567-foot missile cruiser who formed the northwestern edge of the protective ring. Churning at barely four knots some eighteen miles off the *Krasnoyarsk*'s bow, Palkov knew the *Gettysburg* was clueless to his presence, just like the remainder of the American fleet. He'd come in so slow, so steady, leveraging the protective benefits of thermoclines to obscure his boat's presence, that *Gettysburg* never had the opportunity to identify a menacing new presence.

It was a benefit of the American taskforce's near glacial speed. Had they been churning at cruising speed, Palkov would have needed to move faster to intercept, and would have made more noise. But with the Americans almost literally standing still, facing down the Chinese...well.

They were sitting ducks.

Slowly, silently, the *Krasnoyarsk* crept onward. The Futlyar deep-water homing torpedoes already loaded into the sub's forward tubes were good from twenty-seven kilometers out, but with the element of surprise so soundly on his side, Palkov wanted to close until there was absolutely zero chance that *Gettysburg* could evade. At fifteen klicks away, sitting silent at 150 meters beneath the surface, he would lock onto his target and deploy a four-torpedo salvo that was guaranteed to wreak absolute destruction.

Seconds ticked by. The control center of the *Krasnoyarsk* was so quiet that Palkov could hear his weapons officer breathing from the next chamber. No man was allowed to speak above a whisper, and no metal implements were to be used. Sailors even removed their shoes and walked in stocking feet along the submarine's narrow corridors.

With this much enemy firepower lurking so close at hand, any mistake spelled certain death.

The navigator whispered to announce that *Krasnoyarsk* had reached final firing distance. Palkov responded with an order to decrease speed to a minimum, allowing for just enough forward momentum to maintain steerage control.

Quiet faded to absolute silence. Palkov looked up, sweat dripping from his nose as he imagined the moon glinting off the whitecaps, a starry sky interspersed with clouds. All of it overhanging the powder keg of a prospective world war, just waiting to blow.

Captain Palkov and the RFS *Krasnoyarsk* were here to light the fuse.

"Contact bearing two-seven zero. Confirmed US warship *Gettysburg*, range of eight thousand, eight hundred meters."

The sonar officer spoke in a whisper, but Palkov heard him clearly and responded just as quietly.

"Designate US warship as *Target Alpha*. Maintain tracking, set combat readiness to condition one."

In many ways, the orders were superfluous. The fish were already loaded into the tubes—everyone knew why they were here. But protocol ensured flawless execution, and Palkov couldn't risk a mistake at the pinnacle of his operational career.

All those years of training. All that dedication and sacrifice to earn command of his own boat. It all came down to this.

"Control to weapons," Palkov whispered, activating an intercom. "Confirm status."

"Captain, weapons." Palkov's weapons officer answered right on cue. "Tubes one through four loaded and pressurized. Torpedoes set to passive homing mode at depth one-five-zero meters."

Palkov mashed the intercom switch a second time. "Very good. Set salvo interval of two seconds. Prepare to fire on command."

Moments passed. The weapons officer returned to the intercom to confirm orders executed. Palkov glanced once to his sonar officer for an update. The officer knew what Palkov wanted to know, and simply shook his head.

No change in contacts. No threats to monitor.

The ocean was full of warships...yet none had discovered the *Krasnoyarsk.*

Palkov straightened his aching back, twisting until his spine crackled. He glanced once to his executive officer, and noted the XO's lips tightening, just a little. Not quite a smile—both men were too professional for that. But visual satisfaction.

Palkov mashed the intercom.

"Control to weapons. Fire tubes one through four on my mark. In three...two...one...*fire.*"

The reaction was immediate. A shudder of the attack boat as the first torpedo raced from its tube. Two seconds later, a matching shudder. Then a third. A fourth.

"Weapons to control, *torpedoes away*. All fish confirmed. Time to impact, five minutes, twenty-two seconds."

Palkov didn't bother to answer his weapons officer. Now that the fish were free, the easy part was over. In mere minutes, the success or failure of his attack would be made manifest—for the moment, the name of the game was to break for safety.

"Starboard rudder," Palkov hissed. "Depth of two-two-zero meters. Silent running."

The crew sprang into silent action. The nose of the *Krasnoyarsk* dropped—hard right, hard down. Metal groaned but otherwise the boat remained as quiet as moments before. Palkov clung to an overhead hand rail and braced his feet, his gaze once more passing upward.

And he counted. One second. One minute. Two minutes that bled into three. The *Krasnoyarsk* leveled off some four kilometers from its original shooting nest. The crew, in unison, leaned back from their controls and looked upward along with Palkov. They seemed to be holding their breaths, biding their time. Hoping and not daring to hope.

Waiting. Waiting.

Then a sound like thunder. Palkov felt it in his shoes before he actually detected the rumble in his ears. The sonar operator clamped hands around his headset and smiled. He looked to Palkov and nodded.

The powder keg had blown.

17

Rublyovka, Russia

Ivan reached the house on the hill without detection, circling wide through thick shadows and slipping right past the parked limousine. He entered the carport, his weapon held low, moving with near perfect silence on the balls of his feet.

He detected one sentry pacing just beyond the sprawling back porch at the rear of the house—tall and dark, armed and equipped exactly like the man Ivan had taken down near the exterior fence. Ivan could have shot him through the head, dropping him in place without ever being detected.

But that would have removed another link in the FSO security chain, and Ivan had already removed one. With the captured radio earpiece fit into his ear canal, he shrank against a wall and turned the radio volume up, just a little.

He checked his watch to confirm the passage of time—six minutes had elapsed since he'd taken out the guard near the fence, and Ivan knew that the FSO security cycle couldn't be much longer than that. When the guy didn't pass the guard shack, they would give him a little buffer—time to pee, maybe.

But then six minutes would bleed into seven, then eight. A radio check would be made, just to make sure everything was on the up and up. When the radio check went unanswered, a practiced emergency sequence would kick into gear—and it was that emergency sequence which would allow Ivan full access to the dacha.

"*Station Four, situation check.*"

The radioed command crackled through Ivan's earpiece, sounding every bit as routine as he expected. He knew it would take a few moments longer before reality kicked in. Ivan counted ten more seconds.

Then the voice returned, and this time, the tone had changed. There was some hint of urgency.

"*Station Four, report your status.*"

Ivan leaned out of the shadows in the carport, twisting just enough to look through a doorless passageway into the backyard. The guard who paced there had stopped pacing, his head ducked and both hands wrapped around his submachine gun as he seemed to be suspended in space, waiting for something.

Then the final radio call, five seconds after the last, crackled through Ivan's ear.

"*All stations, Code Eagle. Repeat: Code Eagle.*"

It wasn't a radio code that Ivan recognized, but he knew exactly what it meant. In essence: *something may be wrong, so secure your position and put eyes on the primary.*

It was that last part, *put eyes on the primary*, that had led Ivan past the main entrance and into the carport. He knew that natural instinct would compel the Russian security officers to focus on the most obvious point of attack—the gate, and the road beyond. That meant that the guard stationed at the front door would dig in, pointing his weapon outward toward the main drive.

The guard in the rear, meanwhile, would be the one to put eyes on the primary.

Right on cue, the man Ivan had been watching spun on his heel. Still holding his weapon, he vanished from sight, his boots thunking against wooden porch steps. Ivan gave him barely two seconds' lead, then glided out of shadows and through the carport corridor to the backyard. He leaned low and spun left, also keeping both hands on his weapon as he circled to those same porch steps. Ran up them just as the windowless back door of the house closed—but didn't lock.

Ivan reached it and held the pistol grip of the sub gun with his right hand while working the knob with his left. Sheltered by the door post, he pushed the door open and held his breath, ready to return a burst of fire in the event that anyone he couldn't predict waited inside.

But there was no fire, there were no shouts. Ivan counted two beats, then swung through the door, stepping into warm yellow light and onto a bearskin rug. He stood in a mud room with a single brick step leading up to what appeared as a kitchen. There was a breakfast table and chairs, and a hallway directly beyond them that led all the way to the front door. He didn't see the guard, but Ivan didn't expect to.

The guy was inside, marching straight to whatever room Maxim Romanov occupied. Placing eyes on his primary, just to be certain. Then—probably after being cursed at—he would return.

Ivan wouldn't be visible when he arrived. He slipped smoothly to the left, past rows of boots and a coatrack, all the way to a utility closet. One twist of the knob and Ivan ducked into the shadows. He closed the door and breathed easily, his heart settled into a resting rhythm after the momentary stress of running up the hill.

One check of his watch and Ivan found the count reaching the nine-minute mark. It was time for the second domino to fall—and again on cue, it did.

"All stations! Sentry down. Repeat: sentry down. Secure your posts and lock down the house."

A dry smile stretched Ivan's lips as boots pounded from the hallway. A moment later the sentry he'd followed inside passed by the mudroom—Ivan heard the man speaking from beyond the door only a split second before his words crackled through the earpiece.

"Walrus confirmed secure. Barricading back door."

Then the dacha's back door opened and the man hurried out. He shut the door behind him and a keypad beeped. The lock slid into position, and whatever motion-sensing security apparatus was mounted outside the house kicked into gear.

But the wolf was already inside the henhouse, with nothing standing between Ivan and *Walrus*—a pretty suitable call sign for Romanov, Ivan thought. He exited the closet, finding the mudroom as empty as before. The earpiece now crackled with constant commands, but Ivan was no longer interested in the useless scrambling of the FSO team. He switched the radio off and pulled the earpiece free. He lifted the submachine gun into his shoulder and ascended the single brick step into the kitchen, clearing it before advancing down that hallway.

On his left, a stairwell reaching to the second level. Romanov might be up there, in his private suite, preparing for bed.

But Ivan didn't think so. The guard had moved quickly, confirming Romanov's security in under sixty seconds. Ivan hadn't heard him ascend any stairs. Most importantly of all, the corridor that led to the stairs also led right, just a few feet past a bathroom to a heavy oak door.

The door was closed, and a band of yellow light leaked from beneath it.

Ivan lifted the sub gun and started down the hall, creeping without a sound over smooth hardwood. As he drew within two paces of that final door, he slowed, straining to listen past the hum of a gas-powered heating system.

There were voices, maybe more than two. Ivan glanced back once, then slipped the final two meters to the door and put his ear against it, holding his breath. The words became clear.

"...but he *can't* be reasoned with. That's what I'm saying, Maxim. Speaking to Nikitin is a practice in stupidity, like speaking to a fence post!"

Ivan's mouth dropped open, but he still didn't breathe. A murmur of agreement sounded from beyond the door, none of the voices recognizable. Then an opposing voice broke between them, and this time, Ivan *did* recognize it.

It was Prime Minister Maxim Romanov.

"This is why we need the list—ahead of time. We need to know who supports us. Who can be counted on. We need a coalition."

Another argumentative burst ended Romanov's plea, but Ivan was already withdrawing, his mind spinning. Momentary disbelief collided with equally brief hope.

The informant was right.

Ivan lifted the sub gun into his shoulder. He put one hand on the knob and breathed deep.

Then he shoved into the room.

18

Ministry of Defense Headquarters
Moscow, Russia

Word arrived just before midnight—not from the *Krasnoyarsk* or the *Novosibirsk*. Direct communication from the two stalking submarines was an absolute non-option, not only because of the risk of enemy interception but because the subs ran too deep to communicate at all.

That didn't matter. The moment the United States warship *Gettysburg* lurched sideways in the South China Sea, erupting into flame as mangled steel hurtled into the still night air, Russian military command knew. They witnessed the events via spy satellites, circling just outside the atmosphere far out of sight of both the Americans and the Chinese. They waited with bated breath, staring and not blinking, watching for what would happen next...

Then the USS *Hopper*, an Arleigh Burke–class guided-missile destroyer took a hit to the stern some fifteen kilometers south of the burning *Gettysburg*. Another torpedo attack, another eruption of flame and twisted body parts.

And just like that, all hell broke loose. The Americans opened fire—the Chinese opened fire. Missile trails arced across the black water as

Gatling-style machine guns dumped lead into the skies in a desperate attempt to shoot them down. Some missiles shattered and tumbled into the night—others struck their targets.

In mere minutes, fires burned everywhere. Aircraft were exploding off the decks of the Nimitz-class US carrier. Across the room, a Russian analyst monitoring activities on the Chinese mainland reported a flight of Chinese fighter jets racing to respond.

It had happened. The pressure had finally boiled over—and neither the Chinese nor the Americans had fired the first shot.

Makar Nikitin stood in the back of the room, sipping dark Russian tea while his sharp eyes passed from one workstation to the next, accepting updates in silence.

Both the *Gettysburg* and the *Hopper*—sunk. Two Chinese frigates and one corvette, sunk. Three American destroyers burning. Another American guided-missile cruiser listing hard to starboard and immobile in the water. All this...and the air battle hadn't even begun.

"The Chinese are deploying additional destroyers from Yulin Naval Base."

It was Golubev—he approached like a shadow, same as always, speaking just loud enough for Nikitin to hear.

"And their carrier?" Nikitin asked.

Golubev snorted. "Still in reserve."

Cowards.

Nikitin kept the disgust to himself. There was no need to underscore the point. The Chinese would hold their prized *Shangdong* in reserve because their only other operational carrier was a retrofitted Soviet boat originally built in the mid-eighties. Hardly a threat to the American naval war machine.

This was why the Chinese dragged their feet on engagement. The bulk of the world's "largest navy" was nothing more than missile boats and attack submarines. High in quantity, low in quality, and mostly untested.

Oh, but they were being tested now.

Nikitin's heart rate spiked. In his mind, he heard the order—his own order, reserved for so very long. Repeated in silence over and over until his body quivered with anticipation, adrenaline flooding his veins and pure, animal delight overcoming his mind.

A moment he'd waited so long for. The culmination of *years* of strategy and sacrifice and patience.

Was the moment here?

Nikitin looked to Golubev, and saw in the cold dark eyes of his right-hand man the same question. The same lethal excitement.

Yes, Nikitin thought, just the hint of a smile curling his lip. *It was time.*

"Give the order," Nikitin said. "Assault Ādaži."

19

The White House
Washington, DC

Maggie couldn't complete the set.

She wanted to, so desperately. She sat on the incline bench with a pair of fifteen-pound rubber-wrapped dumbbells and managed three out of four shoulder presses but *could not* force the final rep. With her eyes clamped closed and her body throbbing from her scalp to her toes, she gritted her teeth and focused on the objecting muscles. She visualized the completed motion. She blocked out the pain and the nausea boiling in her stomach and told herself it was all in her head.

She did *all* the things. The weights trembled in her hands and she planted her feet against the floor to block out the sensation of a pitching ship deck. She inhaled half a breath through her nose and pushed—

Then the pain came. A burst of it, exploding from her transplanted liver. Maggie doubled over, dropping the weights. She clutched her middle and shook, fighting back the urge to scream even as the door to her private gym exploded open and a Secret Service agent rushed inside.

"Ma'am? Are you okay?"

Maggie couldn't answer, she was too focused on managing the pain. It still throbbed from her middle, but wasn't quite so bad. She could deal with it—she did *not* need the painkillers.

"Ma'am? I'll call medical."

"No," Maggie managed. "No medical."

The agent hesitated just inside the doorway. Maggie measured her breathing and forced herself to sit up, looking into the full-body mirror mounted just in front of her incline bench.

She saw herself—ghost white. Frail. Muscles shrunken to near invisibility after so many months of disuse. Only thirty-six years old, but she looked fifty. She looked half alive. She looked—

"Ma'am?" the agent said again. "Please let me call medical."

Maggie glanced right. She inhaled slowly and forced a smile she didn't at all feel.

"Just muscle cramps," she lied. "Your boss lady is out of shape."

It was a poor joke, and the agent didn't smile. He didn't call medical, either. Maggie swabbed her face with a towel and chugged water, noting that the agent still hadn't left. She was just about to complain when footsteps tapped on the floor—short and sharp strides, impossible to misidentify.

Even before Easterling spoke, Maggie knew it was her.

"Ma'am?" A hesitation. Then a curse. "Are you all right?"

Easterling rushed into the room uninvited. Maggie waved a hand.

"I'm *fine*. Geez. Could I have *ten minutes* to myself?"

Easterling didn't answer. Maggie chugged more water and then looked up.

What she saw in her chief of staff's gaze was enough to erase any further concern about the failed rep. Maggie even forgot about the ghost of herself staring from the mirror.

"What is it?" Maggie said. "What happened?"

"We need you downstairs," Easterling said simply. "The Chinese have engaged."

"Downstairs" was the Situation Room, and within minutes of arriving—still sweaty and dressed in baggy workout clothes—Maggie received the rundown of a developing situation from a Pentagon aide.

It was all about the South China Sea. About two sunken American warships, many others heavily damaged, and erupting air combat that might cost the lives of dozens more. It was a full-fledged battle, and nobody knew exactly how it started.

"Sucker punch!" It was the first thing General Yellin said as he barged into the room, dressed in slacks and a collared shirt with the Westpoint logo embroidered over his chest. He was red-faced, he was strained. He was rushing down the length of the table to overlook a battle map that marked the progression of the conflict.

American ships depicted in blue, Chinese in red.

"I told you," Yellin said, shaking his head.

From her position at the head of the table, Maggie wasn't quite sure who Yellin was addressing, but she thought it was Secretary of Defense Steven Kline. The only member of the emergency meeting dressed in a suit, Kline looked both cold and angry.

"All this discussion about NATO, NATO, NATO," Yellin said, jabbing a finger at the screen. "I *told you* this would happen."

"Nobody ever questioned you, General," Kline snarled. "When half the house is on fire, you can't worry about the burglars breaking in through the garage."

"And how about now?" Yellin said. "Turns out those burglars have a mean right hook!"

"General, *please*." It was Easterling. "We don't have time to bicker. The president needs a recommendation."

Yellin was ready for that. He turned right on Maggie.

"Madam President, between eighty and a hundred Chinese warplanes are launching from air bases across the coast of the Chinese mainland. They'll be joining the fight within the next half hour. While our warships are engaged with the Chinese Navy, we've kept the USS *Springfield* held in reserve. She's a Los Angeles–class fast-attack submarine fully equipped with enough Tomahawk cruise missiles to turn those airfields into rubble. I recommend we fire immediately."

The room fell silent. Still seated, still sweating from her failed workout, Maggie's gaze darted from one screen to the next, monitoring the battle map in real time. Noting the disappearance of one Chinese icon, followed by a flag that read *Confirmed Sunk.*

Missiles were flying. Ships were on fire—American warriors were dying. And yet...

She couldn't shake the feeling. Something didn't feel right.

"You said they sucker punched us, General?"

Yellin blinked. "Ma'am?"

"The Chinese. They sniped two of our ships."

"Torpedoed, likely from a stalking attack sub. There's so much noise and chaos now, there's no telling. We *really* need to get those missiles in the air—"

"Why?" Maggie said.

"What?"

"If this was a planned attack, why are their fighters still half an hour away?"

Pause. Yellin glanced to Kline, but the SecDef didn't have an answer.

"I am not qualified to advise on Chinese psychology," Yellin said. "All I can tell you is that they're killing our people and we've got to hit back hard. *Now.*"

The room boomed with Yellin's voice—his face was beet red. Aides and Easterling and Lisa Gorman, who had just stepped in, all stared.

Maggie didn't blink. She fixated on the screen, her mind churning, her abdomen aching...and that feeling deep in her gut refusing to leave.

"All these weeks," she whispered, almost to herself. "Nothing, nothing, nothing. Now this?"

"Madam *President,*" Yellin said. "I'm asking you to—"

The phone call cut Yellin short. A blaring ring from his end of the table —one of the few phones that wasn't set to silent. Linked to the watch officer two doors down in another portion of the Situation Room complex, it was for use only in dire emergency.

Kline responded first. He snatched up the handset and spoke in a clipped monotone.

"Yes? Where? *Now?* On screen, immediately."

Kline hung up, a sharp snap of plastic on plastic. He spun to Maggie.

"It's the Russians," he said. "They're assaulting Ādaži Military Base in Latvia. They're bombing American troops."

American troops.

The words rang like gunshots, and Maggie's spine turned rigid just as one screen at the end of the room flashed to a map of the Baltic. The Ādaži Military Base was marked in red, with arrows indicating the Russian assault.

Aircraft. Cruise missiles. Artillery. Straight into American's mouth.

Yellin swore and snatched up a phone. He barked for a connection to Naval Command at the Pentagon.

"We're getting those birds in the air."

"General," Maggie said.

Yellin ignored her—flatly ignored her. Through her peripheral Maggie observed Easterling shooting her a look, already half rising from her chair.

Maggie beat her too it. Her knees locked and she slapped the table.

"General Yellin, you have *not* been authorized to give that order!"

Yellin's face flushed, knuckles turning white around the handset. His mouth opened—Maggie cut him off.

"If you launch a full assault on the Chinese mainland, we'll be in open war by midnight—no turning back. With Russian troops storming Europe we *can't* afford that. We're not prepared to fight on two fronts."

"Ma'am—"

"You heard me, General! I've got one war on my hands already. I won't rush into a second. Order the fleet to disengage from the Chinese."

"*What?*"

"You heard me. Defensive fire only."

Yellin looked ready to explode. "They *sunk* two of our ships. This is the second time they've attacked us! If we don't crush them now—"

"Then we can crush them tomorrow, General. Give the order—do it now, or I'll find somebody who will."

The room froze over. All eyes pivoted between Maggie and Yellin—the two of them only stared at each other. Maggie endured the ache that consumed her entire body, but for the first time in days, her mind was sharp. She saw it—somehow, she saw it.

And she knew.

"Withdraw our ships far enough to initiate a cease-fire, but don't surrender the region. The objective is to restore a standoff. Those are my orders—we will not allow this to become a world war. Do you understand?"

No answer. Yellin's jaw was clenched so hard his flushed cheeks quivered. He stared, wide-eyed and furious.

"Tell me you understand," Maggie demanded.

"I understand, Madam President." The words were spat like venom, but at least they were loud and clear. "And the *Russians*?"

Maggie's gaze switched back to the screens—that map of Latvia and the arrows tracing a full-frontal assault on Ādaži. Once again, her gut was loud and clear.

"I want you to hit them," Maggie said. "I want you to hit them now. I want you to hit them *hard*."

20

Al Udeid Air Base
Near Doha, Qatar

Reed snuck into the command center.

It wasn't as hard as it should have been. An Army jacket stitched with captain's bars, swiped from the back of an office chair just outside the secure-access door, was all it took. The door opened—somebody exited, and Reed slipped in. He knew he didn't look Army. He didn't even look like the Marine he used to be.

But nobody cared, because nobody was actually paying attention. Reed could feel the vibration of the expansive, darkened room even before he entered. Officers of every military branch rushed in and out, and everyone seated at a workstation seemed to be wearing a headset or talking on a phone. The place felt like the interior of a beehive, literally buzzing with frantic activity as wall-to-wall screens mounted at the end of the room explained the source of the raw energy.

Al Udeid Air Base was launching. Not part of what they had, but *everything* they had. Reed heard the jet fighters and high-level bombers screaming off the tarmac outside, which was what prompted him to slip into the command center in the first place. One after another after another. Exploding off the tarmac while the next jet in line ramped up its engines.

America was striking back. From Qatar the target had to be Iran, or at least the Iranian Navy spread across the Persian Gulf. The F-35A Lightning II stealth jets, visible via camera feeds displayed on large monitors, held their payloads in concealed compartments, but the F-15E Strike Eagles bore death mounted directly to their wings. They were *heavily* loaded.

And returning to base empty.

Sliding into a darkened corner near a water cooler where Reed could plausibly stand without drawing undue attention, he poured himself a paper cup and sipped, dark eyes switching from one exposed monitor to the next while he sifted through the chatter of air traffic commands that he mostly didn't understand. It was Air Force speak, not ground operator speak. The end result, though, wasn't so different. There were targets identified, targets engaged, targets eliminated. And yes, he'd been right. The target *was* Iran, specifically the Iranian Navy, which wasn't much of a navy, but it stood in the way of full American control of the Gulf, and Washington finally had an excuse to kick that problem permanently into the abyss.

Support of Isreal, namely. Distracting Iranian military authorities from their drive through Iraq, probably. And yet…

Reed bit his lip, mind spinning as the screens blurred together, the chatter fading to background noise he barely registered. There was something else here, something else happening in real time that felt bigger than everything he saw on these screens. Almost as if the aircraft ripping over the Persian Gulf were little more than a sideshow, a spinoff from a larger, more uncertain conflict. The officers packed around workstations and rushing in and out of the ops center were animated, flushed, snapping at one another.

They were *angry*. Aggressive. Barely celebrating each report of a sunk Iranian patrol boat, but instead merely demanding the next and the next. It was as though the whole room was consumed by bloodlust, as though they weren't here for tactical execution so much as the satisfaction of raw, unchecked destruction.

As though they wanted *revenge*.

"What happened?" Reed addressed an Air Force lieutenant who stopped by the water cooler, bending to fill a bottle. The guy looked up, glancing to Reed's shoulder patches, then back to the wall.

"You haven't heard?"

"I was occupied," Reed said—which meant nothing. The truth was, he was out of the loop.

The lieutenant flicked the water valve off and chugged from his bottle. He wiped his lips.

"The Russians hit one of our bases in Latvia—the Chinese engaged our fleet in the South China Sea. The war has started, man. Americans are dying."

There was something in his voice when he said that last bit—the part about Americans dying. It was cold. It was nasty. The words carried a razor edge that reminded Reed of the way people talked just after 9/11. He'd only been a child then, but the voice of unbridled rage is not one that you forget.

"We've engaged in Europe?" Reed asked.

The lieutenant shook his head. "That's outside my pay grade. I just know they hit us, and then orders came down the pipe for us to hit the Iranians. You shoot the guy in front of you, right? I gotta go."

The lieutenant bustled off, leaving Reed in the shadows with his water. He felt the cup trembling in his fingers as the screens came back into focus. He watched the bold red Xs that marked each sunken Iranian patrol ship stacking across a map, a small column of four blue Xs tallying American aircraft lost. Maybe pilots lost with them.

American lives—American blood.

Reed pictured soldiers lying mangled and lifeless, and he felt the rage also.

21

Rublyovka, Russia

There were four men in the room, and every one of them panicked as Ivan entered.

Sitting at the head of a long table laden with documents, tumblers, and a half-empty bottle of vodka, Maxim Romanov's unhealthy bulk was jammed into a chair at least six inches too narrow for him. He startled as Ivan entered, and so did the other three men.

Two on Romanov's left, one on his right. It was the one on the right who reacted most judiciously, one hand dropping beneath the table and into his jacket.

Ivan put the muzzle of the sub gun right on him before any weapon could appear, snapping a single command in cold Russian.

"Don't move."

It was a simple order, easy to understand and easy to follow. Wide eyes stared at Ivan and cheeks drained pale, but nobody spoke or moved. They followed orders, and Ivan used one boot to kick the door closed behind him, isolating the room from the FSO team outside.

Only then did he pause to actually identify each of the men joining Romanov at the table—and as he did, his stomach fell.

To Romanov's left sat Leonid Voronin, Minister of Internal Affairs. To his right, Vasili Zaitsev, chairman of the State Duma Committee on Defense or Security—a legislative officer of middling importance.

Last of all was Alexei Lebedev, mayor of Moscow. Three men of debatable importance and relatively minimal power, each significant in their own little worlds...but *little* was the right adjective.

"Put your hands on the table, Zaitsev," Ivan said. "I don't want to shoot you."

Slowly, Zaitsev withdrew his hand. It was empty—his face was hard. Ivan could see in his eyes that the chairman recognized the intruder. In fact, they all did.

Why shouldn't they? Ivan Sidorov was a wanted man.

"Anyone want to pour me a drink?" Ivan asked.

Nobody answered. Romanov sweated.

"Fine," Ivan said. "So I'll do that myself."

He lifted the half-empty vodka bottle—Green Mark, one of his favorites—and poured into an empty tumbler using his left hand. His right hand still managed the submachine gun.

The liquor burned his throat. It burned in his esophagus and lit a fire in his stomach. Ivan appreciated the warmth. He lowered the glass, and at last Romanov spoke.

"What...what are you doing here?"

Ivan licked the vodka from his lips, studying Romanov for a long moment, but he didn't answer. Instead he circled the table, still wielding the submachine gun, and inspected every document he passed. Every notepad scratched with Cyrillic handwriting.

They all watched him. Voronin was the most visibly alarmed. By the time Ivan reached the end of the table where he had started, the minister was mumbling.

"Whatever you think this is—" he started.

"*Silence*." That was Zaitsev.

Ivan looked from one man to the next, then toed a chair back and sat down. He rested the barrel of the submachine gun on the table, pointed at Romanov.

Ivan didn't put his finger on the trigger.

"Why don't you tell me what this is, Mr. Minister?" Ivan said.

Voronin swallowed. His wide eyes switched to his companions and his mouth opened, but he didn't answer.

Ivan shook his head, unable to stop himself. The one word he couldn't stop thinking was: *coward.*

"Seems like an insiders club to me," Ivan said. "Three federal officials and a mayor...my, what a coalition. And you really think you can overpower a president."

The final words rang like gunshots, and all four men—even Zaitsev—flinched. It was as good as a total confession.

"Whatever you think you see, Mr. Sidorov—" Mayor Lebedev began.

Ivan snorted, cutting him off. "I know exactly what I see. Four men flailing to prevent global catastrophe...and I am here to help you."

That caught them off guard. Ivan could tell by the sudden tension of indecision. One glanced to another but nobody seemed to know what to say. Mouths opened, then closed.

Nobody was willing to take the leap.

With a frustrated sigh, Ivan shifted the gun into his lap and reached for the bottle. He poured himself another glass, savoring the fresh rush of warmth, then set the tumbler down with a smack and looked straight at Romanov.

"Enough child's play. Cards on the table—you want to replace Nikitin."

The room froze over. Romanov didn't so much as blink. Finally it was Zaitsev, the warrior of the group, who voiced the obvious.

"What you suggest is treason."

"And here I thought saving the Motherland was patriotism," Ivan retorted.

He swigged more vodka. Raised his eyebrows.

Still, nobody would engage. It angered Ivan. It made him wonder if all of this, his desperate hope to avert disaster...maybe it was only a fool's errand.

"Fine," Ivan said. "If I'm the only man in the room, I'll do the talking. Nikitin wants to kill me anyway—I'd welcome him to try in person. That might clean this mess up the quickest."

Lebedev and Zaitsev stiffened. Zaitsev and Romanov remained as still as statues.

"I will tell you what you already know," Ivan said. "That a madman has hijacked your country. That he is charging head-first into a needless war justified by a web of lies. That his conquest of the Caucasus and the Baltic, and his partnership with China and Iran, is nothing more than a mechanism to build an empire for his own glory. The result can be only one thing—absolute destruction. Perhaps for Russia. Possibly for the entire planet. Certainly for whatever nations become battlegrounds between Nikitin and his enemies. I say *his* enemies, because he picked this fight. Not the Russian people. That is a distinction that will be lost forever in another week, maybe less. If we do not move before then, it will be too late to reverse the catastrophe—it will be over."

Romanov blinked, very slowly. He sipped from his own glass. Voronin looked ready to speak, but Romanov lifted a hand. He took his time.

Then he said: "Why are you here, Mr. Sidorov?"

"I already told you. I am here because I love my country. Just as I always have, and always shall. I have dedicated my life to her service, sworn oaths to her protection. Fought her enemies around the planet...and returned home to find her greatest enemy occupying her most powerful office. I am here because Russia stands on the brink of the abyss, perhaps closer to annihilation than she has ever come, and there is still some hope in my heart that good men remain."

Another round of exchanged glances. Voronin leaned forward, no longer awaiting Romanov's permission.

"However you snuck in here, you cannot possibly expect to leave with our goodwill. We could have you shot. Bring Nikitin your body. Prove our loyalty."

"Indeed you could," Ivan said. "Which is why there is no risk for you in being honest now."

One more final hesitation. All eyes turned to Romanov. It was an airtight argument—Ivan knew that. It was his final push to get the truth out in the open.

Another long ten seconds dripped by. Romanov swallowed.

Then he said: "We have met to stop the madness."

"And?" Ivan prompted.

Romanov gritted his teeth. He stood from his chair and locked chubby fingers behind his back. He turned to face an ornate world map that stretched between book cases, the Russian mainland depicted front and center.

When he spoke, his voice sounded nearly broken. "And we may already be too late. It is as you say—there is a madman in the Kremlin. We all saw it coming, but we ignored the signs. We never thought he would actually assault NATO. We convinced ourselves that we could pacify him with the Caucasus—distract him with third-world proxy conflicts. Maybe it worked for a while, but Nikitin..."

"Is insatiable," Lebedev said. "Insane."

"Now he invades the Baltic and confronts the Americans," Romanov said, turning from the map. "In the coming weeks he will launch invasions of Poland and Moldova while his allies in Beijing and Tehran keep the West stretched thin. He is counting on weakened leadership in Brussels and Washington to stall, never fully committing to war, and never even considering a nuclear option. Meanwhile Nikitin will keep pushing West until..."

Romanov trailed off. Ivan filled the gap.

"Until he is king of the world...or until that world burns."

The room froze over. Romanov stared at Ivan.

"We're short on men," the prime minister said. "We're short on support."

"Russia is full of good people, comrade," Ivan said. "So is the Kremlin, perhaps. They are cowed and afraid. But if given hope of success..."

"That is why we're *here*," Zaitsev said, finding his spine. "To orchestrate *something*. To pull a miracle out of a hat. To...to throw our bodies before the machine!"

"And will you?" Ivan challenged.

"Will we what?" Zaitsev snapped.

"Will you throw your bodies before the machine? Will you risk everything—your very *lives*—to save your country? Or is it not only the West who refuses to commit?"

Every back stiffened. Chins lifted. Romanov returned to the table and placed two thick hands on the back of his chair. His gaze turned hard.

"Do not question our courage, Sidorov. There is more risked here than you know. We have families."

Ivan nodded. He finished the Green Mark and the glass hit the table.

"Very well, then. You are the men I hoped to find."

"Hoped to find?" Lebedev said. "To find for *what*?"

"To pull a miracle out of a hat, Mr. Mayor. To forestall the end of the world."

"And how do you plan to do that?" Romanov suggested.

"There is only one way. This snake has grown too large to be contained —we must remove its head."

Romanov's eyebrows shot skyward. Voronin spoke first.

"You want to *assassinate* our president?"

"I do."

"Are you insane?"

"Quite possibly. But there is no better option, and everyone here knows this. If Nikitin is removed, and certain powerful leaders stand ready to seize control—leaders such as yourselves, for instance—there may yet be time to reverse history. But we must move quickly. Days, not weeks. Time is already against us."

Zaitsev shook his head. He muttered a curse. "Even if that were *possible*, which it is not—"

"It is," Ivan said flatly.

"*Even if that were possible*," Zaitsev repeated, dropping his tone, "Nikitin has already engaged in open conflict with the West. If he is removed, and Russia is weakened, NATO will counterattack. They will sweep our armies back and invade our heartland. They will *dominate us*."

Lebedev grunted in agreement. Ivan shook his head.

"You do not know the Americans. Their people have neither the taste nor the stomach for conquest, and besides, their economy stands on the edge of a knife, and their hands are full with China and Iran. We have the opportunity to back out of this war—but that will not be true if this war turns nuclear. Despite your dismissal of their commitment, you cannot think that if Nikitin uses nuclear weapons in Europe, the West will not respond in kind. Then it is truly over...for everyone."

"So what?" Voronin said. "We are just supposed to murder our own leader, and then *hope* the Americans let us bow out?"

"Of course not," Ivan said. "We will guarantee the arrangement ahead of time."

"We will what?" Lebedev said.

"We will work *with* the Americans," Ivan said. "They will help us cut the head off the snake."

22

Langley, Virginia

Silas Rigby worked separately from the rest of his team, segmented in a glass office behind a bank of computer screens, reviewing the same simulation reports pumped out by the war gaming supercomputer...but focusing on one key strategy. A strategy undeclared to the rest of the team, managed by Rigby alone.

He input the requests. He reviewed the results and made adjustments. He communicated directly with the AI engine that slowly computed complex responses, complete with predicted military fallout, diplomatic chaos, and ancillary risk.

The question was always the same: Would regime change terminate the Russian offensive?

The answer: *It could...depending on who took Nikitin's place.*

Rigby sat frozen as the latest batch of predicted military moves and counter-moves loaded across his screen, red lines of Russian offensives spilling steadily westward until the moment Makar Nikitin was removed from power. Twenty-two theoretical days ticked by while those red lines remained frozen in place. The world seemed to be holding its breath. The computer spun, calculating for Russian civil instability while power players in the Kremlin struggled to seize control. NATO waited, hoping for a moderate Russian leader who would advance to the negotiation table.

And then, in a flash, resolution was reached. Dimitri Smirnov, deputy chairman of the Security Council, displaced the acting Russian president and seized control of the Federation. Thirty-two hours later, and the offensive was back on.

Forty-six hours later, and the first Russian tactical nuke detonated in Poland.

Rigby swore and tore his headphones off, slinging them to the floor before slapping Control + P. His office printer whined to life, spitting out the simulation summary as Rigby ran both hands through his hair.

It was the third time the AI had predicted Smirnov as Nikitin's likely successor. While the Russian constitution stipulated that in the event of a president's unexpected death, the prime minister would serve as acting president, the AI doubted whether Russian PM Maxim Romanov possessed either the fortitude or coalition to *remain* in power. Not much was known, in fact, about Romanov's foreign policy or his perspective on Russian expansion. It was thought that he might be little more than a puppet on strings for the Nikitin administration, meaning that he could be easily displaced or at least bullied by the war hawks loyal to Nikitin's agenda.

And that left the West right back where they started—standing on the edge of nuclear apocalypse.

Patton was right, Rigby thought, snatching the print-off from the printer tray. *We should have kicked the Soviets in the teeth the moment the Nazis fell.*

Barging out of his office, Rigby ignored the calls of his deputies from across the SCIF floor and exited into a hallway. He took the elevator to the executive floor, gritting his teeth as he walked.

Ready to *quit*. Aimes herself had tasked Rigby with his special operation, and he understood the value. But at some stage, what was the point? Rigby saw no eventuality short of a divine miracle which would save the planet from nuclear war. Maybe the best defense was a good offense. Convert Moscow into a glass parking lot before the Russians could ever pull the trigger.

Additional voices called Rigby's name as he marched to Aimes's office.

The automated blinds were activated, and the door closed. Rigby barged ahead anyway, finding the interior of the executive suite dimmed to near midnight darkness—likely because Aimes was suffering from another migraine.

The director of the CIA sat stooped behind her computer screens, her face illuminated in electronic blue. With a phone clamped to one ear, she snapped her fingers for silence, and Rigby stumbled to a stop.

The office was cold. Dead quiet. Aimes listened to the phone without blinking, finally saying "update at soonest" before hanging up.

She didn't say anything. She settled slowly back into her chair, still eyeballing the phone. There was something on her face—Rigby hadn't seen it before. Churning gears behind her eyes, detached focus. It was as though, for the first time in Rigby's chaotic tenure as Deputy Director of Operations, he was witnessing his boss thinking about *one thing*.

Undivided. Undistracted. Like nothing else on planet earth mattered.

Rigby was smart enough to shut up and wait. He settled into a chair, twitching in the chill while Aimes just sat.

Finally, she blinked once. She turned, and she was back to the present. She looked to the papers in his hand.

"Well?"

"It'll work," Rigby said. "With Nikitin out of the picture the AI predicts a stalled Russian war machine in eighty-seven percent of simulations."

"But?" Aimes pressed. She knew there was a *but*.

"But we don't know who will take his place. Romanov's politics are a question mark, and if he's not strong enough to maintain control, one of Nikitin's surviving war hawks might displace him. In seventy-two percent of simulations, the war resumes and even worsens within weeks of Nikitin's death—especially in the event that whoever seizes control is able to accuse NATO of an orchestrated assassination."

Which would be true.

Rigby kept that last thought to himself. Aimes extended a hand.

"Let me see."

Rigby handed off the paperwork and Aimes flipped through it, reading by the light of her computer screens. Dark eyes framed by crow's feet squinted behind smudged glasses. She looked exhausted—she looked ten years older than she had when Rigby first reported for duty as her deputy.

Maybe that didn't matter. Maybe, in another six or eight weeks, they would all be vaporized anyway.

Aimes finished with the documents and rested them on the desk. She leaned back and removed her glasses, clicking the tip of one stem between her teeth as she stared at the phone.

And the gears spun.

"If we remove Nikitin, we create a vacuum," Rigby said. "It's happened with every case of regime change the United States has ever instigated. Iran in 1953, Iraq in 2003, Libya in 2011. We take the bad guys out, and chaos ensues. Nine times out of ten, a worse guy takes their place. Only, this time, we're talking about a nuclear power. Fifty-five *hundred* warheads. Over a *million* active troops. I mean...this isn't a powder keg. This is..."

"The end of the world," Aimes said.

Rigby nodded. Aimes clicked her teeth with the glasses again. It was a steady ticking sound, and it made Rigby want to throw something. He shifted in the chair, his body a nucleus of contained tension.

"But if the status quo remains," Aimes said, "that's also the end of the world. Right?"

Rigby considered, the reel of AI-generated war simulations playing on repeat in his mind. Endless flashes, all ending the same way—mushroom clouds and radioactive fallout.

"I guess we could surrender," he muttered.

Aimes stopped with the clicking. She stared at the glasses, her mouth open. He couldn't tell if she was about to laugh or scream.

Instead she lowered the glasses. Aimes cocked her head.

"But what if we *could* know who would seize power? What if...we could guarantee their political strategy ahead of time?"

Rigby snorted. "You holding out on me? You got a crystal ball somewhere?"

"Nope. But I've got a chief of station in Moscow."

Rigby squinted. "We evacuated Station Moscow along with the embassy."

Aimes said nothing. Rigby swore.

"You *are* holding out on me. Boss—I'm the director of operations. This is *literally* my department. I have to know this stuff."

Aimes said nothing, and Rigby swept the deception aside, choosing to focus on the subject at hand.

"So this nonexistent chief of station. What did he say?"

"She. Natasha Kirov, Russian American doctorate student at Moscow State University, and longtime undercover asset. She's built quite the cover as a faux Russian nationalist—I think Nikitin himself would trust her. It can't hurt that she's hot."

Rigby snorted. "It never does. So what does this super hot, super smart, super undercover asset have to report?"

Aimes squinted, and when she spoke, she didn't directly answer his question. "What if we're not the only ones thinking of displacing Nikitin?"

"Huh?"

"What if a sizeable portion of the Russian government doesn't even support the war? What if there's a coalition, buried inside the Kremlin… just waiting for an opportunity?"

Rigby's heart rate quickened. He sat forward. "That's what Kirov reported?"

Again, Aimes didn't answer directly. Her gaze switched from empty space to lock with Rigby's.

"Remember our old pal Ivan Sidorov?"

23

The White House

The withdrawals were back, and worse than ever.

Coursing through Maggie's body, racking her with alternating hot flashes and chills, her vision wavering when she stood too quickly. Nausea came in waves, accompanied by bouts of diarrhea and abdominal cramping.

Then there was the emotional instability. Mood swings, anxiety and irritability. It sounded like a small thing, but working in tandem with the physical afflictions, the mental turmoil made focus nearly impossible. It compromised clear thought. It waylaid Maggie's every conversation and difficult decision.

It left her wondering. Second-guessing herself. Disbelieving her own eyes. Doubting everyone around her.

And yet...she was unable to relinquish control. Unable to deny the pressure in her very soul, the demand that she *keep going*. Without the meds. Without surrender. This was her *duty*. She'd come so far and given so much. How could she quit now?

The Oval Office was no sanctuary for quiet work. With doors that seemed never to be closed, an endless stream of aides and meetings and phone calls kept Maggie scrambling just to keep up. Her orders to General Yellin had been executed—American warships had disengaged from the Chinese, only firing enough to protect themselves as they withdrew fifty miles across the South China Sea. The Chinese, meanwhile, had accepted the cease-fire. They had remained in place, not attempting pursuit—licking their wounds and brooding. Denying the US State Department's phone calls and making no public statements of their own.

Silent. Menacing. An unanswered question parked on a dusty shelf for another day.

Russia, meanwhile, was offered no such luxury. The NATO air raids launched out of Poland and Romania began on Maggie's command and had run back to back every hour since. Pounding Russian forces in Estonia and Belarussian forces in Latvia. Striking armored columns and bridges, engaging enemy air power over the Baltic in dogfights that—thus far—had left more Russians dead than Americans.

Meanwhile, NATO ground troops already stationed in Poland were mobilizing in preparation for deployment. When given the order, they would meet Russian and Belarussian forces on the field of battle in Latvia—a country who was about to be brought to its knees.

It was horrific, catastrophic. And yet that wasn't all. Maggie learned just before heading upstairs to her residence that General Yellin, unprompted and without direct executive approval, had launched similar air raids out of Qatar, targeting Iranian warships and patrol craft occupying the Persian Gulf. As yet, no declaration of war had been made against anyone—Congress would be screaming their heads off by morning.

What did that matter? Formalities would follow. The House could launch articles of impeachment, if they wanted. Maggie couldn't wait any longer to act—she was barely maintaining control of her own military as it was. America needed blood for the lives lost in the Russian assault of Ādaži Military Base. The nation would demand blood for the loss of American sailors in the South China Sea, also.

One problem at a time.

Maggie wrapped herself in a thick cotton robe and shivered as she left her private bathroom. It was nine p.m., and she wasn't headed to bed—not for hours yet. A workstation erected in a sitting room off her main bedroom stood stacked with memos and notes from her aides. Things she hadn't been able to attend to during the day and couldn't ignore any longer. Seated at the desk with a cup of decaf coffee, her toes curling around the fibers of an ornate rug, Maggie gave herself sixty seconds to just breathe.

In, and out. As deep as she could manage, ignoring the throbbing pain and the ceaseless voice of craving—constant craving. She forced her exhausted mind into gear and began with the top note, a memo from her press secretary, Farah Rahman, suggesting that Maggie appear for a brief press conference as soon as possible. It had been two weeks since Maggie had shown her face to the American people—it wasn't a good look. The country was already coming apart at the seams.

Fifteen minutes, Maggie wrote on the memo. *Tomorrow at 2 PM.*

Then she moved to the next. Intelligence briefings from the CIA counter-terrorism division detailing concerns of repeat terrorist attacks inside the United States while so much attention was directed overseas. There was no action item, it was purely an FYI.

As though Maggie needed more to worry about.

She shuffled onward, chugging coffee and barging ahead under brute force. She reached her call log and scanned missed calls from foreign affairs departments around the world. Japan, Italy, Germany. Israel called twice in the same day. Prime Minister Elad Ben-Ari wanted to speak. Maggie made a note to call him back the next day.

Then her eyes caught on a name she didn't recognize—Hugh Sumner. He'd called her office four times over the past two days, with no explanation or message left. She wrinkled her nose and searched her tired brain, mining for any memory of the name. Maybe a congressman, some kind of Agency official…

But no. Anyone like that should be labeled and would have left a message. What was this about?

Maggie lifted the phone from her desk and pressed the shortcut key for her secretary's office—not one person, but multiple, working around the clock on rotation.

"Good evening, Madam President. This is Denice. How can I help?"

"I'm looking at my call log. There's four missed calls from some guy named Hugh Sumner? Five-seven-one area code. He didn't leave a message?"

"Let me check, ma'am."

Pause. Keys rattling. The phone shifted.

"Yes, it looks like he called twice today. He...didn't leave a message for you. The memo here says that he's an attorney."

"An attorney?"

"Yes, ma'am. Private council for...uh...James O'Dell?"

Maggie's heart skipped a beat. She sat upright, her gaze snapping back to the page. Her mind raced as she fixated on the name.

James O'Dell's attorney. What on earth?

"Would you like me to conduct some research, ma'am?" Denice said. "We can find out more about him, or block the calls if you prefer."

"That won't be necessary. Thank you, Denice."

Maggie hung up. She chewed her lip and reached for coffee but didn't lift the mug. She was still staring at that name. Curious, yes. And also confused.

Why on *earth* would James O'Dell's attorney be calling her? After Easterling had reported that O'Dell had been arrested, Maggie was concerned. Distressed. Confused. She'd ordered Easterling to have someone investigate and then update her. To keep it quiet.

And then?

Then Russia invaded NATO, and nothing else mattered.

Four calls.

Maggie punched the 571 number in—she couldn't help herself. She lifted the phone and it rang...and rang. She leaned back in the chair as her mind kept spinning and she *knew* she should hang up. Whatever this was, she shouldn't be touching it. If O'Dell was in trouble, she would help him. Of course she would help him. But she had legal counsel for that. Insulation. Distance. She should be—

"This is Hugh Sumner."

The voice was deep, confident, East Coast. The guy *sounded* like a lawyer.

"You called my office?"

Maggie didn't identify herself. She wasn't sure why. It just felt like a good idea.

"Madam President," the attorney said. "Thank you for returning my call."

Maggie waited. She was starting to get a very bad feeling in her stomach. Maybe that was just the withdrawals, but what was she doing? She should hang up.

"I'll get straight to the point," Sumner said. "I'm a defense attorney representing Mr. James O'Dell in a capital murder case involving a Washington, DC, man named Jacob Grover. Maybe you've heard of him. The FBI believes you now possess his liver."

"*What?*" Maggie said it before she could stop herself. She was sitting upright again, blinking, stunned. The words didn't even make sense, at first.

Sumner kept talking. "Grover committed suicide just before your transplant surgery. His liver was a match. I'm not sure how those medical records were breached—obviously, they're supposed to be sealed. My guess is that the FBI played dirty, which wouldn't be the first time. The point is, they believe that Grover didn't commit suicide at all, but was murdered by Mr. O'Dell. That's their argument."

Maggie sat frozen. Her lips were parted, the breath sticking in her throat even as her mind raced.

Murder?

"I'm not calling to comment on the prosecution's theory, Ms. Trousdale. The fact is, this case was assigned to me by the court and I'm just doing the best I can to defend my client. The FBI wants to cut a deal. I don't yet know specifics, but when I broached the subject with Mr. O'Dell, he demanded that I call you. That's all he would say."

Cut a deal.

Maggie pictured O'Dell in prison, and even in the monochromatic film real of her mind, his hands were stained in crimson. He was handcuffed to a table.

No, it wasn't in prison. It was *here*. In this room, only feet away from her. She could *see him*. He was shackled and shaking the chains, eyes wide as blood dripped from his lips.

"*Help me, Maggie! Help me.*"

"Ms. Trousdale? Why would James O'Dell ask me to call you?"

"I..." Maggie started, stopped. She swallowed. The vision of O'Dell danced in front of her eyes—she blinked and it vanished.

"I don't know," she said. "Don't call me again!"

Maggie hung up. She buzzed her secretary's office. Denice picked up.

"Yes, ma'am?"

"Block that number," Maggie hissed. "No more calls."

She hung up again, breathing fast. Swallowing over a dry throat, she placed both hands on the desktop as the floor tilted beneath her. Her gaze darted, moving from one darkened corner to the next. Searching for the wide eyes and bloody lips.

There was nothing, but O'Dell was there. Just out of reach, orbiting on the outskirts of her life, just as he had for so many years.

Now haunting her.

24

Kalorama
Washington, DC

The townhome was small by neighborhood standards—just thirty-two hundred square feet—and yet the three-story residence still cost Senator Matthew Roper north of two and a half million dollars.

Mortgaged, of course, but with a sub-market interest rate, compliments of a friend of a friend who ran a mortgage brokerage and valued public servants such as Roper. Perhaps, one day, the favor could be returned when some crucial real estate legislation hit the Senate floor. That understanding wasn't explicitly stated, of course—Roper wasn't nearly so stupid. But he knew how the game was played, and he played it better than most. He entered Congress with something like eight thousand dollars in his bank account, one small house in Des Moines and another in his home town of Cedar Rapids, both financed to the hilt to help fund his campaign. His net worth was well in the negative.

Now, just a decade later? He was a multimillionaire boasting record returns on a stock portfolio inflated by "gifted" shares. Life was good—but money alone hadn't brought Roper to DC. He came to this town in search of true power, the kind that swelled under its own exponential energy, leading to ever larger opportunities.

First the House, then the Senate. From a junior senator to a senior, chairing the Senate Select Committee on Intelligence. A very powerful force in Washington.

But not powerful enough. Matthew Roper sat on the Hill, but he very much wanted to descend it. The office he had his eye on sat at 1600 Pennsylvania Avenue, and nothing short of that goal would ever suffice.

"I spoke with her," the attorney said, his voice ragged with exhaustion. "She wouldn't say much. Barely identified herself. Then she hung up."

Kicked back in a leather chair with both feet on his desk, Roper relaxed with his tie tugged loose. The room was dark, the walls of bookcases lined by tomes Roper had never touched standing like shadows on every side. Across from him, Jim White, Roper's chief of staff, leaned close to the desk with a tumbler of whisky clutched in one hand.

White smelled, just as he always did. Like sweat and rotting onions, his hair disheveled and greasy. His gaze was fixated on the phone resting between them, the speaker button illuminated bright red.

"Did she express any fear?" Roper's voice was calm as he probed, his index fingers steepled beneath his nose. Internally, his mind raced—it always raced. He was working the angles and estimating the odds. Evaluating a developing strategy like a chess player working three and four moves ahead.

"Not directly," the attorney said. "She sounded…I don't know. Wound tight."

I'd hope so.

Roper thought of the endless news reel that played on a muted TV in his office. The burning and sinking warships in the South China Sea. The bombed American troops in Latvia—the fighter jets screaming over Europe amid racing missiles. The world was flying apart, and the president of the United States hadn't been seen in weeks.

"And how did she sound after you told her about O'Dell?" Roper said.

A sigh. "Like I said, she hung up on me, and I can't say that I blame her. Look, this is all very unusual. Maybe even a breach of protocol. If my client knows something incriminating about the Trousdale Administration, the last thing we should be doing is warning the president. She'll lawyer up—she might file an injunction. How could that *possibly* help my client?"

I'm not interested in helping your client, stupid fool.

Roper kept the thought to himself. He dropped his feet off his desk and swallowed whiskey. It was good—fifteen year Pappy. Elite, just like his future home office.

"I'm writing the checks, Hugh. How about you let me stress the details?"

No answer.

"Go back to Mr. O'Dell," Roper said. "Tell him you spoke with the president. Tell him that she hung up on you. Then tell him that if he doesn't work with the FBI, they will *bury him*. Right? He'll never be seen or heard from again. He'll die in a concrete box."

"You're asking me to push a plea bargain when I don't even know what my client has to offer."

"Again, Hugh, you're stressing the details. I wrote you a five-figure check—aren't you looking forward to a Caribbean vacation with that high school girlfriend of yours? What's her name...Kaylee? Kayla? Kay-something. Cutsie names are back in vogue, aren't they, Hugh?"

Dead silence—not so much as a breath. From across the desk, Jim White's lips stretched in a wolfish grin.

"James O'Dell is my client," Sumner whispered. "I told you from the start, I'm obliged to do whatever is in his best interest—"

"So make him *talk*, Hugh." Roper's voice turned suddenly sharp, like an ice-cold scalpel slicing through flesh. "You get him on record with the FBI and have him spill everything he knows about Maggie Trousdale—about her entire administration. That's the only way he cuts a deal. It's the only way he doesn't spend the rest of his life in prison. *That's* in his best interest."

Roper ended the call, heart thumping as sudden frustration boiled through his body. It wasn't desperation—he knew he held the high ground. He knew that he lay behind a rifle, one eye focused behind a sniper's scope with Maggie Trousdale fixed in the crosshairs. He *knew* he had her, cornered and helpless.

Yet, for the sake of plausible deniability, Matthew Roper couldn't be the one to pull the trigger. Why was it *so hard* to get other people to do their jobs?

"He may be right, you know," White said. "Calling Trousdale may have been unnecessary. Possibly even dangerous. She'll lawyer up."

Roper shook his head. He rose from the table and walked to a minibar beneath a window. Moonlight streamed in as he poured himself another three fingers of Pappy. One deep swallow, staring out at nearly silent Kalorama streets, and his body loosened.

"Did you ever read about the Red Baron?"

"The pilot?" White said.

"Right, from the First World War. He painted his plane bright red, and somebody warned him that it would make it difficult for him to surprise his enemies. To that, he said: *I don't want them to be surprised. I want them to be afraid.*"

Roper drank again. White's chair creaked. "I think that's only in the movie."

Roper rolled his eyes. He turned from the window.

"Good grief, Jim. Read the metaphor. The point is that Trousdale will lawyer up no matter what we do. Didn't you hear what Sumner said? She's strained. She's starting to crack."

"And?" White said.

"And we're gonna dump fuel on that fire until the house of Trousdale *burns to the ground.*"

White considered that. A sticky, ratlike tongue crossed his lips. Then he lifted his own glass, and Roper lifted his.

"To ashes," White said.

"And what rises from them," Roper replied.

Both men drank.

25

The Kremlin
Moscow, Russian

Nikitin couldn't believe his eyes—the Americans had not taken the bait.

With three US warships already rusting at the bottom of the South China Sea, several more belching flames, and numerous aircraft shot down, the damage inflicted by a brief but savage engagement with the Chinese Navy *should* have been enough to lock America in a death struggle with Beijing. Certainly, there were no indicators that the Americans knew who had really torpedoed their ships, initiating the conflict. Both Russian submarines tasked with the attack had slipped away undetected and were now safely back on patrol in the deep waters of the open Pacific.

So *why* had the Americans withdrawn from the battle? And, perhaps just as importantly, why had the Chinese *let them*?

"Cowards," Golubev snarled, barreling into Nikitin's office as though it were his own. The uncharacteristic demonstration of emotion was far more shocking than Golubev's unceremonious intrusion—Nikitin's right-hand man almost always let himself in without knocking, and Nikitin didn't care.

He didn't care about the outburst, either. In truth, he felt much the same.

Unbelievable.

"Useless *dogs*," Golubev continued. "We should wipe them off the map when we're finished in Europe."

Gazing at his computer screen and the map of the South Pacific that it depicted, Nikitin was more than a little inclined to agree. Just the mental image of Russian intercontinental ballistic missiles raining over China's proudest cities was enough to unleash a little rush of maniacal satisfaction into his chest. He could actually picture the smug little runts burning—he *wanted* them to burn.

But what good would his anger do now? China had betrayed their unwritten agreement with Moscow and Tehran. Even in the face of open military conflict with the Americans, they seemed eager to disengage. Maybe they *were* cowards, just as Golubev declared.

Or maybe they were simply smart, because in the short period during which America had lost two dozen planes and three warships, China had lost three times as many aircraft and eight warships. Granted, they were smaller vessels than what America had lost, but the point remained. Chinese equipment, Chinese technology, and Chinese pilots were proving to be vastly outmatched by American warfighters. It wasn't a battle China could really win. If America had kept pressing, she might have wiped out the bulk of what Navy Beijing had allocated to the region.

Instead America had withdrawn—all while unleashing wave after wave of brutal, unrelenting attacks across Eastern Europe and the Persian Gulf. Obliterating the Iranian Navy, smashing critical roads and bridges across the Baltic, and raining hellfire on Russian positions.

Not backing down.

"They know the Chinese lack the will to fight," Nikitin said. "They're focusing their assets on Europe and the Middle East."

"Which is exactly what Beijing was *supposed* to prevent," Golubev snarled.

Nikitin shot him a glare over the top of the computer screen—a harsher, colder look than maybe he had ever pointed at Golubev. It wasn't that Golubev was wrong. It was just that stating the obvious served no purpose for Nikitin. He needed to focus, now. He needed to get back ahead of the game.

He needed to think about Europe.

Smacking a key on his computer, Nikitin switched screens. He surveyed a display of Russian positions spread from just east of Tallinn, Estonia, and spilling south toward the town of Tartu. Nearly one hundred thousand Russian troops had already penetrated enemy territory, and half a million more stood ready to deploy on Nikitin's command. Meanwhile, the Belarussians were doing a fine job of occupying NATO in the south-eastern reaches of Latvia, shelling military installations and seizing strategic high ground even while Russian air power pummeled Ādaži Military Base...or had, anyway. For a while.

Now America and NATO were striking back. Missiles, bombs, and hundreds of fighter jets were sent to engage Russian air cover and hammer Russian ground positions. Thus far the damage was moderate, certainly within acceptable levels, but the momentum of the Russian advance had stalled.

That was not acceptable.

"We focus on Europe," Nikitin said. "We get the troops moving again."

"It's dark," Golubev objected. "Progress along broken roads will be slow. NATO air cover will tear them to pieces."

Nikitin chewed his lip, still studying the map. Considering—and reaching the only obvious conclusion.

Escalate.

"Initiate Order Seventeen," Nikitin said. "Authorize immediate air and missile strikes of NATO bases in eastern Poland. If the Americans want to launch planes, we'll decimate their runways."

Golubev didn't immediately answer. Nikitin's gaze flashed up.

"Did you hear me?"

"It's...early to hit Poland," Golubev said. "We had planned to secure the Baltic first. With our air power stretched thin—"

"The Americans' airpower will be stretched thin to confront us," Nikitin said. "Meanwhile our ground troops will finish securing Estonia and pivot to join Belarussian forces in Latvia. In two weeks we'll be marching into Riga and NATO will still be scrambling."

Golubev still didn't appear convinced, but Nikitin wasn't asking for permission. He stood from the chair.

"Give the order. We *will not* lose the initiative."

Golubev ducked his head. "Very well. I'll make the call."

Nikitin reached for his coat, sliding it on with a silky rush. He clipped on a Rolex watch and turned for the door. "NATO was unprepared, Anton. They still are. By the time the Americans know what is coming, we'll be kicking down doors in New York City."

26

The White House

Maggie held the meeting not in the Oval but in the vice president's office.

At face value it was an odd choice. She didn't actually know if she'd ever *been* in this office before. Since ordering Stratton out of the West Wing, the office had sat vacant, the White House staff learning to walk right past it as they grew to accept the VP's absence.

That was what made the room so desirable. Maggie could bar the Oval Office if she chose, blocking out the majority of her administration while holding a private meeting with the only two people invited inside. But to do that would draw attention. Literally everyone would know that something was up—questions would be whispered, and Easterling would likely press Maggie about the issue later on.

Maggie didn't want to deal with any of that. Ideally, nobody would even know about her clandestine meeting with CIA Director Aimes and Deputy Director Rigby. Maggie herself slipped into Stratton's vacant office twenty minutes ahead of time, sitting in the dark and alternating between torrents of sweat and racking chills.

The withdrawals were back. Harder than the night before, she *couldn't* shake them. She could barely focus. She desperately needed relief...but relief would have to wait. Aimes had contacted her office requesting Maggie's private line. That was the only touchpoint between Maggie's staff and the CIA for this entire conversation. After that, everything was off the books.

And it needed to be. Aimes hadn't delved into any specifics on the phone, private or otherwise, but Maggie knew what the meeting was about. She requested Aimes to meet her in the VP's office. She sat breathing in measured cycles and sipping water, waiting in the semi-dark.

The director and her deputy arrived five minutes apart, and Rigby arrived first. He seemed surprised to find Maggie waiting in the shadows. He reached for the light switch, then paused.

"Uh...good morning, Madam President. Should I...should I wait outside?"

"No."

It was all Maggie said. Rigby still hesitated, then left the lights off and sat across from Maggie. He shifted in his seat. He unbuttoned then rebuttoned his suit jacket. Maggie watched him twitch, his gaze flicking around the room to every dusty memento that adorned Stratton's shelves and walls. Anything *but* her.

Rigby was young—even younger than Maggie. Late twenties, maybe just about thirty. *Way* younger than the average deputy director, but Maggie understood Aimes's rationale in selecting him. Rigby's youth made him an outsider of the intelligence establishment—unformed clay, moldable in Aimes's hands. Flexible, creative, aggressive.

Had choices like those led America to the brink of destruction? Or would they save her?

"Do you like music, Silas?"

The question caught Rigby off guard. He blinked.

"Uh...yes, ma'am. I do."

"What's the best concert you ever attended?"

Another hesitation. A momentary flush of red to Rigby's cheeks. Then he said: "U2, I guess. Sophomore in high school."

"Stop lying."

"Ma'am?"

"Everybody says U2. Who was it, really?"

Rigby forced an awkward smile. "Taylor Swift, Reputation Tour. I went with my girlfriend."

Maggie laughed. It was a soft, dry sound. Even to her own ears it sounded unhealthy. "But you would have gone alone."

Rigby shrugged. "The production is incredible, like nothing I've ever seen."

"So I hear."

Another awkward silence. The AC kicked on, hissing somewhere overhead. Rigby cleared his throat.

"What about you, ma'am? If you don't mind me asking."

Maggie didn't mind—not at all. It had been *months* since she'd held a conversation like this. Just two people chatting about nothing. She only wished she could ask Rigby to call her Maggie.

She knew she couldn't.

"Olaf Dahl."

"Who, ma'am?"

"Swedish techno artist. He toured the US while I was in college at LSU. A bunch of us rented out an abandoned warehouse to host him. Partied until three in the morning—first time I tried ecstasy."

Rigby blinked. For a moment his mind seemed to deadlock. He breathed a half laugh.

"Uh...seriously?"

Maggie laughed too. "Seriously. I saw things, man."

Rigby laughed again. Maggie sipped water and shook her head. She was shivering, a little. Even in the dark, she thought Rigby could tell.

And it didn't matter. Just like her narcotics confession didn't matter. What was anyone going to do, anyway? Arrest her? Print her name in the tabloids? Torpedo her approval ratings?

It had all been done before, and there was zero chance that the Trousdale Administration would be reelected, anyway. Maggie wasn't even sure she could survive the campaign.

Why not throw her cards on the table?

"Wow," Rigby said at last.

"Yep," Maggie said. "Wow."

She lifted her cup in salute. Then the door opened and Aimes slipped inside. Rigby's back turned rigid as the lights flooded on. Maggie squinted and Aimes looked only temporarily apologetic. She didn't switch them off.

"I'm sorry I'm late, ma'am. I thought it would be best for Rigby and I to arrive separately. Minimize attention.

"It's fine," Maggie said. "Sit."

Aimes did. She carried a locked briefcase but didn't open it. Rigby, his smile evaporated, sat stiff alongside her, waiting. Maggie crunched ice from her water and licked her teeth. She rattled the cup.

"Well?"

Aimes cleared her throat. She set the briefcase down.

"We'd like to update you on our previous discussion. The one about..." A hesitation.

"About parking a bullet in Nikitin's brainpan," Maggie said. "Right?"

What were they gonna do to her?

"It's...a little more complicated than that," Aimes said. "We prefer the term *regime change*. But, essentially, yes. The strategy you asked us to investigate involves removing Makar Nikitin from power."

"And?" Maggie pressed.

Aimes turned to Rigby. He stepped right in.

"We ran 2,062 simulations involving Nikitin's death by non-natural causes. In eighty-seven percent of cases, the Russian offensive stalled or even collapsed while the Kremlin descended into turmoil. Per constitutional protocol, Russian PM Maxim Romanov takes power for a three-month period until a special election can be called. That's...where things get hazy."

"Hazy how?"

"We can't be sure what happens while Romanov is in power," Aimes said. "Whatever members of Nikitin's inner circle survive his death—we assume most of them would—are likely to launch competing bids to take his place. Legal protocol or otherwise, open war with NATO would create a constitutional crisis—a power vacuum. Anything could happen. Russia could become a de facto dictatorship overnight."

"They already are," Maggie said.

Aimes rocked her head. "You could say so. It's mostly a case of *the devil you know*. We can somewhat predict what Nikitin will do next. Absent of Nikitin we—"

"Are you hedging?" Maggie cut in.

"Ma'am?"

"Are you covering your ass?"

No answer. Maggie's gut tightened, unleashing a wave of throbbing pain. It did nothing to soften her mood.

"Sarah, I didn't appoint you to dodge bullets. Give me the truth or I'll find somebody who will."

It was strikingly close to the statement Maggie had fired off at General Yellin, and everyone in the room knew it. Aimes straightened.

"We've received intel from an asset in Moscow. Somebody buried deep. She's connected with a former Russian SVR agent who is now a pseudo-partner of the CIA. At least...when he wants to be."

"Explain it to me like I'm five, Sarah."

"He's a Russian traitor. That's their perspective on him. My perspective is that he's a Russian patriot—one of the few who remain. He's obsessed with protecting his country from annihilation. He believes that open war with the West will lead to annihilation—at least with Nikitin at the helm."

"He's right," Maggie said.

"Our simulations certainly think so."

"So what does this Russian traitor have to say?"

Pause.

"Well?"

"It's impossible to verify any of this. But according to Mr. Sidorov—that's our contact—a coalition to displace Nikitin has already assembled inside Moscow...and it's led by Prime Minister Romanov."

Maggie settled back into her chair. A headache developed behind her eyes, pulsating through her skull, but she barely noticed. She wasn't even looking at Aimes anymore. As her heart rate accelerated, Maggie's mind spun.

Had Aimes *really* just said that?

"I have to reiterate—we can't prove any of this," Aimes said. "Mr. Sidorov has proven trustworthy before, but his allegiances are clear. If he helps us at all, it's only because he wants to help Russia. That makes him predictable only so long as we know as much or more than he does, but if we miss something—"

"Reed Montgomery," Maggie said.

The room turned cold. Aimes glanced toward Rigby—Rigby shook his head, just once.

"I'm sorry, ma'am?" Aimes said.

"You reactivated Reed Montgomery. You deployed him into the Caucasus and then India."

Maggie knew it was true. She'd been blindsided by the fact, initially ready to rip Aimes limb from limb when the truth was exposed. Nobody knew Reed as well as Maggie—nobody had witnessed firsthand his potential for animal savagery. Nobody had been stained by that blood spatter worse than her.

And yet, as the smoke cleared, Maggie saw it. Like she'd never seen it before, as though every collision between herself and the man they called *Prosecutor* had all boiled toward this exact moment. This precise need.

"Mr. Montgomery is offline, ma'am," Aimes said. "His team is badly banged up. Honestly, I'm not even sure where they all are."

"So find them," Maggie said, sitting forward. "Assemble them and build out the mission."

"What mission?" It was the first time Rigby had spoken since Aimes arrived.

"The mission to stop this war," Maggie said. "The mission to remove Makar Nikitin from office."

27

Umm Bab, Qatar

The setting sun faded into the Persian Gulf, an endless shimmering horizon with Saudi Arabia somewhere far beyond. It was hot on the beach. Lucy sweated as she sat cross-legged in the sand, all alone, nothing but desert and palm trees at her back.

And one dusty and dented Suzuki Carry—a gas-powered micro truck used by an Air Force contractor at Al Udeid Air Base. Lucy had sweet-talked the contractor into letting her borrow it for an errand off base. He hadn't been enthused, but was eventually convinced.

Funny—so much had changed in Lucy's life since she came to faith. She felt like an entirely different person. Yet she still maintained that old charm—albeit a less savage version. She still knew how to smile and bat those eyelashes and talk a bear out of his honey pot.

Now seated on the beach, breathing in the salt air and basking in the glow of the sun, the aches and pains of Lucy's recent ordeal in India faded to the back of her mind. When she closed her eyes, she was back in that chair. She was jerking, turning rigid under blasts of muscle-contorting electricity. She was screaming. Choking. Tugging against her bonds to no avail.

The horror was so fresh in her mind that she would have expected nightmares. Panic attacks. Sleeplessness and desperation and mental deadlock—all the symptoms she had suffered after similar torture in Southeast Asia, the agony that originally led to her opioid addiction and subsequent rehab.

And then conversion. Newfound faith. Hope—for the first time in her life. Had so much really changed that she could close her eyes and be back in that chair in an Indian pit and just...accept it? Release herself from the obligation to be terrified or desperate? Acknowledge the pettiness of that moment in the context of a history-spanning story bigger than all of humanity?

But really that was giving herself too much credit. Lucy Byrne knew that she hadn't grown stronger, but something dwelling in her had taken over. Armored her. Calmed her spirit and comforted her mind.

Yes, that was it. And Lucy had never been so okay with not being in control. With eyes closed and palms turned upward, she remembered the torture...and simply let it go. She breathed, basking in the warmth and the gentle rush of the waves. Communing with her Creator in silence and stillness—the best way she knew how.

It was more than prayer, it was spiritual vulnerability. A deliberate opening of her own heart to be invaded by a greater spirit. A healing, changing, loving God.

No opioid had ever touched her this way. None of the yoga or shallow meditation or physical exertion she used to practice so religiously could sooth her soul or erase the clamor in her mind.

This was rebirth.

Lucy met Jesus Christ in her mind and prayed for the world. For the lost, the suffering, the warriors bleeding on the battlefield. She prayed for her friends—for the fractured Prosecution Force, and most especially for its leader. She didn't pray for comfort or removal. She didn't ask for safety or security. She asked for strength. For purpose. For Reed and his little army to be hurled like a cruise missile straight into the face of whatever fight God had waiting for them.

And if they never walked away?

She only asked that Reed and Co would know redemption the way she had. That they could walk into eternity confident, steady, believing.

Lucy prayed and the sun set. The desert wind grew cool on her back, but she barely noticed. She was so lost in her own spiritual dialog that she barely felt the shudder in the sand beneath her—barely detected the distant churn of rotor blades storming in from the east. It wasn't until the helicopter was barely a thousand yards away that Lucy's eyes opened, and she twisted her head to look back.

The aircraft was storm gray—an HH-60G Pave Hawk with US Air Force markings on the tail. It blazed directly overhead at barely two hundred feet and Lucy shielded her eyes from a wash of damp sand exploding off the beach. The chopper didn't fade over the Gulf—it turned instead, nosing back toward her and dropping rapidly a hundred yards from her position.

Lucy scrambled out of the sand, still squinting as heavy tires sank deep and the rotors wound down. A rolling door was already open. Shadows moved inside.

Then Reed Montgomery dropped out. Dressed in ill-fitting Air Force cargo pants and a PT shirt, he bent as he jogged out from beneath the rotor blades, followed close behind by an Air Force airman in a utility uniform.

Lucy didn't move. She stood with one hand over her eyes as Reed approached. Surf rolled in from the gulf and splashed up to his ankles, but he didn't seem to notice. He marched ahead with a light in his eyes that Lucy hadn't seen in days—not since India. It was a focused, burning intensity. Like a laser sight fixated on a target.

Reed Montgomery had a mission. Lucy knew it even before he spoke. Her prayer had been answered.

"Where?" Lucy said simply.

"Cyprus. Right now."

"Do we know why?"

"Not yet. They'll brief us when we arrive. You…don't have to go."

Lucy glanced over her shoulder, back toward the Suzuki Carry. There was no question in her mind as to whether she would go. Only a slight logistical snag.

"I borrowed that truck."

"I can return that for you, ma'am."

The airman pinned his cap down with one hand, holding it against the blast of the rotors. Lucy dug the keys out of her pocket and dropped them in his hand.

"Motor pool—ask for Sammy."

"Got it."

The airman jogged for the truck, apparently eager to step out of the rotor wash. Lucy turned back to Reed.

"I want you to know something before we leave," Lucy said.

"What?"

"God loves you, Reed. He always has."

Reed said nothing. The laser focus in his eyes broke, for just a moment. He blinked. Lucy tilted her head toward the chopper.

"Let's roll!"

28

Moscow, Russia

Natasha Kirov met Ivan at Novodevichy Cemetery, an eighteen-plus-acre facility parked just west of Novodevichy Convent near the heart of Moscow.

It was an apropos place to discuss the end of the world. With graves interlaced by walking paths and overhung by spidery evergreen trees, the rush and churn of the nearby city was nearly silenced, the graveyard frozen in pre-winter frost. Ivan slipped in wrapped in a thick trench coat and threaded his way along the marked paths as though he knew exactly where he was headed.

In fact, he did. Along Path 8, near the core of the property, a wall of grave vaults towered four coffins high, adorned with scrollwork and covered by a metal roof. The vault wall was built of brick in a shallow U shape, allowing a concave of privacy in its middle.

Ivan found Kirov waiting for him behind a statue of a girl in an ankle-length dress, walking and looking to the ground, appearing very sad. Kirov also appeared sad, wrapped in a puffy coat as she stared at a grave marker with all the lost and heartbroken affectation of a young widow.

A convincing actress.

"Thank you for getting back with me so quickly," Ivan said, standing beside her with his hands in his pockets.

Kirov shot him a sideways glance. Her eyes—bright green—sparkled like gemstones, the corner of her mouth twisting into just the hint of a smile.

"It's kind of an emergency."

She spoke in relaxed Russian—no discernible accent. Ivan merely grunted.

"You communicated with your bosses?"

"I did."

"And?"

Kirov looked back at the grave marker, not answering as footsteps padded behind them. Ivan already knew who it was—a pair of teenage lovers skulking through the cemetery, likely looking for a quiet place to make out. He'd identified them upon entry and dismissed them as not a threat. As soon as they saw the pair standing at the grave wall, they hurried on.

"We are prepared to help," Kirov said.

We. As though she wasn't half Russian. It annoyed Ivan, but he let it pass. At least he had the answer he wanted—hopefully.

"You're prepared to do the work?" Ivan questioned.

"We are prepared to *assist*," Kirov clarified, shooting him another sideways look.

She was beautiful, no doubt about it. Striking, even. In his younger years, Ivan might have been stricken himself. As it was, he just wanted her to get to the point.

"So what do you need?" he said.

Pause. Kirov took a half step closer to the wall. She brushed dirt and developing moss off the top edge of the grave marker—as though it really were her late husband's final resting place. As though she could still hear his voice in her head.

"Langley is still developing a strategy," she said. "For now, we need all the intel we can get. Specifically, the whereabouts of the...subject."

The subject. That was the kindest name Ivan had heard for Nikitin in some time.

"So you're looking for an opportunity?" Ivan said.

Kirov showed him a piercing glance. "We're looking for *options*, Ivan. Just like the rest of the world. Work with your contacts—find out what you can. If Langley decides to move, they'll be most interested in travel plans outside of Moscow. Outside of Russia, if possible. Someplace a little more exposed."

Ivan snorted. "You think he's stupid?"

"We think he's insane."

Well. Ivan couldn't argue with that.

"Find out what you can," Kirov said. "You know how to reach me."

She turned. Ivan cut her off, placing his bulky body between her and the exit. She was so close he could smell her perfume, but she didn't so much as flinch. She merely lifted both eyebrows.

"I don't need Langley to get this done," Ivan said. "I need Langley to guarantee, *when it's done*, that they won't exploit our turmoil. The object here is to save Russia...*our* people."

Kirov's faint smile returned. "Relax, big man. I work for the good guys."

She stepped around him and Ivan let her go, turning as she passed the statue and reached the walkway. Coat swishing, head hanging. As though she was still consumed by grief.

All Ivan could think was: *No—you just work for the other guys.*

29

Department of Corrections Central Detention Facility
Washington, DC

Faces—James O'Dell saw their faces.

Not only Jacob Grover, that convicted pervert blubbering on his couch with a cheap revolver pressed to his temple, but also Victor O'Brien, prior director of the CIA and sworn enemy of Maggie Trousdale.

Grover had died in his living room, a .38 caliber entry wound drilled into his temple. O'Brien had died in his backyard pool, a belly full of hard liquor as he thrashed to break free of O'Dell's grip, his face held beneath the water.

And then...the life left him. It left Grover, also. O'Dell hadn't felt anything at the time other than raging adrenaline and breathless focus. He hadn't seen the lights go out, he hadn't watched souls depart their mortal cages.

But now, in his nightmares? He saw them all the time. He stood at the edge of the pool and watched himself holding O'Brien down, not one but two bodies thrashing in the water. The first was flesh and blood, the second looked more like a ghost. It was tangled around O'Brien's body, like a blurry image shot with a slow lens. The longer the body thrashed, the messier the blur became, until at last...

The spirit separated. O'Dell watched it break free as the body grew still. He staggered back from the edge of the pool and looked up to find the ghost staring at him—wide, black eyes. Drifting slowly into a midnight sky, its vapor mouth opening and closing, teeth clicking. Eyes glaring hatred. Wispy fingers reaching out but not touching him, falling just short.

O'Dell fell, pitching into the pool. He thrashed, colliding with O'Brien's lifeless corpse. The ghost hung over him, still drifting toward the sky but leaning down. Lunging with one smoky hand that turned mortal for only a split second.

Just long enough to shove O'Dell under the water. Down into the dark. He choked, and O'Brien's body floated over him. He couldn't get back to the surface. The body held him down.

And now those lifeless eyes came alive. They turned fiery red, and O'Brien's mouth opened to swallow him.

Like a grave.

O'Dell broke out of the dream as though he were breaking out of the water. He sat bolt upright, heaving and shaking from head to toe. He was drenched, not with pool water but with sweat. His prison jumpsuit stuck to his skin, and shivers racked his spine. He couldn't breathe, he couldn't see. Everything was pitch dark, and if he blinked, he saw the corpse.

Devouring him.

O'Dell threw his legs off the bed and tore at the metal snaps that held his collar closed. The jumpsuit opened down to his stomach, exposing a chest that gleamed with sweat, still quaking with each breath. He grabbed the edge of the bedframe and dropped his head, forcing himself to breathe more slowly even as sweat dripped from his face.

He couldn't hyperventilate—he couldn't afford to pass out. He was terrified of the nightmares. He couldn't face the bodies again. He needed to *calm down*.

Minutes ticked by before O'Dell lifted his head. The tiny prison cell which encased him contained only the bed and a stainless steel toilet/sink combo. The floor was bare concrete, O'Dell's prison-issue flip-flops resting along one block wall.

He was alone—no cellmate. Maybe because he was a relatively high-profile prisoner, or maybe because O'Dell had scared the piss out of the only guy they'd ever bunked him with. He'd been alone ever since, nothing but his own thoughts to break the silence. Nothing but blank walls to stare at, a hard mattress to lie on.

Alone.

O'Dell exploded off the bed and reached the cell door. He wrapped both hands around the bars and pressed his face into the gap. The hallway was dark, the other cells quiet. O'Dell shouted for the guard. Nobody answered, and he shouted again, louder this time. From another cell an inmate cursed, calling for O'Dell to shut up.

O'Dell didn't shut up. He kept shouting until at last a light flashed on, and a correctional officer appeared. The CO wore a wrinkled shirt and carried an energy drink. He looked exhausted, disgusted. Ready to rattle the teeth out of O'Dell's head.

"What's the problem?" the CO demanded.

"I need a phone," O'Dell said. "I need to call the president."

The CO blinked. He snorted a half laugh. "What?"

"She'll take my call—I know the number. Just give me three minutes on the phone. I'll make it worth your while."

"What, you think this place is a phone booth? You think I'm a concierge?"

"*Shut up!*" It was the irate inmate again, louder than before. The CO glanced over his shoulder, then closed on O'Dell's cell. He gulped the energy drink and wiped his lips with the back of one hand. His voice lowered—it didn't soften.

"I guess you don't get the news in here. World War Three is kickin' off, dude. The Russians are storming Europe—the Chinese are sinking our ships. And that swamp rat president of yours? *She's got nothing.*"

O'Dell's fingers tightened around the bars. The breath whistled between his teeth.

The CO only smiled. "You ask me, she's got the next bullet coming."

O'Dell shot a hand through the bars and just missed the guy's throat. The CO danced back, laughing as his drink spilled. O'Dell's shoulder slammed against the bars and he flailed for the guy. It was too late. The CO scrubbed his wet hand across his pant leg, still grinning.

Then the other inmate started shouting again, and the grin faded. The CO drew a whistle from his pocket and blew two ear-piercing blasts. Loud enough to wake *everyone* up.

"All right!" he screamed. "Any more noise and I'll throw the lot of you in solitary!"

The whistle, plus the threat, was enough to light the whole hallway on fire. In an instant, everyone was shouting. Everyone was screaming curses and spitting at O'Dell's cell. O'Dell stepped back from the bars just as the CO shot him a wink.

"Sleep well, big guy."

30

RAF Akrotiri
Akrotiri, Cyprus

The Air Force transported Reed, Lucy, and Turk from Al Udeid to Cyprus using the jump seats of a KC-135 Stratotanker. It wasn't a purpose-built transport plane—it was actually a midair refueler, one of half a dozen that were being emergency transferred from Qatar to Europe to feed a mushrooming airborne offensive against the Russians.

Designed to draw fuel not only from its wing tanks but also from the fuselage bladders built for refueling other aircraft, the Stratotankers were capable of flying nonstop for sixty-five hundred nautical miles and could have easily reached their European destinations without interruption. Cyprus, however, wasn't too far out of the way, and one of the Stratotankers broke off from the pack to deposit three members of the Prosecution Force on a wide RAF runway in the middle of the night.

Jet engines howling, airframe throbbing, the Stratotanker was taxiing for takeoff the moment the door closed behind Reed. He shot the pilots a two finger wave, then ran alongside Turk toward a waiting Land Rover Wolf parked at the edge of the tarmac. Painted in NATO green, the Wolf was a British vehicle used by the Royal Air Force, sort of a modern-day version of the old Wyllis Jeeps. Lucy already sat in the front passenger seat, covering her ears against the howl of the Stratotanker.

Reed had barely noticed the noise. His ears were shot anyway after so many years of gunfire and hand grenades. All he could think about was the next step—reuniting with his team and finding out why the CIA had moved them to Cyprus.

"Mr. Montgomery?"

A sharp-dressed RAF Flying Officer—roughly equivalent to the US Air Force's first lieutenant—stood by the Wolf awaiting Reed and Turk's arrival. He didn't seem to know which of them was Reed—he extended a hand and Reed made it easy on him, accepting a confident grip.

"Welcome to Akrotiri. I've been ordered to drive you across base."

"Great. Thanks."

Reed and Turk swung into the Wolf's open back seat, bracing themselves on the roll cage as the flying officer powered them away from the airstrip. It was nearly two a.m., but the base was hardly asleep. Small vehicles rushed along winding roads while lights shone from every passing office building. In the background, smaller, nastier aircraft than the Stratotanker roared off the runway, their afterburners appearing as hot white dots before they vanished into the sky.

Pointed east—toward Israel and Lebanon and the onslaught of Iranian aggression.

It's already a world war.

The Wolf squealed to a stop at the base of a three-story building marked with a letter and three numbers. The flying officer left the engine running as he rushed to open Lucy's door. He was beaming at her, actually bowing as she stepped out. He made no such ovations for Reed or Turk.

They proceeded past a secure-access door and into a hallway manned by a British military policeman who asked for ID. Reed didn't have any—none of them did. All those things had been lost somewhere amid their stint in the Caucasus. The flying officer was prepared, however. He told the policeman who to call, and the call didn't last long. Then Reed, Turk, and Lucy were ushered to an elevator, with the flying officer babbling the entire time. He asked Lucy about her hometown and whether she enjoyed beaches and seafood—Cyprus could offer the best of both.

Reed glanced sideways and found Lucy blushing, curling one lock of her hair absently around her finger. He rolled his eyes, suddenly thinking of Banks. Of a bar in Atlanta. Of a pit in his stomach and words falling flat on his lips. It felt like a *lifetime* ago—really just a few years.

But he still remembered that feeling, and thinking of Banks...he remembered why he felt it.

The doors rolled open and the flying officer led them to a room with a locked metal door. He stood awkwardly outside, shifting on his feet and trying not to look at Lucy. Reed cocked an eyebrow.

"The door?"

"Oh. Right, right. Here you are, old boy." The officer swiped a card and pushed the door open. Lucy fired off a smile that seemed to melt him in place, and Reed led the way inside.

The room was small—maybe ten feet by twenty—with two windows overlooking the base outside. Tables lined one corner, and the moment they entered, Reed's gaze settled over Wolfgang and Corbyn. They rose from metal chairs, Corbyn rushing straight to Lucy and wrapping her in a big hug while Wolfgang staggered a little on his way to Reed and Turk.

He looked older than when Reed had last seen him, on a hospital ship just prior to the India operation. Wolfgang hadn't participated in that mission—he was too badly banged up. He still looked banged up, with streaks of gray in his hair and an ill-fitting prosthetic leg that squeaked as he walked.

But there was iron in his gaze. He extended a right hand that clamped tight around Reed's, then around Turk's.

"Good flight?" Wolfgang said.

"The best the Air Force could offer." Turk made no effort to disguise the sarcasm in his voice—there was a little pain in it, also, born out of the bullet wounds Turk had suffered in India that were a long way from fully healed.

And yet he was here. They were all here, in pieces or staggering or whatever. The unchecked anger in Corbyn's eyes told the reason why.

"So what's the deal?" Reed said.

Wolfgang squinted. "They didn't tell you?"

"Tell us what?"

"I don't know. We were told to sit here and wait—I assumed you guys knew why."

Reed didn't know. He'd only been told to get on a plane and fly to Cyprus—not eventually, not later that day. *Now.*

"I don't know," Reed said simply.

A sequence of exchanged glances passed around the room. Reed looked over his shoulder to the closed door, hands in his pockets.

Then he simply sat down. What else was he going to do? If he'd learned anything at all from the Marines, it was how to hurry up and wait. With a restrained grunt through gritted teeth, Turk sat also. Lucy stood by the window and overlooked the road outside—maybe searching for her new RAF crush. Wolfgang paced on his squeaking prosthetic leg, and Corbyn crunched peanuts. There was a bowl of them resting on a table, in their shells. She smashed the shells and ground the nuts between her molars, as loud as a horse with an apple, but nobody said anything.

"They wouldn't have brought us here just to send us home," Turk said finally.

Reed grunted. Wolfgang stopped pacing and folded his arms. Then interlaced his fingers behind his back.

Everyone was strung out. Everyone looked like they hadn't slept well in days...maybe weeks. Reed's gaze passed across his battered team and he couldn't help but marvel at how much had changed in such a short period of time. How much this war had cost them.

Was it war from the start? From all the way back to a flaming Air Force One streaking out of the sky?

It was starting to feel that way.

"Anybody got an update on Europe?" It was Wolfgang, but before Reed could answer, sharp footsteps rang from beyond the door. They all turned just in time for the lock to buzz. Voices murmured outside, but only one person stepped in.

He was white, about average height and average build. Not more than thirty years old, with streaks of faint gray in his hair that contrasted youthful eyes. He wore a suit wrinkled by the familiar marks of air travel and carried a messenger bag in one hand. He let the door close behind him, and for a long moment, he said nothing.

Reed had never seen him before, and yet he could tell by the look in his eyes that this guy had seen them, at least in photographs. His gaze switched from one face to the next, as though he were taking inventory.

Nobody spoke. Nobody greeted him or extended a hand. Corbyn continued to crunch peanuts as the newcomer advanced across the room and rested his bag on an table. His gaze settled on Reed.

"Mr. Montgomery?"

Reed's mind clicked—the moment the guy spoke, he recognized the voice. He'd heard it before, on the phone during the India mission. This was the guy who had communicated on the CIA's behalf, never identifying himself but sticking with the Prosecution Force right to the end.

"Who are you?" Reed said simply.

The guy had refused to answer before. This time, he didn't hesitate.

"My name is Silas Rigby, and I'm Deputy Director of Operations for the CIA."

Deputy director. Way, way up the chain. Yet this guy was here, in person. *Why?*

"I'd like to express my gratitude on behalf of the nation for the heroic service each one of you have rendered. Your courage, your fortitude, your focus...they're unmatched."

They were the kind of words every politician spews at Memorial Day fundraisers, but Rigby's tone was calm. Measured. He looked each of them in the eye as he spoke, and Reed somehow believed that he meant every word.

Corbyn crunched another peanut. She must have gotten a piece of the shell in her mouth because she spat, right there on the floor next to the table.

"Brilliant pep talk, Clever Clogs. Why are you here?"

Her voice cut. Reed understood why. For his part, Rigby took it right on the chin. He rested both hands atop the messenger bag, his gaze settling on Reed as he replied.

"I'm here because the Free World needs you—one last time, for one last mission. The most important operation anyone in this room has ever attempted."

31

Ministry of Defense Headquarters
Moscow, Russia

The Russian air strikes against NATO bases in Poland were a mixed bag.

Some air strips and missile silos lay smashed and worthless, their locations marked by red Xs scattered across the digital map that Makar Nikitin surveyed. Those marks he liked—they were what he was hoping for.

But other NATO military sites had been successfully defended, with Russian missiles and aircraft shot out of the skies. Even now, NATO was already returning fire. Ballistic missiles screamed out of Poland toward Russian positions across eastern Estonia and Belarussian positions in Latvia, while Poland continued to serve as a staging ground for swelling NATO ground power.

The war had arrived, most definitely. Even as America withdrew from confronting the Chinese, she was dumping on the heat in both Europe and the Middle East. United States Marines, landing by the tens of thousands in Beirut, were wiping Hezbollah from existence while US aircraft did the same with Iran's Navy in the Persian Gulf.

It was all preliminary, little more than an initial wave of gratification for NATO. Nikitin had been around long enough to appreciate the ebbs and flows of war. Luck would swing his way again...

But Makar Nikitin had spent most of his life waiting. Either for his single meal a day as a starving peasant child, or for his orders as a Red Army soldier, or for his opportunities as a rising political star in Moscow. With all that practice, he should have been an expert—instead he was only worn. Stretched. Pushed to an invisible limit that strained his mind and inflamed his natural lust for blood.

He'd tasted blood in the Caucasus. Again in in the Baltic. Things had been going *perfectly* before the Chinese chickened out. Now the whole thing felt like a chess match, when it should have felt like total domination.

Enough.

"Send orders to all ground commanders in Estonia," Nikitin said. "They are to advance immediately against Tallinn. I want the city seized by the weekend. Belarussian forces should advance against Riga."

Dead silence fell across the sprawling command center. Nikitin's gaze was still fixated on a map of the Baltic, his mind racing as he calculated the angles. Estimated timelines, the strength of Estonian and Latvian domestic defenses. The realities of burning capital cities and a unified Russian/Belarussian offensive.

"Could you...repeat, sir?"

The Russian general who voiced the question sounded a great deal more tentative than Nikitin would have expected from a senior military leader. He spun from the map, teeth gritted.

"You heard me! Advance against Tallinn. Launch ballistic missile attacks against the city to soften defenses, and prepare an air assault to clear the skies. We will blitz them like the Germans—wipe NATO out of the Baltic before American troops arrive."

The general didn't answer. He glanced sideways, away from Nikitin and toward Anton Golubev, who lurked in a darkened corner. The junior officers in the room fixated on their monitors, making themselves small at their workstations. Nikitin's hands clenched. The blood rushed to his face.

"You have my orders! *Execute*. Immediately."

"Yes, Mr. President."

The general ducked his head. Nikitin spun back to the map as Golubev slipped to his side. When he spoke, the Ghost of the Kremlin kept his voice low. Only Nikitin could hear.

"This is not well-advised, Makar. It was already a risk to assault Poland so early—advancing our ground forces now will isolate them from their supply lines. If the Americans launch air strikes—"

"The American's aren't *here*, Anton. They're still scrambling to assemble ground troops. They will hesitate, just as they have hesitated against the Chinese. Our chance is *now*. We seize Tallinn and then Riga. We unify our forces with the Belarussians and pivot straight into Lithuania. By next month, we confront Poland with an iron foothold in the Baltic. We'll have all the momentum."

Golubev didn't answer. He stared at the same maps Nikitin obsessed over until at last Nikitin glanced left. Golubev simply shook his head.

"We could falter in Tallinn—falter across Latvia. There are too many variables, too much resistance. We should wait for heavy armor and overwhelming force—"

"Bomb the resistance!" Nikitin screamed, snapping like a dry tree branch. "Smash their cities and smash their defenses. Pour fire from the skies—I don't care if a man, woman, or child survives. You will *erase* them, Anton. You will hit them, and you will hit them now. Do you understand me?"

Nikitin's voice boomed off the walls, spittle flying. Golubev stood frozen, staring at his boss, unblinking and uncowed, his face flushing in just a little indignation. For a long moment the two men locked into a staring contest, Golubev's head rocked back to meet the president's gaze. Across the room, nobody dared to breathe. Golubev's jaw clenched.

Then, very slowly, he lifted a hand to his brow. The salute was short and sharp. It came without comment. Nikitin watched it, then exploded around Golubev and hurtled out the door—slamming it behind him like a gunshot.

32

Department of Corrections Central Detention Facility
Washington, DC

The staff at the prison admitted Senator Matthew Roper without requesting ID. Without asking him to sign the visitor log or remove his hat or even submit to a pat down. They only ran him through a horseshoe metal detector before a correctional officer led Roper down a narrow corridor that somehow smelled of both bleach and body odor at the same time.

It took three phone calls to arrange access. A friend of a friend of a friend—a chain of favors called in, the entire way. Roper arrived at the tail end of third shift, which ensured that all the on-site guards were tired and inattentive, eager to conclude their lengthy rotations and clock out for breakfast before bed. They didn't know his name, and he doubted whether anyone recognized his face. People like this, in Roper's experience, were unlikely to recognize their own senators, let alone a senator from five states west.

They only knew that he was a VIP. That he was here off the books, and that he should not be spoken to. Safely ensconced in an interview room where all cameras were switched off, Roper took a seat in a stainless metal chair but left his sunglasses on, just as he had since arrival. He interlaced his fingers in his lap and twiddled his thumbs, first in one direction and then the other, doing his best to ignore the sour stench and the hard chair and the overt bleakness of the room.

He would snap in a place like this—he knew he would. Given a few months, maybe just a few weeks, he would go crazy. He would be one of those prisoners who beat his own head against a wall or laughed like a maniac as he broke his own fingers. Clinical insanity ran in Roper's family—he'd felt its siren call in his own mind when life became most stressful.

How long could even a stable person last in this pit? How long could James O'Dell last?

The door opened after eleven minutes ticked by on Roper's Rolex. The same guard who had escorted him in now escorted a prisoner, dressed in a jumpsuit and corrections flip-flops, his hair uncut, his face covered in rough stubble. O'Dell wore handcuffs but no leg shackles. He stopped just inside and stared at Roper in squinted confusion, then turned to the CO.

"That's not my lawyer."

"Never said he was," the CO grunted.

He pushed O'Dell toward the table without another word, then departed the room and locked the door, leaving Roper still twiddling his thumbs as he looked up at the oversized Cajun...the president's personal man.

How about that.

"Sit down," Roper said.

"Who are you?"

Roper took his time answering. He'd game-planned this entire conversation, even roll-playing with White before arrival. White thought the visit was a terrible idea. He'd lobbied Roper to stay in DC, to let White himself visit O'Dell in his place.

But Roper knew that White, for all his cunning talents, wouldn't break a man like O'Dell. He'd be lucky not to be broken himself. O'Dell was too smart for cunning, too savvy to be played. He needed to be *won*—like a skeptical voter.

In that activity, Roper excelled.

"I'm a friend," Roper said. "I came here to help you."

O'Dell snorted, and Roper finally broke off his twiddling long enough to remove his sunglasses. He folded them and slipped them into the interior pocket of his jacket.

"I know my friends," O'Dell said. "It's a short list. You ain't on it."

"Call me a prospective friend, then. A candidate."

O'Dell shook his head. "You're a politician."

"Maybe."

"Definitely. I can smell it on you, like cheap cologne. You're all the same up here. All the same smell."

Roper smiled at that, one side of his mouth curling upward. "I assure you, Mr. O'Dell. I'm not the same. Why don't you have a seat?"

Another few seconds ticked by as O'Dell glanced over his shoulder toward the door. There was a security glass pane, about four inches wide and a foot tall. No sight of the correctional officer. O'Dell's gaze next traveled to the ceiling, toward the cameras.

No lights gleamed or blinked. The only light hung over the table.

O'Dell seemed to consider that. At last, he advanced to the chair on his side of the table and tugged it back with is cuffed hands. He sat, leaned back, staring at Roper.

And not speaking.

Fair enough.

"They tell me you're in quite a pickle," Roper said. "Charged with capital murder in the death of one Jacob Grover...an organ donor, no less. Isn't that interesting?"

Roper waited, but O'Dell didn't answer. He didn't even blink.

Ice cold, just like the president.

"I'll be frank with you, James. Is it all right if I call you James?"

Again, no answer. Roper shrugged.

"James it is, then. As I was saying, you're way, way up the creek...and there's not a paddle in your universe. I had a look at the FBI's case against you, and it's nothing short of damning. Video footage pulled from traffic cams places you near the scene of the crime. One of Grover's neighbors claims that she saw a large, angry black man emerging from Grover's house not long after she heard a gunshot. And then, of course, there's the weapon itself. Crime scene technicians found a hair trapped inside the crane of the revolver that killed Grover...Turns out, it matches your hair."

The last two portions of Roper's monologue were complete fabrications. The FBI had neither a witness statement nor a hair, but Roper wasn't obligated to tell the truth, and O'Dell couldn't be certain that the evidence was false. Even now, he might be wondering about neighbors and hair. Obsessing over those questions. Working them through his strained mind as the psychosis of so many days alone in prison worked their catastrophic magic on his better judgment.

All to Roper's benefit.

"They're going to convict you, James. Capital murder in Washington lands you with life in prison, no chance of parole. Meanwhile the country will move on. Nobody will remember you or your story. You'll just be packed away in a windowless box, eating stale food and watching your back in the yard. All alone for thirty or even forty years."

Roper never took his gaze off O'Dell as he spoke. He watched as a vein pulsated in O'Dell's thick neck, bloodshot eyes beginning to twitch as the picture Roper painted clarified in real time. A vivid, striking reality. A *certain* future. It was working on O'Dell's mind the way rust works on a car frame back in Roper's home state of Iowa—all that salt and melted snow, just eating away at the surface and penetrating to the core. Getting to him, however slowly.

Fast enough?

"I can help you, James," Roper said, his voice softening. "You're right, I'm a politician. I have friends in high places. The fact is—and I really hate to say this—nobody cares about you. You're a small fish and this is a big ocean. My friends at the FBI seem to think that you know about much bigger fish...but you won't talk. I can't imagine why."

Roper stopped again, waiting. O'Dell's disposition had shifted as Roper pivoted to the punchline—to his offer of aid. The pulsing vein had grown still, the shoulders somehow more relaxed, but at the same time, O'Dell didn't look interested. He was slumping back in the chair, breaking eye contact with Roper, his mouth a hard line.

What was Roper missing? He'd found a weakness in James O'Dell's ironclad defense—he'd felt the tremors as his words struck home. And now, somehow, he was losing ground again. O'Dell saw a way out...and wasn't responding.

Roper leaned over the table, hands still in his pockets, eyes narrowing. He evaluated O'Dell for a long time but could no longer see behind the man's eyes. O'Dell's guard was back up. He was iron.

What had Roper said that shook him before? Was it the thought of being alone? Or maybe...

"Forty years," Roper said again. "That's...a *really* long time. How old will Holly be by then?"

O'Dell's gaze snapped toward Roper, his nostrils flaring. In an instant, his eyes were wide again. The vein was pulsating harder than ever. Sweat appeared on his brow. He looked like a caged bull, just waiting to be released into an arena.

Bingo.

"We're talking high school, James. Unprotected, fatherless. You know what seventeen-year-old football players call a girl like that? *Easy money.* Rocking pickup trucks and teenage pregnancy—and that's *before* she tries drugs. Forty years from now, I bet you won't even recognize her. She'll be a life wasted—all because her daddy capped some dumb pervert for no apparent reason."

As Roper spoke, O'Dell breathed harder. His hands clenched inside the cuffs. His shoulders trembled.

But when Roper reached the punchline—*some dumb pervert for no apparent reason*—O'Dell finally snapped. He exploded out of the chair, and both hands smacked the table together. The stainless steel popped like a gunshot. O'Dell snarled through his teeth.

"I killed for *her*!"

As soon as he said it, O'Dell's eyes widened. His mouth hung open, frozen. His body stiffened. Roper could see the dread cascading over his face like a waterfall.

But the words were already said—and *her* didn't mean Holly.

Roper smiled.

It was more than enough.

33

RAF Akrotiri
Akrotiri, Cyprus

"Are you *insane*?"

Turk was the first one to say it out loud. Spread around a table with Silas Rigby seated at its head, the Prosecution Force had listened in silence as the deputy director had slowly worked his way up to the point—the big ask, the actual mission. Reed hadn't spoken a word during the entire spiel, but he knew where Rigby was headed from two minutes in.

He could sense it—but even more than that, his mind had raced ahead and unpacked the pieces and arranged them in clear sequence. There was only one logical end that Reed could see. The only thing that actually surprised him was the fact that the CIA had been willing to acknowledge the same reality. That they had flown all the way here to communicate in person to a battered and broken black ops team that might already be on the edge of imploding.

How desperate was America?

"You want us to *murder* the Russian president?"

Now it was Lucy who spoke. She sounded just as incredulous as Turk—maybe a little more indignant.

Rigby interlaced his fingers. When he spoke, his voice was methodical.

"We're going to lose this war. Whether by inches or by a wave of thermonuclear destruction, it's only a matter of time. If we land enough troops into Europe to push Russia out of NATO, our analysis guarantees that Nikitin will resort to nuclear weapons. If we assault Russia directly, or box them in, or eviscerate their economy and sabotage their next election, Nikitin *will* use nuclear weapons. He'd rather see the world burn than accept even marginal defeat—which is why our only options short of nuclear war are to either surrender Eastern Europe and hope that he is satisfied, or..."

"Or park a .30 caliber in his brain," Reed finished.

Rigby said nothing. Turk muttered a disbelieving curse and shook his head.

"You really *are* insane. Did you people learn *nothing* from Iraq? From Libya? From Laos? The results of regime change are always the same. One bad guy goes down, and six months later a dozen worse guys take his place. You leave a power vacuum, an opportunity. Only, this time, you want to do that with a *nuclear-armed nation*. One of the most powerful militaries in the world. I mean, just imagine that we'd tried this with Adolf Hitler. You really think that would have changed anything? You really think the war would have just disappeared? It's not just the guy on top, genius."

Turk spat the words and Rigby took them right on the chin, displaying no hint of defensiveness. Before he could reply, Wolfgang interjected.

"That's not exactly true."

Turk squinted. Turned on Wolfgang. "What?"

"That thing about Hitler—the way you described it. It's not exactly true."

"What does that mean?"

Wolfgang leaned forward. He looked terrible—like he'd just survived a war, which he kind of had. But Reed could see something in the Wolf's eyes that defied the exhaustion and abuse. Wheels turning, thoughts spinning. Maybe an idea.

"There were multiple attempts within the German government to remove Hitler," Wolfgang said. "Even attempted assassinations, all of which failed. But outside Hitler's core circle, beyond the scope of the most fervent Nazis, there were men who maintained some semblance of reason. They wanted to seize control and stop the war from the inside."

"And they *failed*," Turk said.

"Yes. But the point is, there were men inside the German government who weren't totally bought into Hitler's insanity. If we had known about them, and somehow been able to help them, we might have ended the war early. Saved thousands of lives."

Corbyn snorted. It was a harsh, disgusted sound. "And in that case, to this very day, Germany would be a military superpower and a menace to the entire world. Just one election away from starting the whole mess over again. Maybe it's easy for you Yanks to say from across the pond, but there's still bomb scars in London. You don't neutralize an enemy like that —you completely destroy them. That's the only way the problem ends for good."

"You might be right," Wolfgang said. "Only, this time, the enemy has nukes, and they can launch those nukes even up to the moment that NATO troops are storming the Kremlin. We could be six inches from victory and watch the entire planet evaporate before our eyes. Not thousands of lives, but millions. *Billions*, even."

"Wait. Are you saying you *support* this idea?" That was Lucy.

Wolfgang shook his head. "I don't know. It's a huge gamble. I'm just saying that Russia is an altogether different situation than Nazi Germany, and the status quo isn't tenable. If Nikitin is truly willing to use nuclear force, then he'll hold the world hostage until he owns it. There's no recovering from that."

"And yet a power vacuum would be even worse," Reed said. "A nuclear war machine without a leader would be a nuclear-armed terrorist cell."

"That's why we have to ensure that the machine is never without a leader," Rigby said. "That's why we have to control who takes Nikitin's place."

A chill fell over the room. Reed's gaze swept left, toward Rigby. Everybody was looking at Rigby—and waiting.

"We have an intel source deep inside Moscow," Rigby said. "Somebody you may remember. Mr. *Ivan Sidorov*."

The chill running up Reed's spine turned to a tingle. He glanced back to

Wolfgang, and found Wolfgang sitting up straight—all eyes and ears. Everyone else recognized the name, too. They hadn't seen Ivan since just after the Azerbaijan disaster. He'd departed the Prosecution Force at that time.

He'd gone to *Russia.*

"What has Ivan done?" Reed said.

"Mr. Sidorov has penetrated the government in Moscow. He's made contact with one of our agents and is feeding us insider intel from the Kremlin. He believes..." Rigby broke off, seeming to search for the right words. "He believes that there is a core of the Russian government and the Russian populace who support neither Nikitin nor the war. They are led by Prime Minister Romanov, who would be first in line to the presidency should anything happen to Nikitin."

Pause. Reed watched his team. Wolfgang was calculating. Lucy still seemed stunned. Corbyn was a blank wall.

Turk shook his head in disbelief. "Are you serious? You *believe* this guy?"

Rigby frowned. "What?"

"A disgraced Russian intelligence officer just asked you to help him seize power in Russia," Turk said. "And you're just gonna *trust* that he'll be Mr. Nice Guy when the smoke clears? That you won't be right back where you started—or, worse, watching Sidorov and his pals turn the Russian army against their own people for a revenge tour?"

"Hey!" Wolfgang snapped. "Ivan was in that dungeon also. He suffered just as much as the rest of us."

"All *because* of the war," Turk retorted. "Because of Russia, directly or otherwise. I've known Sidorov as long as most of you, and—"

"*I've* known him longer than any of you," Wolfgang cut in. "I knew him before you knew me. I've watched him confront terrorism and tyranny and madness in every form. If there's one thing Ivan Sidorov loves, it's his country. He'll do anything to protect Russia. Everything Rigby describes is exactly what I'd expect from him. He wouldn't suggest deposing Nikitin unless he had a better option locked and loaded, and there's no chance this is a revenge tour. Most of Ivan's enemies are greasy-fingered politicians. If he wanted them dead, they'd already be dead."

"Geez," Turk said. "I didn't realize you were a lawyer as well as an assassin. How long have you been on retainer?"

Wolfgang's face flushed, his hands falling to the arms of his chair. Before he could stand, Reed slammed an open hand against the table. It cracked, and everyone froze.

"Enough," Reed said. "Nobody is holding a gun to anybody's head. If you don't want to be here, there's the door."

Silence. Turk turned cutting eyes on Reed. Rigby opened his mouth, then stopped.

"I hear you, Turk," Reed said, voice softening. "We all hear you. But the moment the first mushroom cloud rises over NATO, does any of this matter?"

Dead silence. Reed closed his eyes and embraced the silence. He thought of the Azerbaijani dungeon where he and much of his team had suffered so greatly—but only for a moment. His mind traveled west, across battlefields and oceans, all the way to Nashville where Banks and little Davy and Reed's old English bulldog, Baxter, lived in a high-rise apartment at the heart of the city. Not for the first time, he pictured that city on fire.

He pictured a nuclear shockwave shattering that high-rise like a beer bottle. Just blowing right through it, vaporizing everything inside, leaving a city that Banks loved so dearly in ashen ruin. All in an instant, in the blink of an eye...

And that wouldn't be the only city.

Reed's eyes opened. Everyone was still waiting on him. Slouched and bruised, scarred and shaken. They looked like little more than a shell of the team he'd led into Venezuela. Across Lebanon, the Mediterranean, London, the Caucasus, and India.

They looked like a unit in name only. A team that barely stuck together and might fragment at any time. What kept them in this room at all? What had brought them this far?

Reed looked into Turk's eyes and found them bloodshot. He looked into Corbyn's face and found her burning like a volcano, consumed by rage. Wolfgang's jaw was locked closed, pain rippling through his gaze.

Lucy sat like a lighthouse in a hurricane—rock steady but battered by every crosswind.

And then there was Reed himself. Where did he fall? How badly had he let them down?

"You've followed me around the world," Reed said. "You've followed me into war zones. Into the face of hell and the jaws of death. You've followed me when I didn't deserve it—when I didn't appreciate it. You've followed me as I've fallen apart and left you hanging. You've followed me as we've suffered and bled and lost people. I've never said it before—I should have said it every day. I'll say it now even if it rings hollow. *Thank you*. Each and every one of you. For all you've given, for how long you've believed. For the friends you've been. I'm grateful. You're the finest warriors I've ever known...and if you never pull another trigger and grow old on back porches, you'll die heroes."

Reed's gaze passed from one face to the next as he spoke. He found tears in Lucy's eyes. Corbyn blinked a lot. Wolfgang and Turk didn't blink at all, but just stared. A lump rose in Reed's throat. His stomach turned heavy. He thought again of that brilliant flash rising over Music City.

And he couldn't escape it.

"I was born to fight. It's all I know, and maybe the only thing I'm good for. So long as I've got blood left to give, I have to give it. So long as there's even a chance that I can save my country, my *home*, I have to take it. That's my purpose as I know it, but this isn't the kind of mission anyone walks away from, even if it's successful. I don't expect anyone to come with me. I've taken enough, and you've given more than enough. I won't ask for more."

Reed finished and his own eyes watered. Not because he was afraid of the scenario he described but because he remembered her gentle touch on his skin. Davy's melodious laugh as he toddled between fallen toys. Baxter's woof, his loose skin bunching as Reed scratched him.

Home. Home. Home.

He'd fought a lifetime for it. He'd give a lifetime to secure it.

He might never see it again.

"You never asked us to begin with," Turk said. His voice was a little wet, but steady. Reed glanced his way and found Turk sitting upright, his tree-trunk forearms resting on his thighs.

"We *volunteered*," Turk said. "Because it's our home, too."

Reed looked to his oldest friend and found none of the anger from only moments before. Turk didn't look sad or cornered or even all that damaged. He looked like an American warship as the smoke clears and the fires thin—and the engines are still turning. Water is still breaking over the bow. The course is set and progress continues.

Unbroken. *A rock.*

"You said this guy Romanov is next in line to take the presidency."

It was Corbyn who spoke. She was still looking at Reed but clearly addressing Rigby.

"That's right," Rigby said.

"And Romanov is plotting to remove Nikitin."

"He is."

Corbyn at last broke eye contact with Reed. Her tense, angry face turned to Rigby.

"So the moment Nikitin uncovers that plot, he'll kill Romanov. He'll kill everyone who is working with him."

Reed's mind had already made that connection. His gaze switched to Rigby even as he knew what the deputy director was going to say—the only thing he could say.

"That, Ms. Corbyn," Rigby said, "is why we must move quickly."

34

The Naval Observatory
Washington, DC

The email landed in Stratton's inbox just as his morning coffee became cool enough to sip. He lifted a Chicago Bears mug and slurped pure black Columbian roast, squinting at the sender's name and not immediately recognizing it. It wasn't until he scanned down to the actual email address and read the words *@washingtonpost.com* that his mind finally made the connection.

She was a reporter—one of the few that Stratton had connected with directly, not during his time as vice president but during his tenure as a US senator. She knew his personal email address, which was where this message arrived without a subject line. Stratton clicked, still holding the coffee just beneath his lips, his mind moving in slow motion from a restless night.

The message loaded. It contained only four words and a file. The words read: *Going live this morning.*

Stratton double-clicked the file. He sipped more coffee. He swallowed.

And then he nearly choked.

The file was a graphic, a single large image. Bright red and yellow with a bold title, it was the cover of a tabloid with a full-color image of Jame's O'Dell consuming its middle, a headline printed across his chest.

THE PRESIDENT'S MAN: "I KILLED FOR HER."

The coffee smacked the desktop. Stratton stared but didn't quite believe what he was seeing. He double-checked the email address once more just to make sure it was legitimate—not some clever close-fake like *@washngtonposl.com*.

The address was correct. Stratton's fingers rattled across the keyboard, inputting a web search for the name of the tabloid. A website loaded, and there was the same image as before. The same title—a hyperlink for the article. Stratton speed-read the first paragraph.

Longtime presidential bodyguard and suspected lover, James O'Dell, was arrested two weeks ago by the FBI on charges of capital murder. While remaining in federal custody, unnamed sources report that Mr. O'Dell has made a shocking claim—not only that he is guilty of the accusations levied against him but that he killed on behalf of the president herself.

Stratton's fist slammed into the desktop, sending coffee splashing from the mug. He screamed—a guttural curse he'd bottled up for days, maybe weeks. His body trembled and his breath turned hot. The door to his office burst open and a Secret Service agent appeared, one hand already resting on his sidearm.

"Sir?"

"*Out!*"

The agent didn't argue. Stratton copied the link to the article and dropped it into an email of his own. He typed in only the first two letters of the address before the computer filled in the rest—it was a familiar contact. Stratton hit send and then immediately reached for his phone. It rang four times.

Maybe the contact wasn't near their phone. Maybe they were busy reading the article. Then, at last, the call connected. A voice, tense with strain, answered.

"I just read it."

"Is it true?" Stratton demanded.

"How would I know?" The voice edged with anger. "She's locking me out of everything—holding meetings off the books and only using her private phone line. I barely recognize the West Wing. We're cartwheeling into a *war*."

Stratton knew. He'd already read his daily briefing, which included headlines from the *New York Times* and global media outlets. He knew about the naval battle in the South Pacific and the warships America had lost. About the fall of Bagdad and the pivot of Iranian ground forces toward Israel. About the US Marines battling for control of Beirut and the two hundred thousand US Army infantry the White House had deployed into central Europe—all without any declaration of war from Congress.

It was happening *so* fast. One domino slamming into the next, setting off a chain reaction that couldn't be reversed. The final effect seemed inevitable. A third world war, all but official.

And now *this*?

"Do you have a TV?" the voice on the phone said. "Switch on CNN."

The remote lay close to hand. Stratton jabbed the power button and his office TV blinked to life. The moment the screen loaded, Stratton's stomach twisted into knots. His heart hammered. He wanted to hurl the coffee.

It was an outdoor shot overhung by a bright blue sky with polished white marble as a backdrop. There was a podium—cameras flashed and a light breeze rustled the edges of a drooping American flag.

Standing behind that podium in a pinstripe suit and a face that could barely conceal his own smug satisfaction was Senator Matthew Roper of Iowa.

"I've called this press conference to address the deeply troubling rumors of President Trousdale's possible involvement with an alleged murderer. While these reports are as yet unverified, America's current state of de facto war—a state which has been neither authorized nor endorsed by Congress—leaves no room for questions of character on the part of our leader. Even as I speak, American heroes stand ready to sacrifice their lives for the cause of freedom...all while wondering whether their commander in chief is herself a killer? It's unconscionable and absolutely un-American. This country has suffered *tremendously* under the leadership of the Trousdale Administration—how much more will we tolerate? How much more can we afford to lose?"

Stratton slammed the remote into his desktop, inadvertently muting the TV. It was just as well—he could already guess what Roper would say next. The man had hated Maggie since day one. He was the only *nay* vote in the entire Senate during Maggie's confirmation as vice president. He'd challenged her every step of the way during her presidency.

What did he want?

The White House. Stratton was sure of it. This was nothing more than a pre-campaign stunt—a method of familiarizing the American people with a name and a face long before Election Day. Even with the TV muted, the headline scrolling across the bottom of the screen confirmed Stratton's suspicions.

SEN. ROPER (D, IOWA) CALLS FOR RESOLUTION TO EVALUATE PRES. TROUSDALE'S FITNESS TO LEAD AMERICA.

The key phrase was *fitness to lead*, a modern-English echo of the 25th Amendment's terminology—*unable to discharge the powers and duties of his office*.

Or *her* office, in this case. Stratton was familiar with the line. He'd read and reread those words until he practically had them memorized, his gut twisting a little tighter each time.

Could this *really* be happening?

"We're reaching a crossroads," the voice on the line said.

Stratton closed his eyes. He didn't *want* to ask what he was about to ask. He'd rather say nearly anything else.

But Roper's question just happened to be a good one. How much more could America afford to lose? How much longer would Stratton stand by and watch America careen toward the abyss?

"If I called today," Stratton said, "how many votes would I have?"

Silence. Moments ticked by. Then: "I really have no idea. I've kept this matter strictly between us. We can't be the only ones considering the option, but...nobody is speaking out loud."

And there it was, the real fulcrum of the issue. To speak out loud was to risk everything—the entire integrity of the administration. This wasn't something that could be casually discussed and then discarded. Once anyone voiced those fatal words, they had to go through with them.

"Sir, I don't want to be blunt, but you have to make a decision."

Right.

"Begin with top officials," Stratton said. "Gorman, Kline, West. One-on-one, as covert as possible. Test the waters if you can. Get a temperature—then report back by tomorrow evening. We'll go from there."

A pause. Then: "If you start the ball rolling…we may not be able to stop it."

Stratton's gaze switched back to the TV, no longer to find Roper and his podium but a panel of political analysts and a headline that declared: *Should the president be removed from office?*

"It's already rolling," Stratton said. "Call by tomorrow afternoon."

Then he hung up.

35

The White House

Brett Portermeyer reminded Maggie of an old-school boxer from a seventies action flick. Tall, muscular, and unreasonably handsome, the White House chief counsel had piercing blue eyes and bright blond hair, always swept back in a way that she supposed was meant to look careless, but actually required precision combing each and every morning. He wore premium suits but never sat up straight. He always addressed her as "Madam President," even in private, but would also cross his legs while sitting on an Oval Office couch, almost as though he were kicked back watching a football game with friends from college.

He was the picture of quiet confidence—or, at least, he always had been. Through terrorist attacks and an attempted assassination and enough legal headaches to drive any White House counsel into an early grave.

Today, however, something was different. Maggie felt it from the moment Portermeyer entered her office alongside Jill Easterling. He greeted her with his customary "Good morning, Madam President" and extended his hand as though they were meeting for the first time. He sat and helped himself to a donut from a silver breakfast tray, eating with customary nonchalance that was somehow still produced.

But for all that ease and looseness, something was off about Portermeyer. As Maggie took her chair at the end of the coffee table, her gaze switching from Easterling to her lawyer, she couldn't help but notice that neither seemed eager to break the ice. Both seemed to be hanging in reserve, waiting for Maggie to speak first, even though it wasn't Maggie who had called this meeting.

Portermeyer in particular felt vaguely...removed from the room.

"You can ask," Maggie said. "The whole world is asking."

Portermeyer and Easterling exchanged a glance. Still, they wouldn't say it.

"*No*," Maggie said. "I did not ask James O'Dell to kill Jacob Grover and procure for me a donor liver. I knew nothing about Jacob Grover. The first time I heard his name was this morning, the same as you."

Portermeyer smoothed his suit pants leg. He didn't cross that leg—he seemed subtly on guard, as though he might be planning a rapid exit.

As though he didn't believe his boss.

"Of course we believe you, ma'am."

That was Easterling. Her voice was calm but not altogether convincing.

"So why are you here, then?"

Maggie's own tone was semi-accusatory. Maybe it was simply impatient. Exhausted.

She didn't have *time* for this. None of them did. Easterling should be busy running the administration, orchestrating the meetings that mattered, while Portermeyer should be engaged doing what he was hired to do.

Digging through federal law and finding new applications of executive power—tools to get America out of the international mess she had crashed headlong into.

"We're here to discuss legal strategy, ma'am," Portermeyer said. "I'm sure you must be aware that Mr. O'Dell's statements, if they were actually made, bear ramifications for the administration far greater than bad press."

Maggie squinted. She heard the words—she thought she knew what

Portermeyer was driving at. But why should she before forced to decode? Wasn't that what her attorney was for?

"Speak plainly, Brett."

Portermeyer adjusted his suit jacket. He and Easterling exchanged another glance.

Then he finally spilled.

"The FBI is on a witch hunt. I don't know who started it, I don't know who's driving it, but Director Purcell is no longer returning my calls. In fact, nobody outside of the executive liaison will return my calls. They won't comment on the James O'Dell investigation, they won't comment on their concerns about the administration. They've shut us out in the blink of an eye. I'm not an expert on the issue, but when the FBI goes dark on somebody, in my experience it almost always means one thing."

"That person is being investigated," Maggie finished.

She wasn't afraid to say it. One look into Portermeyer's cutting blue eyes and she knew she was right on the money.

So part of her administration had turned on her. The DOJ was going rogue, and Bill Purcell was flying beneath the radar.

But *why*? Portermeyer was reasonable to question who was driving the train. Purcell was a decent enough FBI director, but he wasn't all that independent as a personality. He followed orders, and he followed the White House's lead...or he followed *somebody's* lead. If that wasn't Maggie, who was it?

Matthew Roper.

It was the first name that came to Maggie's mind, and the notion wasn't quickly dismissed. At the same time, she knew it didn't matter. None of this mattered. It was all just a distraction—an objective waste of time.

Americans were dying in Europe. They were dying in the South Pacific and in Lebanon and in the Persian Gulf. The American economy was on the rocks and the American people needed a leader—not tabloid drama.

"We should prepare a statement," Easterling said. "My advice is to hit this head-on. Denounce O'Dell's claims and distance yourself from the investigation against him. Seize the narrative before the narrative runs wild—"

"No," Maggie said.

Easterling blinked. "Ma'am?"

"You heard me. I said *no*. I won't be making a statement, and I won't be denouncing or addressing this issue in any form."

Portermeyer cleared his throat. "Speaking as your counsel, that may not be the best—"

"I don't care what's *best*, Brett. I'm not here to save face. Have any of you read the news this morning, or only the tabloids?"

No answer. Maggie rose from the chair. Her head was light and her stomach churned with nausea, but she made it to her desk. She found the folded copy of the *New York Times* and returned to the sitting area, slamming it down on the coffee table.

The headline was two inches tall and printed in bold: AMERICAN BODYCOUNT RISES IN EUROPE.

"Eighteen airmen and forty-six ground troops—that's how many soldiers we've lost since the Russians struck Ādaži. Sixty-two Marines dead in Lebanon, nearly three *hundred* service members slain in the South Pacific. And you want to waste my time with trash press?"

No answer. Maggie's gaze snapped from Portermeyer to Easterling.

"That *wasn't* a rhetorical question!"

Portermeyer stiffened, his gaze turning hard. Easterling spoke first.

"Nobody is dismissing the international crisis. We're merely attempting to balance perspective. If you lose the domestic fight—"

"Perspective? You want to talk about perspective? Here's my *perspective*, Jill. My presidency is finished with this term. It's been shot, literally and figuratively. I'll spend the rest of my life debating whether that was fate or bad luck or pure incompetence, but the fact remains that in this moment, *it doesn't matter*. I'm not here to protect myself, I'm here to save my *country*. That's my job. So you can burn the tabloids and stuff the gossip rags where the sun won't shine. Don't waste my time with this high school drama. The next time you step into this office, I expect to hear counsel on how to *stop* World War Three. Do you hear me? *Nothing else*."

Maggie screamed by the time she finished, her voice hoarse and her throat dry. Neither Portermeyer nor Easterling answered—Portermeyer sat like a statue, iron and angry, and Easterling gazed with eyes wide. The moment lagged and still nobody spoke.

Maggie snapped.

"Get out. Both of you. Don't come back with anything but answers."

She pointed to the door. Slowly, Portermeyer rose and buttoned his jacket. He left the room walking tall with his chin lifted. Easterling lagged a moment longer, standing but hesitating.

"Ma'am—"

"You heard me, Jill!"

Easterling ducked her head and left via the same door Portermeyer used. As Maggie watched them go, her vision wavered—her stomach conducted a somersault and a fresh hot flash coursed through her body. She suddenly felt like the floor beneath her was a pitching deck in an open sea. She returned to her desk and nearly fell into the chair, blinking as the room faded in and out of focus. The portrait of George Washington hung over the mantel danced right before her gaze—George seemed to be smiling. To be smirking, really. Like he was mocking her.

Maggie clamped her eyes closed and breathed deep. She guzzled from a glass of water. Then she reached for the phone and speed-dialed her secretary.

"Ma'am?"

"Get me the White House physician. I need to book an appointment."

Easterling barely made it back to her office before the tears came.

Crashing into her desk chair with the door shut, she ignored her ringing phone and the bustle of aides from just outside. She ignored the bubble alert on her computer, indicating ninety-six unread emails since the previous evening. She ignored the news reel playing across the bottom of a muted CNN feed on the TV hung across the room.

She ignored it all, clamping her eyes shut as the tears came hot and slow, an overwhelming wash of sadness.

And anger.

Easterling gave herself five long minutes to feel that way, ignoring a knock on her door and breathing in steady cycles. She replayed the Oval

Office meeting in her mind, visualizing the crazed fire burning in Maggie's gaze. Hearing once more her cracking voice.

But it wasn't just Maggie's voice that was cracking. It wasn't just her hand that shook. This whole administration, the entire West Wing…it was falling apart right in front of Easterling's eyes.

What was she going to do about it?

"If you start the ball rolling, we may not be able to stop it."

It was the last thing she had said to Vice President Jordan Stratton during their most recent off-the-books call. His response rang in her ears, landing as hard in her mind as it had when he first spoke it.

"It's already rolling."

Easterling looked to her computer and noted the stacked emails, the alerts on her calendar warning her of approaching meetings and reminding her of those she had already missed.

None of it was important. It was like Maggie said—the only thing that mattered was saving the country.

The ball was rolling.

Easterling reached for her phone. She dialed a number from a contact displayed on her computer. The dial tone rang twice in her ear.

Then: "Jill?"

"Madam Secretary, good morning. I'd like to arrange a meeting as soon as you're able—just you and me. Off the record."

36

Nashville, Tennessee

Banks arrived home after midnight, dragging a carry-on bag and nearly sleepwalking her way to the Gulch apartment that she called home. With travel grit from four cities sticking to her like an invisible sheen, and the last eighteen hours fueled almost exclusively by energy drinks and sheer willpower, she was ready to drop.

She wanted a shower, a chilled glass of wine, a dark room with a large bed and unbroken hours to disappear into it. She wanted to sleep until her ears stopped ringing, until her eyes no longer burned from the stage lights. But more than anything, she wanted to see her son.

She hadn't seen Davy in nearly three days. With a schedule of back-to-back shows across NYC and Boston, Banks had made the difficult decision to let her mother come get Davy and fly him back to Tennessee. Mercifully, Sharon O'Hara had since proceeded back to Texas, leaving Davy with the twenty-something Belmont University student who dreamed of being the next country music superstar and served as an intermittent nanny in the meantime.

As Banks slipped into the apartment, she found that student camped out on the couch with a true crime show on mute and her boyfriend on

FaceTime. The door clicked and the twenty-something looked up, her gaze a little glossy from the half-empty wine bottle next to her, that adoring-but-semi-jealous look that she always shot at Banks barely concealed beneath a perfunctory smile.

"Welcome home!"

Banks returned the smile, but she didn't feel it. She left the bag in the foyer and ran a hand through her hair, trying to remember when she'd last set foot in her apartment. When she'd last eaten a home-cooked meal. When she'd last been *alone*.

Where's Davy?

It was the only question that really mattered in the moment. Banks left the nanny to her inebriated FlirtTime call and slipped down the hall. She found little Davy sleeping soundlessly in a race car bed, curly brown hair spilling into his face. Even as a toddler, Davy loved cars—the passion was no doubt fueled by the battered 1969 Camaro that Reed kept parked in the garage. An artifact of Reed's youth, a token from Davy's grandfather.

Davy giggled at the Camaro's rumble. He loved to go on long rides with his daddy. But Reed hadn't seen his son in weeks, and just the thought of that sent an arrow through Banks's heart. She bent and lifted Davy close, whispering love as he groaned in his sleep. The moment his head hit her shoulder, Davy was out again. She rubbed his back and kissed his head and lost herself in the smell of toddler shampoo.

It was *so good* to be home. Better than roaring crowds and surging adrenaline and all the highlights of the *Not Afraid* tour experienced on repeat. Those were the things Banks always *thought* that she wanted—had coveted with the same passion as the drunken nanny in the living room. And yes, they were amazing.

But this? It hit on another level.

"Mama's home, baby," Banks whispered.

Davy only snored in reply, the most beautiful sound Banks had heard in days. She contemplated placing him back in bed, thinking of the shower and the chilled wine. But she couldn't bring herself to let him go. The comfort of his touch was too real.

Banks carried Davy to a nearby glider rocker and settled in. She rubbed his back and leaned her head back and tried not to let the anxiety crush in. The questions. The loneliness. The desperation.

Where was Reed? *When* would he be home?

As if in answer to her question, Banks's phone rang. She nearly ignored it, expecting a "just wanted to make sure you made it home safe" call from her agent that was really a "let's plan a new tour call" in disguise. The guy was making money hand over fist from Banks—heck, *Banks* was making money hand over fist from herself. She didn't need to talk about that right now. She just wanted to be home...

But Banks checked the caller ID anyway, and the moment she saw the words *Limassol, Cyprus*, her heart jumped. She couldn't swipe to answer fast enough. She pinned Davy to her chest and sat up.

"Hello?"

"Banks...it's me."

Reed's voice sounded like the creak of an old boat just sailing in from a hurricane. Like the groan of the hinges on the Camaro's doors. It sounded tired, it sounded battered. It sounded almost as good as Davy's snores.

Tears bubbled to Banks's eyes. "I was so hoping you'd call."

Long silence. In the background Banks thought she heard truck engines and shouts—some busy military base, she thought, although she had no idea what bases might be in Cyprus. Perhaps the call was forwarded. For all she knew, Reed might be anywhere in the Middle East—or in Europe.

"Are you safe?" Banks said. "Where are you?"

"I'm safe," Reed said, ignoring the second question. "Had to relocate yesterday. We met up with Wolfgang and Corbyn."

Banks knew the names. She'd known Wolfgang since way back in North Carolina when the assassin then known as *the Wolf* had tried to kill both her and Reed. Their journey from that point to partners and even friendship was a lengthy one—and complex. Those memories played through Banks's mind in a whirlwind as she struggled for something to say.

She really just wanted to hear Reed talk. Not about the war or their place in it—she'd rather him talk about home or their son or that stupid car. *Their* things.

Yet she couldn't keep herself from asking, one more time.

"Are you coming home?"

Long pause. Banks's heart fell. She knew better than to hope. What did she expect?

She didn't expect what Reed finally said.

"I want to. Man, I want to."

It was like water in the desert. Banks's body turned warm at the words and a heavy tear slipped down her cheek. She smiled despite herself and savored the moment for whatever it was, even as her mind whispered an uglier truth.

He didn't say yes.

"I…I need to talk to you," Reed said.

"Yeah?"

"I've been asked…*we've* been asked to do something. I can't say what. I can only tell you that it's very important. Maybe the most important thing I've ever done."

Banks's stomach tightened. Her stroking hand grew still on Davy's back.

"That…sounds dangerous."

No answer. Banks knew she was right.

"I…" Pause. "I know I should be asking your permission."

Banks began to cry again. The words cut her like bullets. They bit and they just kept biting. With every fiber of her being she wanted to scream: *"I don't give it, I won't give it. You've done enough. Come be with your family—be with your son!"*

The words rose to her throat and her lips parted, but she couldn't get them out. Her mouth turned dry. She swallowed once, and then she said something she didn't want to say but knew she believed.

"You've never needed my permission to do the right thing."

Stupid. Why had she said that?

Even as Banks questioned herself, she knew the answer, and she hated herself for being so good. For being so stable, so supportive, so selfless. Why couldn't she focus on herself, just once? Why did so many other women have their husbands close and warm while she—

"I was thinking about that bar," Reed said, his voice soft.

The words caught Banks off guard. She squinted, momentarily confused.

"What bar?"

"The bar in Atlanta...where we met."

Banks remembered. It came to her in a tidal wave of flashing images. Alone on a stool with a guitar, fighting for a foot in the door of the music industry, she hadn't actually seen Reed standing in the back. The lights were too bright, and she was too nervous. It wasn't until after, when she packed up her gear and was headed for her Volkswagen, that Reed caught her eye. Offered her a drink. Attempted a sloppy pickup and then, just as she was walking away...hit her with the truth.

"*I like you.*"

It was the raw honesty that made Banks turn back. A stark departure from all the phonies and frat bros who usually serenaded her with bad pickup lines and sour beer breath. There was a sincerity in Reed's eyes which would quickly come to contradict the reality of his life, yet Banks couldn't help but smile at the memory.

"I remember," she whispered.

"You were so beautiful on that stage. I'd never heard anyone sing that way."

"You looked like a hired gun," Banks retorted.

That brought on the faintest hint of a laugh, which was maybe all the joke deserved. Another long minute crept by. When Reed next spoke, his voice was hoarse.

"I never got over that night."

Banks blinked hard. The tears were coming faster. Her face and the top of Davy's head were wet with them. Her son slept on.

"Me neither," she whispered.

"I love you, Banks. I always have. I'm so sorry for that."

Banks squinted. "What?"

No answer.

"Why are you sorry?"

"If I had kept walking that night...you would have never known this darkness."

"*What?*"

"I think it's all I am, Banks. Maybe all I've ever been."

"Reed. What are you talking about? I'm holding our son. Right now, in my arms—*our son*. In *our home*. Do you hear me?"

Her voice choked. She swallowed and wiped one eye with her thumb. She hated herself again for being so selfless—for telling him the truth instead of begging him, screaming at him, to come home. To face these lies with her. To be with his family.

I can't make him.

"You're not darkness, Reed," Banks said. "You've lived in some very dark places, but I won't leave you there. Do you understand? You're going to find your way out. You're going to find the light. Tell me you believe that—tell me you'll fight through, and you'll make it home. Please."

An audible swallow. "I'll make it home, Banks—I promise you."

37

RAF Akrotiri
Akrotiri, Cyprus

Reed finished the call and stood in the glare of early morning, the sat phone in his hand as RAF vehicles whizzed by on every side. He replayed his wife's voice in his head, savoring every word. Longing to dial her again, even though he knew it was late in Nashville, and circling the problem while never directly addressing it wouldn't help anyone.

Even though he felt it in his bones, no matter how hard he denied it—this might be the last time he ever heard that voice.

Alone on the sidewalk for a long time he just stood with the sat phone pressed against his forehead, his face pointed at the ground. He closed his eyes and tuned out the noises of war. He pictured Banks in her glider rocker with Davy held close, his entire world all wrapped up together.

How *long* had it taken him to see that? How much had he risked in the meantime?

If this was the end—if he never walked away from what the CIA was asking him to do—Reed was grateful to have seen it for a moment. To have understood and appreciated it. To have been grateful.

"Montgomery?"

Reed looked up to find Turk standing right next to him, a sat phone of his own held at his side, his eyes a little red. It didn't take a rocket scientist to guess what call Turk had just placed. Reed thought of Sinju and baby Liberty and figured Turk must be feeling the same things.

What was there to say? He stared at Turk and didn't know. Turk stared back, mouth open, but silent. He shifted awkwardly on his feet.

Then he wrapped Reed in a bear hug. Sudden and tight and prolonged, pulling him close and squeezing the way only battle buddies ever can.

"They're ready," Turk said, finally releasing him.

Reed simply nodded and the two men went back inside to find everyone else gathered around a table. Each of them had been offered the chance to make a final call—only Reed and Turk had taken it. Standing just inside the darkened room and surveying his battered little army, Reed couldn't help but think of all the Marine fire teams he'd led back in Iraq. Some good, hard, reliable warriors. The best America could offer.

But none better than these.

"Thank you," Reed said simply. There wasn't anything else to say. Lucy offered a tight smile, and Corbyn grunted. Wolfgang just stared, expectant.

At last, Reed turned to Rigby. The deputy director waited in a corner, arms folded, an unspoken question on the air.

"You want this guy dead?" Reed said.

"That's the idea," Rigby said.

Another pause. Reed pushed his hands into his pockets.

"So make the call. We're ready when you are."

38

Moscow, Russia

"We've found you a dance partner."

Ivan's second rendezvous with Natasha Kirov occurred at the Church of St. Nicholas in Khamovniki, a district of Moscow looped by the Moskva River and sitting southwest of the Kremlin. Residential, historic, and quiet, Khamovniki was home to Leo Tolstoy, to say nothing of several embassies and a number of ornate Russian Orthodox churches.

The Church of St. Nicholas in particular was a statement piece of not only the district but the city at large. Constructed in the late seventeenth century, the opulence of golden onion domes and teal roof tiles were put to shame by an interior drenched in gold, paved in stone, and featuring dozens of wall murals stretching up to arched ceilings.

Unlike in Western churches, there were no pews. Lining the nave were a series of chapels and small alcoves featuring the flickering glow of candlelight, many hung with icons of the saints. Outside of standard service times, the church was mostly empty, dim and quiet with only the tap of gentle footsteps to break the stillness. Ivan slipped inside with ease and found Kirov standing in an alcove with her head bowed before an icon of the Virgin Mary, apparently praying.

He didn't say a word as he slipped up beside her. Crossing himself, Ivan extended a thin candle and lit it with the dancing flame of another. He then placed it in the candlestand before the icon, crossed himself a second time, and bowed his own head. It was only several seconds later, after nearby footsteps grew distant, that Kirov had spoken.

Dance partner, she had said. Not what Ivan had expected, and certainly not what he'd asked for.

"I never needed a partner," Ivan said. "As previously stated, what I'm looking for is an *understanding*."

"Oh, but you'll like *this* partner." Kirov lifted her face toward the Virgin—crossed herself, then bowed again. There was a grace and familiarity to her movements that left Ivan wondering if she really was Orthodox.

Or maybe, once more, just a great actress.

"He's an old friend," Kirov continued.

Ivan didn't turn his head. He stood a yard to the right and one step back, a natural distance for two parishioners venerating the same icon, but separately. Using his peripheral vision to monitor the passageway to their left, Ivan kept his voice barely above a whisper as he replied.

"Montgomery."

Kirov clicked her tongue, head still bowed. "I'm told you've danced together before."

It was true—Ivan doubted if Kirov had any idea how *much* it was true. He'd met Reed Montgomery via a mutual acquaintance, Wolfgang Pierce. Their paths had now crossed and recrossed, weaving into a web that always led back to the same core problem.

Makar Nikitin.

"Again," Ivan said. "I never asked for help."

"No?" Kirov glanced sideways and Ivan caught her piercing gaze. "But you're going to *need it*."

From not far away, footsteps grew louder down a passageway. Someone, perhaps a cleric or another parishioner, was headed their way. It was already time to conclude this meeting.

"Montgomery and his team are en route to Europe," Kirov said. "They'll train and prep while awaiting intel. It's your job to find that intel. Do you have access to the Kremlin?"

Ivan did—not himself, not directly. But he could find what Montgomery needed.

"Romanov," Ivan said simply.

Kirov grunted. She lifted her head and crossed herself one final time.

"The sooner the better," she said.

Then she was gone, fading like a ghost just as a shuffling old lady with a cane slipped into the alcove and ducked her head. Ivan took another step back, head still bowed, but gave Kirov a three-minute head start. Then he himself slipped from the church, back into the biting wind of the encroaching Russian winter. With a hat pulled low and his collar flipped up, he turned northeast.

Back toward the heart of Moscow—and the bear's den.

39

35,000 feet over the North Atlantic

Maggie could have sent Lisa Gorman to Brussels, or perhaps a team of diplomats and military advisors from the State Department and the Pentagon. The emergency NATO summit called in response to Russia's invasion of Estonia and Belarus's invasion of Latvia was likely to last days, not hours, and would involve multiple meetings spanning every subject from direct military response to logistical support of countries whose infrastructure was about to be erased like chalk from a blackboard.

This was the real deal. Not a preparedness meeting, not war games. NATO was under attack and scrambling to do the thing that it had been founded to do but maybe never actually believed would be necessary. The resulting discussions would be less strategic and more tactical. Maggie could have led America's involvement via proxy, taking short and frequent phone calls to give simple yes or no answers to various military and diplomatic requests.

But she wanted to be in Brussels. Maybe because Maggie had never been the type of leader to direct from afar—maybe because her image as the leader of the Free World had taken a beating, and she found value in making a confident appearance.

Or maybe because the four walls of the White House were closing in on her—crushing her. Suffocating her with a storm of tabloid headlines, TV talking heads, and shouting reporters from the West Wing press room. They all wanted to know the same thing, all demanding details of her association with James O'Dell and the truth of his claim that he'd murdered on her behalf.

The noise and the pressure left her no room to think or to hide or even to regroup—and that was on top of the crushing misery of the endless opioid withdrawals. She needed an eight-hour flight to lock herself in an airborne office and to claw a miracle out of thin air—some way, *any way*, out of this disaster. Ninety minutes outside of Washington she had completed a review of half a dozen military briefs and Pentagon memos, held three conference calls, and spoken with two heads of state—the presidents of Poland and France.

She was no closer to an answer than when she'd taken off. The situation already felt hopeless—Russia's advance already felt unstoppable.

How had it come to this?

Maggie ran both hands through her hair, and her palms came away sweaty. It was another hallmark of the withdrawals. Her scheduled appointment with her White House physician, from whom Maggie hoped to obtain a limited supply of hydrocodone to finally erase the fog, wouldn't occur until after the NATO summit.

That wasn't good—it left Maggie exposed and her body pushed to the brink for another twenty-four hours. But what were her options? Her private physician was the only person Maggie thought she *might* be able to trust with this request. If she let her staff know that this was an urgent matter, and that she couldn't wait for her personal doctor to return from a brief vacation, then they would schedule her with somebody else. Heck, there was probably a supply of hydrocodone available on this very plane.

But that would mean exposure. It would mean the truth leaking out. Maggie told herself that she wasn't ready for that.

In truth...maybe she just wasn't ready to surrender to the little orange bottle. Maybe she was still hoping against hope that if she pushed on for another day the cravings would end and her body would balance. Her mind would clear. She could *do her job* without a relapse.

Wasn't she strong enough?

Maggie's phone rang and she snatched it up, grateful for the distraction from her mental war. An aide announced a call from Langley—it was Director Aimes, seeking Maggie's private line. She authorized the connection. Aimes's voice was clear despite the distance.

"Good afternoon, ma'am. Sorry to call on your flight."

"What is it, Sarah?"

Aimes didn't answer immediately. Maggie turned away from the window.

"*What is it?*" She repeated, her voice snapping more than she intended.

"I wanted to update you on our previous discussion," Aimes said.

Maggie sat up a little in her chair, but this time she didn't pressure Aimes. She waited.

"I've received confirmation from Europe," Aimes said. "The team you requested is en route to Poland. They'll be on the ground and prepping by this evening. We have contacts in Moscow evaluating leads. We're looking for...an opportunity."

It was a horrible euphemism, something Maggie recognized in an instant as Washington/Pentagon/intelligence sector speech for "we're looking for a chance to murder one of the most powerful men in the world." And yet Maggie didn't blink.

"What do you need?"

"I just...wanted to check. One more time. I don't know how quickly things will move, and..."

And you're giving me a chance to back out.

Maggie's gaze drifted back to the window and the storm clouds sweeping beneath. A roiled mess of menace and potential destruction—both a picture of her tangled insides and a metaphor for the world's predicament.

And here she was, a swamp girl from outside of New Orleans caught in the eye of the storm, literally flying right through it. Given a chance, however slim, to hold the planet back from certain destruction, what else was she going to say other than *full speed ahead*?

"Sarah," Maggie said. "I'm finished. When this term is over, whether the world is saved or the world burns, my presidency is over. This job was never about me to begin with, but it certainly isn't about me now. The *only* thing that matters is that we end this war before it ends us—every one of us. Do you understand?"

Aimes's voice was subdued. "I do."

"I'm trusting you now in a way I've never trusted you before, and maybe in a way I've never trusted anyone. I'm not going to micromanage or second-guess you. My only order is this—if you get the shot, *do not miss*."

A long pause. Again, Maggie gave Aimes the time—she gave herself the time to fight through another wash of pain in her stomach.

Then she summarized in direct English, because the time for indecision was long gone.

"This is your green light," Maggie said. "Go save the world."

40

Moscow, Russia

Maxim Romanov couldn't stop his heart from thundering.

It was a problem—it had been a problem long before present events drove him to drastic measures. Overweight and overfond of red meats, red wines, and all things fried, Romanov's heart had been a concern for years. He'd even suffered a minor heart attack not long after achieving the office of prime minister. His physicians had pronounced a full recovery but also warned him that if his diet and lifestyle didn't change, this would only be the first of a number of such medical events which would only expire when he did.

Romanov knew they were serious. He knew he needed a better way to manage the stress of his career—he just never had the time to find it. Long hours stacked in Moscow, resulting in his third divorce and another twenty-two pounds of gut fat. He rose early and worked late, a strangled sleep schedule only compounding existing problems.

He didn't have time for exercise, he didn't have an appetite for leaner, healthier food. The priorities of the Federation consumed him, and now he had one more fear to stack on a wobbling tower of existing concerns...

The terror of a madman driving Russia straight off a cliff.

Arriving early at the Kremlin, Romanov barely acknowledged the greetings of passing government officials as he navigated toward a secure conference room where Russia's minister of Internal Affairs, deputy prime minister, and deputy chairman of the Security Council all waited. Ostensibly, Romanov was here to chair a meeting regarding the internal security of Russia's major cities during a time of war—a bureaucratic, paper-shuffling sort of discussion that did not warrant President Nikitin's appearance. Romanov could have held the meeting at the Russian White House, which wasn't a house at all so much as the seat of Russian governance.

He chose the Kremlin—again, *ostensibly*—for the benefit of the secure conference rooms the executive complex offered, and also for the convenience of other attendees. Romanov was generous that way.

But actually, Romanov just needed an excuse to be near Nikitin's office. He knew the president was scheduled to be on conference calls with Iran, Belarus, and Russia's CSTO allies that morning. If Romanov could rush the internal security meeting, he would venture into the presidential secretary's office for an impromptu "check-in." He would be declined—Nikitin would still be on the phone.

And that would be all the opportunity Romanov needed to achieve the real objective of his entire visit to the Kremlin—gaining a look at Nikitin's personal schedule.

Bustling inside the secure conference room, Romanov grunted greetings at the other attendees and took the head of the table. He sipped dark tea and did his best to accelerate the discussion without appearing to do so. Mostly the other attendees wanted to waste time bloviating about the war. As staunch allies of the president, their verbiage was entirely positive, entirely enthusiastic.

Romanov focused them back on the topic of escalated policing in St. Petersburg—a liberal city with *less* enthusiastic support of Nikitin. There were whispers of protest riots. Romanov emphasized the need to squelch opposition before it caught fire. The other three officials heartily agreed—nothing should be allowed to stand in the path of Russia's best interests. Clearly those best interests included Nikitin's war.

Eventually, Romanov concluded the meeting just as his Rolex ticked past ten a.m. He shook hands and snapped his briefcase closed. He strolled back into the marble hallways and turned first toward the exit.

Then, as if triggered by an afterthought, he reversed course. He headed back toward the core of the complex, his leather-soled shoes clapping as he ducked a head at passing members of the Nikitin cabinet. With every stride closer to Nikitin's executive office, Romanov's heart thumped harder. It might be his mind playing tricks on him, but his chest felt a little tighter. It almost...Yes, it hurt.

But that was probably just acid reflux from Romanov's sausage breakfast. He breathed deep and forced his mind to calm, reminding himself of Ivan Sidorov's words at their last meeting.

We need him outside the country, Maxim. We'll never get Nikitin inside his fortress.

Romanov knew it was true, maybe even better than Ivan did. Nikitin had so militarized the police force of Moscow, literally encircling the Russian capital in a barrier of heavily armed defense, that any hope of assassinating him at home or at the Kremlin would require a hydrogen bomb.

And wasn't that the point? To *avoid* a hydrogen bomb?

Romanov reached the exterior door of Nikitin's office suite. He placed his hand on the gold handle and breathed deep, attempting to burp to alleviate the pain in his chest.

It *was* reflux, right? Just greasy sausage.

Romanov entered. He flicked on a high-wattage smile as Nikitin's secretary looked up from her computer. She rose when she recognized him, returning her own tight-lipped smile.

"Good morning, Mr. Prime Minister. May I help you?"

"Just stopping in for a word with the president," Romanov said, not so much as slowing as he turned for Nikitin's office door. "He's in, right?"

"I'm sorry, the president is on a phone call right now. He asked not to be disturbed."

Romanov stopped mid-stride. He looked back, frowning.

"Oh."

"Yes, sir. Perhaps I could put you on the schedule?"

Romanov feigned annoyance, grumbling as he approached her desk. The secretary resumed her seat, twitching and nervous, skinny little fingers dancing over the keyboard.

"What's his schedule later this week?" Romanov asked.

"I'll check…" She clicked and spun the mouse's scroll wheel. Clicked some more. Shot Romanov a nervous smile.

"The president is quite booked. Is this a pressing matter? I could speak with him—"

"No, no." Romanov waved an annoyed hand. "Just an informal thing. What about next week? I'd like to catch him before he leaves Moscow."

"Leaves Moscow?"

"Wasn't he headed out of town?"

The secretary squinted. Shook her head. "Not that I'm aware of…"

Romanov's chest tightened a little further. The reflux was really flaring up. He refocused his mind on the task at hand and decided to push his luck. This girl didn't seem like the kind who would be smart enough to sniff out his true intentions.

"I thought the president was headed to Minsk," he said. "To meet with Zhukov."

The secretary glanced back to her screen as though the answer might be hidden on whatever calendar app she used. She scrolled once, then shook her head.

"I'm sorry, you must be mistaken. President Nikitin has canceled all travel plans until further notice. He'll be leading the war effort from here in the Kremlin. Perhaps I could book you for a lunch meeting?"

Romanov blinked, his eyes suddenly burning. He heard the girl, but everything after *until further notice* was a blur. His chest was *really* hurting. The reflux, or whatever it was, wouldn't relent. Mumbling something even he didn't understand, Romanov stumbled out of the office. His vision wavered as he reached the hallway—sweat rolled down his forehead. He steadied himself against the wall and breathed deep. Blinked hard. Ignored a passing FSO agent who inquired about his condition. Started down the hallway again, headed for the door.

The pain was subsiding. Romanov's mind returned to the task at hand

—to thoughts of rendezvousing with Ivan and updating him on the latest. It wasn't good news.

Romanov, Ivan, and their allies had a huge problem.

41

Department of Corrections Central Detention Facility
Washington, DC

This interview room wasn't like the last—the one where O'Dell met with Senator Roper. Located outside the core of the prison and inside the administration complex constructed next door, the walls were still faded and the ceiling still hung with suspended tiles, but in place of dirty industrial tile the floor was covered in worn commercial carpet. Bookshelves and a coffee bar lined the perimeter. A conference table filled the center.

O'Dell was led inside dressed in the same prison garb he'd worn since his arrest. Shackled hand and foot with a chain wrapped around his waist, he was flanked by a pair of CO's who never took their eyes off him as he was ushered to a chair in the middle of the table and directed to sit.

They hadn't explained why he was there. They hadn't explained who he was meeting, or offered him a phone call to his lawyer, or even told him if he was meeting anyone at all. Truth be told, it had crossed O'Dell's mind that he might be headed for a van and a long drive into rural Virginia. A quiet dirt road, a muffled gunshot.

And then blackness—the end. It was a horrific thought, but the pragmatism of the approach made sense to him. Could he really blame Maggie if she took that route? O'Dell had become a magnificent liability. That was never his intention. He *wanted* to help her. He had literally killed for her...

And then admitted it to Senator Roper. O'Dell had kicked himself every moment of every passing hour since then. He'd hated himself. He'd literally smashed his fist against the block wall of his cell, bloodying his knuckles and maybe breaking a finger. It was swollen now, and ached, but he deserved that.

He'd let the emotions get to him—he'd exposed Maggie. It was his fault.

A door opened and O'Dell's gaze snapped up just in time to see his lawyer enter. Hugh Sumner looked exactly as he always looked, tired and haggard, dressed in a wrinkled suit and an outdated tie. He nodded once to O'Dell before dragging back the chair next to him and plopping down. He didn't carry a briefcase or a computer bag or so much as a pen.

Even before Sumner had settled in, he was already checking his watch. Tapping one finger on the table. Looking to the door.

"Why am I here?" O'Dell said.

Sumner glanced his way. Snorted and shook his head.

"Because I'm a miracle worker," Sumner said.

O'Dell didn't know what that meant. He wasn't so naïve as to be excited. He simply waited until the door opened a second time, and three men entered.

All were dressed in black government suits, and all marched with the impatience and efficiency of men who wanted everyone else to know exactly how important they were. O'Dell knew the first two were FBI agents without recognizing them. They just had that bearing. But if he had any doubts, the identity of the third man—a man he *did* recognize—erased them in a heartbeat.

It was FBI Director Bill Purcell.

"Good morning, James," Purcell said, pulling back a chair from the table. "Did they offer you any coffee?"

O'Dell sat momentarily stunned. His gaze flicked toward Sumner, and Sumner only smiled a tight-lipped, impatient smile. O'Dell looked back to Purcell, flanked by agents that O'Dell now thought might be bodyguards.

He hesitated, then for no particular reason he lifted his wrists above the table and exposed the shackles.

Purcell frowned. He gestured to the COs still standing by the door.

"Remove those, immediately. Get Mr. O'Dell some coffee—and some donuts, or something. He must be hungry."

O'Dell didn't think that Purcell was actually aware of his meal schedule. In truth, he was hungry. The food at the detention center was something beyond terrible, and he knew he was losing weight. He made no comment as the COs reluctantly uncuffed his wrists.

They left his leg shackles. They poured him coffee and dropped a stale muffin onto a paper plate. Then Purcell motioned them out.

"Sir, we're not supposed—"

"To eavesdrop on a confidential witness interview?" Purcell cut the CO off. "I know. So get out."

There was no room for debate in his tone. The COs left while O'Dell sat with his liberated hands in his lap, ignoring the coffee and the muffin. He couldn't eat if he wanted to—his stomach was in knots. He looked from one face to the next, waiting for *somebody* to say something.

Nobody did.

"So now the FBI's my best friend?"

It probably wasn't the smartest thing for O'Dell to say, but it was at least rational. Purcell didn't seem offended.

"Mr. O'Dell, who's my boss?" the director said.

O'Dell squinted. "What?"

"It's a simple question."

O'Dell glanced to Sumner. His attorney nodded, encouraging him on.

"The attorney general," O'Dell said.

Purcell shook his head. "No. Try again."

O'Dell squinted. Then shrugged.

"The president."

"Wrong again. Any third guess?"

O'Dell was tired of playing games. He didn't answer. Purcell interlaced his fingers and leaned forward.

"My boss is the American people. That's who I swore my oath to. You've sworn a few oaths in your own life, so you should understand. Whoever sits in the White House is just a temporary installment of executive power. Ultimately, I answer to the citizens of this country. That's how it's meant to be—it keeps power in check."

O'Dell could already tell where this spiel was headed. He wasn't interested in fueling it, so he just stared.

"I won't waste any time describing your predicament," Purcell continued. "Clearly, you already understand it, and clearly, you don't care. Maybe you think it's noble to throw your life away on behalf of somebody else. The fact is, the FBI has come to believe that Maggie Trousdale may have committed serious crimes—violations of her oath, in other words. We believe you have knowledge of those crimes. I'm not asking you to assist our investigation in trade for immunity. I'm asking you to assist because it's the right thing to do, and because *you* swore an oath. Do you understand?"

Still, O'Dell didn't answer. For the first time, one of Purcell's associates spoke—a cutting voice and a condescending glare.

"Maybe you're confused, Mr. O'Dell. Maybe you assume that your loyalties to the president are reciprocated. Is that it?"

Still, O'Dell said nothing. The agent shook his head, feigning sudden sadness. He reached into his jacket and produced a phone. He tapped and sighed...then rotated the device.

"A stone-cold savage, that swamp girl. Geez."

O'Dell looked to the phone—he couldn't help it. The screen displayed a full-picture video. It was a news reel branded with a national media outlet's logo, and depicted a sweeping airstrip with Air Force One parked in the background. The scrolling caption read: PRESIDENT TROUSDALE DEPARTS FOR NATO SUMMIT, BRUSSELS.

And then—there she was. Stepping out of the Beast, clad in one of her best pantsuits, dirty-blond hair torn by the wind...

She looked terrible. Worse than the last time O'Dell had seen her, somehow weaker and more frail. Large sunglasses couldn't hide the sag in her cheeks or the pallor of her skin. Her wide smile seemed forced even as she glided toward a pool of reporters just the way she had approached similar pools a few hundred times before.

Only now that stride was labored, however subtly so.

"Good morning," Maggie said, keeping the sunglasses on but allowing the smile to fade. "It's a difficult day for our allies in Europe. I'm headed to Belgium to meet with leaders from every NATO member state. I can't promise instant fixes, but I want Russia to hear me loud and clear when I say that the aggression stops *today*. We will not tolerate a broader European or global conflict. We will not tolerate further military expansion. President Nikitin would be well advised to—"

"Madam President! What if Russia goes nuclear?"

"Madam President! Where have you been? You haven't held a presser in weeks. How's your health?"

"Madam President! What can you tell us about your association with the accused murderer James O'Dell?"

It was that last question that broke through Maggie's armor. O'Dell recognized the moment the bullet sank in—she visibly flinched, however momentarily. She hesitated, breaking her train of thought. Then she swallowed.

What are you doing? O'Dell's gaze was riveted to the screen. He hadn't realized it, but he'd stopped breathing. He wasn't budging—neither was Maggie. The press grew quiet, circling sharks who smelled blood in the water. They wouldn't offer her a detour. They wanted her in this trap.

"Madam President, did you direct James O'Dell to kill on your behalf?"

Maggie's mouth closed. She seemed deadlocked, frozen in time. Every second that dripped by heightened the tension, worsened the effect...

"Madam President, are you a killer—"

"Let me be perfectly clear." Maggie's voice turned hard, her body stiffening. "I have never, would never, and *could never* associate with a murderer. Mr. O'Dell was nothing more than a bodyguard from my days in Louisiana. I brought him to DC in appreciation of his service—I've barely spoken with him since. Whatever he's accused of, I fully support the Justice Department in their inquiry."

"Does that mean you believe he's guilty?"

"That means exactly what I said—I know nothing about the situation and I support the Justice Department. Thank you, everyone."

Maggie turned away, marching hard toward the plane, and the video clip ended. The FBI agent whistled softly and shook his head.

"'Nothing more than a bodyguard,'" he quoted. "*Ouch.* And we all *know* you slept with her."

Blood surged to O'Dell's face. His heart thundered. He looked away, hands clenching into fists despite himself. The room turned silent and O'Dell wanted to be anywhere else—he wanted to bury himself in a hole. To scream where nobody could hear him. To throw something.

It's not true—it can't be true. She's just saving face with the media. She doesn't have a choice.

"She's sold you out, James," Purcell said, sounding almost sad. O'Dell's gaze switched his way, and he saw a much older man than the FBI director he first met while following Maggie to the White House. A much more battered man.

This place—this *city*—was killing them all. Draining the life away.

And who had it drained more than Maggie?

O'Dell pictured her stepping out of the Beast, looking like little more than a walking skeleton. So thin, so weak, so weary. Torn apart by injury and stress and—yes—addiction. O'Dell knew about the opioids.

What he hadn't known about—what he was just now seeing clearly for the first time—was the betrayal.

"You want me to talk?" O'Dell said, jaw tightening.

"Very much," Purcell said.

"Fine. I'll talk—I'll do it at the Capitol."

Purcell squinted. "The Capitol?"

"Before Congress, with the American people watching. You said it yourself, Bill. I swore my oath to the citizens. I'll tell the citizens the truth."

42

Moscow, Russia

Ornate and historic, Café Pushkin sat on Tverskoy Boulevard overlooking Novopushkinsky Square only two kilometers northwest of the Kremlin.

Ivan had eaten there many times during his tenure as a senior SVR officer. The style and menu wasn't his favorite—as the child of peasantry, he preferred basic, hearty foods over the complex flavors and paltry servings of the rich and famous. Café Pushkin was a place of pomp and circumstance, elegance and pretense. Popular with tourists and Russian socialites, the restaurant was almost always busy, which made it an unlikely choice for a covert meetup...

And in that respect, the perfect choice.

Ivan slipped in through a back door, taking a narrow stairway to the private dining rooms on the second floor. This wasn't his first time rendezvousing with a VIP contact in this way. He was familiar with the routes and routines of the servers and staff, and knew how to avoid them. At the top of the stairs a maître d' in a silky black tux guarded a door, but Ivan was expected. Neither man said a word—the maître d' guided him down a hallway to a windowless room stocked with a mahogany table, crystal stemware, and china dishes.

And only one occupant—Prime Minister of Russia, Maxim Romanov.

The maître d' closed the door and Ivan removed his hat. He pulled back a chair without a word and sat next to Romanov. The PM was already eating, his plate loaded with minced beef cutlets, roasted potatoes, and pickled cabbage. The drink was red wine, and by the flush of his face Ivan guessed that it wasn't his first glass.

"Hell's angels, Maxim. You'll kill yourself."

Romanov said nothing. He speared beef and a potato on his fork and shoved both into his mouth, sloppy wet lips smacking, wine dripping down his cheek. One hand trembled—the other rolled a steak knife. Around and around, chewing and swallowing and jabbing up another bite.

Ivan shook his head. He reached for the open bottle of Bordeaux and poured his own glass. It was weaker than he liked—he would have preferred vodka. But Ivan needed something. He hadn't slept in nearly twenty hours. Earlier that day on his way back to the hostel where he'd established temporary residence, he was delayed by a traffic jam.

The jam was fortunate—he arrived late at the hostel to find two unmarked government sedans parked outside. The suits who exited the building were most definitely FSB officers, and Ivan didn't think they'd come to the hostel looking for any of the unwashed hippies who slept there.

The noose was tightening. Perhaps word had leaked that Ivan was back in town. The government's plate was loaded down heavier than Romanov's, but that didn't mean they wouldn't make time to hunt Russia's top traitor.

"What did you find?" Ivan said.

Romanov shot him a look, gulping more wine. He speared another chunk of potato.

"*Maxim*," Ivan snapped. "Get yourself together. Answer the question."

Romanov wiped his lips with the back of one hand. "Nothing. I found nothing."

"You didn't see the schedule?"

"I saw it. I mean he's not leaving—not in the next month. Nikitin has barricaded himself inside the Kremlin. He's running the war from within his fortress."

Ivan's jaw tightened. Romanov crammed more beef into his mouth and nearly choked—the man was shaking, hyperventilating, moving on autopilot. He was *panicking*.

Ivan struck the plate with a sweep of one arm. Beef cutlets, cabbage, and potatoes rained over the floor. The plate shattered and shards of china skated over polished hardwood. Romanov swallowed hard and started to choke. He dropped the knife and put a hand to his throat—something was stuck inside.

Ivan exploded out of the chair. He circled behind the PM and wrapped two bearlike arms around his chest. Romanov was still gagging, his face turned cherry red. Ivan interlocked his hands at the base of the PM's sternum and yanked.

Once, twice. On the third pull, the PM spat up a soggy chunk of beef, gasping and falling over the table. Ivan shoved him from behind, smashing his chest against the table edge and driving the air from his lungs.

Romanov couldn't speak. It was exactly what Ivan wanted.

"Now," Ivan said, resuming his chair. "So long as you're fighting for air, listen closely. I didn't come to Moscow to watch Russia's last hope of survival eat himself to death on rare meat and greasy potatoes. To be here at all is to risk my life—but that's all part of the job, what I swore an oath to do. It's what *you* swore an oath to do, and 144 *million* Russians are counting on us to stand in the face of unchecked tyranny and stop the madness. Do you understand?"

"What...what do you want me to do?" Romanov snarled. "I told you he isn't—"

"*Lower your voice*," Ivan snapped. "And wipe your face. You are the prime minister of Russia—act like it."

Ivan shoved Romanov a cloth napkin. The PM scrubbed his lips and cheeks, still flushed. He jabbed a finger at Ivan.

"You're out of your depth—"

"We're *all* out of our depth, Maxim," Ivan cut him off. "Either rise to the occasion or get out of the way."

That was enough to slow the PM's roll. His jaw clenched and he stared at the table a long time, eyes closed. Breathing deep.

At last, Romanov said: "We can't kill him inside the Kremlin. A slaughter so obviously internal would never be accepted by the people. We would be murderous traitors—Nikitin would be a martyr. It can't be done."

Ivan didn't answer right away. He drained his glass, swishing the wine before swallowing. Of course he knew that Romanov was right. Ivan had already completed the mental math himself. As much as the Russian populace might not support Nikitin, they wouldn't support perceived murderers any more.

No. This *had* to look like an outside job.

"We will move him," Ivan said. "We'll get him outside the city—outside the country, if possible."

"*How?*" Romanov said. "Do you have any concept of who you're dealing with? Makar is a law unto himself. He doesn't take orders from anyone, and nobody questions him. You can't *tell* him what to do."

"Then we won't try," Ivan said, voice lowering. "We'll just plant a sword in the ground, and let his pride throw him on it."

"What?" Romanov's brow furrowed. "What does that even mean?"

"It means we make Makar his own worst enemy, Maxim. If he wants to be God, let him try. We'll bait him straight into hell."

43

Langley, Virginia

The report arrived at Aimes's office first thing in the morning.

Passed from Ivan Sidorov to Natasha Kirov, the update from Moscow was then transmitted to a US satellite by Kirov using an encrypted, one-way burst transmission. From there the message was downloaded directly into Langley, decrypted, and supplied to Aimes via internal secure messaging.

Quick, discreet, and as secretive as modern espionage technology could manage. The contents of the missive were just as succinct.

Nikitin not leaving Kremlin. Need assistance in flushing him out—suggest baiting him. Operation inside Moscow not a politically viable option.

That was all. No suggestions for exactly *how* assistance could be supplied, or further information about the nature of Nikitin's daily patterns.

More impossible obstacles.

Aimes thumbed her intercom and directed her secretary to get Silas Rigby on a secure line. Her deputy director was still in Europe, escorting the PF into Poland for pre-op preparation, but inside a NATO country, the communications available to Rigby were far more advanced than what was available to Kirov. She and Rigby could talk over an encrypted line without risk.

While waiting for her phone to ring, Aimes punched out answers to emails and scanned additional reports of developing military action across Lebanon. Fourteen US Marines had died the night before via rocket strikes from Hezbollah. The militant group was already gasping its dying breath under joint pressure from both the Corps and the Israelis, but were inflicting pain all the way into the grave.

And Iran was still coming. Only days from securing Iraq and penetrating farther west, that hurricane would drive that KIA report into triple digits...if not higher.

The phone chirped just as Aimes was scanning news headlines regarding President Trousdale's trip to Brussels. The reports were not positive, and given the fact that the substance of the NATO summit was classified, Aimes thought the tone of those articles said more about media perception of Maggie than events in Europe.

More headwinds.

Aimes punched her speaker phone button. "Yeah?"

"It's Silas."

In only two words Rigby's voice transmitted more exhaustion than Aimes had heard the entire time she'd known him. He sounded like he hadn't slept in days—and maybe he hadn't. The trip to Cyprus and then into mainland Europe was no vacation.

"I sent you an email," Aimes said. "Let me know when you've read it."

Twenty seconds passed. In the background Aimes heard echoes and the hum of heavy machinery. Rigby was likely inside an aircraft hangar at Powitz Air Base, which had been roaring for days with incoming C-17 Globemasters loaded with US ground troops.

"So..." Rigby hesitated. "They don't want him killed him inside the city...and he won't leave. What exactly do they want us to do?"

"Apparently they want us to *bait* him," Aimes said.

"What does that mean?"

Silence. Aimes rubbed her eyes—she was *so* tired.

Think, Sarah. Come up with something.

"Where's the PF?" Aimes said.

"I parked them at the Polish Special Operations Unit facility. They're out of sight."

"Condition?"

Rigby didn't answer.

"Silas?" Aimes pressed.

"Not good," Rigby said at last.

"Meaning?"

"Meaning they're shattered. Exhausted, injured, and in very questionable mental state. I've spoken with each of them individually, at least for a moment. I'm getting radically different vibes from everyone. Pierce seems to be barely holding himself together. Turkman is distracted. Byrne is like...in some kind of spiritual fourth dimension. Corbyn wants to see Russia totally destroyed, and Montgomery I can't get a read on. He might be zeroed in or he might be approaching a total collapse. I have no idea, but whatever the case, this team isn't anywhere *close* to being ready for this kind of op. I mean they're months away, if they're capable at all. Azerbaijan...really wrecked them."

Aimes sucked her teeth and forced herself not to panic. Not to be overwhelmed or to snap. More than ever in her life she *needed* to focus.

"Silas, they're our only option," Aimes said. "The *only* way this works is plausible deniability for all sides. The world is going to know that we killed Nikitin, but they won't be able to prove it, and that might just be enough wiggle room to establish non-hostile relations with the replacement Russian regime. If we send the SEALs in there—"

"I know," Rigby cut her off. "I've already considered that."

"Sidorov is right about Moscow, also. It can't happen at the Kremlin. The Russian people would perceive it as a homeland assault—or worse still, they would know that Romanov was involved, and they'd never accept his legitimacy as Nikitin's successor. This *has* to be done outside the city, and it *has* to be done by a nonexistent team. If you have something better than the PF..."

Aimes trailed off, not needing to finish. She already knew the answer. So did Rigby. There was nobody other than the PF—not in structure or capability or availability.

This *was* the last-ditch play.

"What are my orders?" Rigby said.

"Do whatever you can to get them ready. Give them everything they need—anything they want. I'll authorize any expenditure."

"Okay. And Nikitin?"

"That's on me," Aimes said. "You get Montgomery's people ready—I'll flush out their target."

The call ended without further debate. Aimes ran her hand over her face and keyed her intercom again, requesting coffee. Already her mind was spinning ahead to her insane commitment, and how she could possibly deliver.

One step at a time. Get the caffeine.

The coffee arrived and Aimes reached for sugar free sweetener—then scrapped that idea and poured in the real thing. She inhaled rich Colombian brew, her gaze drifting to the silenced wall-mounted television...and then she froze.

The newscast was from CNN. The headline played on repeat.

WHITE HOUSE INSIDER JAMES O'DELL SET TO TESTIFY AGAINST TROUSDALE BEFORE SENATE.

44

Air Force One
Somewhere over the Atlantic

The NATO summit was chaos.

Held behind closed doors, Maggie could at least be reassured that the media would be insulated from the exact extremity of that chaos, but the panic displayed by European representatives was impossible to fully conceal.

The world would know, whether by fact or instinct, that NATO was reeling.

Poland, Finland, and all the Baltic states demanded immediate declarations of war against Russia by every NATO nation. Germany, Italy, and Hungary—countries heavily reliant on Russian energy exports—were less enthusiastic. France called for diplomacy. Turkey wanted to shelve the entire matter, referring to the invasion of Estonia and Latvia as "a regional dispute."

And everyone else, caught in the middle or else too afraid to know what to think, looked to the United States to work a miracle.

Maggie left Brussels early without committing to any stronger a military response than what was already in process. Tens of thousands of US infantry and armored units were streaming into Poland around the clock, and US naval presence in the North Sea and the Norwegian Sea had reached an all-time high. American air strikes could continue against Russian ground forces in the Baltic, and pressure could escalate as necessary.

After Korea, Vietnam, Desert Storm, Iraq, and Afghanistan, who needed a declaration of war, anyway?

Maggie boarded Air Force One with her head swimming, an empty stomach threatening to eject bile through her throat. For six hours straight she had forced her body via sheer willpower alone to perform—to keep her upright, keep her voice steady, and keep her mind focused not on the endless cravings but on the business of preventing global destruction.

The effort, she felt, almost broke her. Twice during the meetings Maggie's head spun so badly that she knew if she stood, she would pass out. She couldn't eat and made an excuse with the British PM to avoid a lunch meeting that would have exposed her digestive problems. Leaving early, in the end, was a very bad look and would certainly cost her with America's allies and her people, but what was Maggie going to do?

Delaying her meeting with the White House physician's office had been a mistake. Maggie should have found somebody other than her regular doctor. She should have asked somebody on her staff—maybe asked Easterling.

No. She couldn't ask Easterling. Maggie felt that in her gut. There was something broken there...some hint of mistrust. All Muddy Maggie could really do was *keep going*.

Inside her private quarters on Air Force One, Maggie showered and changed into sweats. She sat with her eyes closed as the jet took off, confronting the misery head on for half an hour until Easterling buzzed her room to remind her of the post-summit cabinet meeting to be held via conference call.

Secretary Gorman was in New York, meeting with NATO. SecDef Kline and the Joint Chiefs of Staff would phone in from the Pentagon. Everyone wanted an update on the plan moving forward.

Maggie entered AF1's conference room to a welcome wash of icy air conditioning. She was sweating and lightheaded. The hot flashes blended with waves of nausea and a buzzing sensation in her fingertips that made it difficult to perform precise tasks.

She ignored it all and took a seat at the table. Coffee waited, and she tried not to allow her hand to tremble as she poured.

"Are we ready?" Maggie asked.

From across the table Easterling didn't answer. She sat with her mousy features framed by gold-colored glasses, unblinking and a little...pale?

"What?" Maggie said.

By way of answer Easterling slid an iPad across the table. Maggie took the device and scanned the screen—a headline from a major media outlet, printed in bold over a photograph of a familiar face.

James O'Dell.

President's rumored lover to testify before special Senate committee—Quote: "I have a lot to say."

Maggie read the headline and looked to the photo. It was an old picture taken from sometime during her last campaign, before she was shot. Maggie was visible in the backdrop, beaming at the crowd and lifting a hand. O'Dell stood just behind her, his iron jaw closed, his gaze hidden behind dark sunglasses. Ever a hawk.

I looked amazing.

It was an ironic, inconsequential thought, but the first one Maggie could clearly process. She noted the rosy tint of her skin, the twenty-odd pounds of healthy weight she now lacked, the clarity and energy in her eyes...

"Ma'am?"

It was Easterling. Maggie looked up.

"What?"

Easterling didn't say anything. She seemed to be waiting, as though the topic of her concern should be obvious.

Maggie simply switched off the tablet. "Don't bother me with tabloid gossip, Jill. You should know better."

Easterling frowned. "It's the *Senate*, ma'am. The special committee will be chaired by Matt Roper. This is the furthest thing—"

"From our concern," Maggie cut in. "Europe is on *fire*, Jill. I couldn't care less what Matt Roper is wasting time on. Now start the call."

Easterling looked shell-shocked—for a long moment she didn't move.

Then she reached out a hand and pressed a button on the desk-mounted phone. The operator announced the attending members of the secured call. Maggie nodded for Easterling to lead.

After another moment of stunned silence, Easterling did.

"Secretary Gorman, would you update us on the situation in New York?"

"I just finished a call with Ambassador Renard," Gorman said. "I don't know what the French said in Brussels, but their position with the UN is unequivocal—they're resisting any escalation of military force, and they're refusing to deploy additional troops into Poland. They want a diplomatic solution."

Nobody answered that, but Maggie easily identified a disgusted snort as belonging to General Yellin. She couldn't say that she disagreed with him.

"Forget France," Maggie said. "They'll join the party when their borders are threatened. I want to know about support *outside* of Europe."

"Mixed, ma'am. BRICS is obviously opposed, but their voice was louder than I expected. Brazil and South Africa in particular spoke at length to condemn NATO aggression—they sounded like they were reading right off of Russia's teleprompter. India joined Australia and Japan in support of diplomatic pressure and sanctions but maybe not increased military action. Everybody in the Middle East couldn't care less about the Baltic. They're all wrapped up with the Iran-Israel conflict. Most of Southeast Asia is similarly preoccupied with China."

It was pretty much the summary Maggie expected. She nodded again, and Easterling summoned Kline to report on military action.

"We're gaining ground in Lebanon," Kline said. "One hundred eighteen Marines dead thus far, another four hundred injured. But in the next seventy-two hours we expect to have Hezbollah all but neutralized and Beirut secured for additional deployments. From there we can partner with Israel to confront the Iranian advance."

"Europe?" Maggie said.

"Our situation in Europe is much less positive," Kline continued. "Russia's incursion into Estonia is practically irreversible. They'll hold full control of the country by this weekend. Belarus, meanwhile, has hammered the Latvians into retreat and is driving them straight into Russia's line of fire. We could parachute a hundred thousand troops into Latvia tomorrow morning and I don't know if we could do better than delay the inevitable. Russia and Belarus hold all the strategic high ground. They're just moving too fast."

"And Lithuania?" Easterling said.

It was the obvious next question. As the last member of the Baltic trio, Lithuania was sandwiched between Latvia to the northeast, Belarus to the south and southeast, Poland to the southwest, and worst of all the Kaliningrad Oblast directly to their west—a Russian holding.

"They'll be next," Kline said. "And that's really where we have a choice to make. Do we want to confront the Russians on the ground in Lithuania, or concentrate a larger force in Poland, and dig in? If we move now we can occupy Lithuania before the Russians are ready to assault, but I doubt we have enough time to fully fortify the country. Our resulting casualties will be extreme—Lithuania will almost certainly be destroyed, and there's a strong possibility that we'll still lose ground. On the other hand, if we stall in Poland, we can build a stronger wall to halt their advance...but we also give them more time to develop momentum."

Maggie recognized the dilemma—she understood the give and take, at least logically. But she couldn't force her mind to focus on the problem. She kept seeing the entire situation from the outside, not on the tactical level but the strategic level—and even that was through a haze of brain fog.

War, she kept thinking. War was the real enemy. Bigger than Russia, Iran, China, or the three of them combined. Nobody could win this thing, even if they declared victory. The slaughter would be unprecedented.

"Madam President," Kline said. "Whatever we decide to do, we need to do it with congressional approval. We need to ask for a declaration of war."

Maggie's gaze flicked to the phone. "What?"

"We haven't formally declared war since World War Two," Yellin said, joining the conversation for the first time. "Every conflict since then has been one foot in, one foot out. If we're honest, we've lost most of them. Nikitin is expecting the United States to pursue this confrontation in the same way, applying pressure only by degrees and never fully committing. He's *depending* on that. We need to send a resounding message to the world that this won't be like Iraq or Vietnam. We're *all in* right from the opening gun."

Opening gun.

It was a horrible metaphor—or a perfect one. Maggie pictured a revolver lifted into the air, cracking with a thunderclap and spitting out a mushroom cloud.

"I agree with the SecDef and the general," Easterling said. "Pursuing military action against Russia separate of a declaration is tenuous and... pointless, honestly. I don't know what the exact vote count would look like, but Congress really has no choice but to stand behind us. America is terrified."

And they should be.

"Are you really asking me to declare war on a nuclear power?" Maggie said.

The room fell silent. Yellin cleared his throat, awkwardly, but it was Kline who stepped in.

"Ma'am, if we're unwilling to confront Russia because of their nukes, we may as well surrender now."

"But it's not *Russia* that we're confronting, Mr. Secretary. It's Makar Nikitin. Tell me you understand the difference."

No answer. Maggie's mind spun—her head began to spin with it. All she could think about were those satellite images the Pentagon had provided of nuclear blasts rising first over Panama, then Azerbaijan. Hellish glimpses of what was to come—and who would it punish most?

Not Nikitin. Not even Maggie. *The people.* From the farmlands of Eastern Europe to the mega cities of Western Europe and all the way to the swamps of Maggie's homeland. The people would die by the millions, and those who survived might wish they hadn't. It was a mortal spiral that nobody could control, nobody could stop.

Unless.

"No," Maggie said. "We won't be declaring war. We aren't there yet."

"Madam President, the Baltic states are NATO allies—"

"And we will *defend them*, Mr. Secretary. We are defending them now.

We will confront Nikitin's aggression and pummel his regime day and night until it crumbles, but we will *not* make the Russian people our enemy. The moment we do that, this thing doesn't end until the world burns."

"Are you..." Kline hesitated. "Are you really counting on Russia's populace to resist Nikitin?"

"I'm not counting on anything, Steven. I just know what happens when ordinary people feel threatened. Rationale, justice, even morality all goes out the door. It becomes us versus them, and I *will not* allow that. The enemy is the monster behind the wheel—we drive that point home and we keep our heads cool. Back me up, Lisa."

Silence. Maggie waited for Gorman to express support, to champion the diplomatic angle she had so often expressed. But Gorman didn't rush to respond. She only spoke after the silence became overbearing, and when she did, her voice was quiet.

"I cannot agree, ma'am."

So there it is.

Maggie looked to Easterling and found no reassurance, just a calm and unblinking stare—proof that Maggie was at last on her own.

"Well, it's a great thing that this isn't a democracy, or we'd be burning by next weekend," Maggie snapped. "Steven, proceed with deployments into Poland. Air strikes will continue over Estonia, but not one American boot will cross onto those battlefields without my express direction. Is that clear?"

By the time Maggie finished, her abdomen was hurting again. She was short on breath, and nausea washed through her in waves. But she didn't second-guess anything.

Knotted or otherwise, she was following her gut. She was *not* taking the bait.

"Understood." Kline's voice boiled with restrained frustration, maybe anger. Gorman and Yellin didn't speak at all. The call ended and Easterling just stared at Maggie.

"What..." Easterling started. Shook her head. "What are you *doing*?"

It was the bluntest question Easterling had ever asked her, and while Maggie had an answer, she wouldn't voice it.

She couldn't voice it.

"Give me the room," Maggie said.

Easterling didn't move for a long moment. Then she collected her computer and departed without a word, leaving Maggie staring out a window, head pounding and hands trembling as she remembered Aimes's wild strategy, and thought:

Gambling. I'm gambling like a maniac.

45

Moscow, Russia

The Western headlines were like crack cocaine for Nikitin—they flooded his body with adrenaline and dopamine, actually spiking his heart rate and leaving him desperate for *more.*

Embattled Trousdale Refuses to Acknowledge Murder Scandal.

Who is James O'Dell, and Why Did He Kill for the President?

Senator Roper: O'Dell Hearing Will Dwarf Watergate Tapes.

It was like a perfect storm—like a gift that Roper hadn't even thought to ask for. In the midst of his incursion into the Baltic, with Iraq toppling and American naval assets in retreat out of the South Pacific, a miracle bomb was detonating right in the heart of Washington. A scandal Nikitin knew nothing about and had neither orchestrated nor influenced...and yet it was playing right into his hand.

Maggie Trousdale was a mouse caught on a griddle, and the temperature was rising.

"What do you know?" Nikitin barked the question the moment Golubev entered his office. With unwashed hair slicked back from his forehead and bags hanging beneath his eyes, it was no great secret that Golubev hadn't been home in days, or showered in just as long.

He was running Nikitin's war like his own personal agenda, keeping his thumb on generals, politicians, and allies alike. Every order from Nikitin came through Golubev—every request back up the line was filtered by the same. He was the bottleneck.

He was *getting it done.*

"First I've heard," Golubev said, helping himself to the teapot on Nikitin's desk. "Apparently this guy killed the man whose liver was transplanted into the president."

"And that's a crime?" Nikitin snorted.

He was in a good mood. Why shouldn't he be? Military success across Estonia and Latvia was unchecked despite the intermittent NATO air strikes. Western resistance, in fact, had been even weaker than he expected. Troops were swelling inside Poland, but nobody was moving to directly challenge Russian ground forces.

And now this—like a cherry on the cake.

"It can't hurt us," Golubev admitted. "The spectacle will distract the American populace from our advance and further undermine the integrity of Trousdale's administration. It might buy us more time."

"We have all the time we want," Nikitin said. "She's even weaker than we supposed."

"She's deploying troops to Poland," Golubev countered. "And American naval assets are advancing past Denmark."

"So let them. What do we care? We want the dirt, not the water. Once we hold the Baltic we can blast them right back into the Atlantic."

Golubev grunted but didn't otherwise respond. Sitting behind his desk, Nikitin was still scanning at the American news stories but was no longer really thinking about them. His mind was spinning ahead to another idea —a big, bold idea. It was a card he'd planned to play all along, although certainly not so soon.

But with America in such chaos and the ground advance proceeding so well...why not press his advantage?

"Initiate the air assault of Lithuania," Nikitin said. "Let's begin phase C."

Golubev blinked. Looked up. "What?"

"We have both the momentum and the advantage. NATO is stalling and Trousdale is drowning. Let's exploit their weakness and hit the Lithuanians before those troops in Poland even think about deploying. Let's bomb them now."

Golubev set his tea down. He rocked forward in his chair.

"Makar, please. This is too soon. Our ground troops are still a week, maybe two from merging with the Belarussians and fully securing Latvia. We're a month at *best* from invading Lithuania. If we initiate an assault now—"

"We can pummel them into submission before we ever put boots on the ground," Nikitin said. "Don't you see? Lithuania stands alone. The Americans and NATO will do nothing but deploy air strikes. If we pound the Lithuanians now, we can drive back their defenses before we even arrive. We're rolling out a red carpet for ourselves."

Golubev was shaking his head long before Nikitin finished the spiel. "No, Makar. It's too far. I've supported your escalations all week, but this is much too aggressive. We should deploy those bombers over Estonian and Latvian forces—double down on our existing battlegrounds. This is exactly how Hitler lost in Stalingrad—"

"By confronting Russia," Nikitin barked, cutting him off once more. "By defying the Russian people! *We* are the force of Europe, Anton. Not Germany and certainly not NATO. We have exposed their weakness, and now you would have me pull punches?"

"I would have you stick to the plan."

"The plan is evolving, right along with the war. Am I not still in charge?"

No answer.

"*Well?*" Nikitin nearly shouted.

"Of course you are in charge."

"Then trust me, Anton. Trust my instinct. We are killers—the Russian people are killers. There is meat on the table and it is time to feast. Initiate the air strikes, as ordered. Concentrate on Lithuania's military bases and key infrastructure. Send the message loud and clear—Russia is coming. Russia will not be defied. If they'd like to surrender...the phone lines are open."

Nikitin finished with a wolfish grin. He couldn't help it. Golubev stared a long time—obviously longing to resist.

But Nikitin knew he wouldn't. Not only because Nikitin was in command but because Golubev trusted his boss. He had followed Nikitin like a faithful bloodhound for decades.

Now was the climax of their journey together. The thing Nikitin had worked toward his entire life.

"Do it, Anton," Nikitin said. "Do it for Russia."

Golubev set his tea on the desk. He nodded once. "For Russia."

Then he left. Nikitin looked back to the screen. He read the headlines again and the wolfish grin stretched a little wider.

The whole *world* would be a slaughterhouse.

46

Langley, Virginia

There were only three people in the room besides Aimes. Outside of Silas Rigby, these were the officers of the Agency that she trusted most—all hand-picked upon her confirmation as director. They each worked for different directorates but were all absolutely loyal to Aimes's leadership, and together they understood more about the intelligence sector than most people could learn in a lifetime.

Most importantly of all, they were absolutely trustworthy. They were the sorts of people who would take Aimes's secrets to an early grave, if asked.

Aimes shut herself and her "three musketeers" inside a secure conference room and directed her secretary to hold all calls and refuse all meetings. Lunch would be catered in and an attached bathroom provided necessary functions for the extended work hours ahead. Aimes sat her people around the table and stood at the head, her hands resting on the back of a chair.

She told them why they were there in direct terms.

We're going to kill Makar Nikitin.

Nobody blinked. Nobody freaked out. The lone guy leaned back and scratched his cheek. One of the two women sat with her coffee halfway to her lips, then slowly set it down.

But they didn't object or argue, because the combined fifty-four years of CIA intelligence experience sitting around that table had weathered far crazier ideas than this, and the logic of Aimes's explanation was irrefutable. It was the best idea the AI supercomputers had generated in weeks, and not without reason.

It was the world's best option.

"We need the target outside of Moscow," Aimes said. "Actually, outside of Russia, if possible. Someplace where a hit could be lightning fast and plausibly deniable for both ourselves and the Russians—an unexplainable act of war. The problem is that Nikitin doesn't plan to leave Moscow. It's our job to figure out a way to lure him out."

That was the directive. All three of her musketeers exchanged a glance —then they went to work. Around the clock, with a pair of couches set along one wall for limited but necessary rest.

No idea was a bad idea until proven to be. Strategies to bait, cajole, trick, or drag Nikitin out of Moscow were all considered and eventually scrapped. Nobody could think of anything that wouldn't link directly back to the US, or wouldn't otherwise rely on an astounding volume of luck to work.

They needed something totally outside the box. Something nobody would suspect. Something that played on Nikitin's greatest weaknesses...

Then the phone rang, and Aimes placed it on speaker. They were twenty-two hours into her brainstorming lockdown and she'd directed her office to not disturb them unless Trousdale herself was calling, or else a major new development demanded her attention.

In this case it was the second, not the first. Russia was bombing Lithuania, an analyst reported. Dozens of Tupolev Tu-22M strategic bombers and Sukhoi Su-34 fighter bombers were launching hundreds of cruise missiles across Lithuania's Švenčionys Region, targeting supply depots, fuel storage facilities, and military outposts. Early reports of the damage were limited but this did not appear to be a probing assault—this was the real deal. A full-fledged roundhouse kick to the last remaining member of the Baltic trio.

"Already?"

It was one of the musketeers who spoke, and Aimes shared the disbelief evident in their tone, but she didn't comment. She simply concluded the call and withdrew into a long moment of silence, unchallenged by the three other occupants of the room.

This is out of control. We have *to respond.*

A chair creaked. Aimes glanced down the table to see one of the musketeers stepping across the room, frowning at a large-scale map of Europe. Her finger rose to the Baltic, and she tapped the Švenčionys Region. She left her hand resting there...then slowly slid it.

Down to Vilnius. Then west.

To the Kaliningrad Oblast and the city of Chernyshevskoe, which rested on the border with Lithuania. A slow smile stretched the musketeer's face, and she turned to Aimes.

"I think I have something."

47

The White House

"I'm...not sure what you're asking me, Madam President."

The presidential sitting room was small, decorated in a twenties-noir style with framed prints of New Orleans street cars and Canal Street palms. Sometimes when Maggie sat alone with her back to the window, she would lose herself in the aroma of imported Café Du Monde chicory coffee and pretend that she was back in the Crescent City. That she wasn't snatching a few precious moments of solitude, fighting back the quakes of pain in her gut, and scrambling for answers that she didn't have.

It was a futile fantasy, always short-lived, always brought back to earth. Today in particular Maggie wasn't even alone. Her White House physician was present for Maggie's twice-weekly physicals—Dr. Sally Guidry, another Louisiana native. Maggie appreciated the doctor for that. She often wished they could spend less time discussing blood panels and more time arguing LSU football.

Today wasn't that day, and the look in Guidry's eyes wasn't what Maggie wanted to see. Her question reflected confusion, but there was no actual confusion in her face. She knew exactly what Maggie was asking.

"I have back pain, Doctor. Substantial back pain."

Guidry, fifty-something and graying, still made Maggie jealous with her healthy skin and full body. She didn't look like a walking skeleton, and she wasn't begging for a fix, either. Maggie hated herself for the position she was putting Guidry in—hated herself for needing this. For being so weak. For—

The mental tirade broke short as a fresh wave of pain pulsated from Maggie's gut.

Yes, she was legitimately in pain. She'd only lied about where the pain originated because liver pain was an indicator of the same stress that had already driven Maggie to the point of needing a transplant, and could now indicate that the transplant was failing. Guidry would demand that Maggie step back from the White House if she knew.

Maggie *couldn't* step back.

"If you're asking for painkillers..." Guidry started. Stopped. Looked at her iPad.

Maggie leaned forward, wincing a little but hiding it well—at least, she thought so. She kept her voice soft.

"Doctor?"

Guidry looked up.

"We're at war," Maggie said. "I need to do my job. Do you understand? Please *help me* do my job."

There was a lot more pleading in Maggie's voice than she was proud of. Guidry's unblinking stare told her that the doctor saw right through her—that she'd probably seen right through her for weeks. Maybe the doctor knew that Maggie had been still taking opioid painkillers long after her prescribed supply had expired. Maybe she even suspected that somebody from Maggie's inner circle—in this case, James O'Dell—was providing an illicit source.

But now that source was gone. Maggie had fought her way through nearly ten days of brutal withdrawals. She couldn't go any farther. She *needed* the relief.

"Hydrocodone?" Guidry whispered.

"Please."

Guidry swallowed. Then she nodded. She tabbed across the iPad screen and mumbled about a two week prescription. She collected her blood pressure cuff and bag and departed without looking Maggie in the eye.

The room was quiet. Maggie leaned back into the chair and breathed deep. Her gut burned as she did. Her head felt like it was floating.

But she told herself it was okay. It was all okay. She was doing what needed to be done. She would figure all this out when the crisis abated. If she could just push America through the gap...

The phone at Maggie's side rang. Her eyes blinked open, that black-and-white view of Canal Street slowly clarifying. She sat up, wiping sweat from her forehead, and looked to the door. Guidry was long gone.

The pills will be here soon.

Maggie lifted the receiver. She cleared her throat. "Yes?"

"Ma'am, I've got Director Aimes on the line for you requesting an immediate conference."

Aimes.

Maggie's heart beat a little faster as the pain faded from her mind. "Put her through."

"Madam President?" Aimes's tone was clipped with a nervous energy Maggie had seldom heard from her usually calm, cool, and collected chief of intelligence. It added a little more tension to Maggie's chest.

"Tell me something good, Sarah."

"Russia is bombing Lithuania."

Maggie's heart sank right to the floor. Her face fell and she wanted to disappear. She wanted to melt right into the chair. Instead, she simply said: "That's not good."

"No, it's not. We expected an eventual Lithuanian assault but not nearly so soon. Moscow is moving even more aggressively than we anticipated. My gut tells me they sense our weakness."

And if we don't strike back now, they'll push even harder.

Aimes didn't say that last bit—she didn't have to. Maggie knew.

"Tell me you didn't call just to fill in for my watch officer," Maggie said.

Pause.

"Regarding our...previous discussions."

Maggie knew exactly what Aimes was referencing. She straightened, a tinge of hope washing through her body.

"Yes?"

"As directed, I've been assembling options. And...we think we might have something. Russia's attack might actually be an opportunity."

Maggie squinted. "*How?*"

"Are you familiar with the Kaliningrad Oblast, ma'am?"

48

33rd Air Base
Powidz, Poland

"One, two, three, one!"

Turk's voice, strained as it was by physical exertion, still boomed across the hangar in a cadence that Reed would have recognized in his sleep.

On *one* they all went down—Reed, Turk, Wolfgang, Corbyn, and Lucy. Shaking under strained muscles, chests nearly brushing the sweat-stained concrete. At *two* they were back up, into plank position, but already headed down again for *three*, and back up for *one*.

Combined, it was a single USMC push-up—and Turk wasn't even started.

"One, two, three, two! This is what we asked for—United States Marine Corps."

Whether Wolfgang or Lucy or Corbyn appreciated the Parris Island heritage, Reed didn't know. He didn't really give himself time to wonder—none of them had time. It was seven a.m. in Poland and they had been going since just after five, led by Turk on a four-mile run before returning to the hangar for jumping jacks, crunches, lunges, and now the push-ups.

It wasn't a pretty sight. Of them all, Turk might have been in the worst physical condition, and yet he performed the best with his usual superhuman grit. Reed did the best he could, sore muscles and a pounding head fighting him through every rep. Corbyn crushed the run with ease but struggled under the body-weight exercises. Lucy was focused but slow—and Wolfgang...

The replacement prosthetic leg provided by the CIA didn't quite fit. Reed could see the agony on Wolfgang's face with every stride over packed dirt and poured concrete. For the push-ups, Turk had quietly suggested that Wolfgang drop to his knees.

That had earned Turk a withering glare, but by the fifth cycle of the USMC cadence, Reed could tell that Wolfgang was barely holding on, shifting the majority of his body weight to his good leg while his entire core shook like a tree in a hurricane.

He wasn't ready for this—none of them were. And none of them had a choice.

"One for your mother!"

Down, up. Down, up. Reed called the cadence back through gritted teeth.

"One for your brother!"

Down, up. Then a metallic snap cracked through the hangar like a gunshot, and Wolfgang went down with a slam. Everyone froze in place, then Lucy was the first to respond. She rolled to her feet and grabbed Wolfgang by the shoulder. He swore and fought to regain his footing.

But he wasn't getting up. The prosthetic leg was twisted, the composite foot turned ninety degrees. Flushed and out of breath, Wolfgang's feet were tangled and he kicked angrily, shoving when Lucy again attempted to help him.

She stepped back without comment. Nobody else moved. Wolfgang managed to sit upright and jerked his shorts leg up, wrenching on the mechanism that locked the prosthetic to his severed leg.

Then the prosthetic went flying across the hangar, and Wolfgang screamed—loud, long, guttural. It wasn't even a word. He finished and his head dropped. He panted—his eyes were closed.

Reed exchanged a look with Turk.

"Let's take five," Reed said.

Nobody argued. Water was dispensed. Reed and Turk retreated to a workbench twenty feet away littered with greasy tools belonging to the Polish Air Force.

"He can't handle this." Turk's voice was just loud enough for Reed to hear, but Reed didn't answer. He was watching his team—not just Wolfgang, but Lucy and Corbyn, also. The two women were in much better shape than Wolfgang—at least. Corbyn had finished her water and already donned fingerless fighting gloves. She was pounding on a heavy bag as though it were personally responsible for Kyle Strickland's torturous death.

Even Lucy looked dark.

"I don't need them to be okay," Reed said. "I just need them to be willing."

Before Turk could answer, a shadow fell across the open mouth of the hangar, signaling the arrival of one of the air base's many Melex electric cars—Polish golf carts, essentially. Reed's gaze snapped toward it in time to see Silas Rigby dismount. He wore slacks and a polo, removing his sunglasses as he stepped in.

His gaze went right to Wolfgang. Then Corbyn, still wailing on the heavy bag.

Then to Reed and Turk. They only drank more water as Silas approached, drawing an iPad from beneath one arm. His voice remained low.

"Everything good?"

"Perfect," Reed said. "Get a line back to the States and order Wolfgang a new prosthetic. No junk this time—I want the Lamborghini model."

Rigby shot another glance over his shoulder, then simply tilted his head toward the workbench. A shifted box of wrenches allowed room for the iPad. Rigby signed in with a thumbprint and a sixteen-digit passcode. The screen unlocked to reveal a map.

It was northern Europe.

"There's been a development," Rigby said. "Maybe nothing. Maybe an opportunity. We're still working on it. Before the ball rolls too far, we wanted your input."

Reed and Turk leaned close. Rigby zoomed on Poland...then moved north.

"It's called the Kaliningrad Oblast. It's a little like Alaska for the US—a detached but sovereign territory of Russia. Bordered on the south by Poland, and on the east by Lithuania...a NATO state."

Rigby tapped on each nation. Then he zoomed on the Kaliningrad-Lithuania border. The screen clarified around a small town, just across the river from NATO. It featured a clean grid of roads and a handful of buildings. Not much visible military infrastructure.

Fully exposed.

"Chernyshevskoe," Rigby said. "It's just across the border from the Lithuanian town of Kybartai. The river you see running between them is really more of a stream—about twenty feet wide, not very deep. But there's a ditch steep enough to block vehicles, and only three bridges providing access between the two towns. Both communities are reasonably isolated from neighboring Russian and Lithuanian municipalities, also."

Rigby zoomed out. Paused. Lowered his voice. "Supposing that we could get Nikitin there..."

He looked to Reed and lifted both eyebrows.

Reed took the iPad and studied both towns. He panned with two fingers and studied the surrounding Russian and Lithuanian landscapes.

Then he nodded. "You get him there, and this war is over."

49

The Naval Observatory
Washington, DC

The trio of cars arrived individually, and no less than ten minutes apart.

Jill Easterling was first. She drove herself—a jet-black Volkswagen sedan that matched her petite frame and subdued style perfectly. A Secret Service agent guided the car into a concealed parking place, and Easterling waited alone in a sitting room until a pair of black Cadillacs delivered two more government officials from their back seats.

Secretary of Defense Steven Kline and Secretary of State Lisa Gorman. Each were ushered in and joined Easterling. No handshakes or greetings were exchanged. They waited another three minutes, then were guided by a member of Jordan Stratton's security detail to the second floor, and into the VP's office.

The place was expansive, and reeked of cigar smoke. A broad mahogany desk stood laden with printed documents and a pair of computers—a tumbler of untouched bourbon and an ashtray still smoldering with the stub of a Cuban.

Stratton himself stood with his back to the room, facing the windows that overlooked a sprawling yard. He held his hands behind his back, clasped together. His posture was neither stiff nor relaxed. He looked pretty much exactly as composed and focused as the day that Easterling first met him, and just that thought was enough to put a lump in her throat.

How had it come to this?

Stratton turned from the window only after leaving the three of them standing for an awkward sixty seconds. He met each of their gazes, then proceeded to the head of a compact conference table without comment. They all took their seats—Stratton at the head with a fresh Cuban withdrawn from his jacket. He cut the cigar and placed it between his teeth, but didn't light it. He didn't say anything at all. He just sat, rotating the cigar with two fingers, and stared at the middle of the table.

He doesn't want this, Easterling thought. *He actually hates it.*

Maybe that made Stratton noble—his loyalty to his own president. Or maybe he just didn't want to be the first vice president in American history to exercise the powers granted to him by the 25th Amendment and forcibly remove a sitting president from office.

"Mr. Vice President."

Kline's voice was stable, maybe a touch stern. Stratton blinked but didn't look up. He simply spoke around the cigar.

"Is she better?"

There was a hint of hope in his voice that sounded sincere.

"She met with Dr. Guidry this morning," Easterling said. "Obviously I don't know what the content of their discussion was, but...the Walter Reed pharmacy dispatched a courier to the White House immediately after."

Stratton's eyes closed. He breathed deep.

"Mr. Vice President, we should all be clear." It was Kline again. "What we're meeting here to discuss can't be a half measure. Regardless of what happens next, our careers are likely over. Even if we succeed in stopping this war and restoring American security, we'll always be the cabinet that backstabbed their own president. We'll never live that down."

Easterling's gaze flicked to Kline. She narrowed her eyes. *Was he...*

Kline sat forward. "What I'm saying is that political calculous no longer factors into this decision. Not for myself—not for any of us. The only question we should consider is what is best for the country. And then, once a choice is made, we have to maintain our course no matter what happens. Fall on our swords if needs be. But we cannot hesitate, we cannot second-guess. It's all or nothing."

"I agree," Gorman said.

Stratton lowered the cigar. "If we assembled the cabinet tomorrow, how many votes would we have?"

"We need at least eight votes to declare Trousdale unfit to discharge her duties," Kline said. "Jill doesn't get a vote, so assuming Lisa and I are in agreement, we're starting with two. Attorney General Thomas has privately expressed grave concerns to me—I think he would count as three. Neither General Yellin nor National Security Advisor West can vote, but West is firmly in our camp and would help to lobby the cabinet. That influence could be significant."

"So you're telling me we've got three yeses and twelve question marks?" Stratton said.

"No, sir." Easterling rejoined the conversation. "You've got three yeses and ten question marks. Carmen Silva and Stacey Pilcher are both loyal to the president and far enough removed from the crisis in Europe to be counted as confident no votes. I don't know how hard they would lobby the undecideds, but I would be very surprised if they supported us."

Stratton's jaw tightened. He tapped one finger on the desktop.

Once again, Kline jumped in. "Sir, this isn't the Senate. We're unable to rally tentative support and sway undecideds ahead of announcing an initiative. At some point we just have to take the plunge and let the chips fall where they may."

"Are you telling me to buck up, Steven?"

"I'm telling you that Europe is *burning*. I'm telling you that the Middle East is engulfed in chaos, and Marines are dying. That the Chinese have withdrawn but only long enough to let the Russians determine our actual strength. The moment Beijing feels comfortable, they'll be back, and this time we may not be able to stop them. I'm telling you that our president is addicted to opioids, and whether by physical impairment, mental overload, or sheer incompetence, she is *not* up to the task of leading us through this fire. I'm telling you that if you don't act *now*, the blood will be every bit as much on our hands as hers."

Silence. Easterling's heart thumped. She hurt—not physically, or maybe not *just* physically. It was the ache of crushing defeat. The reality that she had failed. Somehow, some way. The train had left the tracks and the smoke was so dense that Easterling could no longer tell what had gone wrong or when.

It was carnage. It was abject collapse. It was everything she'd given her life to build snatched away in a second. A country in crisis, and the horse Easterling had bet on...flailing.

"This is your choice," Gorman said, addressing Stratton. "Now or never."

Slowly, Stratton returned the cigar to his lips. He rolled it once, then produced a torch lighter from his pocket. The flame rushed—the cigar smoldered. For two slow puffs nobody spoke, a haze of gray swirling around Stratton's head.

Then he said: "Make the preparations."

50

Vilnius, Lithuania

Dovilė Petrauskienė loved her country more than life itself.

More than her family—her husband and young son. More than her home town on the Baltic Sea. More than her career, even, remarkable though it may have been. It was love of country that drove her fresh out of college to pursue politics. She didn't want the power, and could barely stand the mudslinging war that was the election cycle. Dovilė ran because she both recognized and understood the challenges facing her beloved Lithuania, and if she wasn't willing to confront them...who was?

Her initial commitment was only to serve as a civil servant to an elected member of the *Seimas*—the Lithuanian parliament. That job was meant to last four or five years, after which Dovilė would return to her passion for visual arts and seaside sunsets.

But the *Seimo narys* she served under, as ambitious and principled as he first appeared, turned out to be completely corrupt, and it was Dovilė herself who uncovered his treachery. The people were predictably outraged—less predictably, they called for Dovilė to take his place.

So she ran. She didn't expect to win. She triumphed by a landslide. By her early thirties, Dovilė had served six years in the Seimas and was tapped by an incoming presidential administration to serve as minister of finance. Leading reforms across Lithuanian's banking sector and broader economy, Dovilė's reputation as an incorruptible voice for the people made her almost as many enemies as it made her friends.

And the momentum kept growing. She returned to the Seimas as the leader of the opposition party, and at forty-one she was elected prime minister. Her tenure was swift, loud, and effective. She championed more reforms and spearheaded a surge in GPD growth and infrastructure development. Her popularity with the people outpaced her *un*popularity with the establishment. The next thing she knew, she was running for president. She was winning again. She was taking her seat at *Prezidentūra*, the presidential palace. She was on top of her beloved world...

Then came war. Eight months after her inauguration. Two nuclear blasts and Russia steamrolling the Caucasus and then, in a heartbeat, smashing into the Baltic. Estonia fell and Latvia shuddered under Belarusian attacks.

Dovilė ordered Lithuanian Defense Forces to assist their neighbors, but as NATO stalled and leadership from across the pond failed to reinforce flailing Baltic states, Dovilė was forced to recall those troops and precious aircraft. She was forced to order her people into a state of military readiness—braced for bombs and missiles, for the incursion of ground troops. With the Kaliningrad Oblast directly to Lithuania's west, Russia was already a constant menace.

Now the threat was tangible. It was boiling straight toward Vilnius, even while the Poles and the Americans and the rest of NATO gathered troops in central Europe but refused to directly commit to a ground war against Russia.

What were they doing? Would they really leave Lithuania to wither and burn, all by herself?

Dovilė stood alone at a second-story window, overlooking the primary courtyard of the presidential palace complex. Featuring a large fountain, landscaped paths and colonnades, it wasn't as beautiful as her hometown, but somehow even more special. It was the seat of Lithuanian governance

—the hope of a proud people so recently liberated from the scourge of international dominance, and now facing that threat once more.

On the desk behind Dovilė, the stack of memos from her military and intelligence divisions described the Russian/Belarusian advance in brutal detail. They detailed the endless air raids that pounded key Lithuanian infrastructure all through the night—literally thousands of bombs and missiles, all smashing bridges and road beds, airfields and fuel depots.

The attack had just begun, and already Lithuanian was losing.

A single tear slid down Dovilė's cheek—the first she had allowed since the crisis began, and it wasn't even for herself. It was for Lithuania. For the innocent farmers caught in the crossfire. The young children who would grow up fatherless. The mothers who would scrounge through trash bins to find food for their families. The homes and communities that would be laid to waist under the wrath of the next barrage of air attacks.

Dovilė would fight straight to her own death. But she already knew, even if NATO finally responded and the full might of American and European military power rushed to their aid, Lithuania was still going to lose. They were a small dog in a giant war, and Makar Nikitin wasn't accepting anything less than total surrender.

"Madam President?"

Dovilė barely heard the soft knock that proceeded the address. She deftly thumbed her cheek to wipe the tear away, lifting her chin before turning.

"Yes, Aldona?"

"I have a call for you."

"I'm about to step into a meeting. It'll have to wait—"

"It's from President Trousdale, ma'am."

Dovilė blinked. Her heart thumped. For a brief moment the announcement caught her so much off guard that she didn't know what to say.

Then Dovilė's honed crisis response instincts kicked into gear, just like they always had. She'd been attempting to reach the White House for weeks. She'd only penetrated so far as the secretary of state.

No *way* was she missing this call.

"Seal the room," Dovilė said. "I'll take the call here."

"Yes, ma'am."

The door closed. Dovilė hurried to a desk where a ten-inch-tall figurine of Vytis—a white knight seated on a rearing horse, bearing both a sword and shield—represented the fighting spirit of the Baltic. The double cross printed on his shield was the only portion of the figurine painted.

It was gold, a symbol of pride and sovereignty and the traditional Christian faith that had drawn Lithuania out of pagan days fraught with savagery and chaos.

Days which can never return.

Dovilė breathed deep. She lifted her head, reminding herself that she was Trousdale's equal. That Lithuania needed America—she needed NATO. But she didn't have to grovel.

Dovilė lifted the receiver.

"Good morning, Madam US President."

Dovilė spoke in English. It wasn't perfect—she'd only practiced for about three years. But she wanted to meet Trousdale halfway. She *needed* to.

"Dovilė, good afternoon. I'm so sorry it's taken me this long to reach you in person. It's been...a lot happening at once."

Trousdale sounded exactly like she did on the television. Relaxed, informal, with that peculiar Louisiana swamp accent that reminded Dovilė a little of distorted French and a little of musical Polish and a lot of...she had no idea what.

Dovilė liked it, if she was being honest. She instinctually found herself wanting to trust Trousdale's transparent persona. But Dovilė had also read the many headlines about the US president, and really, did it matter if she trusted Trousdale?

It only mattered that Trousdale sent the troops.

"I appreciate your expression of support, Madam President," Dovilė said. Her words sounded stilted even in her own ears, but maybe that was the language barrier.

"Please call me Maggie," Trousdale said.

Dovilė hesitated, unsure what to say next. She wanted to dive right in to the question at hand—the question of *when* she could expect a strategic NATO response—but Trousdale had called her, not the other way around.

Maybe Dovilė should play this call from the high ground. Not appear too much the beggar that she was.

"What can I do for you, Maggie?"

The dice landed. Dovilė waited, her body as tense as the frozen posture of the Vytis. She almost immediately regretted the move.

But Trousdale remained calm as she responded—not the first hint of offense.

"I'm calling about the war, Dovilė. We're deploying additional troops to Poland as we speak. My military officials are evaluating strategies to cut Russia off before ground troops reach your borders."

It was amazing news, all of it. Dovilė wanted to breathe a sigh of relief...but she felt the punchline coming. She noted the lack of specifics in Maggie's statement—the lack of timelines.

"We'll do everything we can to protect your sovereignty," Maggie said. "The United States is committed to all our NATO allies. I've ordered additional air strikes to begin within the hour against Russian positions in Estonia."

But...

Dovilė knew it was coming. She found herself holding her breath.

"Dovilė..." Trousdale's voice softened. "We're stretched thin. It could take months to confront Russia on the ground, and maybe much longer to reverse their incursion. We're talking about years, in total. A full-scale, European ground war."

"Lithuania is not afraid," Dovilė said, her blood turning hot for the first time.

"I know. Neither are we. But..."

There it was. The line fell silent. Dovilė's heart pounded.

"I need to know if you trust me," Trousdale said at last.

Dovilė squinted. It wasn't the statement she expected. She evaluated various responses that might progress the conversation without placing herself as a vassal of Trousdale's administration.

In the end, she went for the truth. "I barely know you, Maggie."

"That's true. And I barely know you, which makes what I'm about to say extremely dangerous. If you choose to reject my request and disclose my strategy, I can't stop you. It will cost America dearly. It will cost the world just as much. But honestly, I would understand."

Dovilė squinted. She leaned closer to the desk.

"Madam President...*what* are you asking me?"

Another long pause. Then:

"I'm asking you for a favor, Dovilė. The scariest thing you've ever been asked to do by anyone. But if you do it, and if it works...it might just save your country."

51

Moscow, Russia

Ivan's latest meeting with Natasha Kirov wasn't a meeting at all, but a *brush pass.*

He brushed past her in a crowded subway station, and she passed him a wadded-up gum wrapper, all without either of them making eye contact. Then Kirov boarded the next train and Ivan climbed back to street level. He walked two kilometers, using passing windows and the side-view mirrors on cars to monitor the sidewalks behind him and check for tails before he at last ducked into a tea shop. He ordered black tea to go, no sugar, then slipped into the restroom while it was steeped.

Only then did he unwad the gum wrapper, reading the message written in tight Cyrillic. Two lines, only five words. Ivan's body rushed with adrenaline and he wadded up the paper once more. He dropped it into the toilet and flushed. He took his tea and took his time winding across the city, south of Red Square and the Moskva River, deeper inside the Zamoskvorechye District.

This was old Moscow—the seat of governmental power, and a region often used for the construction of state government buildings. Many of those buildings dated back to the Soviet era, and many more were now abandoned or only partially occupied.

Ivan selected a records building constructed in the nineteen thirties which had once been used by the KGB to house files on "enemies of the state"...which was kind of the same thing as enemies of the party, or enemies of Stalin, or anybody who didn't fall into line. Present use of the building included the housing of federal records and some ancillary government offices—the kind of places where a prime minister was unlikely to visit but wouldn't raise too many eyebrows if he did.

The building was large. Ivan knew firsthand that only about sixty percent of it was occupied, the rest abandoned in dusty ruin. He slipped inside without drawing attention and found his way down a darkened corridor to a room barely large enough for the metal desk it held.

There were still Soviet posters on the walls. Propaganda against the West, and propaganda in favor of the revolution. Ivan ignored it all as he settled onto the desk's edge and sipped his tea for twenty-four minutes. Then Maxim Romanov arrived, alone and a little out of breath, casting a glance over his shoulder as he eased the door closed.

He sneezed on the dust. Ivan gave the disgruntled PM time to collect himself.

"I only have a few minutes," Romanov said. "What couldn't wait?"

"It's done," Ivan said. "The Americans found a way."

Romanov squinted. "What?"

Ivan sipped tea.

"What do you *mean*, 'found a way'? He's not leaving Moscow!"

"He'll leave Moscow for this."

"For *what?*"

Ivan straightened from the table. His voice softened to barely a whisper.

"Kaliningrad, Maxim. Chernyshevskoe."

"Chernyshevskoe?" Maxim shook his head. "Why on earth would Makar go *there*?"

Ivan didn't answer. He just lifted both eyebrows. Romanov's mouth hung open...then his eyes widened.

"No."

"Yes."

"And Lithuania will *do that*?"

"That's America's problem. Our problem is to make sure Nikitin takes the bait."

"You want me to suggest it?"

"Certainly not. I want you to oppose it. I want you to volunteer to travel in his stead."

Romanov's mouth closed. Ivan could actually see the wheels spinning behind his eyes. The debate, the evaluation.

And then the conclusion.

"That just might work," Romanov said.

"It will," Ivan said. "And your job, Maxim, is to be *ready when it does*."

52

The West Wing
The White House

Easterling returned to the White House following her morning meeting at the Naval Observatory and didn't so much as glance at Gorman as the two passed each other in the lobby.

Gorman didn't glance her way either. She was stiff, strained. Appeared exhausted...and Easterling knew what she was thinking. The same thing Easterling was thinking.

Are we really going to do this?

Easterling reached her office and ignored a barrage of questions from aides. She shut the door and flicked the lock—something she never remembered doing. With the lights off she settled behind her computer. She breathed deep, eyes burning, and looked to a scratch pad list of fifteen names.

The chief members of Maggie's cabinet—votes to be swayed just like members of Congress. Except this time...

Easterling's phone buzzed. It was one of her deputies calling. She almost ignored it, but also wanted the distraction. She slapped the answer button.

"What?"

"Sorry to disturb you, ma'am. I just wanted to remind you that James O'Dell is set to testify before the special Senate committee in fifteen minutes. He's arriving at the Capitol now."

Easterling's gaze flicked to the wall-mounted TV. For once, it was switched off. A quick application of her remote called up CNN. The broadcast was predictable—a black Chevrolet Suburban rolling up at the Capitol steps, James O'Dell stepping out dressed in a full business suit and handcuffs. He was escorted by two federal marshals who held him by the elbows. He was marched up the steps under the blink of a hundred news camera flashbulbs like a man advancing to the gallows.

Theater. It was pure, perfect theater. The kind only a conniving political genius like Matthew Roper could orchestrate, but *wow*, what a job this was. Easterling couldn't deny it. She didn't even bother switching to the other major news outlets—they would all be carrying the same feed. The eyes of the nation would be fixated on it.

"Keep me posted," Easterling said.

"You're not…going to watch?"

"It's a circus, Kelcey. Dancing monkeys and elephants on tightropes. We have a government to run."

Easterling reached for the button to hang up. Her deputy caught her at the last moment.

"Ma'am, one other thing."

"*What?*"

"President Trousdale."

"What about her?"

"Nobody can find her. She hasn't reported to the Oval all day."

"She's sick?"

"We don't know. I thought maybe you had spoken to her…"

Easterling hadn't, not since departing Air Force One the day prior. Something about Maggie's absence felt wrong—a cold chill rippled up Easterling's spine.

She shelved the feeling. She had work to do, and if Maggie wasn't in the West Wing, well. That made things easier.

"Handle your schedule, Kelcey."

Easterling hung up. She ran both hands over her face, then scanned the list again. She settled on a name near the bottom—not a prominent member of the cabinet, but Easterling's gut told her that the secretary of Homeland Security might be a yes vote. Maybe.

She lifted her phone and dialed just as the TV on the wall displayed James O'Dell stepping into the United States Senate.

53

The United States Senate
Capitol Hill, Washington, DC

"This special hearing of the Senate Select Committee on Presidential Conduct will now come to order."

Matthew Roper's voice boomed against marble walls, his seat on an elevated platform making O'Dell feel like he was being overlooked by a judge in federal court.

In many ways, the simile was accurate. O'Dell's hands were still cuffed, one federal marshal sitting to his left while another stood directly behind, and his attorney sat at his right. There was a pitcher of water at hand. A microphone on a flexible boom that stretched to O'Dell's lips. An auditorium full of civilian witnesses and press.

Everything O'Dell had hoped for.

"This committee has been assembled on behalf of the People of the United States of America to evaluate claims of gross misconduct, high crimes, and misdemeanors on the part of the Trousdale Administration, possibly to include President Margaret Louise Trousdale herself."

The pomp and circumstance in Roper's voice was overbearing, a smug smirk only barely concealed on his lips. O'Dell sat, unblinking, as Roper droned on for the benefit of the press and the cameras, using a lot of large and fancy words but saying very little.

Hinting. Baiting. Whetting their appetite but never delivering a true, juicy slice. He was a master showman.

"Mr. James O'Dell of Louisiana, longtime bodyguard and personal attaché of the president, is called as our first witness. Mr. O'Dell, please rise and raise your right hand to receive your oath."

O'Dell rose. He had to lift his left hand along with his right, but his voice was clear and strong as he swore to speak the truth, the whole truth, and nothing but the truth—so help him God.

"Thank you, Mr. O'Dell. Please be seated. And can somebody kindly remove those cuffs? Mr. O'Dell is no threat to any person in this room."

The faux generosity in Roper's tone didn't fool O'Dell for a moment. He knew Roper had deliberately waited to make the request, ensuring that every camera in the room focused on those cuffs while he took the oath.

Just another splash of drama in a stew already boiling with tantalizing flavor.

"Mr. O'Dell, before this committee commences with questioning, do you wish to offer an opening statement?"

O'Dell didn't answer. Didn't so much as blink. Roper waited, and a flash of confusion crossed his face. His eyebrows dipped, just a fraction of an inch.

But enough to show his hand. O'Dell kept staring.

"Mr. O'Dell, I would remind you that you are present for this hearing by your own volition, under no pressure of this body or any other. As such, it is reasonable to expect that you answer our questions."

O'Dell still didn't answer. Now the frustration flickering behind Roper's eyes passed a shade closer to anger. He cleared his throat and shifted a stack of papers on his desk, then slurped water.

"Very well. As the witness has refused to accept an opportunity for an opening statement, we will proceed. As chairman of this committee, I recognize myself to begin questioning."

More shuffling of papers. Roper cleared his throat again. He was stringing the audience along—more baiting. More luring. But O'Dell knew what was coming, because all of this was rehearsed. O'Dell had broken from the agreed script, not by declining to make an opening statement but by refusing to speak at all.

Now it was Roper's turn to drop the atom bomb.

"Mr. O'Dell. Isn't it true that you murdered Jacob Grover of Washington, DC, under direction of President Trousdale's administration, for the express purpose of securing her a donor liver to save her life?"

A gasp exploded through the crowd. Instant murmurs from the spectators and C-SPAN cameras zooming on O'Dell's face. Roper would have been justified to call for order, but he didn't. He *wanted* the shock wave. He'd waited months for this, O'Dell knew that. Looking into the senator's face, O'Dell could tell that Roper was fighting not to laugh.

"Isn't that true, Mr. O'Dell?"

O'Dell said nothing. He didn't twitch under pressure. He just stared, and he thought of Maggie. The swamp girl who ran an opposition campaign for governor—a once in a million shot-in-the-dark pitch to reverse decades of Baton Rouge corruption. A race nobody expected to be victorious, but Maggie *just kept winning*.

Debates and town halls. Speeches and interviews. Gaining momentum by degrees until she took the oath. She pledged to fight for the little man, the lost and forgotten. People like O'Dell's own family. He'd met her after she was sworn in—O'Dell himself had sworn to protect her with his own life, his own body and breath. Not just because the promise came with a paycheck, but because James O'Dell *believed*.

From Baton Rouge to the Naval Observatory and then the Oval Office. He'd always believed. He'd always loved.

And now he sat in the Senate, and he *said nothing*.

"Mr. O'Dell." The first hint of unchecked frustration entered Roper's tone. He leaned forward. "I would remind you again that you are *here voluntarily*, and should answer my question. Isn't it true that you killed James Grover on behalf of President Trousdale?"

Still, O'Dell said nothing. The murmurs and shuffling continued. Reporters were texting and whispering into each other's ears. Roper's face reddened.

"Mr. O'Dell, isn't it true that two days ago while agreeing to this hearing, you stated privately that you had indeed killed Jacob Grover on the president's behalf? Isn't that *true*, Mr. O'Dell?"

Still, O'Dell didn't answer. The current of crimson rising up Roper's neck turned maroon. His jaw tightened. His lips opened.

Then, finally, O'Dell spoke.

"You want to know what's true, Senator?"

In a moment the room fell silent. All eyes swiveled to the witness. All cameras steadied and phones lowered. O'Dell leaned toward the mic.

"I can tell you what's true."

Another long pause—now it was O'Dell's turn to bait the audience. To draw this out. Hadn't he learned from the best?

"It's true that I'm looking at an American traitor," O'Dell snarled.

Another gasp from the crowd, but O'Dell wasn't done. He hadn't even started. He had rehearsed this speech in prison for hours, refining and adjusting every word, every inflection. He was ready to dive for the killing stroke.

"I'm looking at a panel of pork-bellied, backstabbing liars who have sold out their president because they sold out the American people *decades* ago, and Margaret Louise Trousdale is the friend and champion of those people. I'm looking at cowards who wouldn't know justice from genocide, and are happy to endorse either to win the next election. I'm looking at so-called leaders who couldn't lead a fish to water. I'm looking at—"

"*Mr. O'Dell!*" Roper shouted. "You are out of order, sir!"

O'Dell exploded out of his chair, abandoning the mic and allowing his natural voice to boom across the room. "I may be out of order, Senator, but I am not finished—I'm not even close to being finished. You want to know the truth? I killed Jacob Grover. I did it for the president, without her knowledge and without her consent. I did it because unlike the slithering slime in this room, I'm not afraid to make hard choices and put my own neck on the line on behalf of this country. Maggie Trousdale is the *people's president*. They elected her. I swore to protect her—"

"*Mr. O'Dell!*"

"I'd do it again if I had to. Jacob Grover was a child predator and a sorry excuse for humanity. Maggie Trousdale is a hero—a woman who took a bullet for her country. A lover of freedom, a champion of the forgotten, a heroine of America's darkest hours—"

"*Sergeant at arms!*" Roper bellowed, rising out of his own seat. "Detain the witness and remove him from this chamber!"

Everyone was on their feet. The rush of voices drowned out the slam of O'Dell's body against the desk as the marshals yanked his hands behind his back. In a moment he was cuffed again and being dragged out, but O'Dell didn't care. He was actually smiling, looking dead into Roper's eyes.

He was going to prison. He would never see freedom again. But it was *worth it*.

"This committee will come to order!" Roper shouted. "The press and audience will take their seats, or the sergeant at arms will have them removed. *Come to order!*"

Roper kept shouting, but nobody was listening. As the marshals led O'Dell out, he suddenly noticed that nobody was looking at him, either. Nobody was snapping photos. Nobody seemed to care about the hearing at all. Every face was directed at a phone, fresh murmurs of shock and horror preceding a tidal wave headed for the exit doors.

O'Dell's body tensed. He felt the shift in the room, and his dark eyes swept the crowd. He caught the face of a smartphone screen just before its owner switched the device off—O'Dell read the headline printed there.

PRESIDENT OF LITHUANIA ANNOUNCES SURRENDER TO RUSSIA.

54

The White House

Maggie sat alone, the doors of her sitting room closed, the volume on her TV turned down low as Matt Roper's special hearing unfolded in the high drama style of a soap opera.

O'Dell was sworn in. He was seated. Roper began with the questions and Maggie watched in silence, ready for anything. Expecting that O'Dell would likely cave—and could she blame him? Hadn't she demanded *so much* of her oldest friend? A man who'd given his life to her cause and had been used and abused more often than not.

But O'Dell didn't speak. He sat stone-faced while Roper slowly lost his cool. The questions came louder, harsher. More demanding.

Then O'Dell leaned toward the mic...his voice soft at first, then also growing louder. Filling the chamber and booming from the TV speakers. He exploded out of his chair. He jabbed a finger at Roper, and didn't stop. He careened like a freight train smashing right through the United States Capitol.

And Maggie cried. She couldn't help it. The hint of a smile curled her lips and she shook her head, barely believing what she was hearing. A warmth started in her stomach and carried through her chest, and it wasn't the result of the opioid painkillers that had *finally* calmed her body.

This was deeper. It meant so much more.

O'Dell was halfway out of the room before the broadcast abruptly switched. "BREAKING NEWS" flashed across the screen, then an anchor appeared alongside a photograph of Dovilė Petrauskienė, President of Lithuania.

"From our correspondents in Vilnius, we've just learned that President Petrauskienė has asked Moscow for terms of immediate surrender."

The smile faded from Maggie's face. The warmth left her body, a cold chill taking its place. She watched the broadcast for two minutes, photos of Petrauskienė displayed alongside a printed statement announcing her desire to preserve Lithuanian life and property from certain destruction.

"A stark and shocking condemnation of NATO," the anchor declared.

If only you knew.

Maggie lifted her phone. She reached her secretary and named the person she wanted to speak to. One ring, then Director Aimes picked up.

"Ma'am?"

"The ball's in your court, Sarah. Let's get it done."

55

Moscow, Russia

Makar Nikitin was beside himself—Romanov had never seen the man this way.

News of the Lithuanian president's declaration reached the Kremlin just as Romanov returned from an early dinner. Even before he knew for sure what was happening, he could feel the buzz in the air. The raw elation. Pushing his way into Nikitin's private offices, Romanov found the president, half a dozen aides, and—of course—Anton Golubev, all crowded around a Russian news media broadcast.

Photographs of Dovilė Petrauskienė filled the screen along with Cyrillic copies of her statements. "Lithuania is a peaceful country and does not wish to risk any further bloodshed. I hope to speak directly to the government in Moscow to discuss terms of mutual cooperation."

Translation? *Surrender.*

"It's unbelievable," Nikitin hissed, his body fairly trembling with delight. "She's turning on all of NATO!"

Romanov's own blood pressure was up, although for a very different reason. He was sweating—his hands felt cold. His gaze swept across the room, searching to see if anyone was watching him.

All eyes were on the TV. The aides looked as thrilled as their president. Golubev, in typical style, appeared slightly suspicious of the news out of Lithuania.

But what was he going to say? The bait was there, like a raw slab of beef hung before a starving lion. How could anyone resist?

"Mr. President?" Another aide stuck his head into the room. "I have the Lithuanian foreign ministry on the line. They are requesting an immediate cease-fire and a meeting on the ground with a Russian delegation."

Nikitin's head snapped toward the door. His tongue, long and darting, actually swept his lips. He *looked* like the lion salivating before that hunk of beef. He looked ravenous.

"Put them on hold," Nikitin said. "All of you, clear the room!"

The aides hurried out. Romanov and Golubev, already knowing themselves to not be included with "all of you," remained behind. Nikitin turned back to the screen and Romanov saw the wheels spinning behind his eyes.

"This doesn't feel right," Golubev said. "Only two days ago Petrauskienė promised to fight to the last man. Now she wants to surrender?"

Romanov's mind tensed, but he was smart enough not to contradict Nikitin's right-hand man. He waited instead, leaving room for Nikitin to take the first step.

"It's Washington," Nikitin said. "They are weaker than we supposed. NATO isn't committed to defending the Baltic—Petrauskienė knows this. She fears total war."

Golubev shook his head, still not buying it but also not voicing further disagreement. Nikitin was still thinking, a slow smile stretching his face. Romanov could almost *see* his mind fixating on that side of beef. Being consumed by it.

"We'll hold all the Baltic by the end of the month," Nikitin said. "With Lithuania fallen, we'll consolidate our forces against Poland before the first snowfall. The momentum will be on our side."

Golubev was still shaking his head. "It's too simple, Makar. Too easy."

"Was Georgia too easy?" Nikitin barked with sudden, unexpected aggression, turning on Golubev. "Was Armenia? Was Azerbaijan? I am not my predecessor, Anton! We've planned this for years. Why do you inspect the teeth of a gift horse?"

Golubev stared, motionless, an didn't immediately respond. Romanov felt the break in the conversation, and remembered Ivan's words.

Resist him.

This was the moment.

"I agree with Anton, Mr. President," Romanov said. "It feels too easy. I recommend caution—"

"*Caution?*" Nikitin fairly bellowed. "Did caution win the revolution, Maxim? Did caution drive the Nazis out of Stalingrad? Did it put Sputnik in space? I'll tell you what caution did, Mr. Prime Minister. Caution brought us *perestroika*. It broke the Soviet Union and gave a foothold to the West. It lost Afghanistan and it snared us in Ukraine. Fools advise caution —champions seize the moment."

It was there—right in Nikitin's eyes. The wild craze. The bloodlust. Everything Ivan had predicted and Romanov had hoped for. All that was missing was the nail in the coffin, and before Golubev could interject, Romanov swung the hammer.

"At least let me go, Mr. President. Let *me* meet with the Lithuanians. We can pick neutral ground. Someplace on the Lithuanian/Oblast border... Chernyshevskoe, for instance. We can keep it quiet, keep you protected in Moscow—"

"*Silence*," Nikitin snapped. "Enough sniveling, Maxim. You will not steal this moment. I have led the Russian people to victory over NATO—*I* will be the one to accept Lithuania's surrender. *In person*, before the world. That decision is final. Do you understand?"

Romanov stood with his mouth open, heart still pounding. Slowly, he closed it. He never nodded or said a thing. Beyond Nikitin, Golubev didn't speak either. The Russian president looked back to the screen, and that crazed light returned to his eyes. He swept away toward his office. Golubev exchanged one angry glance with Romanov, then stormed out the other way.

In a moment, the Russian prime minister was alone. He was sweating hard, his chest throbbing. And he was headed out of the building.

Headed to pass one final message to Ivan Sidorov and the Americans.

56

33rd Air Base
Powidz, Poland

"It's confirmed. The place is Chernyshevskoe, in the Kaliningrad Oblast."

The Prosecution Force joined Silas Rigby in a windowless meeting room off the same hangar that they had trained in for the past few days. The room was dark, with a locked door and towels stuffed at its base to mute any sound leak. Rigby's voice was low as he stood in a shadowy corner, a projector screen displaying a map of northern Europe.

The point of focus was the border between Lithuania and the Kaliningrad Oblast, a Russian federal holding.

"It's a town of somewhere between five hundred and a thousand residents—little more than a settlement, really. Situated along the A229 highway, Chernyshevskoe mirrors the Lithuanian town of Kybartai, which is only slightly larger at under five thousand residents. In short"—Rigby turned from the projector screen—"this is an isolated place. Low volumes of civilians and minimal military presence. The border is fortified but not significantly so. Russian President Makar Nikitin is expected to land it Khrabrovo Airport and take a helicopter to Chernyshevskoe, while

Lithuanian President Petrauskienė will be waiting in Kybartai. We expect Nikitin to make Petrauskienė cross the river."

"So we don't have a target building?" Wolfgang said. "We don't even know for sure where Nikitin will be?"

Rigby cleared his throat. "Uh, no. Not at this time."

Wolfgang swore. Corbyn crunched potato chips and tossed the bag.

"Help me out here, brainbox. If we know what city he's going to be in, and it's only a stone's throw away from Poland, why don't we just bomb it to ash the moment he lands? Tell the old girl from Lithuania to stay at home and burn this man alive. Drop a nuke on his head, for all I care. One big beautiful mushroom cloud and call it a day."

Silence. Reed swept each face, knowing that they were all wondering the same thing. For his part, Reed already knew the answer, and figured they would all reach it in time.

He was right. Turk was the first to speak up.

"Because then everyone knows that America was responsible. Then 144 million Russians, pro-Nikitin or otherwise, are confronted with the reality of their own president being murdered by a foreign power. That will leave the Nikitin opposition without any legitimacy to seize control and end the war. The radicals will frame them as American puppets—and the war will only escalate."

"That's correct," Rigby said. "For this to have even a prayer of working, we need to remove Nikitin without any direct fingerprints connecting America *or* the Russian opposition to the assassination. It has to look like an anonymous third party just appeared out of nowhere, eliminated Nikitin, and then vanished just as quickly."

Wolfgang snorted. "You actually expect anyone to believe that?"

"It won't matter what they believe," Reed said. "It will only matter what they can *prove*. Uncertainty breeds fear, and with Nikitin dead, Russia will run wild with fear. That's a good thing. It will hand the opposition a brief window of opportunity to seize control and pitch the Russian people with a narrative of security. Of backing out of the war and returning to normal life. They'll have to pretend to be outraged at Nikitin's death, but with no certain knowledge of who to blame, that fire will die out, and the conflict can wither on the vine."

Rigby nodded. "Exactly. It's all a balancing act—a diplomatic tightrope maneuver."

This time it was Corbyn's turn to laugh. She sat with her arms folded and shook her head.

"You want us to bump off the second-most powerful man in the world…and you're calling that a *diplomatic maneuver*."

"You got a better idea?"

"Sure. How about *operation suicide*?"

Silence. Wolfgang shifted in his seat, grimacing as he adjusted his stump of a leg. Finally, it was Turk who spoke—not without a hint of irony in his voice.

"I mean, it's got a nice ring to it."

Corbyn laughed again, sounding a little maniacal. Reed looked down the line of his battered team and saw insanity in their eyes. A little blood thirst, a lot of battle rage. Some calm focus, in Lucy's case.

But not one trace of fear or resistance. They were shaken, but there was no better team on earth to attempt this.

Reed turned back to Rigby. "Let's say, just for kicks, that Nikitin shows up in this little Russian town whose name we've already forgotten. Let's say he's in an armored car with two hundred of his best bodyguards and Russian fighter jets streaking overhead—Russian attack helicopters on standby, and maybe some tanks too, because why not? Let's say it all works out exactly like you hope, and there we are standing at the Lithuanian border like the last five honest gunslingers in the Old West. Let's even say that we're not worried about coming out alive—that this really is a suicide mission. Just *how* do you expect us to have a shot?"

Rigby's gaze dropped. He lifted a coffee mug, drank a slow sip, then cleared his throat.

"Well, Mr. Montgomery. That's your problem. But I do have one piece of good news for you."

Reed lifted both eyebrows in mock anticipation. "Do tell."

"The full resources of the United States military stand at your back. I've been instructed to offer you anything short of a nuclear warhead. Consider this an all-expenses-paid trip to the Baltic—you've got a black credit card to the Pentagon, and nobody's double-checking the bill."

Reed looked down the line of faces one more time and made eye contact with each one. Measured their gazes—waited for questions or objections. Gave each of them an unspoken opportunity to back out.

No shame. No resistance.

But nobody did. Reed addressed Rigby.

"Done."

57

Langley, Virginia

The latest encrypted report from Poland didn't put a smile on Sarah Aimes's face—it didn't even relieve the tension in her chest. If anything, it only increased it, because with every grinding step of this insane charade, the world drew closer to a resolution...or the abyss.

And there was less and less likely wiggle room between the two.

Aimes confirmed Rigby's message but didn't otherwise reply. Already she was on her feet and stepping to the conference table where the three musketeers had assembled—those trusted members of the Agency who were in the know about what would happen next. Aimes stood at the head of the table and crossed her arms, staring at the circled point on a digital map.

Chernyshevskoe, with the Lithuanian town of Kybartai just across the stream. A random spot on the map that just might be the most important place in world history.

"Okay," she said. "Here's what we're gonna do."

58

Vilnius, Lithuania

Dovilė Petrauskienė expected outrage. She expected resistance—widespread protests, maybe even calls for her ouster as president. She expected the Lithuanian people to be hurt, maybe to feel betrayed. Wouldn't she, if she were in their shoes?

Whatever she expected, the sheer passion of the backlash following Dovilė's statement of intended negotiations—*surrender*, really—came faster and harder than even she was prepared for. The Lithuanian people, literally overnight, rose as one unit to resist her decision. To voice their outrage, their humiliation, their *refusal* to suffer the degradation of defeat.

They wanted war. They *wanted* the fight. It actually warmed Dovilė's soul to stand at the presidential palace window and hear the ferocious chants just outside. It made her prouder than ever to be Lithuanian—to be the leader of this great people. It made her ache to know that 2.8 million citizens who so recently trusted her so deeply now believed her to be a traitor.

But despite all those conflicting emotions, Dovilė didn't stray from her adopted course—not for a second. Because the plan that Maggie Trousdale had sold her on was insane, yes. Pure madness. Maybe just crazy enough to save the lives of tens, even hundreds of thousands of her people.

And if not? Well. The Lithuanian people would still have their war with Russia. What was the difference?

The door opened and the clicking footsteps of Dovilė's chief of Presidential Administration—roughly equivalent to Trousdale's chief of staff—rang over the marble floors. Dovilė recognized the sound without needing to turn. She could sense the tension in those steps, the pending confrontation.

The door closed but Dovilė didn't turn from the window. She was watching a swarm of protestors waving homemade signs...and smiling sadly.

"We just heard from Moscow." The voice was subdued, a little shaky—but not with sadness like Dovilė felt. This sounded more like anger.

"We have a timeline for the meeting?" Dovilė asked.

"Yes. Nikitin will arrive in Kaliningrad tomorrow afternoon. They want to hold the meeting on their side of the border...They want you to cross the river."

Of course they do.

Dovilė had expected nothing less, as had Trousdale and the Americans. Dovilė wasn't sure exactly what American preparations were underway to confront Nikitin in the Kaliningrad Oblast—Trousdale had been deliberately vague, and perhaps that was for the best. Dovilė would need to claim ignorance later. Shock and surprise, maybe even expressed sympathy for the Russian people...right before she pivoted hard back into the waiting arms of NATO and the American super-army building in Poland.

Whatever the case, if all went well, Dovilė herself would never need to cross that border. She could remain semi-safe on the Lithuanian side while the fireworks detonated...not that she would hesitate for a moment to throw her life away in the service of Tėvynė—her homeland.

"Dovilė."

The chief of Presidential Administration addressed her boss by her given name, and that wasn't unusual. Many of Dovilė's staff were informal with her behind closed doors. Dovilė encouraged it. She appreciated an openly communicative environment.

Now the tone in her chief's voice tore at Dovilė's heart. She turned, finding the tall but thin woman dressed in a conservative gray suit standing just a meter away.

"What are you doing?" the chief whispered.

Each word was like a needle straight through Dovilė's chest, but she didn't show it. She didn't falter for an instant.

"Do you trust me?" Dovilė whispered.

The chief blinked. Swallowed. But eventually nodded.

"You know that I do."

"So believe me when I tell you—everything I do, everything I am, is all for Lithuania."

The confusion was still there. The alarm, the hurt, the anger. But the chief didn't say anything more in objection.

"Call the Air Force and have them prepare a plane for my trip to Kybartai," Dovilė said.

"You won't take a car?"

It was a logical question. The trip was under three hundred kilometers, and the highway route was direct. Lithuania did not maintain any helicopters for executive travel, but Dovilė's armored BMW 7-Series was very comfortable.

She turned back to the window, and as soon as her face was safely concealed from her chief, the sad smile returned to her lips. She looked to the protestors, already doubled in number from an hour prior. Not just young students but old men and middle-aged mothers also. Children. Working class and white collar.

One young man wore a Lithuanian flag wrapped over his shoulders, lifting a sign that read: *RUSSIAN BY BLOOD, LITHUANIAN BY HEART. NEVER, EVER SURRENDER.*

"They will block the roads," Dovilė said, and there was pride in her voice.

59

The Situation Room
The White House

It was the first time Maggie had ever been alone in the SitRoom.

Seated in her usual chair at the head of the table, facing a screen that was now blank but had so often displayed so many high-stakes operations that Maggie had long ago lost count, she couldn't help but think back over the last three years.

And *wow*—had it only been three years? It felt like a lifetime ago that she first arrived at Camp David to meet the then-president, William Brandt. His offer for Maggie to assume the vacant vice presidency was the career jump of a lifetime. An unthinkable opportunity, a remarkable personal accomplishment.

But then Turkey. Then Air Force One was down—then Maggie became president herself, and the three years that followed involved so many late nights and early mornings spent in this same room that they all blended together.

North Korea. Venezuela. Terrorist strikes in the heart of America. A nuclear blast in Panama, then Azerbaijan. A lot of political conflict sprinkled in between, and numerous weeks fighting for her life in various stages of recovery from the assassin's bullet that should have killed her.

Now this. The final stage. Was it really the final stage?

Behind Maggie, a door opened, and heavy footfalls marched in. General John David Yellin, chairman of the Joint Chiefs, made it only two strides inside before stopping cold.

Maybe because he expected to see a full cabinet. Maybe because he was already in the dark about why this meeting was even called, and the shocking silence and near emptiness of the cabinet room threw gasoline on the fires of confusion.

Maybe because he was angry—deeply, fiercely. Burning up inside. Maggie had seen it in his eyes for weeks, and she understood. She even respected him for it.

What warrior in his right mind could tolerate watching the world burn while his boss repeatedly ordered him to stand down? To wait. To trust her.

Yellin had reached his limit—Maggie knew that. Now it was time to put all her cards on the table.

"Hello, John," Maggie said, still staring at the blank screen. "Would you shut the door?"

A long moment passed. Yellin never answered—but he did close the door. Slowly he advanced across the room and tugged back a chair directly across from Maggie. He sat, and she turned to face him.

The weathered general wore a button-down shirt with a West Point logo embroidered on the chest. No uniform, no tie. This was his off-duty wardrobe—it seemed he was finally taking a breather.

And yet Maggie had never seen the general look angrier. Stiff-backed and glaring, he appeared ready to explode.

"I won't apologize for calling you here this way," Maggie said. "I doubt you'd accept the apology, and frankly, I wouldn't blame you."

Yellin's jaw locked. He was otherwise as still as a statue.

"I want you to know how much I appreciate your service—from day one, through every crisis, your leadership and dedication—"

"If you're going to *fire me*," Yellin growled, "have the courage to hit me between the eyes."

Maggie squinted, genuinely confused...then just as quickly, understanding. She shook her head, sitting up and placing both hands on the table.

"I'm not going to fire you, John. I asked you here to apologize for something else—for keeping you in the dark."

Yellin blinked. His brow wrinkled, just a little. He still didn't speak.

Reaching into the chair next to her, Maggie produced an iPad and input a code. She sat with the screen facing her, looking over its top to Yellin.

"This past week an operation commenced which I have not disclosed to the Pentagon. In fact, I've not disclosed it to anyone. Only the CIA is aware, and I can understand how angry that must make you. Hopefully, when you see what's involved...you'll understand."

Yellin didn't respond, but Maggie noted a spike in his emotional temperature. She passed him the iPad without a word and the general took it. He held her gaze a moment longer.

Then he read. And read. One finger sliding, his brow still wrinkled in a glare, then gradually loosening. His mouth falling open, just half an inch. He scanned through a document that included everything Maggie wanted him to know.

The CIA war game reports. Their theory on regime change. The communications with assets in Moscow who advised on the status of anti-Nikitin politicians inside of Moscow. The details of the orchestrated surrender setup with Dovilė Petrauskienė.

And, finally, the position of the Prosecution Force. Training and planning. Ready to go into action.

Yellin finished and he looked up. The iPad fell from his fingers to the table. For a long moment Maggie couldn't tell if he was about to scream or simply stand and walk out of the room.

She was risking everything in this moment. Maggie might be Yellin's boss, but the truth was that she couldn't proceed with this operation without his support. If he wanted to sabotage it, to cancel it, to disclose it for the world to see...she couldn't stop him.

She needed him to *believe*.

"You've manipulated a sovereign state into feigning a surrender in order to lure the Russian president into an assassination attempt?" Yellin said finally.

Maggie evaluated her answer, taking her time. She wanted to say that she was returning the favor, because she still believed that Nikitin had a direct hand in her own attempted assassination.

But this wasn't about her. This wasn't personal. This was about the life and death of millions—nothing less.

"Yes," Maggie said. "That's exactly what I've done."

Yellin's face dropped back to the iPad screen. He shook his head in disbelief, and Maggie still couldn't read him. She decided to risk a push.

"Our troops have massed in Poland in case it doesn't work," she said. "The worst-case scenario is that we're still at war...in which case, I promise you, if I'm still president, I will take you completely off the leash."

"If you're still president?" Yellin repeated.

Maggie didn't explain. She didn't need to. They both knew how many ways this could backfire—at least half of them included a mushroom cloud.

But also, this operation might just save the world.

Once more Yellin looked to the iPad. He rubbed his face and studied, and Maggie thought she saw wheels turning. Gears spinning. Calculations and war plans, all blending together.

Finally: "You really think you can lure him into a trap?"

"He's already on his way."

"And Montgomery?"

"Banged up," Maggie admitted. "But he's never failed us before. He'll just need backup once the smoke clears—Lithuania will need backup. Fast and overwhelming...heroes raining from the skies."

Yellin's gaze snapped up once more, and this time Maggie knew exactly what she saw. It was fire—the blazing war spirit of a man who had dedicated his life to the battlefield, and now saw his enemy stepping into a field of crossfire, only moments from being eviscerated.

A war dog, with the scent of the battle flooding his nostrils.

"That, ma'am," Yellin said, "I can handle."

60

33rd Air Base
Powidz, Poland

Silas Rigby was as good as his word. The list Reed handed him was long and demanding, and Rigby didn't so much as blink an eye. Within hours, the equipment began arriving at the hangar in nondescript olive-drab boxes.

Small arms. Communications gear. Shoulder-fired ordnance. A *lot* of explosives. Every bit of the gear was American-sourced but Silas tasked two bearded guys who didn't wear uniforms with scrubbing serial numbers and labeling from each item.

Like Rigby, they didn't ask questions, even though Reed could tell that they desperately wanted to. They completed the work while Reed and Turk met at a table spread with tablet computers and detailed maps of the Kaliningrad-Lithuanian border. The rest of the team was scattered around the hangar eating the dinner that Rigby himself carted in. It was always Rigby who supplied the food, a measure of operational security that Rigby himself had imposed.

Each time the deputy director arrived, Corbyn tacked on another zero to her "suicide fee." The total had reached seven digits and Rigby had only said "sure thing" each time.

Maybe because he knew Corbyn wasn't serious—or maybe because he knew a dead woman wouldn't collect.

The brunt of the tactical planning fell on Reed's and Turk's shoulders. They were the only two with city-wrecking experience. Corbyn had flown combat helicopter missions, and Wolfgang and Lucy knew more about piano wire and sharp knives than anyone should, but this wasn't a question of covert action or subtle death.

This was a wholesale attack. Sudden, brash, overwhelming...and fatally flawed.

"We *need him* on our side of the river," Turk said, his voice quiet enough that only Reed could hear. "There's no way we'll get guns on him from the Russian side. He'll be surrounded by troops, covered from every angle. A dozen routes of possible escape, and his men will know them all—we'll know nothing. It's too many question marks."

Reed didn't say it, but he knew Turk was right. He'd had the same thoughts himself ever since Rigby proposed the plan, but he also knew that there was absolutely no logical reason for Nikitin to cross into Lithuania. Even if he wanted to, his security team wouldn't allow it. To do so would be madness.

So where did that leave the Prosecution Force?

Reed didn't know. He'd wrestled with the problem all afternoon until his mind hurt. Every time he accepted the variable of hitting Nikitin inside the Oblast, he struck a block wall of obstacles exactly as Turk described. Likewise, every time he considered hitting Nikitin in Kybartai, he knew the Russian president would never cross the river.

So, what, then?

"You're right," Reed said. "We've got to get him across the bridge. Once that happens, it's easy money. Three blasts"—Reed tapped a map of the border in three places, marking each of the bridges between the two towns—"and then we've got a window of maybe five or eight minutes before air cav arrives. Should be more than enough, with the right perimeter. I like it here."

Reed traced his finger to another spot on the map and tapped.

Turk sighed—he sounded very, *very* tired.

"Right. But *how do we get him across the bridge*?"

Reed was still working on that. He wasn't any closer to an answer—but he also knew that a battle plan with a hole was better than a battle plan that would never work in the first place.

"Let's call that my problem," Reed said, straightening and smacking Turk on the shoulder. "You work on the explosives. I'll figure it out."

Turk shot him a look that said the big man was neither convinced nor particularly enthused about the arrangement...but maybe just worn out enough to go along with it.

"Call your wife," Reed said. "Get some sleep. We launch at zero hundred."

Turk hesitated only a moment longer, than tossed a casual salute and walked off—limping a little, and trying very hard not to show it. Reed looked once more to the map and hit the problem again, pushing his mind to produce a miracle...

And once again coming up empty-handed. It was just the reality of the situation. He needed rest as bad as anyone—maybe something would come to him in his sleep.

"Reed?"

It was Lucy, stepping up softly alongside him. Reed switched off the iPads and shoved them into a waiting backpack, the field kit he would use to review the target zone after departing Poland.

"What is it, LB?"

"Can we talk a minute?"

Reed looked into calm green eyes. He'd known those eyes for years, and despite the strain of the impending operation, he couldn't help but think that he'd never seen them look so steady. It was remarkable, really.

"You don't have to go," Reed said. "We won't need a medic."

"I'm not going as a medic."

Reed wasn't sure what to say to that. He hadn't seen Lucy carry a weapon since her Christian conversion—something he neither understood nor judged. War had a way of shattering the foundations of even the most stalwart soldier. Lucy's method of coping and recovery seemed better than most.

"So a priest, then?" Reed asked.

Lucy smirked—just a little. "I think I like *sister* better. That's what they called me at rehab."

Reed nodded but wasn't really thinking about the rehab where he'd sent Lucy to fight a drug addiction, or the change it had produced. He wasn't thinking about Lucy at all, or anyone in the hangar, or even Makar Nikitin.

He was thinking about home. About his bulldog, Baxter. About Davy. About Banks.

And how he didn't deserve to see them again.

"Reed, I really need to talk to you," Lucy said.

Reed blinked, clearing the haze in his eyes. He looked back to the map still spread on the table. "Yeah?"

"I...know you're banged up. I mean, inside. And you have a right to be. I know you're looking for answers—"

"I'm not interested in religion, LB."

Reed's voice was colder than he intended. Then again, he meant what he said.

"I'm not talking about religion."

"Every religious person says that."

Pause. Lucy sighed. She placed both hands on the table.

"Look. If you don't want to hear it, I won't push. I never have. I just want you to know...I found a way out of the darkness. I found the light, and you can too, Reed. You can too."

Reed's gaze snapped up, locking with Lucy's. It wasn't what he expected to hear, and now he wasn't sure what to say or think. His lips parted, but nothing came out. Lucy smiled, very gently. She squeezed his arm.

"If you ever want to talk...I'll be there. *He'll* be there...even in the valley of the shadow."

She left without another word, headed toward Corbyn across the hangar. Maybe ready to make the same offer. Probably about to be shot down just as cold.

But she left something behind. It lay heavy in Reed's gut, like a lead weight. A boiling question pulsating from the heart of the cloud closing around his head.

He swallowed, still thrown off-balance. Then he looked back to the table and closed his eyes. He breathed deep.

He pictured Makar Nikitin with crosshairs hovering over his throat.

Focus.

61

Moscow, Russia

Anton Golubev had a bad feeling, and he couldn't shake it.

From the moment Nikitin first announced his intentions to fly to Kaliningrad and accept President Petrauskienė's offer of surrender in person—a triumphant moment, to be sure—something nagged at the back of Golubev's mind like a worm.

He wasn't quite sure what it was, or what it meant. He'd lain awake for hours wondering and came up empty-handed. He'd reviewed every aspect of the president's travel itinerary and supporting security, double-checking for gaps or exposure. Tugging at loose threads and micromanaging both the Federal Protective Service and the military departments responsible for escorting Nikitin's Ilyushin jet and securing the airport in Kaliningrad.

Maybe it was the timeline that bothered Golubev. Normally presidential travel—even from one point in Russia to another—would involve days of advanced notice given to the ground teams at both ends, allowing for increased security measures and elevated staffing. Such precautions weren't really necessary in Kaliningrad, which was one of the most heavily militarized zones anywhere in Russia. Nikitin should be as safe there as he was in the Kremlin.

And yet...

It was the suddenness of it all, Golubev decided. That was what bothered him most. Everything Golubev knew about President Petrauskienė told him that the move was out of character. That her overnight reversal didn't make sense, even in context of Russia's dominant ground offensive and NATO's sluggish response.

Something just didn't feel right.

Golubev stood at the mouth of a fortified aircraft hangar overlooking Vnukovo-2, the VIP terminal at Vnukovo International Airport reserved for use by Nikitin and other elites. Behind him, the mass of Nikitin's Ilyushin jet gleamed with trademark white, blue, and red stripes. Not far away, a Russian Il-76 cargo jet sat in a similar hangar, already loaded with a pair of heavily armored Aurus Senat limousines, which would be waiting for Nikitin both at Khrabrovo Airport and at Chernyshevskoe on the Lithuanian border. Nikitin would take a helicopter from Khrabrovo to Chernyshevskoe and probably wouldn't need either limousine, but options were never a bad thing.

Why did Lithuania want to surrender?

Maybe Golubev didn't understand because he himself was a warrior, the kind of man who would legitimately prefer death to defeat. Maybe he didn't understand because, truth be told, he didn't *want* Lithuania to surrender.

He wanted Lithuania to burn—he wanted Europe to burn. He wanted the shells to fly and the bombs to drop and the blood to flow, because nothing brought the animal in him to life quite like the carnage of war. Perhaps he was simply feeling deprived.

Or perhaps...

"Show me the ground security again," Golubev said, still staring at the loading cargo jet. Behind him a pair of senior Federal Protective Service officers looked up from a command table laden with computers and radios. They were debating the best motorcade route from the helipad in Chernyshevskoe to the government building where Nikitin and Petrauskienė would meet. Nikitin had demanded camera angles and flashy presentation—his security team was eager to please. Golubev couldn't care less about the news reels. He approached the table and watched in silence while the security team ran him through the particulars once more.

The ground team. The standby helicopter support. The posted snipers and even a battalion of five hundred Russian infantry held at a nearby forward operating post. That battalion boasted a fleet of Typhoon-K armored vehicles and even a pair of T90-M main battle tanks.

It was a *lot* of firepower. But not enough for Golubev.

"Double it," he said.

The nearest officer looked up. "Sir?"

"You heard me."

"Yes...but which part?"

"All of it—everything. I want twice as many helicopters, twice as many troops, twice as many snipers. Put a dozen fighter aircraft on the tarmac with engines burning. Deploy armored units to secure the city from the outside. Post roadblocks and checkpoints in ten, twenty, and fifty kilometer rings. If so much as an unauthorized bicycle crosses within that radius, I want to know about it."

The officers exchanged a glance. One of them shifted awkwardly.

"Sir...it's Kaliningrad..."

Golubev's cutting eyes sliced toward the officer. They were the dead eyes of a cold-blooded killer, rightly called a Ghost.

He was Nikitin's fixer, his silencer, his vanisher of men.

"And?" Golubev snarled.

A swallow. "It will be done, sir."

Golubev nodded. His gaze drifted back across the tarmac—back to the cargo plane and the rushed preparations at hand.

"If ten thousand United States Rangers parachute out of thin air...I want them slaughtered like dogs."

Without another word, Anton Golubev left the hangar.

62

Ramstein Air Base
Rheinland-Pfalz, Germany

Colonel Greg Packer always dreamed of being an airborne soldier.

The obsession began as a child, when his grandfather, a veteran of the US Army's 82nd Airborne Division, told him stories of that unit's heroic paddle across the river Waal during Operation *Market Garden*, a massive European offensive of the Second World War. Old-man Packer, as he was known to friends and family alike, hadn't actually paddled that river himself. With a broken leg, he'd been slated to remain behind.

But when the boats returned to the Allied banks loaded with wounded, nobody could hold him back. He dragged one stretcher after another up the muddy banks while withering German fire raked in from across the river. His leg, already fractured in one place, broke a second time when he tumbled into the water.

Old-man Packer kept going, and years later when he recounted the story, he barely noted his own participation in the battle. All he talked about was the brave men of the 82nd who had crossed that river in collapsible, canvas-sided boats, fully exposed to machine gun fire and nearly helpless to defend themselves.

"But they went," he used to say, tears in his eyes. "They went."

Greg Packer himself, sitting wide-eyed in his grandfather's lap, would beg him to tell the story during every summer visit. Little Packer proudly declared that he himself was someday going to be a member of the 82nd—he was going to *be* like his grandfather.

It didn't much matter that Packer was terrified of heights, a major problem for a would-be paratrooper. He muted his fear by climbing to the top of his grandfather's barn, scaling his middle school gym, and joining the rock-climbing team at his high school. An ROTC scholarship to the University of North Carolina placed him only sixty-five miles from Fort Bragg, headquarters of the 82nd. The rock climbing escalated to skydiving, and by the time Packer finally commissioned as a second lieutenant in the US Army, acrophobia was in his past.

He *enjoyed* the thrill of the jump. He worked hard and impressed his commanding officers. He made it, at long last, to the 82nd. He kept ascending the ranks.

And now, years later, here he was. Stationed in Germany in command of his own brigade of razor-sharp airborne troops. Three thousand, eight hundred, fifty-two by present count, every one of them known personally to Colonel Greg Packer. He drilled them day and night like his life, and theirs, depended on it. He put them in the air and kicked them out of perfectly good airplanes at every available opportunity. He enforced strict academic study, remaining in constant contact with every level of his chain of command, and practicing an open-door policy for any man who reported to him.

Not just because Packer loved the Army and loved his job but because the legacy of the river Waal hung heavy on his mind. A constant motivator to drive harder, push farther, be better—*all the way!*

As Russian ground forces swept the Caucasus, then Estonia and Latvia, Packer was only too well aware that "all the way" might one day mean Moscow. He was determined that his men would be ready for that moment, and that he would bring them home safe, whatever it took.

Training would escalate. Standards would increase. They would drill night and day. Failure would not be an option.

And now this. A call for an immediate, emergency meeting with the division commander, a brigadier general recently appointed to the post. Packer didn't know the man all that well, although the O-8 had a reputation for exacting expectations and relentless standards of discipline. Marching down the corridors of Ramstein Air Base, Packer wondered if he was being called in for some discipline of his own. If he had somehow overlooked something, perhaps crossed the general's radar in an undesirable way.

He wasn't intimidated, he just wanted to be ready. But the moment Packer crossed into the general's office and stood at attention in a room occupied not only by the two-star division commander but also by a one-star brigadier general and two additional colonels, he knew this wasn't that kind of meeting. Everyone looked up as Packer entered. Nobody smiled or extended a hand.

"Morning, sir," Packer said, chin up and body stiff.

"At ease, Packer." The two-star sat at a table spread with laptops and iPads, the modern tool of choice for strategic military planning. In fact, he was the only one seated. The one-star and the colonels remained standing.

Everybody was staring at Packer. He dropped into the "at ease" position, as directed, but didn't relax. He couldn't.

Slowly, the two-star lifted his coffee. Drank. Swallowed and set the West Point cup down.

"I'm sorry we haven't met before—it's been a whirlwind these past six weeks. Usually I like to engage with each of my brigade commanders one-on-one. A peacetime luxury, I guess."

Packer wasn't sure what to say to that, so he said nothing. The two-star cleared his throat.

"They tell me you're a problem."

Packer flinched. "Sir?"

"They tell me you run your men day and night. Drill, drill, drill. You've got planes in the sky every time you can get your hands on them. More training jumps under your belt than any officer of your rank—and it's not close. Seems you've run up quite a tab with logistics."

Packer's gut tightened. *So that was it.* This was a money thing. He knew this day was coming—

"In fact," the two-star continued, "they say there's not another brigade in this Army who can compete with your boys. Highest marks on every metric."

Packer blinked, thrown off-balance. He frowned, looking instinctively to the colonels. One was the two-star's chief of staff. The other was the Division Sustainment Brigade commander—a logistics officer.

No other field commanders were present. Just Packer.

What is this?

"I'll get straight to the point, Colonel," the two-star said. "I've got a job for you. A jump, actually. The biggest of your life...for all 3,852 of your boys."

Packer blinked again. Now his heart was beginning to race. His palms beginning to tingle. The twinge of real excitement flooding his veins.

Without a word, the two-star flicked a hand. His chief of staff extended an iPad. Nobody else spoke as Packer took it and surveyed the screen—the jump plan included. Detailed and organized and fully developed.

A launch point. A route. A drop zone.

Packer looked up, that nervousness now supercharged with a flood of adrenaline and confusion.

"Sir?"

"War, Packer," the two-star said. "I'm sending you to war."

63

The Naval Observatory
Washington, DC

The spectacle of James O'Dell's defiance might have consumed the attention of mass media for days, but the announcement of Lithuania's intention to break from NATO was straight out of left field—and it was *exactly* the nail in the coffin that Vice President Jordan Stratton needed.

Within two hours of the breaking headlines, Easterling had pushed the vote count needed to oust Maggie across the fifty percent mark. The secretary of Homeland Security and the US attorney general had joined Kline and Gorman in a commitment to do the unthinkable. That gave Stratton four votes, but he was still four votes short, and with the entire Baltic standing on the brink of absolute defeat, there was no time left to play it safe.

Stratton himself had to get on the phone. He had to make his intentions clear, risking his own political survival if even one member of Maggie's cabinet refused to participate and announced the developing coup. It was a risk from day one—even a committed *yes* vote could smell a change in the winds and get cold feet.

But this wasn't about politics anymore. It wasn't even about power. It was about the survival of the entire West.

Stratton started with the secretary of Veterans Affairs, a retired Air Force colonel who had a reputation for military pride and would likely be worried about American soldiers being slaughtered in Europe. The call was surprisingly brief, and refreshingly positive. The secretary was behind Stratton one hundred percent, even going so far as to say: "I've been waiting for this call."

That brought the vote to five, with momentum on Stratton's side. Easterling was targeting the secretary of Health and Human Services, and Gorman was reaching out to the secretary of energy. Stratton chose the secretary of commerce and met some resistance, then some uncertainty, and then pushed the sale.

Two hours more work, and the vote count was eight—just enough. Easterling called Stratton to see if he wanted to play it safe or risk exposure and build a buffer. Stratton was feeling almost as bold as he was stressed. They each made one more call.

Easterling made the sale, landing the secretary of labor. Stratton was shut down hard by a horrified secretary of agriculture. He'd forgotten that she was an LSU grad and occasionally enjoyed football games at the White House with the president. The personal connection was too strong, the request too shocking.

So the count was nine, allowing for one defector without losing the vote...but at this point, news of Stratton's actions were almost certain to have leaked.

"We should do it now," Easterling said, speaking over the phone. "Make the announcement before Nikitin lands in Russia. Maybe give Lithuania some confidence in our willpower—talk them off the ledge."

It was a reasonable argument. Stratton leaned back in a leather chair, staring at a muted TV playing news reels of burning Estonia, and he understood the logic.

But we don't know what chaos this will bring.

"No," Stratton said. "Legal needs more time to finalize the paperwork, and besides, moving now could play right into Nikitin's hand. We'll go tomorrow while Nikitin is on the ground with Petrauskienė. It'll catch him off guard."

Pause.

"Word could leak by then," Easterling said.

"So it leaks. I want the paperwork airtight, and I want our allies in Congress ready to receive our declaration. No mistakes, no snags. We've got to get this right."

More silence. Then: "Okay."

"Jill?"

"Sir?"

"I need you with me on this. One hundred percent—from declaration and beyond. I need a chief of staff."

This time, Easterling didn't hesitate.

"I'm with you, sir."

Stratton hung up and look to the clock on his computer screen. It was late afternoon in Washington—late evening in central Europe. Nikitin would land in Kaliningrad sometime the next day.

In eighteen hours, maybe twenty, America would have a new president.

64

33rd Air Base
Powidz, Poland

"Wheels up in five!"

The aircraft was a Polish Air Force PZL M28 Skytruck—a twin-engine, compact cargo plane with a tail ramp and a capacity of five thousand pounds. Both pilots were members of the US Air Force's 352nd Special Operations Wing, short takeoff and landing qualified and cross-trained on international aircraft for wild situations exactly such as this.

Only, maybe not *this* wild.

The plane, painted battleship gray, bore a tail number and NATO markings only two hours prior, but those numbers and symbols had been slathered over with fresh paint, leaving behind a generic airframe. It was more plausible deniability for Washington, but what Reed was most concerned about was the tight fit.

All seats had been removed from the rear of the Skytruck, leaving the seventeen-foot cargo bay only barely large enough to pack a pair of Melex electric vehicles nose to tail with their side-view mirrors removed. More property of the Polish Air Force, the first Melex was a personnel carrier with four seats. The second was a truck model, with a metal cargo bed already packed tight with equipment, weapons, and ordnance—a lot of ordnance.

Both Melexes were four-wheel drive with fully charged batteries offering a range of sixty to eighty kilometers at speeds up to twenty-five miles per hour. Not fast, and despite the four-wheel drive, not overly capable of all-terrain maneuvers. But the electric motors would be dead quiet, and with half his team still limping from their last engagement in Azerbaijan, rucking in the equipment simply wasn't an option.

"You good, Commander?"

The Air Force captain in charge of the flight was as nondescript as his plane. His flight suit was stripped bare of all insignia, and under the glow of nearby airstrip lights, Reed didn't even note the gleam of a dog tag chain around his neck.

Completely off the books.

"Ready," Reed called over the roar of a Polish fighter jet, taking air some five hundred yards away and still shaking the ground.

The pilot smacked his arm and nodded once. There was something in his eyes that made Reed wonder if he had some idea what this mission was all about—if he was wondering, even now, if he was carting five shabby operators to their deaths...or if he was embarking on a flight that would save his grandchildren's future, even if he could never tell them about it.

The pilot disappeared, and Reed stuck his head inside the open tailgate of the Skytruck to check the load one more time. To pull on the straps. To look down a narrow corridor between a Melex car and the curvature of the Skytruck's fuselage that was just barely wide enough for each member of the team to slip through. They would ride seated in the Melex carts, packed in so tight they couldn't turn around.

Only Lucy would be comfortable for this flight—but that didn't matter, because the flight wouldn't last long.

"Montgomery!"

Turk's voice boomed even over the firing turboprops of the Skytruck. Reed turned back to find his worn battle buddy standing alongside Silas Rigby, both men's clothes and hair torn by the whir of propellers. Reed jogged close enough for words to be understood in less than a shout.

Rigby extended a hand. "Good luck, Prosecutor. Nobody will know, but the world thanks you."

Reed took the hand, a pit opening in his stomach even as Rigby squeezed.

"Thank me when it's done," Reed said. He began to turn. Rigby caught him.

"Reed."

Reed looked back. It was the first time he ever remembered Rigby using his first name, and there was something in Rigby's eyes that Reed didn't like. Something dark—menacing. The CIA officer leaned closed, his voice barely loud enough to be heard.

"I don't have to tell you what happens if this goes sideways. If the mission fails, we're still at war. But if the mission fails and any of you are captured...if Nikitin figures this out..."

Rigby didn't have to finish. Reed got the picture, and it featured a horizon full of mushroom clouds.

"I understand."

Rigby reached into his pocket. He produced a small orange bottle, barely an inch long and opaque, but Reed didn't have to ask what was inside.

"If you want it," Rigby said.

Reed looked. He glanced at Turk. Then he shook his head.

"We're not spies, Rigby. We're soldiers—and we won't be taken prisoner."

He smacked Rigby on the shoulder. From the tip of the Skytruck's left wing, red navigation lights flashed once—a signal from the cockpit. Time to go.

Reed jogged back to the open cargo bay and directed the rest of the team up the ramp—Wolfgang with his new prosthetic, Corbyn chewing gum, and Lucy wriggling down the narrow aisle without complaint. They all took their seats in the rear Melex, and then Reed himself fought his way into the driver's seat of the second vehicle.

It was the one loaded down with weapons, gear, and explosives. As Reed slid into position, he double-checked just to make sure the keys still hung from the ignition. Turk settled in next to him, and the vehicle's suspension creaked. Reed cast a glance over his shoulder and made eye contact with Wolfgang. Corbyn. Lucy.

Three thumbs-up. Reed shot a hand over the Melex's roof and closed his fist. A second slipped by, and then the cargo ramp shifted and swung upward. Silas Rigby, still standing alongside the tarmac, faded from view.

Temporary darkness was replaced by soft red illumination. Reed knew that the flight would last about seventy-five minutes, which would be long enough for all of their eyes to adjust, ready for a switch to night vision goggles and full stealth mode.

Touch down in the dirt. Offload vehicles and equipment. And then... war.

"This might be the stupidest thing I've ever done," Turk muttered.

Reed squinted.

"Riding to war on a freaking golf cart," Turk clarified.

Just as Turk said it, the Skytruck lurched and turned. Vibrations tore down the airframe as both engines ramped up. Turk slouched in the Melex's seat like a bored caddy killing time between clients.

And for the first time in a very long time, Reed smiled. Turk smiled with him. Reed started to laugh. Turk laughed louder. The world couldn't hear them over the thunder of the turboprops, and it didn't matter.

Reed threw both arms around Turk and hugged him close. Slapped his back hard.

"If you gotta be stupid, be stupid in good company," Reed said.

Reed pulled away as the Skytruck's nose left the tarmac—he planted his feet in the Melex's footwell even as his body fought to rock out of the seat. Somewhere far beneath him he imagined Poland fading into the darkness, and in the strangest way, he was okay if a lot more was fading with it. If everything faded with it.

"You got any ideas about getting Nikitin across that bridge?" Turk said softly.

"Working on it," Reed said. "Still working on it."

Turk shot him a sideways look—Reed noticed but chose to ignore it. He leaned back into the seat and breathed deep. Grew still.

He cleared his mind and switched into killer mode.

65

The White House

Maggie took the call in her residence.

She hadn't left the White House's second floor all day, conducting business from either her bedroom or her sitting room, effectively isolating herself from the West Wing and all the buzzing officials she might encounter there. Dressed in White House sweats with comfy socks for shoes, Maggie directed her aides to filter all calls.

She would speak to Director Aimes, and she would speak to General Yellin. That was supposed to be it, but when the caller from the Department of Agriculture dialed her executive line, something in the speaker's voice must have rattled Maggie's secretary.

The secretary buzzed Maggie's room and asked if the president would like to make an exception. Maggie said yes, and the subsequent call lasted only three minutes. Most of that was time spent listening to an agitated, babbling voice.

Nothing that voice said surprised Maggie. In fact, if anything, she was only surprised that this was the only call she received. Maybe that was a bad omen—maybe it was fate, or even punishment. Maggie thanked the caller but said little else. She hung up and stood over the phone a long moment, swallowing back a lump in her throat but barely fighting the heavy tear in her eye.

The opioids Dr. Guidry prescribed had made *such* a difference. Maggie felt calm and loose and warm. She knew it was borrowed relief, mortgaged at the expense of future misery and damage. She knew that the drugs, heavy as they were, could reasonably be accused of compromising her mental state and sabotaging her judgment.

But for just a moment, for just one night, she was totally okay with that. She wanted to accept reality for every ugly thing that it was and *stop* fighting it. To be alone in a dark room and remember—reminisce even. That bumpy, chaotic road from a south Louisiana swamp to the governor's mansion in Baton Rouge and then to the White House. A crazy, tumultuous, painful, agonizing trip.

But now this.

Maggie released the phone but didn't wipe her eyes. She stepped to an antique hardwood cabinet carved thick with scrollwork—something she'd brought with her from Louisiana—and withdrew a bottle of Buffalo Trace. She poured herself three fingers, no ice, and took the bottle with her to a desk near a window.

Seated with the burn of the bourbon still searing her throat, Maggie looked out over the White House grounds, completely ignoring the late-night protestors gathered at the fence, and gazed to the sky instead. To the distant glimmer of just a few stars, barely visible beyond the city lights and smog.

Not like Louisiana, out in the swamps where tens of thousands of stars could be enjoyed on a clear night. Maggie rocked her glass back and remembered. She pictured herself stretched out on a blanket in some lonely parish with the same Buffalo Trace and a cheap radio crackling jazz music from down in the Big Easy, and she knew...

She was ready.

Maggie set the glass down and flipped open a leather-bound folder that had lain on her desk for most of the afternoon. She hadn't yet read the contents, but a quick scan was sufficient to confirm their veracity. She signed the document without further thought, and closed the folder. Slid it to one side.

Then she retrieved a single sheet of presidential stationary, complete with letterhead, and arranged it on the leather desk pad. She clicked open a pen with blue ink, and breathed deep. She added the date first and paused for bourbon.

Then Maggie wrote. Quick lines, a smooth and confident hand. A signature as fresh and bold and confident as the day she first took office.

The final word of a whirlwind presidency.

66

Moscow, Russia

"You have to call it off. Golubev has doubled Nikitin's detail."

Maxim Romanov's voice hummed with tension in the restaurant bathroom. With the lights off, Ivan couldn't actually see the prime minister's face, but he could picture it strained, blotchy red and white, sweat trickling down his flabby cheeks.

There was red wine on the PM's breath, and the garlicky odor of the fried potatoes he loved too much. Ivan imagined sludgy blood crashing through a heart so long abused, so long strained, and could only *pray* that this fat fool lived long enough to save his country.

"How many men?" Ivan said.

"*Hundreds*," Romanov hissed. "Not just the FSO—there are soldiers also. Armor and helicopters. Fighter jets on standby. Nikitin is ready for anything. He's encased in pure lead. You *must* call it off."

There was fear in Romanov's voice. Maybe something closer to panic. Ivan could feel it, even in the dark. Easing out of a bathroom stall, Ivan closed to within inches. He leaned close, barely making out the gleam of desperate eyes in the faint glow that leaked beneath the door.

"Keep your voice down," Ivan hissed. "And get control of yourself. You should be ashamed, Maxim. I thought you were a *warrior*."

A snort. Romanov's eyes flicked toward the door as somebody shuffled past—a waiter or an exiting patron. Then all was silent again.

"Your mistake," Romanov said. "This idea was always insane. Now it is pure suicide. We should pull out, cancel everything. Renew pressure on Nikitin from political angles. If he learns what we were attempting—"

A sharp, metallic snap cut Romanov short. The blade, springing from the open top of a metal handle, landed against the prime minister's loose throat with the pinch of razor-sharp steel. Ivan didn't press very hard—just hard enough to draw a trickle of blood and cut Romanov's pathetic babbles short.

"What—what are you doing?" Romanov hissed.

"Do you feel that?" Ivan's tone was as calm and merciless as it had ever been. His *death voice*, he used to call it. A monotone whisper reserved for interrogations where the time for empty threats and intimidation had long passed. Torture was a forgone option. Patience was no longer on the table.

This was the voice Ivan Sidorov used when all the cards were on the table, and it was time for men to make decisions.

"Do you know what that is?" Ivan said.

Romanov swallowed—it was a stupid move. His rippling Adam's apple aggravated the pressure of the switchblade against his skin. The blood flow increased, if only by a little.

"It's a knife," Romanov hissed.

"No." Ivan shook his head. "It's the Russian people, Maxim. One hundred forty-four million desperate souls, *demanding* that you perform your duties. That you rise to this occasion. Fate has appointed me as their representative, Maxim, and if you think for one *moment* that Nikitin is your greatest threat...well."

Ivan leaned closer. He pressed with the knife and Romanov's head collided with the wall. The PM gasped. Ivan's voice descended into a snarl.

"You are indeed a fool," Ivan finished.

Fully adjusted to the darkness, both men could see each other in the gloom. Neither of them blinked. Romanov barely breathed.

Then Sidorov retracted the knife. The bloody blade snapped closed, and the weapon vanished into his jacket.

"Nothing will be called off," Ivan said. "We proceed. Advise me with every update."

Ivan turned for the door. Romanov had a hand on his throat, stemming the blood. He straightened from the wall.

"It is *hopeless*, Ivan," Romanov protested. "Nikitin's forces will slaughter America's soldiers long before they come within sight of him. They're dead men walking."

Ivan, one hand on the door, turned back. He stared at Romanov, and a cold smile stretched his lips.

"Oh, but they're not sending soldiers, Maxim. They're sending *monsters*."

67

Marijampolė County
Lithuania

The Polish Air Force Skytruck flew low and rough, skimming just one thousand feet off the ground as it streaked northeast out of Powidz and passed into the Suwałki Gap. Barely forty miles wide at its narrowest point, this stretch of Polish dirt bordered Lithuania to the northeast but was capped on either end by holdings of the enemy—Kaliningrad to the northwest and Belarus to the southeast.

It was a weak point in NATO's armor and always had been. Military leaders long worried that a coordinated Russian/Belarusian strike could penetrate and seize the gap, effectively cutting the Baltic states off from Allied support—a worst-case scenario.

Nobody actually imagined that Nikitin might ignore the gap altogether and simply blitz the Baltic from the east, depending on NATO sluggishness to buy him time for a full occupation. If Reed was honest, he had to admire the aggression and confidence with which the Russian executed the maneuver.

It was bold, unexpected, relentless.

But two could play at that game.

Safely entering Lithuanian airspace without attracting attention from the nearby batteries of enemy surface-to-air missiles or radar sights, the pilots banked the Skytruck and swung due north, ripping over gently rolling farmland segmented into wheat and potato fields, with patches of spruce and pine forests scattered at random.

Reed caught glimpses through the porthole window to his left, the ground below illuminated by a three-quarter moon while his NVGs rode the top of his head. Vibrations from the plane's twin turboprop engines shook the cargo floor and passed through the Melex's tires, reaching his tailbone and agitating sore muscles. An aching back. A tightened jaw.

Nobody in the plane spoke. It was too loud for casual conversation, but Reed doubted whether his team was feeling chatty anyway. He glanced over his shoulder a couple of times and found Wolfgang dozing in the passenger seat of the Melex behind them. Corbyn slouched behind the wheel, an armor plate affixed to her chest while she chain-chewed apples like a horse. Lucy seated in the rear, head bowed and eyes closed, lips moving silently.

But nobody interacting. Nobody discussing the inevitable, or strategizing, or second-guessing. Reed adjusted in his seat and checked his watch to estimate flight time. They had to be getting close, but the pilots were operating under strict radio silence, and Reed's headset couldn't reach a plug-in to communicate with them via internal intercom. He would know they were about to land when the groan of the landing gear accompanied a sharp decrease in altitude.

"I think..."

Turk started, stopped. Reed glanced right and waited. Turk was chewing gum, relaxed in the undersized seat as though it were his easy chair back in Tennessee. Yet his eyes were alive. His nose twitching.

"I think Sinju is pregnant," Turk finished.

Reed squinted. "What?"

"We've been video calling. She, uh, won't show me anything but her face. And she's gained some weight."

"Why would you see anything but her face?" Reed said.

Turk shot him a sideways look, and Reed flushed. He looked quickly away.

"Right."

Silence. The Skytruck shuddered. They were turning again, maybe gaining a little altitude. That could precipitate a landing, if the pilots needed to get over a hill. Reed wanted to check his watch again. He wanted to press-check his SIG and reseat the magazine in his M4 rifle. He wanted to tap his foot.

He wanted to stop thinking about Banks. About Davy. About that generic little shoebox Nashville apartment that he would never complain about again if he could only make it home.

"Well, congratulations, buddy," Reed said, realizing that he'd left Turk hanging. "You hoping for a boy?"

Turk didn't answer. Reed looked right again and found something he'd only seen maybe twice in his entire life. From Iraq to America and the carnage everywhere in between.

There were tears in Turk's eyes. He didn't answer the question—he didn't have to.

Then Reed heard the landing gear. Groaning out and locking with a thump. The plane shuddered and Turk looked quickly away. Both men sat up. Reed looked over his shoulder and made eye contact with Corbyn, ensuring that she felt the gear also. Wearing her trademark aviator sunglasses slid halfway down her nose, only a portion of her dark eyes were visible, but Corbyn nodded. She placed a hand on the Melex's roll bar, bracing herself for the impact.

The Skytruck started down. The engines wound back. Reed looked out the porthole window and noted more sweeping farmland with the distant lights of a small town barely visible over the horizon. It was Kybartai, he knew. That spec of a Lithuanian town parked on the frontier with Vilnius's greatest enemy—the side of the river he *needed* to lure Nikitin onto.

But how?

Reed still didn't know.

"Remember!" Reed shouted. "Full silence. Lights off. Lithuanian cops and farmers are as much an operational threat as the Russians."

Corbyn tossed a sloppy salute. Wolfgang said nothing. Lucy had lifted her head and strapped her little body in place. The Skytruck nosed down and Reed felt the elevation bleeding away as his stomach rose toward his throat. He breathed deep and reached for the Melex's keys. The battery activated, but the headlights remained dead, already disabled back at Powidz. Reed rocked his NVG's down and adjusted the fit.

Then the Skytruck touched down. A bounce of grippy tires against an unpaved surface, followed almost immediately by a second impact. The plane shuddered and stayed down. The brakes squeezed, and the aircraft ground to a stop in under three hundred yards—well beneath operational standards. These pilots knew exactly what they were doing.

Reed reached for the hand brake. It disengaged and the Melex rolled forward an inch, catching on its transmission. He eased his foot to the accelerator and waited, breathing deep.

"Definitely a boy," Turk said. "I'll teach him to golf."

Reed smirked. The Skytruck shifted again as the tailgate lowered with a hiss of hydraulics. A field opened beyond—distant grain stalks and an empty, dark horizon.

Reed mashed the pedal and led the way into the jaws of death.

68

They reached their first destination in Kybartai in eight minutes—exactly as estimated by Reed's calculations when he first charted a course between potato fields. The target was a barn, standing alone amid the row crops with the nearest streetlight several hundred yards away.

Pitch dark. Empty. Isolated. And yet within barely two klicks of "downtown" Kybartai.

Reed drove his Melex straight through the open barn door, the second vehicle rolling just behind. Gravel turned to dirt, a cloud of dust exploding from all-terrain tires as the barn door rumbled shut behind them.

Only then did the lights kick on—a buzz of aged fluorescents. Reed was already out of his seat, his M4 rifle riding a one-point sling with his finger a twitch away from the trigger.

The men who stood ready to greet the Prosecution Force were Lithuanian military—Reed recognized the yellow, green, and red flag patches on the arms of their green fatigues. None were armed, but Reed didn't relax his grip on the rifle as the lead man of the trio stepped forward.

"Commander?"

It was what the Lithuanians had been told to call Reed. They didn't know his name—they didn't know anybody's name, or where they came from, or the details of their plan. That was all by design, ensuring plausible deniability for Vilnius when the smoke cleared.

One way or the other.

Reed simply nodded, ignoring the proffered hand. The soldier slowly lowered it. He scanned the other four members of the team, already dismounting and unpacking gear from the bed of the lead Melex.

Rifles. Submachine guns. Body armor and encrypted radios. Smoke and frag grenades. One Mark 19 40mm grenade launcher in a case. Two LAW rocket launchers.

And C4. A *lot* of C4.

"This..." the soldier started. Stopped. Then looked back to Reed. "This is it?"

What did you expect? SEAL Team Six?

Reed kept the thought to himself. He left his team to their work and accompanied the Lithuanian soldier to a nearby table already spread with a map of the region. On the Lithuanian side of the border, Kybartai served as a farming and railroad hub—brick and stone houses, a lot of quiet streets lined by trees and cafés. Classic small-town Europe, not remarkable in any exterior way except for one thing.

It's proximity to Chernyshevskoe—and Russia.

The Liepona River ran between the two, barely twenty feet wide and really more of a stream. There were three bridges, only one of which was strong enough to support anything larger than a civilian vehicle. Crimson marks on the map depicted known Russian military installations, including an airstrip stocked with fighter jets and helicopter gunships barely five miles distant. One garrison of ground troops and a battalion of twenty-two Russian artillery pieces pointed dead at Lithuania...and NATO.

"The Russians are increasing military force all along the border," the soldier said. "Fast infantry and light armor. Troop transports, even mechanized artillery. It's like...they plan to invade."

"They do," Reed said simply. He was sweeping the known troop entrenchments and filling in the gaps with guesswork. Not where the Lithuanians *knew* there to be Russian ground troops, but where Reed assumed them to be. Where he would have stationed them himself, if he were in charge.

It was a lot of firepower, but it all had one thing in common—it was on the *Russian* side of the river, and in the event of an emergency, it would take precious minutes to get a beast so large moving.

"Here." Reed pointed. The soldier frowned.

"That's…inside Lithuania. The meeting is to take place in Kaliningrad."

Reed shook his head. "It'll take place there."

"How can you know that?" The soldier's voice brimmed with frustration. "Why would he cross the river?"

Reed folded his arms. Studied the map. Turned over an idea in his mind that had been slowly developing for hours—something so vague that he didn't even know it was there, at first, but now it was coming into focus. It was metamorphosing, clarifying, taking shape in real time.

And maybe, just maybe…it was the idea he'd been waiting for.

"Because he's invincible," Reed said, finally answering the Lithuanian. "And because the whole world is watching. Now find something to write with—this is what we need."

69

Kybartai, Lithuania

Infiltrating Kybartai was easy—even easier than Reed expected. Whatever military official the Lithuanian president had placed in charge of facilitating the Prosecution Force's operation, that official knew what they were doing.

Doors were unlocked where they should be. Lithuanian ground troops looked the other way at every turn. The implements Reed had requested—bolt cutters, rolls of electrical wire, camouflage netting—were resting in place exactly where he wanted them.

And most importantly of all, there were no civilians. The entire core of the town had been cleared out, forcibly evacuated to temporary mobile housing east of town in the name of securing the site for the upcoming diplomatic meeting. That left the entire core of Kybartai, and all the houses, offices, and apartment buildings it contained totally accessible to the Prosecution Force.

They ran the Melex cars from the barn straight into the heart of town, slipping into darkened garages at the base of a three-story apartment tower which would serve as "Building A" for the remainder of the operation. From there, equipment was unpacked and the team split up.

Wolfgang took Corbyn and half the explosives and went north—Reed and Turk took the remainder of the C4 and went south. Lucy assumed a position at the third floor of Building A overlooking J. Basanavičiaus gatvė, Kybartai's main street, and provided constant overwatch while communicating via encrypted radios.

There weren't many Lithuanian troops in town, which was exactly what Reed had requested, but he still thought there was likely more to the story than his own preferences. He imagined that the scenario were reversed, and that it was Maggie Trousdale, not Dovilė Petrauskienė, allegedly meeting with Makar Nikitin for the purpose of surrender. That it was happening in some isolated village in Alaska.

Every Marine, every airman, every Army GI and sailor had better be stripped from that place ahead of time, because there was *no way* they would stand silently by while their president folded like a cheap suit. For all Reed knew, there was already a coup underway inside the Lithuanian military or government, ready to strip Petrauskienė of her office and launch an offensive against the first Russian detachment they could find.

The Charge of the Light Brigade—a fearless, foolish, doomed endeavor, but Reed couldn't blame them. He understood. Even as he and Turk slipped silently through tall grass, leveraging shadows all the way to the banks of the Liepona River, Reed didn't think about the mathematical certainty of death bearing down over his entire team like the blade of an executioner's ax.

He couldn't afford to. It didn't matter. Death was an acceptable outcome...just so long as the Prosecution Force took their target with them.

The river work took two hours—not because it was complicated work but because Reed and Turk were forced to proceed in glacial slow motion, maintaining concealment from the Russian border barely a stone's throw away. With the water only rising to Reed's chest, it wasn't much of a hinderance, but it was icy cold and it tightened his muscles. It left him shivering, his fingers numb. He fumbled the finer motor movements of some of the work, but didn't rush or relent.

In an hour he and Turk had the first bridge wired, and a chirp from Reed's encrypted radio, fed into an earpiece, signaled that Wolfgang and

Corbyn were finished with their bridge also. Reed returned the beep with a single chirp of his own, both acknowledging their message and signaling for the pair to proceed with additional explosive setups in the zone labeled "Main Square" before securing operational positions at buildings labeled "B" and "C." Then he and Turk crept out of the river. Slipped south for the final bridge. Began the cycle again.

By four a.m. the job was done, and everyone assembled inside the third-floor apartment of Building A where Lucy had hot coffee and MREs waiting for them. Everyone who was wet changed clothes, and Wolfgang and Corbyn briefly reported on the details of the explosives they had wired and the setups at Buildings B and C.

Both locations had been selected via satellite imagery, without the option to inspect them in person ahead of time. The original site for Building B, it turned out, lacked the line-of-sight vantage that Reed had expected, and Corbyn had subsequently improvised with a two-story house across the street, recently vacated by evacuated locals.

Reed marked the updated spot on a map, along with Buildings A and C, then traced the lines between all three to form a misshapen triangle.

It wasn't perfect—a long, long way from it. But maybe it was enough.

If Nikitin crossed the river.

Taking a pair of binoculars equipped with night vision, Reed advanced to a west-facing window and parted the blinds just enough to look through. Turning right—northwest—he saw the border crossing, then the middle bridge, which was also the widest and largest of the three.

Kaliningrad spread beyond, vast and gray and overtly bleak compared to its Lithuanian neighbor. Reed couldn't actually *see* the vast instillations of Russian ground forces concealed in concrete bunkers and behind walls of planted pine trees, but he knew they were there, spring-loaded and ready to launch at a single word.

A problem? Not really. If everything went according to plan, long before the first Russian infantry unit reached the river, it would be too late. The attack, fast and savage, would be over. Reed might be left breathing to face the onslaught of vengeful Russian masses...

But so what? This had always been a suicide mission. He wasn't scared of that, even if the reality of his own brutal end sank into his chest like a knife.

He was so much more scared of the alternative. Of failure—and the world that would leave his family to suffer in.

Turning from the window, Reed suddenly realized that the room had grown nearly silent. His team, scattered around a living room occupied by worn furniture and adorned with family photographs, all sat avoiding each other's gazes. Wolfgang and Turk picked at MREs. Corbyn rolled a stick of gum in one hand, but for once, she didn't unwrap it. Lucy sat with her arms wrapped around her legs, chin resting on her knees.

There were tears in her eyes—but she didn't look afraid.

A lump swelled in Reed's throat, and he lowered the binoculars. For a long moment he looked from one face to the next, taking his time and not minding that they refused to meet his gaze. Thinking of the first moment he'd met each of them, and what the circumstances had been, and everything that had transpired in the bloody years since.

There wasn't a man or woman in this room that Reed wouldn't comfortably trust his life to. His wife's life. His son's life. Not a man or woman he wouldn't toss the keys of his beloved Camaro to, fully prepared to never get them back.

Not a man or woman he wouldn't willingly, thoughtlessly, give his life for.

What a team.

"I'm..." Reed started, then stopped. His throat felt thick, his mouth dry. He searched, but all he could come up with was: "I'm not good at moments like this."

Nobody answered. Wolfgang and Turk seemed to have forgotten their MREs. Lucy still sat with her legs pulled up to her chest.

Finally, Corbyn said: "You know, I'm beginning to wonder what you *are* good at."

She said it without a trace of humor in her voice, but Reed smiled. He looked to each face one more time, and stopped at Turk. Hesitated.

Then, for reasons Reed himself didn't even understand, he extended his left arm. Stood silent. Turk locked eyes with him, confusion playing across his face...then, maybe, the vaguest hint of a smile.

He stood. He limped as he crossed the room. He met Reed and extended his own right arm, sliding it behind Reed's neck and grabbing his opposite shoulder. Squeezing hard.

Then Turk extended his own left arm, and looked to Wolfgang. Reed looked to Lucy. Both moved to join the growing circle, leaving room for Corbyn.

Still seated in an armchair, Corbyn looked away, hiding the tears in her eyes.

"Bloody hell, guys. I'm British. We don't do this crap."

"Get up, Corbyn."

There was no give in Wolfgang's voice. Corbyn rose. She joined the circle. Lucy had to stand on her tiptoes, arms straining.

But the strength in that loop was unlike anything Reed had ever felt. Forged of iron. Tested by blood.

And probably about to be blown to pieces—but what was the shame in that?

"Nobody I'd rather be with," Reed said simply.

It was all he could come up with—maybe it was enough. Everyone but Wolfgang had tears in their eyes. He looked only seconds away, dropping his face and trembling a little on the new prosthetic. They all just stood, and nobody answered, but that last moment of silence was more than enough.

"What could go wrong?" Reed said.

"Literally everything," Corbyn snorted.

"We could all be killed," Wolfgang said. "Nikitin could launch a nuclear war."

"Billions dead," Turk said. "And no more baseball."

"Russia could rule the world and outlaw all drinks but vodka," Lucy mused.

"But that all happens if we *don't* act," Reed said.

Another moment of silence.

Then a wry smile from Corbyn. "Well if that's all, stuff it. Let's go kill a president."

Reed smiled. He squeezed Lucy's shoulder and slapped Turk on the back.

"*Hoorah!* Let's do it."

70

Moscow, Russia

Makar Nikitin's presidential plane departed the Russian capitol in a rush of hot jet exhaust and a scream of escorting Sukhoi Su-35S fighter escorts. Banking west in the midmorning sun, the glimmer of bright paint was lost in mere moments as the aircraft faded into the horizon, headed toward Kaliningrad and a meeting that Anton Golubev could still barely believe.

Surrender of a NATO state. An unthinkable defeat for the West. An unexpected glory for Russia. Nikitin had every reason to be thrilled, every reason to want to accept the victory in person.

And yet that nagging feeling was still there. Not just the instinct that this was somehow too easy, too simple—there was a deeper, more concrete notion at the root of his mental discomfort. Some particular detail his subconscious had noted, filed, and processed, but his active mind had yet to recognize or appreciate.

Standing at the mouth of the same hangar that Nikitin's plane had exited only moments before, Golubev ignored his personal FSO escort and the armored Mercedes SUV waiting to cart him back to the Kremlin. As Nikitin's proxy commander, it was vital for Golubev to remain behind—to keep his thumb on the heartbeat of Russian command and execute

Nikitin's orders as necessary in his absence. Golubev didn't mind that. He had a full workday ahead.

And yet...

Golubev shook a Russian cigarette from a crumpled pack and slipped it between his teeth. The driver was waiting and the engine running, but he felt no pressure to rush. He was in command. He was the boss. He was Russia's de facto second-in-command even if Prime Minister Maxim Romanov was legally her designated replacement leader—

Romanov.

Golubev's mind ground to a halt. It ratcheted hard back to the three-way conversation between himself, Nikitin, and Romanov the moment that news of Lithuania's intended surrender reached the Kremlin. He thought of how Romanov had volunteered to go meet with President Petrauskienė himself. How he had argued with Nikitin, trying to keep the Russian leader at home.

But what had Romanov *not* done?

He hadn't seemed *surprised*. Not the least bit. The moment the news of Lithuania's unexpected move was announced, the prime minister kicked into gear with Nikitin to discuss a Russian response, but he hadn't once questioned the veracity of the intel. The possibility of a Western trick.

It was as though he *expected* the news. It was the detail that had been bothering Anton Golubev's subconscious ever since.

Could it be possible...

Golubev discarded the cigarette, unlit, and turned for the Mercedes. He rushed to the back seat and slammed the door. His personal bodyguard reached the front seat only a moment later. The driver looked to the rearview mirror.

"The Kremlin, sir?"

"No," Golubev growled, his mind still racing. "Take me to the White House. I want to see the prime minister."

71

The Naval Observatory
Washington, DC

Jordan Stratton rose before sunrise. He dressed in sweats and hit the gym before breakfast for a ninety-minute workout designed not so much to strengthen his body as to silence the storm in his mind.

To bottle the thunder into a barrel, the blasting winds into a bag, and push his escalating heart rate to a strained peak as five miles on the treadmill converted to free weights, a bench press, and push-ups on a rubber mat.

Stratton was alone in the gym and he didn't listen to music. He didn't listen to anything except the hammer of his own heartbeat as sweat ran in sheets from his face and his body grew sore, then tired. When he finally exited he was drenched and panting, ignoring the greeting of his Secret Service detail as he headed for a shower.

Icy cold. Standing beneath the rush, head down, eyes closed. Breathing deep. Reviewing his entire long and tumultuous life in short story form, every strategic decision that had led Stratton from a prep-school childhood to the United States Senate, and then the vice presidency. A meteoric rise, much like Maggie Trousdale's.

Except it wasn't supposed to end this way. It wasn't supposed to end at all. Stratton was meant to serve with Maggie for the duration of her executive career. Then run himself. Set his own standards, his own tempo, his own agenda and branding. He was meant to be a standout American president—a Lincoln, an FDR.

Not the first VP in American history to slide the knife of the 25th Amendment between the ribs of his own boss.

Outside the shower, a fresh shave and carefully applied hair gel preceded a tight undershirt, a pressed white button-down, a four-thousand-dollar suit, and a red power tie. Stratton dressed in front of a mirror and stared himself dead in the eye the entire time—not out of vanity but out of pride. A stubborn refusal, even for a moment, to hide from who he was and what he was about to do.

Because if Jordan Stratton was going to reach for the knife, he would own that decision. No matter the consequences.

Just as Stratton seated the knot of his tie, a door swung and his wife, Carolyn, appeared in her nightgown. With her hair brushed smooth and pale eyes wide and a little bloodshot, she looked a little storm-worn. A little battered.

Carolyn wasn't a particularly attractive woman. Slender to the point of being skinny, a little too pale even with makeup, and a touch awkward despite her silver spoon upbringing. She was also mentally unstable, covertly diagnosed with bipolar disorder and usually medicated to the point of near emotional monotone.

Stratton hadn't married her for her looks. He hadn't married her for her personality, intelligence, or really any form of emotional attraction. He'd married her because Carolyn's maiden name was Presley, and a unification with the powerful Presley family was politically advantageous. Carolyn had to know that, and she'd never complained. She had her own uses for the marriage, mostly involving Stratton's family money. The two of them might go weeks without seeing each other, each pursuing their own lives and, yes, occasionally their own lovers. It was business more than romance. It was calculated, but not always cold.

Yet this morning, Stratton saw something different in Carolyn's eyes. Not quite affection, certainly not desire. She didn't know what he was about to do and he wasn't about to tell her. Yet despite their detached union, Carolyn knew her husband well. She knew his habits and patterns. Maybe she had sensed a disturbance in the waters.

"You're going to be president," Carolyn said, voice soft.

Stratton didn't answer. It wasn't a question. He stood in front of the mirror, turned sideways, his back ramrod straight. Slowly, Carolyn started across the room. She glided on bare feet, the nightgown flowing around her knees, those wide eyes blinking periodically. There was a tension in her posture that told Stratton that her meds were off...or maybe she had deliberately stopped taking them, as she sometimes did.

The decision never ended well, but there were moments between the fog of the drugs and the closing storm of manic episodes where Stratton saw a woman that he barely knew. A woman that, if he was honest, he would love to know. Quiet, confident, complex.

Even...attractive.

Carolyn stopped at his side but didn't touch him. She stared into his eyes. Her own gaze swam with hidden thoughts, disguised not by medication but by her own guile. Stratton looked down, and for the first time since accepting his post as vice president, he pictured his wife as first lady. America's most prominent woman. A demanding, unpredictable job in its own right.

Disaster in the making? Or maybe...

"Will you be there when I am?" Stratton asked.

No smile. No change in expression at all. But Carolyn's voice was steady as she answered.

"You know I will be."

Stratton leaned low. He kissed his wife on the forehead, soft and gentle. She left the room without another word and he looked into the mirror one more time, measuring his own gaze. Lifting his chin.

Jordan Stratton—an American elite. A man ready for the storm.

It was time.

72

Kybartai, Lithuania

Protestors—more than a thousand of them. They mobbed Dovilė's motorcade as she departed her jet and routed toward the heart of town. It was a six-kilometer drive, and tightly packed Lithuanians lined the streets and sidewalks the entire way, waving signs and shouting defiance. Anger. Outrage and flat refusal to comply.

The message was universal, impossible to ignore or misinterpret. Lithuania was *not* interested in surrender. They had slaved under Russian rule before, and they wouldn't go back. They would fight to the death first.

And if their president, Dovilė Petrauskienė, stood in their way, then they would fight her also. Wholeheartedly.

Dovilė sat behind bulletproof glass and watched the passing faces. Most of these people were from Kybartai itself, recently evicted by Lithuanian Defense Forces in the name of securing the region for Dovilė's meeting with Nikitin.

In truth the locals had been evicted for their own safety, but of course Dovilė couldn't admit that, and knowing their ignorance, she understood their rage. She watched as fists shook and listened as chants assumed a life of their own. Ranks of State Security Department agents on motorcycles fought to hold the crowds back, even as the glares of those security agents told Dovilė that they might agree with the citizenry.

She would be dead within a week if she actually surrendered to Russia —and not at the hands of the Russians. The thought actually brought a smile to Dovilė's face. A glow of warming pride to her chest.

She *loved* these people.

"I have an update."

The man seated next to Dovilė wasn't a member of her political staff, but the Chief of Defense of Lithuania, the military's most senior officer. She had known Tomas Vaitkus for nearly two decades, watching him ascend the ranks of Lithuania's relatively small military while she ascended the ranks of its government. Their paths crossed often. Mutual respect was developed—mutual trust, also.

When Maggie Trousdale first voiced her insane idea to end the war, Vaitkus was the only one that Dovilė told. In fact, she told him expecting Vaitkus to reject the proposal for the madness it was. To directly oppose it. To give her some idea how to refuse the American president while also securing American military aid.

But that wasn't Vaitkus's reaction. Quite the opposite—it was Vaitkus who convinced Dovilė that there might be some hope in Trousdale's plan. Perhaps...Lithuania's last hope.

"Our forces cannot hope to repel the Russians alone. NATO is weak— we will be overrun in days," he'd said.

Dovilė knew it was true. She also knew that Vaitkus was the only one she could trust with internal knowledge of her decision, or the necessary preparations to be made to facilitate the team that America was *not* sending. That nobody was sending.

Now Vaitkus was here. Riding beside her to meet Makar Nikitin, and he was holding out a cell phone.

Dovilė accepted it. She scanned the encrypted, internal email from one of Vaitkus's intelligence staff—her only connection with that nonexistent team. The missive was short and straight to the point. It was *more* insanity.

But Dovilė simply nodded. She passed the phone back. "I'll do it."

Vaitkus accepted the phone but didn't look away. He didn't say anything for a long moment. She could see the strain written all over his face.

"There's still time to back out," Vaitkus said, his voice low enough that the driver couldn't hear. "You were never meant to stand in the line of fire. I don't like it."

Dovilė was lost again, staring out the window at row after row of passing Lithuanians. Not just men, but women also. Children, many of them very young. Some so small that their mothers held them as the motorcade rumbled by. Those tiny humans screamed also...

But not like they would when the bombs fell. When the artillery shells rained in like hail. When this village, and so many like it, burned to ash and was crushed under the tracks of roaring Russian tanks. Tens of thousands would die, and many of them wouldn't be military.

Only over Dovilė's dead body.

"I'm standing in front of them," Dovilė whispered, still gazing at the protestors. "Right where I should be. Tell the Americans that I'll do it."

73

The White House

It was six a.m., and Maggie hadn't slept all night.

She'd tried. She'd lain awake in a king-size bed staring at a ceiling that dozens of presidents before her had stared at, and all she could think about was how much she missed the water stain pattern on the roof of that cabin out by Lake Maurepas—the family vacation retreat.

The stains weren't intentional, of course. Somewhere along the line a tin roof leaked and was repaired, but the drywall ceiling was never replaced. As a child, Maggie used to pick out patterns in those swirling stains like some people pick out patterns in the clouds or in the stars. She used to lose herself in whimsy and dreams. She used to imagine...

But she never imagined she'd be here, and now that she was, her only regret was that she hadn't been better. Stronger, somehow. More resilient. Able to serve her country the way she so desperately longed to do.

As Maggie rose and showered, she thought about all those dozens of presidents before her, some failures and some legends, while most were lost somewhere in between. She resolved that if history judged her as a failure, she would understand. She could even accept that reality...just so long as the next hours were a success.

Dressed in comfortable navy-blue sweats with the White House logo stitched over her chest, Maggie dried her hair but didn't apply any makeup. She ate a breakfast of yogurt and granola, leaving most of it on the table. She took her painkiller and relaxed to the welcome wash of warmth through her veins.

Then she went downstairs. Through the West Wing, ignoring the aides who shrank back and whispered at her passage, along with those few who dared to call her name. She reached the Situation Room, like so many times before…but also like no time before.

She entered it to find only two people waiting inside: CIA Director Dr. Sarah Aimes and the chairman of the Joint Chiefs of Staff, General Yellin. Both rose, standing silent as the door closed behind Maggie. The room was very still, and a little cold. Maggie scanned the empty chairs and stopped at Aimes.

"Did Jill give you any trouble?"

Aimes cleared her throat. Tensed. "She's…not in the West Wing, ma'am."

Right.

Maggie knew exactly what that meant. She accepted it with a mere nod, then settled into her usual chair at the head of the table. Poured herself coffee as Aimes and Yellin sat also. Mixed cream and sugar.

She sipped. She looked up.

"Are we ready?"

"Absolutely, ma'am." It was Yellin who spoke, and there was an aggressive confidence in his voice that warmed Maggie's blood. She looked to the wall and the bank of digital clocks hung there. One of them displayed Eastern European Time. It was one p.m. in Lithuania.

Sixty minutes until Makar Nikitin's arrival.

"Okay," Maggie said. "Let's do it."

74

Khrabrovo Airport
Kaliningrad Oblast, Russia

The Ilyushin Il-96-300PU touched down on black tarmac with a scream of tires and a thunder of jet engines.

It wasn't a graceful landing—it wasn't meant to be. From the moment President Makar Nikitin departed Moscow, his directions to his staff and security team were blatantly clear. The object of this trip wasn't purely pragmatic. In fact, it was almost entirely symbolic. Any number of lesser Russian governmental officials could have negotiated and accepted Lithuania's surrender. The point of Nikitin arriving in person was to seize the moment. To draw the attention of a breathless planet.

And to send a message, once and for all. *Russia* was now the world's preeminent power.

With that psychological objective in mind, Nikitin had ordered certain adjustments to the standard protocol of presidential travel. His plane was to arrive like a striking missile, slamming to earth in front of a field of not only Russian news cameras but Western journalists also. After stopping on the tarmac, the jet turned once and ramped its engines to nearly full blast, locked in place by its brakes, roaring like the thunder of the Apocalypse itself.

Then the stairs approached. The door was opened. Nikitin's personal security detail, typically numbering between eight and ten "bubble" agents who shadowed his every public move, had been tripled. Thirty men dressed in all black, each openly wielding PP-2000 submachine guns, rushed the stairs and formed a corridor on either side of a literal red carpet. Six additional agents flanked Nikitin as he emerged from the Ilyushin.

Also dressed in full black—like a minister at a funeral, except it wasn't a business suit. It was a military uniform. Black combat boots and black fatigue pants. A black jacket with matte black epaulettes and matte black braid. Even black buttons—he wore pitch-dark sunglasses and the gray near Nikitin's temples had been muted with dye.

Also black.

He stood at the top of the steps for a glass-shattering moment, conscious that every camera lens from the nearby press corps was fixated on him. Aware of the distant but audible gasps. The murmurings. The jostling of bodies fighting for a better position.

The *shock*.

Nikitin started down the stairs, walking in a clipped military march. Affixed to his right hip, openly visible to anyone looking, was a Tokarev TT-33 pistol, polished to a mirror finish and riding inside a black leather holster complete with a looping lanyard. A relic of the Soviet era, the Tokarev was underpowered by modern standards and only held eight rounds, but statistical lethality wasn't the point.

The gun was a symbol—another reminder to everyone watching of an age come and gone and now resurrected from the ashes. An age of Russian dominance.

Nikitin ignored the cameras and reporters—the brashest of which, all Western, actually shouted his name. He reached the end of the bodyguard corridor and right on cue every one of them turned in unison, boots snapping. They marched not like bodyguards at all, but like trained, elite soldiers.

Like the Nazi SS, Nikitin thought. Hitler may have been a maniac, but he sure knew how to intimidate. These bodyguards weren't actively needed to ensure Nikitin's safety, anyway. Two dozen snipers and enough ground infantry to crush a small town surrounded the airport on every side—one twitch of a threat, and the response would be instantaneous. Crushing.

At the end of the crimson carpet a pair of Russian army officers waited either side of a stocky man dressed in a traditional black suit with a Russian flag pin affixed to his lapel. Nearly a foot shorter than Nikitin, but looking not an ounce less hard, Andrei Vedenin had served as acting governor of the Kaliningrad Oblast ever since the previous governor died in a mysterious car accident nearly three years prior.

Nikitin appointed Vedenin to fill the position. A regular election, for one reason or another, was never held. As a former Russian military officer himself, Vedenin was accepted by most to be a better military strategist than he was a political leader, but nobody questioned his governance because Vedenin was also understood to be an unflinching Nikitin loyalist. Specifically, the kind that had turned an already heavily militarized Kaliningrad into an absolute anchor of Russian military power.

The kind that had NATO second-guessing itself.

"Welcome to Kaliningrad, Mr. President," Vedenin said, offering a salute in place of a traditional handshake. It was another mark of his military bearing. "May I say, your uniform is spectacular."

Nikitin indulged in just the hint of a smile, not visible to anyone more than a yard away. His face turned, and for the first time, he directly faced the press. The wall of so-called journalists was easily distinguishable between Russians and Westerners by their body language and general disposition.

The Russians stood tall—they were professional. Calm. Mechanical as they snapped pictures.

The Westerners, meanwhile, acted like undisciplined children. Actively shouting questions, thrusting microphones even though Nikitin stood a hundred yards away, even hurling accusations of tyrannical abuse. Red-faced and indignant, Nikitin couldn't help but revel in how meaningless their self-righteous grandstanding really was. The world would never see *them*. Never hear their shouted "questions"—really, just thinly disguised propaganda of their own.

But the world would see Makar Nikitin, roaring into NATO. Accepting surrender without a shot fired. And *that* mattered.

"Do you know what I love about journalists, Andrei?"

The governor didn't miss a beat. "The way they smell when their cars explode?"

This time Nikitin couldn't resist a broader smile. "I was going to say how *useful* they are...but you know, I like your answer better."

Vedenin returned the smile. Both men gazed at the press another moment, leering like hungry wolves. Then Nikitin turned. His long strides forced Vedenin to a near jog to keep up, but the governor didn't complain. They marched all the way to a parked Mil Mi-8 helicopter, painted with white, blue, and red stripes just like Nikitin's jet, and specially configured to serve as a VIP transport.

Not far away, a trio of Kamov Ka-52 "Alligator" attack helicopters were already spinning up, ready to provide close-escort services to the Mil Mi-8 on its forty-five-minute flight to Chernyshevskoe and the Lithuanian border. Again, it wasn't a *necessary* protection measure...

Just a matter of intimidation.

"Did you bring any of that Beluga Gold Line you're always bragging about?" Nikitin said, ducking into the helicopter.

Vedenin was right on his heels. The Mil Mi's jet engines howled, even as the door closed. The governor bent and produced an ornate, wax-sealed bottle from a concealed storage compartment.

"Thirsty already, Mr. President?"

Nikitin settled into his seat, ignoring the belt. He looked through the porthole window and across the tarmac, once more to the press. In particular, to a face he recognized from his obsessive review of Western media.

She was a Polish reporter. Brash, defiant, obnoxious. Just now, she looked ready to explode.

Nikitin grinned. "Absolutely parched. Pour us a round."

75

Ramstein Air Base
Rheinland-Pfalz, Germany

"Brigade! *Attennnnn-tion!*"

Seven thousand, seven hundred four individual boots snapped together as the neat rows of US Army paratroopers they were attached to snapped upright. Backs stiff, chins up, arms at their sides and heavy packs at their feet. They were all dressed in camouflage green, helmets held beneath one arm and chest rigs already loaded out with enough ammunition to lay down a small town.

A town like Kybartai, Lithuania, for instance.

Colonel Greg Packer took the low plywood stage at the head of the crowd and tossed a casual salute, ordering his men to stand at ease. In perfect unison, hands dropped behind backs and boots turned outward, a thunder of movement come and gone as every young face remained fixed on their commanding officer.

They called him "Iron Boots" when they thought he might be listening, a reference to his constant threat to personally drive a boot up the ass of any man caught lagging in drill. When they thought he *wasn't* listening the nicknames were a great deal less flattering.

But Greg Packer liked all the monikers because he appreciated the tone of respect in each, no matter how begrudging it might be. He knew that the past eighteen months of brutal training had weeded out the weak from the ranks of this brigade, leaving only the relentless and resilient, those who appreciated the fighting machine he had built them into.

These men would follow Iron Boots anywhere—he knew that. Standing before them with both hands wrapped around the outside edges of a lectern, a sudden lump in his throat, Packer couldn't help but think... maybe he was about to ask them to follow him to their deaths.

Packer swallowed. He swept from one face to the next, noting steady faces, some of them already smeared with camouflage paint. Others sweating despite the Polish chill. None showing any trace of fear—maybe because they didn't know what came next, but Packer liked to think it was because they didn't care.

He smiled at that. He shook his head in mock admiration.

"I tell you what. You boys look ready for the Met Gala!"

That brought just the hint of a smile from a few. The rest remained tense. Focused. Waiting.

Packer breathed deep. He stood a little straighter.

"By now you've all been briefed by your troop commanders regarding the coming mission. It may seem unclear to you as to the purpose of our jump—or why we would be jumping into an Allied country at all while we maintain clear overland access. As usual, the strategic details of this operation were ironed out by men much smarter and better looking than any of us, and I'm not at liberty to share any further details. The most I can tell you—that I can assure you, both as your commanding officer and fellow soldier—is that this jump *matters*. It is, in fact, the jump you have trained for your entire career in the United States Army. The kind of jump that only men such as yourselves, soldiers of the 82nd Airborne, are trusted to perform. The outcome of this mission, if successful, could change the very fate of the world. And if it fails, well..."

Packer trailed off. Resisted another swallow. Forced a dry smile and shook his head.

"It won't fail. Because if, for even a moment, one of you delicate little daises should give anything less than your *very best*...do I need to tell you what happens?"

"*You'll put a boot up our ass!*"

All 3,852 members of the brigade answered in unison, without hesitation. A thunder of shouting voices that echoed off the hangar walls and reverberated across the concrete. A voice of anger, of confidence, of unchecked bravado. The voice of the 82nd Airborne, the proudest parachuting division in US Army history, ready to fling themselves straight into the pit of war.

Packer grinned. "*You better believe I will!* All the way out your throats!"

The grins spread. Packer released the lectern and stood ramrod straight. His voice boomed like cannon fire.

"*Brigade!* Where are we going?"

"*To war, Colonel!*"

"And how *far* are we going?"

As before, the response was instantaneous. Knee-jerk. Instinctual. Absolutely confident.

The proud motto of the proudest parachuting division.

"*All the way!*"

76

Washington, DC

The Eisenhower Executive Office Building sat directly across the street from the Oval Office, but in a place like Washington, DC, Jordan Stratton long ago learned that mere inches could be the difference between absolute power and mere spectatorship.

Such was the case with the EEOB. Housing an army of bureaucrats that served the actual daily functions of the United States executive office, the building was nonetheless removed from the public eye and often overlooked entirely by the swarm of media and other outside forces who infested the White House. Much of the complex, constructed during the nineteenth century, provided space for federal offices and support systems for the president, like the roots of a metaphorical tree, whereas the White House itself was the flowering branches.

Underground. Unobserved. Silent.

The perfect place for a coup.

Stratton hadn't visited his West Wing office since being ejected from the White House some weeks earlier. But in addition to the cramped confines of that room he also maintained a much larger office inside the

EEOB, usually reserved for ceremonial applications or occasional large meetings when West Wing facilities were not available.

This particular meeting was more a matter of flying beneath the radar than a need for the expanded space. Besides Stratton and Jill Easterling, nine members of the Trousdale cabinet gathered around the conference table. A wall of windows overlooked the South Lawn, but all the blinds were presently drawn. The light was dim. Nobody was drinking coffee or sneaking in an early lunch. The AC was switched off and sweat shimmered from the foreheads of more than a few.

And nobody spoke. Nobody wanted to make eye contact. Stratton sat at the head of the table and felt the tension in the air as tight as a banjo string. It compressed around his rib cage, tightening his lungs and making each breath feel shallow.

He looked to Easterling but she avoided his gaze. He looked down the table to Secretary of State Lisa Gorman, but her dark eyes flashed away also. Nobody moved, and Stratton imagined that an entire hurricane could have ripped through downtown DC without anybody so much as noticing.

It was a frozen moment of dread. Of disbelief, perhaps.

But only a moment, and as expected, SecDef Kline shattered it.

"Well. We all know why we're here. We gonna do this, or what?"

Stratton's mind snapped into gear, and he nodded once. The SecDef passed him a leather-bound portfolio emblazoned with the White House logo. Stratton flipped it open and found a single sheet of resume paper printed with his personal letterhead.

To the Congress of the United States of America.

Then a brief paragraph. Plain English. Stratton wanted it that way. In the next few hours this document would circulate around the globe, reprinted by every news outlet from New York City to London to Moscow and Beijing.

He wanted people to comprehend it perfectly. To have no doubt or confusion in their minds. Whether they agreed or disagreed or were just left speechless, at least they would *understand.*

The rest was up to him.

Stratton reached inside his jacket. The Montblanc Meisterstück was heavy in his hand as he spun the cap off, exposing a fourteen-karat-gold nib already wet with ink. He adjusted his grip and lingered over the page only a moment.

Then Stratton signed. He passed the document and—uncharacteristically—the pen to the left. Slowly, one cabinet member after another added the signature beneath their printed name. SecDef Kline was the last one, and he dispensed a signature with three quick strokes of the Montblanc.

Then both pen and document were returned to Stratton. He replaced the cap on the pen and returned it to his inner pocket. He closed the portfolio and passed it to Easterling.

"To be delivered to Congress immediately."

Easterling slid the portfolio into an attaché bag. Still, nobody moved.

"Does anybody...know where she is?"

That was the secretary of commerce. Nobody needed to ask for clarification on who *she* was. All eyes pivoted toward Easterling.

"I haven't been notified this morning," Easterling said.

"I believe she's still at the White House."

Nods. Grunts. Gazes pivoted to Stratton, and he knew—it was time to assume command.

"We'll enter the West Wing at eight a.m., sharp. Lisa, Steven, Jill, I want you with me. Everybody else report to your offices and notify your staff of the change in leadership. Stand by for further instructors. Understood?"

Nods. Silence. Stratton's spine stiffened.

"That wasn't a rhetorical question."

"Understood, sir," Kline said, his voice steady.

Everyone else echoed the acknowledgment. Stratton stood, and they stood with him. Everyone but his chosen three shuffled out. Stratton stepped to the window and adjusted the blinds, allowing a view through tinted glass.

He could see the South Lawn. He could see the West Wing, and even the curtained windows of the Oval Office. No sign of Muddy Maggie or any activity inside—it was as though the seat of presidential power slept, even while the world careened into war.

Lifting his wrist, Stratton checked the polished Rolex.

Fifty-two minutes. Then, for the first time in American history, a vice president would seize control of the White House.

77

Kybartai, Lithuania

Reed heard the helicopters first.

Distant over the horizon, invisible to the naked eye, but impossible to misidentify. Now removed from the third-floor apartment and stretched across the flat roof of Building A, Reed edged to the six-inch brick parapet and lifted binoculars to his eyes, adjusting the focus to look out over the border crossing, the river, and deep into Russia.

There was a haze over the landscape, cloud cover that glimmered in the midday sun. Even as the steady *thwap, thwap, thwap* of rotor blades grew louder, Reed still couldn't zero in on their exact location. He swept distant tree lines, keeping his point of focus just a few degrees above the ground.

It was Turk who found them first. Resting alongside Reed with a matching pair of binos, he whispered just loud enough to be heard above incoming jet engines.

"Three o'clock, high. Four birds."

Reed pivoted to the spot, and he found them. A lead chopper painted with white, blue, and red markings. It was a member of the Mil Mi family of Russian helicopters—a transport craft, not a gunship, but Reed didn't recognize the specific variant.

By contrast the other three aircraft were easy to identify. One flew to either side of the Mil Mi, while a third and final bird raced behind and above. With jutting wide wings hung heavy with armament, and a twin-seat cockpit similar to that of an American Black Hawk, what made the chopper so iconic was neither its silhouette nor its coloring, but the coaxial rotors affixed above its main body.

Two of them, one mounted a few feet above the other, each rotating in opposite directions and thereby eliminating the need for a tail rotor. It was the Kamov Ka-50—the *Alligator*, Russia's premier ground attack helicopter. Racing in alongside the Mil Mi, those three gunships were headed straight for the town on the Russian side of the river.

"That's him," Reed said.

Turk made no answer. Reed lowered his binoculars and watched the helicopters as dots, slowly halting some five kilometers away. Then the Mil Mi descended...but the three Alligators remained aloft.

"And that's a problem," Turk said.

It was, but Reed had expected air cover. He would have preferred jets or even high-level drones, something that wouldn't be able to precisely engage his position once the fireworks began. Now he would have to think about keeping his people away from windows, maybe implementing more smoke...

It changes nothing, Reed thought. *We execute the mission.*

"Six o'clock," Turk said, twisting to look backward. "Two klicks out."

Reed didn't need to look to know what was coming—what he heard told the story. It wasn't the distant pound of the choppers or the nearly silent hum of a precision German engine powering the Lithuanian president's armored BMW.

It was the roar of a thousand distant but angry voices, decrying her betrayal.

78

Chernyshevskoe, Kaliningrad Oblast
Russia

The Mil Mi landed much more softly than the Ilyushin had—there weren't nearly so many people to impress in this isolated spec of a town. Nikitin, in fact, had never been there before. He'd never been to the border of Kaliningrad and Lithuania before. He'd never needed to be.

But after today, the name Chernyshevskoe would be etched in the history books. The first full surrender of a NATO state to the Russian Federation...a domino to start the chain.

Nikitin drained his second tumbler of vodka and buttoned his jacket. He wasn't buzzed—it took a lot more than two pours to get him that far. Accompanied by Vedenin, he marched out of the helicopter and onto smooth tarmac, immediately greeted not only by the thunder of orbiting overhead Alligators but by another *rota*—company—of one hundred heavily armed Russian infantrymen.

A Russian colonel, dressed in field fatigues, saluted Nikitin and welcomed him. He handed off a military intelligence report, which Nikitin scanned before returning.

President Petrauskienė was on schedule. Her motorcade was

approaching the bridge, slowed by storms of Lithuanian protestors, but that was no matter. After their government formally surrendered, those protestors would fall into line...or else.

"We have your car ready, Mr. President. As requested..."

The colonel stepped back. He swept a gloved hand across the airfield toward a line of three heavily armored vehicles—not the Aurus Senat limousines that had been shipped for Nikitin's use but a trio of Russian military GAZ Tigr trucks.

All resting on beefy tires, sporting swivel machine gun mounts...and specially painted flat black with the Russian flag emblazoned on the front doors.

Nikitin shot a glance sideways at Vedenin and noted the governor ducking his head in muted admiration for another tactical triumph.

More intimidation.

"We recommend the rear truck, sir," the colonel said. "Just in case—"

"I will take the front truck," Nikitin cut him off. "Order the Alligators to stand off. I want just enough noise to shake the earth—not so much that I need to shout."

The colonel hesitated a moment longer, then caught a demanding look from Vedenin. That was enough. The entourage started across the tarmac again, Nikitin's heart thumping beneath his jet-black uniform. His fingers tingling with electricity. His body *consumed* by the momentum of the moment.

Within half an hour he would accept Lithuania's surrender and cut Latvia and Estonia off from their NATO allies, all but ensuring their eventual defeat. America had yet to so much as growl, and already Europe was tumbling.

Focus. Drive it home. You are God.

Nikitin reached the lead Tigr and a soldier snapped to attention, reaching to open the rear armored door. Nikitin flatly ignored him, proceeding to the front passenger door and opening it himself.

"Sir—"

Vedenin must have glared again. The soldier's voice fell flat. Nikitin stood in the open doorway, his hat flattened against his head by the downwash of a passing Alligator. He looked back to Vedenin, who wasn't preparing to load up. The governor would remain behind to command military forces along the Lithuanian border—just a precaution.

The two men's eyes locked. Vedenin stiffened and saluted. Nikitin smiled a broad, bloodthirsty grin.

Then he loaded up. The heavy door slammed. The Tigr's engine roared.

The convoy departed to defeat NATO.

79

Moscow, Russia

Anton Golubev was covered in blood—and not his own.

Maxim Romanov's executive political assistant hung from the ceiling walls of a basement vault that didn't officially exist. With thick concrete walls and an insulated ceiling, it had once served as a boiler room for a nineteenth-century internal heating system—thus the insulation.

Now that boiler was long removed. The basement cavity beneath an unused Soviet governmental building was as empty and dirty as all of the offices upstairs. Golubev himself had only ever come to this place for special occasions—usually occasions just such as this.

Long, brutal hours of torture. With chains lifting the body off the floor, and clothes stripped away, Golubev had gone to work on the aide with every tool in his morbid box—pliers, saws, dull knives, a blowtorch. The man had screamed and thrashed even as two of Golubev's secret police soldiers held him. Golubev didn't worry about the screaming. He knew nobody could hear.

He ripped the man apart, one slow piece at a time—not because he knew for sure that the man was hiding something but because the worm in the back of Golubev's brain demanded that he test his suspicions. That he search out any possible threat against Nikitin's regime.

That he *perform* as Ghost of the Kremlin.

That was why he kidnapped Romanov's aide. Why he dragged him here, strung him up, and went to work. The torture lasted for nearly two hours...and then, at last, the political aide did what all men did under Golubev's maniacal talents. He broke. Gasping and half sobbing and pleading for the mercy of death, he spilled everything he knew.

It wasn't a lot. Maxim Romanov had covered his tracks well, and what little he left behind was hardly enough to convict him in a court of law. But in the court of Anton Golubev, Makar Nikitin's right-hand man and the Ghost of the Kremlin, it was *more* than enough. It was solid proof of what Golubev had suspected for months.

It was evidence of treason.

Golubev drove a screwdriver into the man's heart just to shut him up. He spat saliva and blood and stood panting in the glare of overhead lights, his mind spinning.

And then his thoughts landed on the obvious. The thing that had never fit, not even from the start. The thing that seemed too good to be true.

Lithuania.

"With me!" Golubev snapped, turning for the door. "Find the prime minister!"

"What about—"

"Leave him," Golubev snarled. "I want Romanov arrested within the hour. All his staff, too. Notify the FSB and prepare interrogations. Notify the president's staff in Kaliningrad and issue an immediate halt to negotiations with the Lithuanians. From this moment forward, the entire government is to be considered compromised. Do you understand? *Move!*"

There was no further debate from the lieutenants. The body was left to hang, and Golubev led the way up stone steps to the vacant corridors and offices upstairs. He was already reaching for his phone, already sorting through a mental list of *fixers* and selecting names of unimpeachable reliability. Brutal, animal men. The kind who would do whatever they were told, whatever was necessary.

Golubev would seize control of the entire government, if necessary. He would barricade the Kremlin, imprison the entire federal assembly. This was a time of war. Nikitin would back him up. Golubev needed to *hurry*.

But his encrypted smartphone was without signal in the basement. He would need to return to ground level. Another dozen steps and a pivot through a heavy wood door. Golubev's heart was thumping as the bars returned to his phone screen. He entered a corridor, face-down, and began to dial.

Then the boot steps of the men behind him ground to an abrupt halt. Golubev felt the tension in the air spike like a rush of sizzling heat exploding off that old-fashioned boiler in the basement. His face snapped up, the phone still held in one hand, and he froze.

The man standing fifty yards down a corridor was tall—much taller than Golubev. Black hair streaked with gray hung to his shoulders, his oversized nose twisted to one side after what couldn't have been the first breakage. He stood relaxed and alone, a Grach handgun affixed to his hip.

And he smiled. Not a happy smile. Not even smug smile.

This was a *resolved* smile.

"Going somewhere, Anton?" Ivan Sidorov said.

For a long, icy moment, nobody moved. The two men's gazes locked, and in a split second it all made sense to Golubev. That moving player in the shadows that he could never identify—the missing piece of the puzzle.

Golubev's jaw tightened. The phone fell from his fingers. And then, together, four hands flew to their firearms.

80

The Situation Room
The White House

Satellite imagery displayed it all.

From three hundred miles above the earth's surface, a full-color picture of the border between Kaliningrad and Lithuania spread across the wall-to-wall screens constructed at the end of the room. Humans moved as barely perceptible dots, while vehicles crawled like ants along gray roads that led toward the river and the border crossing.

Three vehicles in particular were the focus of the feed. General Yellin informed Maggie that they were Russian Tigr trucks, roughly equivalent to United States military Humvees. They had collected a small number of individuals from the airfield where the Mil Mi helicopter had landed, and even though Maggie had no way of knowing for sure...she believed.

Makar Nikitin was one of them.

Still seated at the head of the table, Maggie slumped in her chair, her body both relaxed by the welcome relief of opioids and also wrecked by them. She had consumed her latest dose in front of both Aimes and Yellin, and nobody had said anything.

What were they going to say? Maybe they already knew, maybe they didn't. By this afternoon it wouldn't matter either way.

"Mildred, can we get some coffee?" Maggie spoke into her intercom. The White House steward enthusiastically agreed, clueless to the operation underway in the Situation Room or what impact it might have. Maybe clueless to a lot of things...or maybe the White House staff knew a lot more than Maggie gave them credit for.

Bless them—they had been *so* good to her. She wished she could return even a fraction of that kindness.

Perhaps, if this operation was successful, she might just save their children from the teeth of war.

"Disappointing showing this past weekend, General," Maggie said, her gaze still fixed on the screen but her voice calm.

From four chairs down Yellin twisted in his seat. "Ma'am?"

"The Army-Navy game. Don't tell me you missed it?"

Yellin looked even more confused, then subtly stunned, as though Maggie were asking him what shampoo he preferred or where he bought his car insurance.

Maggie chose to fill the silence. "That fourth quarter interception should have made the difference. Army's ball at the Navy thirty with only ninety seconds to play. Five points were all you needed...and there Army goes, three and out. Navy kneels through the final sixty. *Wild.*"

Maggie shook her head. Yellin's eyes remained squinted. Sarah Aimes sat with her fingers interlaced over the table, staring down at them. Not speaking.

"I guess you never know when the next play is your last," Yellin said, his voice low.

Maggie smiled, just a little. She didn't feel the smile, but she felt that Yellin deserved it. Maybe he deserved a lot more.

"Sometimes you do, General. Sometimes you do."

Behind Maggie a door opened, and she waited for the rattle of the coffee cart. But no cart came. The footsteps were too fast to be those of a steward. When Maggie looked up, she recognized one of her aides instead —a young woman fresh out of Harvard who always dressed like a fifty-year-old congresswoman. Today her hair was drawn back tight, her back stiff…and her face ashen pale.

"Ma'am?"

"What is it, Cynthia?"

The aide swallowed. She lifted a notecard hastily scrawled in black ink. "From Congressman Lakeland. He wanted you to know…"

Maggie scanned the note. It contained only one line, but that was more than enough. It was exactly what she expected, but the speed and brutality of the message still caught her off guard.

Folding the note, Maggie handed it back. She forced another smile.

"Direct my security detail to seal off the West Wing. I want full operational lockdown—nobody gets in, nobody gets out. Including the vice president."

Cynthia swallowed. Her fingers tightened around the note. "Ma'am, are you…"

She couldn't finish. Her eyes rimmed with red, and she blinked hard. Maggie put a hand on her arm.

"Do what I say, Cynthia. Buy me another two hours. Then you'll understand. Okay?"

A weak nod. Cynthia left, and Maggie heard the door bolt behind her. She twisted in her seat and faced the screen, ignoring the gazes of Yellin and Aimes. Looking instead to that trio of Tigr trucks now approaching the border.

And thinking—she wished the coffee made it before the note.

81

Russian-Lithuanian Border

Something was wrong. Nikitin felt it even before his Russian Army driver applied the brakes of the lead Tigr. They had just reached the bend in the A229 highway and were looking over the bridge into Lithuania. The border crossing checkpoint was there—the humble apartment buildings and business centers of downtown Kybartai rising just beyond.

But there was no sign of the Lithuanian presidential motorcade, the one that was meant to cross the river into Russia and meet Nikitin here at the two-story Russian governmental building which would serve as the official site of surrender.

In fact, there were no signs of Lithuanians at all. No military, no civilians, *nobody*. Not even at the guard post.

"What the hell?" Nikitin said, the Tigr rumbling beneath him. "Where is she?"

The driver shifted, suddenly on edge. He lifted his radio and called to a superior. Nikitin looked into his mirror, noting the other two Tigrs halted behind him. One of the Alligators passed overhead, and his seat shuddered. The driver covered his earpiece as he listened to the radio response. His face was a little pale as he turned to Nikitin.

"The Lithuanian motorcade has stopped, Mr. President."

"What?"

"They're just beyond the border checkpoint. There seems to be some delay."

Nikitin swore, a flush of indignation and embarrassment coursing up his neck and into his face even as he snatched a pair of binoculars from the Tigr's dash. He adjusted the focus and swept across the bridge to the checkpoint and the street beyond. He couldn't see the black BMW or any of its motorcycle escorts. He couldn't see any Lithuanian troops. The street was just *empty*.

And there he was, sitting like a fool. Like a man stood up on a date. It wasn't a rational parallel—there was probably a perfectly legitimate reason for the delay—but Nikitin couldn't help but think of all the Western media on site in Kybartai. Reporters and fields of hostile cameras who would no doubt document this moment for the world to see.

The moment the president of Russia was made to *wait*.

"Put a bird over Kybartai!" Nikitin snapped. "Rattle them loose!"

The soldier communicated the demand via his radio. Moments passed, maybe while Russian military commanders debated the wisdom of the order.

Then one of the Alligators broke off and stormed directly over the bridge. It tore into Kybartai, flying barely fifty feet over the rooftops and dumping rotor wash. Shingles tore loose and blew in the wind—a Lithuanian flag snapped against its tether. The Alligator completed a slow turn, its loaded wings sweeping NATO streets.

Then the soldier's radio crackled again.

"She is moving, Mr. President."

Nikitin didn't smile. His heart was still hammering, his fingers tightening around the binoculars. The Alligator faded from his view even as he fixated on that blank spot in the road on his side of the Lithuanian border checkpoint—the place where Petrauskienė would first appear.

Time itself seemed to grind to a halt. Nikitin didn't breathe, his body frozen in place. Waiting. Longing. Nearly quivering with anticipating.

Then the BMW appeared. It turned the corner, jet black and shiny clean. It was alone—there was no motorcycle escort, no security. Nikitin's eyebrows wrinkled and the first hint of uncertainty twisted his gut. He licked his lips, still hungry.

But the BMW only slowed. It passed the border checkpoint, still a hundred meters from the bridge, and came to a halt. The running lights still shone, but the vehicle didn't move. No other vehicles appeared, either. All was still once more.

"What the *hell*," Nikitin snarled.

Then something did move. It was the BMW's back door. It opened, and very slowly, a leg clad in black pants slid out. Then another. A body emerged.

It was President Dovilė Petrauskienė. She stepped away from the BMW and gently pushed the door shut behind her. Standing alone next to the SUV, she faced the bridge with a bouquet of flowers grasped in both hands. The wind tousled blond hair, tugging at the tail of her blazer, but Petrauskienė didn't move. She stood on the Lithuanian side of the border, as tall and steady as a statue, neither smiling nor quivering.

Looking dead into Nikitin's Tigr. Staring, not blinking or flinching.

And then...her lips began to move.

"What is she doing?" Nikitin snapped, lowering the binoculars. "What the hell is she doing? Does she think this is a game?"

Nobody answered. The driver sat with both hands wrapped tight around the wheel, knuckles white. The two FSO guards in the back seat were rigid and speechless. Nikitin swore again and pushed his door open. Behind him one of the guards shouted and reached for his shoulder, but it was too late to stop the president. Nikitin held the door open, just two inches, admitting a frigid blast of Baltic air swept from across the river.

And with it, just the hint of a melodic voice. Soft at first, barely audible, but growing stronger as Petrauskienė lifted her chin. Her mouth opened wider. Her whole body leaned into the words.

It was a *song*. It was "Tautiška giesmė," Lithuania's national anthem.

Lithuania, our homeland. Land of worshipped heroes!

The words weren't sung in Lithuanian, they were sung in *Russian*, and the moment Nikitin heard them something deep in his chest snapped. It was a breaking leash, a shattering chain. A cage ruptured and bars bent.

It was the animal that had lived inside of him all these years, fed and nurtured and growing more strong and savage by the day, finally bursting free. Completely off the leash, unrestrained and unguided. Taking instant control.

Nikitin slammed the door. He threw the binoculars down. He shouted in the confines of the armored truck.

"*Forward!* Across the bridge. Move now!"

The driver froze. He blinked. He looked back to the FSO officers behind him.

"Sir—"

Nikitin hit him, full fisted, right in the mouth. Teeth crunched. Blood sprayed. The guy's head snapped back, but he wasn't unconscious.

"I said *move*!" Nikitin roared. "I want the whole column across that bridge. Move the choppers in. I want her in *chains*!"

The shouts thundered against metal and glass. The driver was stunned, but he didn't argue any further. His foot slipped off the brake. The heavy diesel engine churned.

The lead Tigr lurched for the bridge.

82

Kybartai, Lithuania

"He's moving! He's moving!"

Wolfgang's frantic call over the encrypted radio erupted in Reed's ear, sending him scrambling for the volume control. From where he crouched behind a window, back inside the top-floor apartment of Building A, Reed couldn't see the road below. He couldn't see the bridge or the Russian side of the border. To grant himself a vantage point would be to expose himself to the sweeping Alligator helicopter or any Russian sniper stationed on the far side of the river. He had to wait.

But Wolfgang was dug into position at Building C, farther inside Kybartai and hidden behind curtained glass with a narrow but critical view of the road, the border checkpoint—and the bridge beyond.

Reed's heart hammered and he twisted on the floor, catching Turk's eye from six yards away. Two LAW rocket launcher tubes lay between them, covered in a blanket. The window they shared offered a clear view of a street that would serve as the Tigr's only route of escape—a definite trap.

But only if they moved quickly enough.

"Hold the line until he's on Lithuanian soil," Reed radioed. "*Do not* blow before. Those charges won't take that Tigr."

"Good copy." That was Corbyn, somewhat less amped than Wolfgang but still dialed in. She and Lucy were the only two members of the team still on street level, hidden behind a row of cars one block to Reed's north, awaiting the signal to trigger the wireless detonators and then run for their lives to Building B.

Reed reached for the nearest LAW and slid it against his leg. He breathed deep, and he felt something he always felt just before moments like this, even if he would never admit it.

Nerves.

"Fifty yards," Wolfgang radioed. "He's gaining speed. She's...she's not moving."

Reed squinted. He shot another glance at Turk.

That *wasn't* part of the plan.

"Report, is she away from the bridge?" Reed called.

"Negative," Wolfgang called. "She's twenty yards back, still facing Russia."

Reed pushed the LAW aside once more. He twisted at the base of the window and leaned out from the frame—just a little. He saw the checkpoint, the street, the bridge. He saw the jet-black Lithuanian BMW parked at an angle, its back door standing open. He saw the column of Russian Tigrs, halfway across the bridge and only yards from Lithuanian soil.

And he saw Dovilė Petrauskienė, standing dead in the middle of the road, a bouquet of flowers held to her chest, defiantly glaring down the oncoming invaders.

And still singing.

"*Move!*" Reed shouted, knowing that Petrauskienė couldn't hear him, and that it wouldn't have mattered if she did. Time was already out. The Tigrs were almost on top of her and they were *not* slowing down.

And then, suddenly, Petrauskienė turned. Her right hand, still clutching the flowers, shot into the air. She faced Lithuania and her face turned hard and she screamed a single word.

"*Kovok!*"

It was Lithuanian. Reed didn't speak Lithuanian. But just this once, he didn't need to. The message came loud and clear, a blend of body language and unrivaled bravery.

Fight!

Then the lead Tigr hit. Dovilė Petrauskienė's body folded over the front bumper, her head snapping back against the hood. The flowers exploded. Blood sprayed. She went under, and the Tigr went over. The vehicle barely lurched. Makar Nikitin was *still* coming. The lead Tigr hit Lithuanian soil—the two others followed.

Then Reed shouted into his earpiece and reached for the LAW.

"*Blow the bridges!* Blow them *now*!"

83

The White House

Jordan Stratton arrived in the back of a government Suburban, flanked by a Secret Service detail and joined by Lisa Gorman, Jill Easterling, and Steven Kline. Tires squealed on the asphalt loop that served the West Wing entrance, and Stratton opened his own door.

His heart hammered. His head buzzed. He wasn't sure if it was anxiety or adrenaline or pure stress, finally boiling over. With the declaration transmitted to Congress sixty-five minutes prior, he expected to have heard from Maggie. He hoped that she would call him, that she would at least *try* to make this easy.

Instead he received radio silence, and that silence was as loud as artillery fire. It transmitted a clear and unmistakable message. Muddy Maggie Trousdale was *not* going down without a fight.

Stratton's jacket snapped, his leather-soled shoes clapping on the asphalt as he approached the door. It was closed—two Secret Service agents flanked it. As Stratton drew near, they moved to block him.

"Good morning, Mr. Vice President. Can we help you?"

"Get out of my way," Stratton snapped.

"I'm sorry, sir." The agent's voice crackled with edgy tension. He swallowed once. "We've been ordered to secure the West Wing. Nobody is permitted to come or go. Security lockdown, sir."

Heat rushed up Stratton's neck. He cast a sideways glance at Kline. The SecDef was less patient. He pushed past Stratton and bulled the first agent right out of the way, sending him stumbling into a flowerbed as the second agent instinctively reached for his sidearm—then froze in confused indecision.

"Yeah, yeah," Kline snapped. "Shoot me, why don't you?"

The agent was still in deadlock, and Kline was already at the door. He shoved it open and Stratton resumed the lead.

Through the lobby. Curving right and passing his own West Wing office. Shoes cracking like gunshots, aides and low-level officials appearing in the hallway with eyes wide and uncertain. Stratton passed at least one TV that displayed C-SPAN footage of the House floor. Congress had called an emergency session and representatives were slowly shuffling in. Already Maggie's enemies were rallying against a dwindling knot of her supporters. It was a national spectacle, the news was out. Maggie *had* to know.

"Where's the president?" Stratton barked.

Nobody answered. Stratton gritted his teeth and hurtled onward, leaving Jill Easterling to trail the group and order her people back into their offices. To switch the TVs off. To stand by for orders.

Then Stratton reached the Oval Office. The door was closed, and he barged ahead. It swung on silent hinges. A rush of cool air hit him in the face—dim lights, and only one occupant.

It was a White House steward with a feather duster. She was agitated, looking ready to cry. Maggie was nowhere to be seen.

"You." Stratton snapped his fingers. "Where's the president?"

The woman stepped back, blinking hard. The first tear leaked out. Her lips parted but she didn't answer.

"Downstairs," Easterling said, catching up. "She's in the SitRoom!"

Stratton spun again, leaving the steward. With Easterling in the lead his column bypassed the elevator and took the stairs, Stratton shaking his head the whole way down.

Unbelievable. She was really dug in. *What* was she up to?

The West Wing basement was quiet, the lights turned down. Easterling shouted down Secret Service agents as they appeared like wraiths from the shadows. Some attempted to block the newcomers—most made barely a protest.

Maybe they'd seen the news. Maybe they no longer knew who their boss was. Maybe they were just as fed up with Maggie as anybody else.

Ahead, the entrance to the Situation Room's primary conference center loomed out of the dark. The door was closed, and the two men guarding it did not immediately step aside. Easterling called for them to open the door—they ignored her, closing ranks instead. Bulky bodies and broad shoulders, these weren't just *any* agents.

They were members of Maggie's personal detail.

"Open the door," Stratton demanded.

The nearest agent stiffened. His nostrils flexed. He didn't move—he didn't look Stratton directly in the eye, either.

"Did you hear me?" Stratton's voice dropped to a snarl.

"I'm sorry, Mr. Vice President. I can't do that."

"I'm *ordering* you to."

"I've been ordered by the president."

"Didn't you see the news? She's not president anymore. I am."

A hesitation. The two agents exchanged a glance. Sweat trickled from the nearest guy's temple.

But he didn't budge. He made a career decision, and stood his ground.

"I don't know about that, sir. I only have my orders."

"Yeah?" Stratton spoke through his teeth, leaning close. "Well, how about this?"

Stratton's hand struck like a snake. He found the man's Agency-issued Glock 19 housed on his right hip. It slipped from its holster and spun in Stratton's hand even as the second guy flailed for his own gun.

Stratton's finger curled around the trigger. The muzzle settled over the first guy's right eye even as he found his balance, hands pressing against the wall, instant fear stretching his face.

"Open the door," Stratton said.

"Sir—" The second agent had his gun out but hadn't yet pointed it at the vice president. The first guy wasn't speaking.

"I said, *open this door*!" Stratton shouted.

The man pinned beneath him swallowed. The sweat trail slipped down to his jaw and ran to his chin. But he didn't budge.

Then the overhead intercom clicked. A soft, familiar voice spoke, just loud enough to hear.

"It's okay, Anthony. You can let him in."

The agent blinked. He looked ready to melt. Slowly, Stratton lowered the pistol. He didn't surrender it. The second man glowered but reached for the lock panel. He input a lengthy code. The electric bolt buzzed.

Then Stratton marched in, the Glock swinging at his side. He entered the conference room where he and Muddy Maggie had shared so many late nights and early mornings. His gaze swept past CIA Director Aimes, General Yellin, and a TV screen that displayed a satellite view of some city Stratton didn't recognize—some city swarmed by smoke and flame.

And then Stratton saw Maggie. Sitting frail and slumped at the head of the table, her face ashen, her hands loose in her lap. Dirty-blond hair fell around her cheeks, and her gaze traveled from Stratton to Kline to Gorman. A flash of pain crossed her face when she reached Easterling.

Then she looked back to her VP. "Hello, Jordan."

Stratton's gaze snapped back to the screen. He read the label in the bottom right-hand corner—it was live satellite feed.

"What the hell are you doing?" Stratton hissed.

"We're saving the world. Would you like to join us?"

84

Kybartai, Lithuania

The three bridges detonated with the voice of thunder.

An oversized application of C4, packed tight against support columns and expansion joints, exploded in the blink of an eye and turned concrete into instantaneous dust and rubble. Clouds of debris hurtled into the sky and the ground shook. Reed felt it all the way at the top of the apartment building as glass cracked and distant screams tore the air.

The bridges were gone—not partially, but completely. Chunks of what remained fell over the road like a meteor shower, nearly obscuring the column of Tigrs from view.

But Reed could still see the lead truck, surging to escape the blast. It was headed up Kybartai's main drag, just as he expected it would.

"Blow two!" Reed shouted. "Blow three and four!"

Even as subsequent blasts shook the town from only yards away from Building A, Reed was already rolling to his knees. He was already lifting the LAW rocket launcher and ramming it's steel mouth through the window. Cracked glass shattered. Reed backhanded the rear of the tube, knocking the cap loose, then grabbed the launcher's tail and yanked it, fully extending the tube.

To his left, Turk moved in lockstep, a second LAW extended and resting over his shoulder. Both me leaned into the window, looking through the haze to the street below.

It only took seconds—a historical blip—and this beautiful, small-town Baltic street had become a war zone.

"I got lead," Reed said, his breath coming quickly but his voice calm.

"I got tail," Turk said.

"Yeah you do, Marine."

It was an old joke—a bad joke. It left Reed's lips without a thought. He sighted down the LAW and found the lead Tigr screaming to a halt at the first intersection, now a five-foot pit as chunks of asphalt from the latest explosion fell like hail. Already the driver was backing up, desperate to evade, colliding with the Tigr just behind him...

Then Reed fired. The LAW cracked like a cannon, spitting a sixty-six-millimeter rocket at 480 feet per second. It raced from the third-story apartment window and reached the street below almost before Reed recovered from the blast.

The rocket struck—forward of the Tigr's crew compartment, at the base of its engine bay. Dead on target. Another explosion and a hail of armor shrapnel. Reed's chest quaked in the ripple of the blast, matched almost millisecond for millisecond by the crack of Turk's rocket striking home against the rear Tigr.

Then both men were on their feet, hurling down the spent tubes and snatching up M4 rifles in their places. They sprinted across empty hardwood, headed for the stairs. Stretching muscles for every inch, leaning low and praying for precious seconds...

Before the voice of the Russian Alligator opened up with a roar like hellfire.

85

Kybartai, Lithuania

It all happened so fast that Makar Nikitin could barely discern which blast originated first.

First he was shouting at his driver, ordering him across the bridge toward the defiant President Petrauskienė even as radio transmissions from Russian ground commanders in Chernyshevskoe frantically called the Tigr column back to safety.

Maybe they smelled the trap. Maybe Nikitin should have smelled it, also, but he wasn't thinking clearly. He wasn't thinking at all. He'd flown to this place to accept surrender, and now he was being toyed with like the diplomat of a third-world hellhole, walking the halls of the United Nations with his hat in his hand. With each trill of Petrauskienė's song, barely audible over the grind of the Tigr's motor, Nikitin's blood churned a little harder. His face burned a little hotter. His vision turned red.

And he wanted her dead. Not maybe, not later—*right this instant*. He wanted Lithuania on its knees, and the driver wouldn't defy his president. Even as the transmission thunked and the heavy Russian war machine blasted into NATO territory, Nikitin wasn't thinking about the uncleared buildings lining the river. He wasn't thinking about anything except the anticipation of flesh crunching over steel. It came with a satisfying slam of Petrauskienė's head striking the Tigr's hood. Heavy wheels leapt over her body. Momentary euphoria rushed Nikitin's chest like the wash of a narcotic.

Then the bridge blew, and a moment too late, he saw it all.

The Tigr slid sideways, tires screaming and the radio blaring. Chunks of concrete blasted the armored walls and Nikitin's body slammed into the dash. He saw stars—he tasted blood. His driver was shouting and the engine roared louder. All Nikitin could hear from the radio was the frantic shouting of the military commander back on the Russian side of the river.

"*Go! Go! Go! Don't stop!*"

The driver didn't stop. He made it past the guard post and three hundred meters into Kybartai, Lithuania. Then the second blast detonated, followed almost immediately by a third and a fourth. Roads exploded on every side, chunks of concrete and asphalt hurtling into the sky and leaving behind craters too deep and too wide to cross. Nikitin pushed himself off the dash as brakes screamed. He coughed and saw the pit. He shouted at his driver to reverse.

Gears ground and the Tigr started backward. Nikitin twisted his head to look through bulletproof glass. The truck behind them was stalling—everything was smoke and haze and broken radio calls. Nikitin blinked and he knew what it was. He saw the trap and hated himself for being so stupid but was already too far behind enemy lines to waste time with panic. He met the gaze of the nearest soldier riding in the Tigr's back seat and shouted the only order that made sense.

"Get the helicopters—"

Then the rocket struck.

86

Moscow, Russia

The first bullet struck Ivan Sidorov dead in the chest—a perfect shot from a FSB agent who had been trained to aim for center mass, had been trained not to hesitate. It landed with a whiz and a slam, sinking past fabric and striking Kevlar with the force of a kicking mule. The breath left Ivan's lungs in a rush, but he'd been ready for the hit. He hadn't even tried to dodge it.

He drew and fired instead, not aiming for the center mass but zeroing straight on the shooter's face—like a KGB killer.

The first slug hit and the guy pitched backward. Ivan pivoted just as the next bullet tore his sleeve and shredded flesh. His second shot was sloppier than the first, landing inches below his point of aim—windpipe, not forehead. The guy went down anyway, gasping and spraying blood even as Ivan forced his body into a run.

Anton Golubev, the Ghost of the Kremlin, was still upright. He'd been slower on the draw than his men, but Golubev had spent his own time inside the KGB, and old skills die hard. He was still quick. He drew aim on Ivan even as Ivan drew aim on him. Both men fired, Golubev swinging wide for cover and Ivan not so much as flinching.

Why bother? He would die or he wouldn't. Ivan no longer cared. He only wanted to see the Ghost of the Kremlin gasp his last breath.

Golubev's bullet hit Ivan in the shoulder, a rushed shot that tore muscles and flesh and scraped bone on its way past the joint. Ivan's bullet, meanwhile, landed right where he aimed it—straight into Golubev's gut, beneath any concealed body armor he might be wearing. Not a kill shot, but that was okay.

Ivan wanted to finish this pig by hand.

Golubev screamed as he went down, his voice echoing off the blank concrete walls. Ivan bit back his own shout, pivoting and firing to finish off the second FSB agent—the one still writhing with blood gushing from his throat.

Then he reached Golubev even as the Ghost popped off another desperate shot. It scraped Ivan's thigh, burning like a hornet sting. Ivan's heavy boot sole landed in Golubev's gut with the force of a battering ram, crushing down on the existing bullet wound and driving the breath from Golubev's lungs. The Ghost choked and fired a third time. The bullet flew into empty air. Ivan slammed down harder with his right foot and kicked with his left, sending the pistol skidding across concrete.

Blood was everywhere—Ivan's, the two agents', and Golubev's. It mixed in crimson trails on the floor even as Ivan relinquished pressure on his target's torso and staggered backward.

Winded—breathing hard. Because he wasn't as young as he used to be.

Golubev choked. Gasped. Blinked with tears streaming down his face. He looked for his pistol but it was out of reach. Ivan still held his own Grach, clenched between whitened knuckles as he placed his free hand over the wound in his shoulder. It was bleeding more than he liked—maybe an artery was nicked.

He didn't care.

Golubev's bloodshot eyes locked with Ivan's. Dark fire consumed his face, and he abandoned the pistol. He bent his leg and clawed for his ankle instead—a backup weapon.

Ivan laughed. A deep, rolling sound. He flicked the muzzle of his Grach and fired once, blowing a 9mm hole through Golubev's palm. The Russian screamed and jerked his hand back. Ivan staggered forward with the muzzle of his handgun dancing.

First to Golubev's chest. Then his gut. Then his face. Then his legs.

Ivan finally fired, driving a bullet into Golubev's kneecap. It was enough to unleash another bloodcurdling scream. A thrash. A burst of curses.

Ivan merely spat—a mouth full of saliva straight into Golubev's face. The gunshot Russian choked and kicked backward, headed for the wall. He was reaching for his ankle again, still with a bloodied and shaking arm.

Ivan shot him in the shoulder. In the elbow. Again in the gut. The Grach barked until it locked back over an empty magazine and gun smoke hung in the air. The thunder of the shots faded into echoes, a storm right in the heart of Moscow.

But nobody came. No sirens rang or boots pounded. There was no response at all, because these walls were insulated. Not just the basement or the lower levels. The whole thing, because the KGB built this place. Ivan had cut his teeth as a young agent amid its corridors.

So had Anton Golubev.

"You know," Ivan gasped, looking up at the arched ceilings. "It's pretty amazing. I must have killed a dozen men in this place...but this is the first time I ever used a gun."

Golubev spat up crimson. He'd reached the wall and was fighting to prop himself against it—maybe to keep from drowning in his own blood. He no longer reached for the pistol attached to his trembling leg. He didn't look ready to fight at all. His face washed pale.

He knew he was dying.

Slowly, Ivan descended into a seated position alongside Golubev. His knees hurt and his shoulder burned. His head was a little light. He dropped the empty Grach and reached inside his jacket, fumbling for the flask of vodka there. One long pull, and the burn took a little of the misery away.

Turning to Golubev, Ivan extended the flask and lifted both eyebrows. Golubev responded with another blast of spit. Ivan grinned and upended the flask anyway, dumping raw vodka into Golubev's nearest gunshot wound. The Russian shouted and jerked. He moved to slap the arm away.

Ivan hit him in the jaw with his good arm, slamming his head back against the wall.

"Scream, you pig," Ivan snarled. "Scream as your life leaves you. Scream to the sky—scream for the Motherland. Your people *deserve* to hear you suffer."

Golubev choked. Gasped for air, and Ivan let him. When at last Golubev could speak, it came as a wet rasp.

"You...you cannot stop him, Ivan. He is a force of nature. He will sweep this world into war—you will be swept away with it."

Ivan swigged vodka. "Maybe."

Golubev blinked, very slowly. His face was growing pale, the lake of blood surrounding him spreading ever wider. His body was weakening, one heartbeat at a time.

But he wasn't dead yet. His gaze traveled across his gunshot body and up to Ivan. There was a hatred burning there like the core of a nuclear reactor. A vibrant, living thing. Ivan recognized it. He'd fought it his entire life...

And mostly lost.

"Sometimes...I think of Chechnya," Golubev hissed.

Ivan stiffened. His body, still throbbing with pain, turned cold. Golubev stared, and didn't look away. Neither did Ivan.

"Do you remember the little ones, Ivan? Those brats from the orphanage? We shelled that place to rubble...and they burned. Can you still hear them scream?"

Ivan's teeth clenched. His fingers tightened around the flask until it flexed. He blinked, and Golubev smiled.

"Or what about...that family in Grozny? We carved that man apart while his wife pleaded for mercy. Chained him between trucks and ripped his legs off. You were *there*, Ivan. We left her shaking on the ground, knowing the infantry would rape her until her body gave out. Do you remember?"

Ivan's arm shook. His mouth was dry. And Golubev was grinning.

"We did it for *Russia*, Ivan. And you want to talk to me about the Motherland?"

Ivan's gaze blurred. His breath tasted hot despite the Moscow chill. His fingers were turning numb.

"You speak of hell," Ivan said. "And now you would usher it back into the world."

"*No*, Ivan. Not back. It never left, and neither did we. You and I sold our souls—we are hounds of hell. There is no saving us, no saving anything. Men who believe otherwise are *fools*."

Ivan's arm trembled. He tasted blood in his mouth. His breaths came faster and faster, his chest tight. He thought he might hyperventilate—might drift into blackness. He *wanted* to drift into blackness.

But not just yet.

His right hand dipped beneath his jacket and found the NR-40 combat knife he had taken from the FSO guard at Romanov's dacha. The stainless steel blade flashed in the dim light. It struck like a viper's fangs, sinking into Golubev's windpipe. Terminating his voice forever, leaving him wide-eyed and frozen in the final moments before death took him.

"Maybe I am a fool," Ivan said. "But I will never stop fighting for my people."

He twisted the knife, and the Ghost of the Kremlin slipped into eternity.

87

Kybartai, Lithuania

The Alligator struck exactly like the reptilian monster it was named for. Sweeping out of the shadows and pivoting on the top floor of Building A, it dumped high-explosive S-8 rockets like salt from a shaker. Windows shattered and explosions shook the building to its core. Reed and Turk were in the stairwell and sprinting down the steps two at a time, dust and collapsing ceiling tiles raining amid the endless thunder.

Reed could barely see. He was choking, radio calls streaming in from Wolfgang, Corbyn, and Lucy in a garbled stream.

"Multiple attack helicopters bearing down—can't see through the smoke—Tigrs invisible—"

The last part was the only thing Reed cared about. He couldn't do anything about the helicopters. He couldn't do anything about the storm of Russian soldiers that would be rushing the river, ready to ford it on foot to save their president. He couldn't do anything about the smoke or chaos or collapsing buildings.

And none of that would matter—not so long as Reed Montgomery won the race to Makar Nikitin's throat.

Reed exploded out of the stairwell and onto the ground level just as a creaking shudder signaled the structural collapse of the apartment tower. It was coming down—the whole thing, rumbling and folding in on itself with gathering speed.

"*Door!*" Reed shouted.

He didn't need to clarify. He and Turk both turned right down a hallway, breaking for an exit that had already been selected during pre-mission planning. At full sprint, time itself seemed to stand still. Chunks of drywall pelted Reed's shoulders and crunched beneath his feet. He saw the door at fifty yards even as an earsplitting snap signaled the failure of some primary structural component. He thought he heard the Alligator still dumping fire—determined to finish the job.

Move!

Another ten yards and Reed hit the door and exploded into open air half a pace ahead of Turk. Behind them the roof came down—not some of it, but all of it, an imploding house of cards. Reed leapt from the sidewalk and rolled onto hard asphalt, covering his head as a tidal wave of dirt and debris blasted over his back. He could barely breathe—all he tasted was dirt. The ground shook as though a bomb had gone off, rattling the teeth in his head.

Then it was over. Reed was gasping and his ears rang. He lifted his head but all he saw was smoke and hanging dust. Somewhere overhead the steady thump of a helicopter indicated the Alligator's survival, but Reed couldn't see it. He couldn't see the Tigrs, either.

"*Reed!*"

It was Turk, clawing his way off the ground and over a chunk of masonry. Shaking Reed by the shoulder.

"I'm good," Reed choked. "All channels, who copies?"

Only Corbyn replied, a distorted garble recognizable by her accent.

"We're hitting the trucks!" Reed said. "Be ready for cover fire!"

It was the obvious command—the only thing that mattered. Reed fought his way to his knees, then his feet. He lifted the rifle and turned instinctively toward the line of trapped Tigrs.

Three vehicles. An unidentified number of tangos inside—and one jackpot, waiting to be drilled through the forehead. Reed sprinted through the smog...

And then the Russian gunfire poured in.

88

Chernyshevskoe, Kaliningrad Oblast
Russia

From the moment the bridge blew, Andrei Vedenin knew exactly what was happening. Exactly what had *been* happening from the moment the Lithuanian president announced her unexpected intentions to surrender. It had never felt right to him. Never felt logical.

But he'd kept his mouth shut, because Makar Nikitin bought it, and the president's opinion was increasingly the only opinion tolerated in the Russian Federation. Now concrete was exploding into the air, joined shortly by asphalt. Then there was gunfire, rocket fire, and Alligator helicopters storming to the rescue.

All too little, too late, Vedenin feared. NATO was making a stand, and not at all in the way Russia had expected. More like a snake striking from the shadows versus a herd of charging bull elephants, this was a bold and actually reckless maneuver. A stunt that could easily end in nuclear war.

But for just this moment? It had Russia by the throat.

Tearing free of his military escort, Vedenin rushed to the windows of the command building on the Russian side of the Liepona River. He snatched binoculars to his eyes even as his staff shouted for him to take cover. He swept the decimated bridge—the only bridge for kilometers to either side—and the smoke-flooded streets beyond. He could barely see the guard post. Kybartai itself was lost in the smog of battle. One building collapsed under a torrent of Alligator rockets.

And he couldn't *see* Nikitin.

"Radio the air base!" Vedenin shouted. "More helicopters, as fast as they can send them. Then order every ground troop we have across the river and into the town—*immediately*."

No answer. Vedenin snatched his face away from the binoculars.

"Did you hear me?"

"Sir…the bridges are blown."

"So tell them to *swim*! Our president is stuck behind enemy lines and is about to die. *Do your job!*"

The governor's voice boomed off the walls and there was no further objection. His men scurried to respond. Radio orders were transmitted. The soldiers gathered in the streets quickly assembled at the riverbank and began to wade in, rifles held over their heads.

Vedenin lifted the binoculars back to his eyes, his fingers tightening around them.

Seconds, he thought. A world at war, and the Russian military had seconds to save their supreme commander in chief.

89

The White House

Jordan Stratton said nothing.

He stood at Maggie's elbow, his compatriots crowded behind him, every eye fixated on the monitor at the end of the room as one explosion turned into two. Three. Four. Then a sweeping helicopter, visible as a twitching blur. Rocket fire. A collapsing apartment building…and a lot of smoke. Too much to see through.

"What are you doing?" Stratton repeated his previous question, his voice hoarse with something that might have been horror, or just disbelief.

By now every newcomer in the room knew what they were looking at. The picture of the Russian trucks and the detonating bombs was clear. The dots had been connected. Both Yellin and Aimes looked to the VP, but neither of them answered the question. Maggie didn't fill the silence, either. She sipped coffee, her gut pulsating. Her head pounding with it. Her whole body feeling very weak.

But she was still there. She was still in control.

Very slowly, Stratton pulled back the chair to Maggie's left. He settled into it, never taking his eyes off the satellite feed. Easterling and Kline sat also. Gorman took more time. She was as white as a sheet, looking ready to drop.

"Drink some coffee, Lisa," Maggie said. "You've got a long day ahead of you."

Gorman turned, her mouth half open. She didn't seem to know what to say. Maggie really couldn't blame her—but she didn't feel any sympathy either.

"This is what you've been doing?" Stratton said finally.

Maggie didn't answer.

Stratton turned, a little burning rage creeping into his face. Maybe terror.

"This will end in nuclear war," he said. "This will be the end of us all."

Maggie wrapped both hands tight around the mug, savoring the warmth. The White House stewards had the SitRoom HVAC turned up to seventy-five, warm enough to leave General Yellin sweating, but Maggie was still cold. She couldn't relax. She was locked on that screen as though the fate of the planet depended on it.

Because it did.

"That's up to Reed Montgomery," she said.

90

Kybartai, Lithuania

Muzzle flash blinked through the haze at forty yards, sixty yards, and a hundred yards. A field of Russian troops bailing from trapped and disabled Tigr trucks unleashed the wrath from their AK-12 rifles.

Reed knew they couldn't actually *see* him. There was too much smoke and dust. But they had the right idea. It wasn't their job to locate and neutralize the enemy—only to buy enough time for the Russian troops on the far side of the river to storm across and take the city.

It was an effort to buy time, and it was Reed's job to shut that transaction down cold.

Sliding to his knees behind a section of fallen apartment wall, Reed swept the M4's ACOG optic across three different points of aim in quick succession, not firing but mapping his targets. When he engaged he would only have seconds—muzzle flash would mark his position as surely as it marked that of his enemy.

"Going left!" Reed shouted. Then he engaged. Semi-auto, not full auto. Two shots per target, flowing from one to the next without ever stopping. To his right Turk was doing the same, covering midnight to three o'clock while Reed covered midnight to nine. Shouts and raw screams burst from the smog, and three guns went silent. Others pivoted on instinct and rained cover fire like hail, a storm that pounded and didn't stop, driving both men for cover. Reed bent low and shielded his face as flecks of concrete pelted his skin. He searched for some identifiable tempo to the fire, some indicator of when it might break or when the shooters might reload.

There was nothing—just the roar. Ceaseless and bearing down right on top of them.

"*Wolf!*" Reed shouted. "Hit 'em!"

Reed wasn't sure if his radio call transmitted. If Wolfgang replied, Reed never heard him. But what mattered most—what Reed needed—was a sound like the slam of a .50 caliber machine gun, except slower and deeper, a steady *choonk* from the second floor of a nearby office building—Building C.

The Mark 19 belt-fed grenade launcher sat on a tripod and spat 40mm high-explosive grenades at a rate of one per second. Wolfgang wasn't specially trained in its use—before this moment, he'd only ever dry-fired the weapon in a Polish aircraft hangar. But at two hundred yards it didn't take a master Marine gunner to pour rounds on target. Each flash of a detonating round served as a beacon to adjust fire, like shooting tracer rounds, only each of these tracers unleashed a five-meter kill radius.

The gunfire from the Russian position died in a mix of earsplitting blasts seasoned with short screams. Reed was still crouched behind the wall, curled into a fetal position as Wolfgang ran through an entire belt of grenades, forty-eight in total. By the time he was done, the smoke surrounding the trapped Tigrs was so thick that Reed could no longer make out the vague silhouettes of bumpers and rooflines. He couldn't make out anything but an inky gray blob, disturbed by the downwash of another Alligator helicopter ripping in from the Russian side of the river.

"*Cover! Cover!*" Turk shouted.

The shout was cut short by the pulsating blast of the Alligator's autocannon, a thunder that sent concrete fragments dancing over broken asphalt. Reed could see the chopper two hundred feed overhead, hovering with its nose down. A split second later, the brass ejecting from its 30mm cannon rained in a gleaming shower, one searing-hot case bouncing off

Reed's exposed hand. He bit back a shout even as Turk's hand smacked him on the arm.

"*Let's go!* We're running out of time!"

Reed didn't need to be told twice. Back on his feet, he ignored the burning pain. He ignored the thunder of death on every side. He didn't worry about Wolfgang, because he couldn't afford too.

He just dashed straight for the Tigr trucks.

91

Kybartai, Lithuania

It was hell. In a moment, in the blink of an eye. The LAW rocket struck the front right corner of Nikitin's tiger and blew the wheel right off. It hurled the vehicle up, sending his head snapping back. Then he was bouncing forward again, slamming hard into the dash.

And he saw Afghanistan. It was 1987, and Nikitin was still a young Red Army officer. The USSR was losing the war and dumping on heat and Nikitin was riding shotgun in a UAZ-469 utility vehicle the moment an Afghan land mine detonated beneath the engine block.

Hurling him up. Turning his world black and bright white and black again. He tasted blood and slammed into the roof. They rolled into the ditch. The driver had writhed and screamed, impaled by the vehicle's steering column.

And Nikitin knew—really believed—that he was going to die. That was the sensation he recalled most from those horrifying moments before a Red Army troop stormed to the rescue. He remembered the abject terror, a certainty of doom.

He felt that way again in this moment. The same haze, the same sudden and desperate fear. It was biological and undeniable. He spat blood and gasped for air and fought to get away from his door.

Because the enemy, whoever they were, weren't coming for the soldiers in the other trucks.

"Helicopters!" Nikitin shouted. "Radio the helicopters!"

It was the obvious order and it didn't need to be made. Moments later the comforting boom of S-8 rockets filled the air. A building was collapsing. Nikitin's driver called for him to lie in the back seat even as the other two Tigrs ejected their personnel to establish a protective perimeter.

"Stay down, Mr. President! Backup is on the way!"

The soldier's shout sounded distant, distorted by the climate of chaos. Nikitin was already lying on his chest in the back of the Tigr, two men literally shielding him with their bodies as a storm of Russian return fire burst from outside the trucks.

It wasn't aimed. It wasn't concentrated. It was desperate, wild, suppressive fire, directed at anything and everything that moved. Brass pinged against the armored walls of the lead vehicle while rifles barked in full automatic. The din was constant, ceaseless, almost comforting.

And then it was answered—one cracking blast after another, followed by screams and silenced rifles. Nikitin thought they were ballistic grenades, raining in by the second, some bouncing off his truck while others zipped right to the feet of the soldiers surrounding him.

It was a slaughter.

"Get off me!" Nikitin roared, throwing back the FSO officer covering his back.

"Stay down, sir! We've got backup—"

"We won't *live* long enough for backup! Are you listening? This is an ambush and we're in the kill zone. Hand me a gun—we're getting out!"

"Sir—"

The objection was cut short by the appearance of Nikitin's Tokarev pistol. It flashed from the holster in an instant, the muzzle thrust into the officer's face even as Nikitin breathed like a winded bull, his eyes wide and wild.

"Do what I tell you!"

There was no further objection. The driver scrambled from the front seat as the two FSO officers in the back reached for their rifles. Nikitin holstered the pistol and accepted an AK-12. He yanked the charging handle, that mixture of sliding metal and the smell of burning gunpowder unleashing further memories of Afghanistan.

Except now it was different. Nikitin wasn't a young army officer anymore. He had so much more at stake than a paltry salary and a pair of greasy lovers back home. His whole *world* was at stake.

Before this was over, he would see Lithuania burn.

"Out the door and secure a corridor," Nikitin ordered. "The rockets came from the south, so we'll move north. Two hundred meters into cover, then we swing for the river. Understood?"

Hesitation. One FSO officer trembled. Another sweated like a waterfall.

"*Understand?*" Nikitin screamed.

"Yes, Mr. President!"

"*Move!*"

Nikitin reached for a Kevlar helmet, and his lead bodyguard reached for the door.

92

Kybartai, Lithuania

Reed and Turk moved in unison—rifles held into their shoulders and ACOG sights sweeping the smoke ahead. They ran straight into the haze, clearing the rubble of Building A and choking on smoke. Somewhere overhead another Alligator thundered by, but it didn't fire—the pilots couldn't see, and even with infrared technology they couldn't tell friendlies from the enemy. The Prosecution Force had one chance, the chance they had flown here to take.

Makar Nikitin was inside one of those trucks, and he would *not* be allowed to escape.

The first target loomed from the shadows as a twisted mound of human flesh, slowly dragging a leg as the wounded soldier fought for cover. Reed put him down with a double-tap to the face at ten yards, swung left and shot another soldier in the back, and then the Russians resumed the fight.

Flashes of rifle fire lit the smoke from directly ahead, but Reed and Turk had already reached the lead Tigr and were diving into cover in the rocket crater at its front bumper. One wheel was blown away—the engine was burning, belching acrid smoke. Reed couldn't see through the bulletproof windshield, and the passenger-side door was closed.

Somebody might still be inside, but for the moment he couldn't concern himself with that question. Half a dozen Russian soldiers still survived, dug in alongside the second and third Tigrs, and they were doing everything in their power to drive the attackers back.

"Frag out!" Turk called.

Reed leaned automatically out from cover, spraying suppressive fire as Turk rose to fling the grenade. It arched into the smoke and disappeared almost immediately. Two seconds later it detonated with a flash, and one of the Russian guns went silent. Two others hesitated, perhaps disoriented. Reed swung back into cover to swap his mag just as Turk darted out to engage one target.

A pained shout. Commands shouted in Russian, then another storm of hot lead rushing in twice as angry as before, driving both Reed and Turk into crouching cover.

"This isn't working!" Turk called. "He could be slipping away."

Reed already knew. He locked his new mag with a slap of his palm, then dropped the bolt on the M4. He blew sweat from his lip, breathing hard, mind racing. Then he seated the rifle into his shoulder and prepared to lunge from cover.

93

Kybartai, Lithuania

From one hundred meters north of ground zero, Lucy and Corbyn crouched on the second floor of a two-story home—Building B. Positioned just behind a window with a clear view of the town's main drag, the house was selected for its clear views of both the thoroughfare and the side street that connected downtown Kybartai with the northern segment of the town.

With Reed and Turk driving from the southeast, the bridges blown to the west, and Wolfgang laying down grenade fire from the northeast, that side street was the only remaining route of escape from the kill zone laid at the core of town. As such, Reed had placed his final two soldiers in position there with a pair of M4 rifles equipped with M203 grenade launchers and one M110 semi-automatic sniper system.

It wasn't a lot of firepower in the face of three circling attack helicopters and so many Russian soldiers on the way, but again, that wasn't the point. Lucy and Corbyn's only job was to hold Nikitin in place long enough for Reed and Turk to finish the job.

"I've got movement!" Corbyn called.

She squatted at the open window, binoculars held to her face while she popped gum, apparently heedless of the roaring gunfire barely a block away. Just to her left beyond the window frame, Lucy couldn't see what Corbyn saw, but she knew she didn't need to. It wasn't her job to engage, only to support.

And to pray—hard.

"What is it?" Lucy said.

"Two tangos on foot," Corbyn said. "Looks to be Russian infantry moving north from ground zero. Reed, are you getting this?"

A long pause. Lucy listened for the Prosecutor to answer through her earpiece.

There was nothing.

"Reed," Corbyn snapped. "Do you hear me? I've got movement at the street corner. Appears to be enemy activity. Confirm your location."

Two more seconds of silence. Still, nothing.

Corbyn swore and tossed the binos down. She extended a hand.

"Rifle!"

Lucy hefted the M110, a twenty-pound weapon system fully loaded with a suppressor screwed to the muzzle and an Leupold optic affixed to the top rail. Before she had it halfway to the window, Corbyn was reaching to snatch it. Drawing the charging handle and blowing a bubble in her gum. Shoving the aviator glasses up her nose and deploying the foldable bipod legs to rest on the windowsill.

The optic lens caps popped open. Corbyn disengaged the safety and settled behind the scope, her face turning hard.

"Come on, you buggers. Who's first?"

Lucy breathed deep.

Then Corbyn opened fire.

94

Kybartai, Lithuania

There was no trick left for Reed except violence of action—hitting his enemy harder and faster than anyone expected.

Swinging out from the nose of the wrecked Tigr, that was exactly the option Reed chose. He didn't communicate with Turk because he didn't need to. Turk would expect the move and either shield him or else join the charge.

Turk joined the charge. They both moved in a full sprint, rifles flicked to full auto, spraying points of known enemy concealment in short bursts before reaching the second Tigr—the one that wasn't wrecked, but trapped. One Russian soldier crouched at the nose, already bleeding from a grenade strike. He swept his AK-12 toward Reed just in time to catch three rounds to the face. The next guy swung out from behind the Tigr, popping off shots that zipped past Reed's arm and grazed his neck. Turk took him down with a blast of M4 fire.

Then they were both ducking behind the bumper of the second truck. Reed was pulling a grenade with a short "*Frag!*" and hurling it over the vehicle's top. Just as it detonated he thought he recognized Corbyn's voice barking through his earpiece. He couldn't understand it—his ears were too numb, his head buzzing. Reed completed a magazine change and was back on his feet, taking the right side of the Tigr as Turk instinctively took the left. From the inside of the vehicle a voice shouted and feet thumped. The back door exploded open just in time to catch fire from both operators, and a bloodied Russian tumbled out.

One vehicle remained—and still, Reed hadn't seen Nikitin. He hadn't seen any presidential bodyguards, either. He wondered for a split, horrifying second...had Nikitin remained on the Russian side of the river? Had he deployed these vehicles merely as a probing force?

No. The response of the Alligators was altogether too immediate and too desperate. They were still churning back and forth above the smoke, searching desperately for a target. Nikitin was *here*, somewhere.

"Nine o'clock!" Turk shouted.

Reed saw the movement and swept his rifle in that direction. He and Turk fired and moved, leaned low. A bullet ricocheted off the concrete and skimmed past Reed's knee, tearing his combat pants. Turk grunted in the way men do when another bullet strikes home, but he didn't stop. They encircled the final, wrecked Tigr, and found the two Russian soldiers dug into a bomb crater, dumping everything they had as fast as they could pull the trigger.

"Cover! Grenade!" Reed called.

Turk didn't need to be told twice. Both men took cover at the nose of the final Russian truck and pulled grenades together, their final two. Spoons dropped, and a moment slipped by as they allowed the fuses to run down.

Then they threw overhand, aiming for the crater. The blasts detonated together and blood sprayed the back of the Tigr. The guns went silent. Reed gasped for clean air and lifted the rifle to his shoulder. His eyes stung in the smoke. He surveyed the Tigr's bulletproof windshield, scarred by blast shrapnel, and pivoted to the driver's door.

It was unlocked. Reed snatched it open, leading with the rifle muzzle. He smelled stale sweat and hydraulic fluid—the international odor of war machines the world around.

But the seat was empty. The back was empty also. Reed dropped out again, pivoting back toward the middle and front trucks, heart hammering as he wondered if he'd missed something.

Then he heard it. Another garbled transmission that sounded like Corbyn's, mixed with the distant pops or rifle fire.

"...position...pinned down...Nikitin..."

"North!" Reed shouted. He spun on his heel and launched into a sprint.

95

Kybartai, Lithuania

Wolfgang ran the Mark 19 grenade launcher through a full belt of 40mm grenades, pounding the Russian position and opening a narrow window of opportunity for Reed and Turk to dash in. Even as they moved from their position of cover, taking first the lead Tigr and then the second, Wolfgang was snapping the launcher's top cover open and fumbling with a new grenade belt. The loading assembly snagged on the belt chain, and he had to force it out again, fingers trembling as he ran through the directions Reed had provided before deploying Wolfgang with the Mark 19.

The launcher was loaded, then. Reed said that Wolfgang probably wouldn't get a chance to reload for a second assault, but prepared him for it anyway. It was "simple," in Reed's words.

For a Force Recon Marine, it likely was simple. Wolfgang had made a career out of killing and was better at it than most, but his usual methods involved sharp knives and silenced pistols—the occasional submachine gun, maybe. He was an assassin, not a soldier. He fumbled the belt a second time even as gunfire persisted from the bomb site below.

"Come on...*come on!*"

Wolfgang seated the chain on the third attempt and slapped the cover closed. He pulled the dual charging handles, his feet pressed against the base of the wall beneath the window that he aimed through. The butterfly handles filled his palms as he swept the muzzle toward the row of Tigrs, quickly locating both Reed and Turk as they advanced to the final truck.

But Wolfgang didn't fire. He couldn't risk it. What Russians remained would need to be neutralized on the ground—the grenades were far too imprecise a weapon to risk firing so close to members of his own team.

"Come on, Reed. Nail this guy..."

Seconds ticked by. More gunfire. A pair of hand grenades. Smoke and blood and *more* rifle fire. Wolfgang could no longer see either Reed or Turk. They had been swallowed by the battle.

Then Corbyn's voice, previously garbled, barked through Wolfgang's headset.

"Multiple Russians approaching my position! I've got them pinned down for now. I think Nikitin may be with them."

Nikitin.

Wolfgang's gaze snapped north, toward Corbyn. As it did, he looked over the river, four hundred meters away...and then he looked back, just as quickly.

There were dots in the river. A swarm of them. It was difficult to see through so much smoke, but as Wolfgang squinted, he thought the dots were moving. Slowly, steadily, sinking into the water but slogging ahead.

They were Russian troops—a couple hundred of them.

"All channels!" Wolfgang said. "Be advised, Russian infantry fording the river. Reed, they're headed your way. Do you copy?"

No answer. Wolfgang snatched up the M4 rifle leaning against the wall and squinted his eye behind the ACOG sight—a fixed, four-time magnifier.

The improved picture only served to confirm what he already knew.

"Reed! Turk! Do you copy?"

No answer. Wolfgang dropped the rifle and grabbed the launcher with one hand. He adjusted its range-marked manual sight with the other. Settled on four hundred yards...

Then pivoted the muzzle toward the river and braced his feet against the wall.

96

Kybartai, Lithuania

Corbyn churned through an entire twenty-round magazine, nailing one Russian in the leg and driving three others into cover behind a dirty brick building.

One of those three she only caught a glimpse of, but he wasn't dressed like the others. In place of dark green camouflage, he wore all black. He was tall, broad, dark haired. He looked an awful lot like Makar Nikitin.

"Reed!" Corbyn shouted. "Does anybody hear me? I think I just saw Nikitin run behind a single-story brick building just beyond the intersection. I don't think I have him pinned. Does anybody copy?"

"I hear you!" Wolfgang called back. "I can't get through to Reed. Be advised, I've got two hundred Russian infantry fording the river. They're assuming offensive positions on our side. I'll do what I can—you've got maybe five minutes."

Five minutes.

Corbyn withdrew from the optic for a broader view of the street. She looked left—east, across houses, backyards, and narrow alleyways. There were a lot of six-foot fences to divvy that space up. The night prior she had scoped the area out and knew that it would provide a staunch obstacle for anyone who attempted to flee on foot. It was also *away* from the river and Russian support.

But if she were in Makar Nikitin's boots, what would she do? Sit tight and wait for a rescue? Or take her fate into her own hands?

It wasn't a difficult riddle to solve. Corbyn withdrew the rifle from the window.

"Come on," she said. "We've gotta move."

97

Kybartai, Lithuania

Reed and Turk reached the end of the smoke cloud and charged into an empty Lithuanian street...to nothing.

No gunfire. No voices. No sign of Corbyn stationed in the second-floor window of the orange house a hundred yards away. With his breath burning in his throat, Reed pressed his body tight against the concrete wall of the three-story apartment building on the corner and slowed—rifle up, Turk stepping automatically at his back and sweeping the street to the left. They didn't need to speak—the predicament was obvious.

And the situation was not moving according to plan. Somehow, Nikitin had escaped the kill zone. Wolfgang's Mark 19 and Corbyn's M110 rifle were meant to hem him in, but assuming he and his guards had made it into the surrounding buildings and faded away...

Through his ringing ears, Reed could make out the distant shouts of Russian troops gathering on the Lithuanian riverbank. The thunder of the Alligators had faded—maybe they were short on fuel, or out of rockets, or withdrawing to regroup with ground forces.

Whatever the case, all of those menaces would be back, and soon. Reed needed to find his target before them. He needed to *hurry*.

"Corbyn," Reed hissed. "Where are you?"

No answer. Reed felt for his throat mic with his off hand and found torn flesh—a bullet had literally whizzed right past his windpipe, tearing away the mic and passing only half an inch from bringing him down. Corbyn couldn't hear him—nobody but Turk could hear him.

"Can you get her?" Reed said, not turning around.

"Blown handset," Turk replied. "I've got nothing."

Great.

Reed slowed at the apartment's corner. He lifted his rifle to scan the second-floor windows of the house across the alley. His body tensed as his peripheral vision detected movement a hundred yards to his left, back on street level. Reed snatched the rifle that way, his finger curled around the trigger.

"*Stop*," Turk snapped. "Green on green!"

Reed relaxed his trigger finger only just in time, his ACOG settling over a petite figure clad in an ill-fitting chest rig with an M4 rifle held into her shoulder. It was Lucy—she was aiming across the street. A moment later Corbyn appeared out of the shadows, also wielding an M4, and sprinting full blast. She reached Reed's side of the street, still a hundred yards ahead, and slid to her knees behind a line of trashcans.

She hadn't seen them. Corbyn pivoted to cover Lucy's crossing. Lucy made the dash a little more awkwardly, her usually agile body struggling under the burden of the body armor.

The moment they were across, Reed whistled, low and slow. The sound drew Corbyn's eye—and her gun. But she didn't fire.

Reed lifted his left hand, palm out, and placed it in front of his face. He moved it up and down, twice in each direction. It wasn't a Marine signal—not even an infantry signal. It was something Reed had seen pilots practice to indicate failure of communications in the air, and he thought Corbyn would understand.

She did. An exaggerated nod, followed by a lifted hand. Reed could make out the details of the gesture through his ACOG—three fingers held up, three men indicated. Corbyn pointed down an alley near her position, where Reed could already detect a dark stain, maybe a blood trail. Then Corbyn extended her right arm and tapped the inside of her sleeve.

Suspect, it meant. In this case, *primary target*.

Makar Nikitin.

"You get all that?" Reed said.

"Roger," Turk said.

"We'll take lead."

Reed lifted his left hand once more and double-tapped the top of his Kevlar helmet—*cover me*. Corbyn nodded her understanding and settled into a kneel, pointing her rifle toward the mouth of the alley. Lucy still squatted sideways, directing her rifle to cover Corbyn's back.

It was as good an arrangement as they were likely to get. Reed seated his rifle against his cheek and started forward…

Then he heard it. Low, slow, and throaty. *Bum-bum-bum-bum.*

It was Wolfgang's Mark 19. He was reengaging the enemy.

98

Kybartai, Lithuania

There were too many—far, far too many. Swarming up the banks and past the border station, fully two hundred heavily armed Russian infantry, still dripping from the river, wielded AK-12s as they fanned out to take key positions along the main street. Already they were within a hundred yards of the original kill zone, the thinning smoke allowing Wolfgang a partial view of their darkened silhouettes.

Body armor. Helmets. Organized tactics. These weren't ground-pounding conscripts, these were elite infantry, some of Russia's best. In another three minutes they would reach the Tigrs and clear them. They would begin spreading throughout the city.

They would strike Reed and Turk from behind.

No way.

Wolfgang breathed deep and dropped his head to align his point of view with the rudimentary sights. They weren't sniper's crosshairs, but in an environment this target rich, they didn't need to be. Wolfgang only needed to strike close, adjusting his point of aim via each blast signature... and get as many as he could.

This is it. And that's okay.

Wolfgang rested both thumbs on the button-trigger and indulged in a dry smile—something he hadn't done in a long, long time. Suddenly, he was thinking of one of his own first encounters with Reed Montgomery, an incident in the North Carolina mountains that had also involved a grenade launcher.

Full circle. Send it.

Wolfgang mashed the trigger.

99

Kybartai, Lithuania

Roof. Find a roof.

It was the only thing that made sense to Nikitin as he and his troops fled the scene of the wrecked Tigrs. They made it only halfway down the next street before raking fire from a second-floor window sent all four of them scrambling for cover.

Only three of them made it. One of Nikitin's FSO officers was shot through the hip and sent cartwheeling to the ground, unable to stand. Without awaiting orders, Nikitin's remaining FSO officer and the Tigr's driver dragged their wounded friend into an alley and left him propped against a wall. They shoved his rifle back into his hands and told him to cover the street.

No goodbye. No apology. No thank you. *Do your job.*

Then they were sprinting again, moving silent as the thunder of the Alligators grew distant. The helicopters had flown straight from Khrabrovo Airport and must be getting low on fuel. Nikitin's precious air cover, once feeling like such overkill, now felt pitiful and somehow vastly outgunned. His soldiers must be storming the river and rushing to his rescue, but how many precious minutes would that take?

This was all spinning out of control. Whoever was on his heels was chasing Nikitin like a pack of bloodhounds, but he still had some advantages. The Alligators would be back, and other helicopters, fully fueled and fully armed, should be on their way. If Nikitin could get to a rooftop, he could be snatched up and flown away, leaving Kybartai to be flattened by the full wrath of the Russian war machine.

But first, he had to buy time.

At the end of the alley there stood a two-story house, grimy and old, with windows on the first and second floors. Nikitin led the way without directing his soldiers. He himself drove a polished black combat boot into the door, kicking it open with his Tokarev pistol drawn—a weapon that now felt like a very *stupid* accessory.

Nikitin wanted a rifle. Better yet, a machine gun. A battalion of main battle tanks, a brigade of air-to-ground Su-25 jets. A *nuke*. Nikitin would set the whole of Lithuania on fire before this was over. He would turn her into a wasteland.

"You, guard the door!" Nikitin shouted to the Tigr driver. "Place a charge, if you have it. You, with me! We're going upstairs."

The driver kicked the door closed and dug a charge from his pack. The FSO officer led the way up the stairs to the home's second level. The building was dark, but not unoccupied. The nearby kitchen still smelled like cooking food. There were toys scattered across the carpeted floor. Pictures on the walls.

They reached the landing and the soldier turned right, his rifle up. Nikitin turned left, kicking a bathroom door open and finding the space dark and empty. There was a closet, also empty. Then a cry from the rear bedroom—the one with the window overlooking the alley behind.

Nikitin spun that way. He shoved through the door to find his FSO officer standing frozen just inside, his rifle hanging static over a young mother and her elementary-aged daughter. The child was crying, shaking. The mother was wide-eyed, petrified and pale. The officer swallowed and turned a questioning glance on Nikitin.

Nikitin shot them both, straight in the forehead, his Tokarev barking. The bodies tumbled and he shoved his officer from behind.

"Take the window, *fool!* Give me your radio and sidearm."

The officer fumbled to pass off his handset and the Grach handgun on his hip. All that remained was the chest plate he wore and the AK-12 in his hands, taken from a rack inside the Tigr.

"Hold this window," Nikitin said. "Whatever it costs, *do not move*. Understand?"

"Yes, Mr. President!"

The officer moved to the window with is rifle. Nikitin turned for the hallway and radioed the army from across the river.

He needed a helicopter—immediately.

100

Kybartai, Lithuania

The first Russian soldier lay half on his back, half propped against a wall just ten yards inside the alley. He was already shot in the leg and had lost a lot of blood. In another five minutes, he might have been dead.

But he wasn't yet, and his position was a point of brutal genius. The moment Reed turned the corner, he stepped into the soldier's line of fire. Unsteady, desperate gunfire ripped across asphalt and whizzed past Reed's body.

The soldier never really had a chance—Reed nailed the guy twice in the face and Turk shot him just above his body armor, four rifle barks stacked so close together that they sounded almost like a cannon blast.

But now Nikitin knew that somebody was coming, and in return Reed knew exactly what to expect.

Full auto fire exploded from the second-floor window of a gunky brick house parked dead at the end of the alley. Bullets raked the pavement as Reed dashed left—behind the tail of a faded black sedan. Turk went the opposite way, taking cover behind a skinny hardwood tree growing at the edge of the sidewalk.

"Throwing smoke!" Reed shouted. He unclipped the grenade from his chest rig and yanked the pin with his free pinky. The spoon popped. He hurled it without rising from behind the car. The grenade bounced twice between gunfire, then hissed a cloud of thick gray.

Reed lifted his head over the car's trunk, peeking through the vehicle's rear window. The windshield was already blown out, but the roofline was too low for him to gain a line of fire against the home's second-floor window. He would need to stand to do that, or else lean out.

"I'll hit him with a grenade!"

It was Corbyn, shouting from fifty yards back. Reed twisted his head just in time to see Corbyn deploying the grenade sight atop her M4 rifle. The M203 grenade launcher attached beneath it was already loaded with a high-explosive charge, but hitting a residential window at two hundred yards would be like sniping with a soda straw.

Better than nothing.

"Ready?" Reed looked to Turk. Turk nodded once. Corbyn fired, a loud pop and whiz of the slow-moving projectile. It smacked the wall three feet beneath the window and detonated with a thunderclap—a similar sound to that of Wolfgang's grenades from two blocks away.

Then Reed ran. Straight into the smoke, rifle up. Turk was on his heels and both Lucy and Corbyn laid down cover fire against the window. For a brief moment the world faded from view as Reed's own smoke screen enveloped him. He held his breath and reached the end of the alley. The gunfire resumed, this time from a lower-level window. Reed took a round straight to his chest plate and choked, half stumbling sideways. The pain was instant and overwhelming, not as bad as actually being shot, but maybe just as temporarily disorienting. Reed gasped for air, knowing he was precious milliseconds behind schedule to respond.

Turk filled the gap, his M4 snarling. The muzzle flash disappeared from the lower-floor window and Reed spun left, instinctively knowing where the door should stand.

He was right. It was closed. Reed approached from the latch side and braced his left foot into the dirt, ready to drive his right foot against the door.

"*Wait!*"

It was Turk. Reed stalled. His battle buddy reached his side once more and shouted into his ear.

"There could be a charge! Let's hit it first."

They both withdrew. Reed and Turk aimed together at the door latch assembly and each drove a three-round burst just above the knob. The force was enough to tear the latch loose and send the door shuddering backward an inch—and that was enough to trigger the planted charge Turk had predicted.

An earsplitting blast ripped the door off its hinges. Reed ducked and Turk swung left. Wood splinters ripped between them along with the acrid flavor of burned C4. Reed's eyes stung and his lungs tightened. He lifted the rifle and dumped fire before fire could be dumped back at them—bullets flooded the darkness and a lone voice shouted from beyond.

Then Reed and Turk charged inside.

101

Chernyshevskoe, Kaliningrad Oblast
Russia

Russian ground troops had crossed the river, and the battle of Kybartai was fully underway.

From the third floor of the command building inside Kaliningrad, Andrei Vedenin monitored the swell of light infantry around the Lithuanian border checkpoint, a force that grew from twenty to fifty and then to over a hundred men. They ascended from the river dripping wet and sprinted for cover behind buildings and parked vehicles, digging in and awaiting orders.

But not advancing. Vedenin wasn't immediately sure why. Then one of his officers handed him a pair of high-powered binoculars, and the Russian governor swept a field of smoke before zeroing in on a repeated flash barely visible through the haze.

Bright orange pops, too slow to be the blast of a machine gun, were nonetheless regular enough to represent some manner of full automatic fire—and when he matched those pops with louder blasts on the ground near his men, Vedenin thought he understood.

It was an automatic grenade launcher, likely installed in the upper floor of a building he couldn't see through the smoke. Hardly a withering weapon against so many heavily armed Russian riflemen, yet those riflemen were held in place, unable to move without risking their lives.

And President Nikitin was still stuck somewhere inside the city... *hopefully*.

"Governor!" A voice shouted from someplace behind. "Governor, quick! We have the president on the radio."

Vedenin spun from the window, eyes wide. One of his subordinates ran in, wielding a handset. Vedenin snatched it and mashed the key before he even knew what to say.

What came out was: "*Makar?*"

"Andrei! I'm pinned inside a house with only two men left. They're almost on top of me. I need a helicopter *now*."

Nikitin's voice crackled with energy, but no fear. Just like the Red Army officer that Vedenin remembered from all those years ago back in Afghanistan, Nikitin locked tight into his battlefield mode.

"Where are the helicopters?" Vedenin snarled, lowering the radio an inch. A nearby Army officer working a makeshift command post of shock-proof laptops lowered a phone from his face.

"We have two Alligators refueled and headed this way—three minutes out. The third is suffering engine trouble. Four additional gunships are inbound from Khrabrovo, along with a Mil Mi-26 loaded with additional troops. They are sixteen minutes out."

Three minutes for the gunships—sixteen for the transport.

It was much too long. The Alligators featured a closed cockpit design that would not easily serve in a rescue function. They could provide close ground support, but their guns were far too imprecise to provide precision defensive fire.

Vedenin's best option by far was still the ground forces dug in at the border checkpoint.

"Mr. President, we have Alligators inbound, only minutes away. We have a transport helicopter coming also, but it's a little farther out—"

"How *much* farther?" Nikitin barked.

Vedenin gritted his teeth. "Fifteen minutes."

Silence. Nikitin could have sworn, but he didn't do so over the radio. He was too good a soldier for that.

"We're moving ground troops to you now," Vedenin said. "They're much closer. Barricade yourself someplace safe—we are *coming*."

Another pause. Then: "You'd better be."

Vedenin thrust the radio back to his subordinate and lifted the binoculars again. The grenade launcher was firing once more. His men had progressed thirty or forty yards but were moving far too slowly.

"Radio the gunships," Vedenin said. "Break one away to the north to search for the president and provide what cover it can."

"Done, Governor. And the second?"

Vedenin lowered the binoculars. His lips lifted into a snarl as he pointed toward the distant flash of the grenade launcher.

"Bring that building *down*."

102

Kybartai, Lithuania

The house was small, but Reed knew from the moment he crossed the threshold that it had once been a happy home.

He could feel it. Something about the smell of a fresh teakettle and warm bread, carrying even through the haze of gun smoke. The toys scattered on the floor. The worn couch and the row of loved books over the mantel. There wasn't a dog curled on the rug, but he could imagine one.

That was before—now this place was hell. The Russian soldier dug in behind the first-floor window spun toward Reed the moment he barreled through the door. Reed's gaze was naturally drawn toward the stairwell directly ahead—the high ground, the most obvious angle of ambush.

He pivoted toward the window only a split second after clearing the stairs, but that split second was enough. The Russian opened fire at twenty feet, a thunder of AK-12 fire so loud and so close that Reed felt the concussions of the bullets even as they missed him. One round just beneath his elbow. Another just over his neck.

Then the third struck home, dead center in his chest plate. Reed choked and was immediately out of air. His body quaked. He was toppling backward and firing at the same time, stitching the soldier across the face, neck, and chest even as a fourth bullet zipped like jacketed lightning and hit Reed in the upper right arm.

He didn't feel the pain, only a dull throb. A creeping numbness. The Russian soldier hit the hardwood as Reed fell against a wall, gasping for breath and fumbling with his magazine release. He was dry again—Turk was exploding into the room shouting, but Reed couldn't hear him. He reached for a magazine and nearly dropped it—his right hand was slick with blood.

"Upstairs!" Reed choked.

Turk was already moving. He hit the steps, rifle held into his shoulder, muzzle sweeping toward the landing. He was two yards away, moving in a steady crouch. Reed was slamming a new magazine into his rifle's receiver.

And then he saw it. A vibration in the ceiling—a subtle shift of a picture frame on the wall. A fleck of the popcorn finish breaking free.

"*Turk!*" Reed screamed. "*Down!*"

Turk's face snapped toward Reed just as Reed flat-palmed the side of his rifle, dropping the bolt. Snatching the muzzle up.

Then the home's ceiling exploded. Bullets burst through the drywall in a hail of zipping lead, wood splinters and insulation raining in a shower from the second floor. It was full auto—a crazed, desperate spray, sweeping the floor and headed up the stairs. Turk twisted and threw himself forward.

Reed opened fire. With his rifle pointed at the ceiling, he dumped rounds, pouring a full magazine into the second floor as dust clouded the air and obscured his vision. He couldn't breathe—he could barely see. The rifle ran dry a second time just as a heavy *thud* slammed into the overhead floor. Reed's bloody right hand slipped on his plate carrier.

He only had one mag left. He dumped the empty and drew the full. His hand shook. The gunfire from the second floor had ceased, leaving Reed's ears ringing so loudly that he couldn't hear anything else. He was dizzy on his feet. He twisted in place, seating the mag. Reaching for the bolt release.

And then finding Turk.

The big Tennessean lay stretched on the steps, his rifle dangling from its one-point sling. He still grasped the pistol grip with one hand, but his other was held against his neck. His fingers were crimson—blood ran down his arm. His face was draining white and he was gasping for air, not shouting. Not moving.

Reed ran. Over the bullet-torn floor, kicking past the toys and nearly tripping on the carpet. Terror took him, propelling him like the boot of a giant. He reach Turk at the base of the steps and hit his knee, the rifle held up toward the second level even as Reed's right hand clawed at Turk's neck.

"Turk! Where are you hit?"

Turk didn't answer. His lips parted, and blood leaked out. His eyes were wide, his body shaking. Reed grasped his hand and finally managed to push it aside only to take a geyser of blood straight to his face. It erupted from Turk's neck like a blast from a fountain—pressurized and unrestricted. Reed couldn't really see the source but he didn't need to.

It was a sliced artery—a bullet to the neck. Reed found the opening drilled by an AK round and rammed his finger in, stretching the skin and fishing to seal the hole.

He screamed over his shoulder.

"*Corpsman! Corpsman up!*"

It wasn't what he should have shouted. Lucy had never served in the Marine Corps—the term she would expect was *medic*. But Reed was no longer thinking. He was falling back on training that was now nearly a decade old—he was locking into desperate automation.

And Lucy didn't leave him hanging. She burst through the door alongside Corbyn, moving low through the smoke and zeroing on Reed's position. In another split second, she was at his side, sliding to her knees and snatching the tear-away trauma kit off her chest rig.

"Where?" she called.

"Neck!" Reed spat blood as he spoke, still holding his left hand in Turk's neck and pointing the rifle up the stairs.

"*Corbyn!*" He shouted. "Clear the second floor."

Corbyn shoved past Reed and hurtled up the stairs, her M4 held into her shoulder. A split second later, gunfire erupted at the top of the steps—the voice of two rifles, followed by the snap of a pistol and a heavy *thud*. Reed's body tensed and he felt Lucy's hand on his shoulder, shaking him.

"Reed! Move your hand. I'll take him."

Reed tore his gaze away from the steps and back to Turk. His battle buddy was chalky pale and growing still. His lips parted, and little more than a rasp escaped. He spat up blood.

"*Reed*," Lucy said. "I've got him. *Go!*"

Reed breathed over dry and cracked lips. He looked into Turks eyes once more. The big man blinked, then hissed a command.

"*Go, Reed*."

Reed let him go. His fingers withdrew from the bullet wound and blood spurted out, spraying his face. Lucy's hands moved like lightning, immediately plugging the wound even as she fought with the med pack with her free hand. She shoved Reed with her shoulder, shouting once more.

That broke him out of it. Reed exploded back to his feet. He swept the rifle hard into his shoulder and charged up the stairs.

103

15,000 feet over the Suwałki Gap, Poland

"Ten minutes!"

The jumpmaster's command echoed down the steel belly of the C-17 Globemaster even as its quad jet engines howled like the voice of a hurricane. The ride had been a rough one all the way out of Germany—pockets of turbulence, heavy clouds rising too high to be flown over, and even lightning. Now the armada of thirty-seven transport aircraft and twelve F-15E Strike Eagle escorts were within minutes of reaching the drop zone.

"One metric ton of airborne whoop-ass," in Packer's terminology, would explode through the jump doors—but he wasn't in the mood to be making jokes now. Strapped down with 140 pounds of parachute, reserve parachute, and combat gear, Packer had to waddle as he moved along the length of the Globemaster, checking in with his men and kicking them in the shins whenever he felt the need to offer emotional support.

They were on edge, but not in a bad way. These men *liked* to be tested. They liked to push the limits of their mental and physical capacities. They liked to shake each other up, to harass one another, to get good and jacked and fling into the great unknown. It was what they were born for—what "Iron Boots" had trained them to do.

Only this time, some of them wouldn't be coming home.

"Hey, Jinks!" Packer shouted. "How far would you go to fetch your wife's boyfriend a cold beer?"

"All the way, Colonel!" the sergeant answered without hesitation, then immediately fired back. "How far would the colonel go to put his boot up our asses, then take credit for our work?"

Packer grinned. "*All the way!*"

A roar echoed down the line as the men rose to their feet. With an overhead clock counting down to that fateful moment, the jokes faded. The jumpmaster was moving through pre-jump prep, a routine so practiced that Packer's men could do it in their sleep.

Stand up. Hook up. Check static lines. Check equipment. *Sound off.*

"Colonel!" The C-17 Loadmaster called from the nose of the plane, lifting a hand. Packer forced his way down the fuselage, using an overhead rail to steady himself. When he reached the Air Force technical sergeant standing just outside the C-17's cockpit, he leaned low to hear him over the thunder of the engines.

"We've got a message from base, a secure drop via SATCOM. I've relayed to your device. It should be ready now."

"Good—thanks."

Packer steadied himself using an overhead rail as he tugged the compact, armored tablet computer from his chest rig. Equipped with the Army's Joint Battle Command—Platform, or JBC-P, it would be his primary method of communication with his bosses once the battle began.

The fact that those bosses had relayed a message through the C-17's SATCOM system instead of dropping it through JBC-P indicated that they wanted him to read it *now*, before the drop.

That couldn't be a good thing.

When loaded the message contained only three lines of text—but three lines was enough.

[SIPRNET // PRIORITY // 1217Z] BE ADVISED: RUSSIAN GROUND TROOPS MOVING INTO KYBARTAI, NUMBERS UNCERTAIN. HELICOPTER GUNSHIP SUPPORT, MULTIPLE JET FIGHTER AIRCRAFT INBOUND. WILL ADVISE FURTHER WHEN DETAILS AVAILABLE.

Packer looked up from the screen. Ran his tongue over his teeth, and switched the device off. Then glanced left at the young Army major who had followed Packer through multiple commands, beginning as a wet-behind-the-ears first lieutenant.

The two men knew each other well, and as with most of the officers under his command, Packer could often communicate his thoughts without needing to actually speak. Just this once, however, he chose to vocalize.

"Well, Joe. Looks like the Ruskies are rolling out a welcome mat. Should we take 'em to the prom?"

The major didn't so much as flinch. "If it's up to me, sir, we'll take 'em all the way."

Packer winked in approval. He looked to the clock overhanging the jump bay just as it switched to the five-minute mark. His men were already on their feet, in position to march through an open door and straight into empty air.

Four minutes, thirty-six seconds to drop.

104

Kybartai, Lithuania

Wolfgang scrambled for the last belt of grenades.

He'd only brought four—he'd already churned through three. His second reload was faster than his first, but the tidal wave of Russians assembling on the Lithuanian side of the river was beginning to overwhelm is limited firepower. He'd taken down maybe half a dozen of them and sent dozens more sprinting for cover. They hadn't done much in the way of trying to return fire except for cracking off a handful of potshots, some of which slammed into the window frame but none of which reached him.

Wolfgang thought that was odd. He knew he was holding them in place, at least temporarily. He wasn't a tactician by trade, but if he were in their shoes, he'd want to dislodge the Mark 19 as soon as possible—get his men *moving*. What were the Russians waiting on?

The last ammo canister popped open with a smell like every aircraft hangar and military supply depot that Reed had dragged Wolfgang through over the past two years. The belt fed into the open receiver of the piping-hot launcher—Wolfgang knew how to correctly place it now. He snapped the cover in place and was just reaching for the dual charging handles, wincing under another slam of lead against the window frame, when he heard it.

Low and pulsating. A concussive thumping sound carrying from someplace beyond the storm clouds, its source as yet invisible but the sound growing steadily louder. A whistling howl of jet engines—a break in the intermittent rifle fire from the street. Wolfgang's fingers froze over the charging handles and his gaze snapped up...

Just in time to see the Kamov Ka-52 Alligator burst through the clouds, one thousand yards distant and racing like a missile. Nose down...and already firing with its auto-cannon.

Lapboard siding exploded, timbers splintered, and Wolfgang just closed his eyes.

105

Kybartai, Lithuania

Reed hurled himself up the stairs.

Rifle up, blood churning, face sweaty hot despite the chill. His body trembled under the deluge of adrenaline, and he moved on instinct. He had thirty rounds of green-tipped 5.56 NATO ammunition locked into the M4—and only one target.

The top of the stairs opened to a narrow landing. A bedroom to his right, a bedroom to his left. An empty bathroom straight ahead...

And Kirsten Corbyn, lying dead on the landing in a spreading pool of blood. She had been shot through the back of the head, twice, and it wasn't difficult for Reed to unravel the riddle of how it had happened.

There were other bodies visible in the front bedroom, three in total. The first two were civilians—a mother and a child who had apparently ignored the evacuation order and remained at home, only for their house to become a battleground. They had each been shot through the forehead and lay wide-eyed and lifeless, visible through the open bedroom door.

The third body was that of the Russian soldier who had shot Turk through the ceiling. He lay twisted over a hardwood floor riddled with holes and slick with blood, multiple wounds in his legs, torso, and arms from where Reed had returned fire.

But it was the bullet hole between his eyes that had killed him, and Reed guessed that shot to have been delivered by Corbyn. She had turned right, engaging a wounded enemy—and been ambushed from behind.

Reed saw it all in a split second, unpacking the tactical implications and then spinning immediately left, toward the final bedroom. The door stood half open, semi-concealing the space beyond and whatever threat of death it contained. Reed didn't know and no longer cared—no longer waited to think or wonder. All he could think of was the face.

The face of a man plastered across the news media. Plastered across Langley's intel files and Reed's target dossier. The face of a man leading the world head-first into the abyss of war—the face of a man who had orchestrated the detonation of twin nuclear weapons, costing tens of thousands of lives. The man who had facilitated terrorist attacks on American soil, slaughtering innocents—even slaughtering Reed's own daughter. Now slaughtering his team.

The face of evil.

The face of a man who was about to *die.*

One boot to the door sent it smashing into the wall, and Reed exploded into the room already firing, driving bullets into any human-sized object that crossed his line of sight.

A chair. A dresser. A painting on the wall. He only stopped when he confirmed that the room to be empty.

But the window was open.

106

Chernyshevskoe, Kaliningrad Oblast
Russia

"My guard is *dead*! Get me a helicopter!"

Nikitin's voice exploded through the radio at Vedenin's command post, and a chill raced up the governor's spine. Not so much because of what Nikitin had said—although that was terrifying enough.

No, Vedenin experienced the chill because of Nikitin's tone of voice. It was a sound Vedenin had never heard before, a desperation he couldn't have imagined even if he tried.

Makar Nikitin was *afraid*. Terrified, in fact. Breathless and on the run. Only a few hundred yards from hundreds of Russian soldiers, and yet hopelessly alone. Hunted by the one thing that no amount of withering mass destruction could account for.

A lethal, precision team, striking from the shadows.

Vedenin snapped the binoculars back to his eyes, surveying a now smoking Lithuanian town. The Alligator hovering between his command post and ground zero of the attack had just dumped half a dozen rockets into the two-story building where the grenadier had nested—the building was on fire, collapsing.

Too little, too late?

"Move the gunships!" Vedenin shouted. "Deploy our troops into the city—*find the president!*"

Radio orders crackled in a maddened flurry. Vedenin's hand tightened around the binos, his heart thumping a snare drum cadence.

This *could not* be happening.

Finally turning from the window, he snatched up a radio handset just as Nikitin called in his latest position, moving east through Kybartai. He was headed away from his troops, but the president had no choice. The hounds were on his heels.

"We're coming, Mr. President. We're seconds away!"

Vedenin's promise was accurate. The Alligators were already converging around the president's probable position. The ground troops were charging ahead...

But were they already too late?

"Governor!"

It was a Russian army officer who shouted from Vedenin's elbow. Vedenin wanted to ignore the man, but the officer was literally jamming a tablet computer into his face.

"What is it?" Vedenin snapped.

"*Look.*"

Vedenin did look. The display was an encrypted messaging app, linked directly with Russian military command outside of Kaliningrad. The missive was brief...and the contents even more chilling than the fear in Nikitin's voice.

Large formation of NATO planes inbound. Fifty or more aircraft, fighters and transport planes. Could contain paratroopers.

Vedenin's gaze locked with that of the Russian officer, and his blood ran cold.

107

Kybartai, Lithuania

Reed saw him.

The man in all black had jumped—maybe fallen—from the second-story window of the back bedroom, landing in another narrow alley directly below. He must have busted an ankle when he struck the concrete, or maybe twisted his knee. Even at a hundred yards his stagger was visible as he held a radio handset in one hand and a drawn pistol in the other. He was turning back and looking toward the sky. He was swerving toward cover behind another house.

But Makar Nikitin was in range.

Reed snatched the rifle up and fired just as the first rocket hit. It slammed into the front of the house, maybe in the bedroom where the second soldier lay shot through the face. Reed recognized the hiss and whizz of the incoming weapon but his mind tuned it out. He didn't even care if it tore right through him, or blew him in half.

He only needed one shot, and Nikitin's face hovered on the far side of the ACOG sights, staring at Reed as though he could see the gaping muzzle of the M4 pointed at him. There was terror in that face—real fear. Reed pulled the trigger.

But the thunderclap blast of the rocket detonated just a split second too soon. Reed's bullet missed by inches as the house behind him erupted into flame and flying wood. Reed was thrown against the wall, the breath stolen from his lungs. Somewhere behind him, the thunder of rotor blades mixed with the bass pound of an auto-cannon. The house was literally exploding, flying apart, caving in. The air swirled with smoke and the kiss of hot flame. The helicopter was storming in closer.

Reed hurled himself through the window. Feet first, dropping straight to the ground. Fifteen feet and a hard landing—pain shot up Reed's right leg as something crunched in his knee. He bit back a shout and rolled to the ground—then kept rolling, back to his feet. Behind him, the house was collapsing and the helicopter gunship was still firing. Reed began to run, staggering and nearly tripping, the rifle clutched in both hands. His lungs burned and fresh blood oozed from the bullet wound in his right shoulder. It was dropping off his fingers, his elbow. He couldn't even feel the pain anymore—his arm had gone numb. He breathed smoke and fixated on the corner where Nikitin had disappeared—two small houses with a narrow street between. Maybe windows to bust and dark rooms to hide in.

Nikitin had a gun. At close range, he might pop off a shot at Reed's face. Reed would just have to be quicker.

Adrenaline. The flavor of the battlefield—of burning timbers, wafting gun smoke, combusting rocket fuel. Somewhere behind him in the haze, multiple Alligator helicopters thundered. Rifles popped. Men shouted.

But Reed only ran. He blinked and he saw mushroom clouds. He saw Nashville, the rolling American heartland. He saw innocent civilians gathered at concerts, county fairs, and school picnics. He saw the terror in their eyes as the same rockets zipping in behind him raced into unprotected crowds of children. Of young families. Of helpless seniors.

He blinked again, and the vision became more specific. It featured the faces of the dead—men and women that Reed had killed over his long years as a soldier, an assassin, a covert operator. Every body like a rung on a ladder that had led him inevitably to this place. This final moment. A bloody, gory, miserable journey.

But in the final blink, it all made sense. Because Reed saw home. He saw his team—those living, those sacrificed. He saw his bulldog, Baxter. His dad's battered old Camaro. And most of all...

His family. Banks and Davy. Two people no more or less important than any other innocent lives on the planet and yet...a worthy representation.

A vision worth dying for.

Reed reached the narrow street and turned the corner. He made it one stride and then took the first bullet in his chest—a zipping-fast pistol round that reignited the pain of fractured ribs and nearly knocked him off-balance. The muzzle flash came from fifty feet away, behind the nose of a parked sedan.

Reed engaged—firing on the move, blowing out automotive glass and knocking away a side-view mirror. The next pop from the pistol sent a bullet whizzing over his head. He gasped for air and leaned low, his right arm so numb from blood loss that he struggled to manage his trigger finger. One shot was rushed—then he failed to extend far enough to reset the trigger. His vision was tunneling. He fired two more bursts at a shadow vanishing behind the car—the same figure clothed in black.

Then the rifle ran dry. The trigger jammed under his finger, the bolt locked back. Reed's left hand swept the chest rig but the magazine pouches were empty—there was nothing left. He dropped the M4 and went straight for the SIG P226 holstered on his hip.

He drew. He found the double-action trigger as the shadow emerged from cover, wielding a pistol of its own. Muzzle matched muzzle—sweat glistened on white skin and Reed locked eyes with his target, just fifteen yards away.

President Makar Nikitin.

108

The world stood still.

From all around Reed, battle thundered like the pound of a hurricane making landfall. There was rifle fire, grenades cracking, engines roaring. The onslaught of Russian infantry was locked in a death battle with some manner of gathering resistance—Lithuanian ground troops, probably, rushing to the site of their president's murder.

Joining that storm of urban combat was the perpetual pound of Alligator helicopters turning and sweeping and dumping fire. Rockets, cannons, guide missiles.

It was hell on earth. The worst thing humankind could do to itself. And yet Reed tuned it all out with ease. He masked the noise and blocked out the shudder beneath his boots. Forgot the pain and erased every instinct of self-preservation or even survival. He was tunnel-visioned in the most extreme sense of the term. He was looking through post-and-notch sights at his target.

Dark hair. Dark eyes. An enraged snarl. A handgun of his own, rising and pointing and twitching even as it spat fire.

Reed fired also. He squeezed the SIG's twelve-pound double-action trigger in one smooth pull, a motion he had practiced maybe a hundred thousand times. No jerks, no hesitations. Even pressure from start to finish. The external hammer rocked back to full action and dropped like the blade of an executioner's ax.

It might as well have been. Makar Nikitin's single shot was well-placed. It struck the very top edge of Reed's chest plate, skipping off the steel and zipping upward. The ricochet punched through the underside of Reed's mouth and tore through unprotected flesh—past his tongue and right through his cheekbone. Reed felt the impact like a punch to the face, knocking him off-balance and sending him stumbling. Flooding his mouth with blood. Threatening to take him down.

But his own bullet was already on the way, and Makar Nikitin took it straight through his teeth, a wad of hot American lead punching beyond his throat and smashing into his brain stem. He froze, eyes wide, blood still pumping. His body in shock. The Grach pistol fell from his hand.

He hit his knees, jaw falling open, eyes still locked on Reed as Reed continued to stumble back, choking on blood.

Neither man spoke. Neither man screamed. The Russian stared with wide eyes, his mouth falling open half an inch, but he seemed unable to move—unable even to breathe. He was paralyzed, suspended in pre-death.

And in his eyes, Reed recognized the fear. Abject terror, rolling like a tidal wave. A million panicked thoughts of disbelief, of pleading, of confusion. All the emotions of a hard charging life stopped short in the blink of an eye.

Reed saw it. He understood it. He gritted bloody teeth and lifted a shaking right arm.

Then, with one more press of the SIG's trigger, he erased it all—a bullet driven straight between Nikitin's eyes just as Reed's numb right arm finally gave out.

The Russian fell sideways to the pavement, and Reed stumbled forward, choking up a spray of crimson. He dropped the SIG and gasped for air, the world spinning around him. The ground pitched, and the sky turned black. He swallowed blood and crashed into the rear of the gunshot sedan. His rifle, still dangling from a one-point sling, was pinned against the busted taillight.

Reed leaned over the deck lid. He opened his mouth and dispensed another cup of blood. His head was going light—it hurt to breathe. He could barely stand.

He looked to the body, folded on the ground.

Haunted eyes—a soul departed.

Mission complete.

Reed heard the thunder from behind and slowly twisted his head. He looked through smoke, through a haze of dust spilling over a town engulfed in war. He heard the gunshots again, a faded scream barely audible through ringing ears.

And he saw the Alligator gunship, five hundred feet up and two thousand yards back. Nose down, sweeping toward him. A flash of orange exploded from its rocket pods.

Reed slumped against the car, and smiled.

109

The Situation Room
The White House

Stratton didn't breathe.

Seated at the conference table, phones and computers and the demanding world of the West Wing totally forgotten, the vice president fixated on the screen at the end of the room just like everyone around him. No longer displaying satellite imagery, that screen now featured footage from a high-level spy drone, and the picture was near perfect, like looking down through glass into a living diorama.

There were the streets, choked by rubble. Soldiers moving like dots, their arms and legs and even the color of their uniforms clearly visible. Muzzle flash from silent rifles, endless clouds of smoke blooming from burning buildings, detonating rockets, and cracking grenades.

Misery. Death. Carnage unleashed. An entire town brought to rubble in mere seconds, the invading troops charging into the teeth of staunch Lithuanian resistance. But all of that was just window dressing—just context.

One battle amid them all stole the show. The surveillance drone tracked it with ease, first to a house at the end of the alley where five men entered but only two came out. Those two fell from a rear window. They ran, the lead man dressed in black and his pursuer dressed in military green.

Both limped. Both staggered. But only one lunged for cover. The second kept advancing, leaned low and firing with first a rifle, then a pistol…

And then not firing. Because it was *over*.

Makar Nikitin, president of the Russian Federation, lay lifeless on the ground under full view of the drone. His face, captured by a million-dollar zoom lens, was clear and crisp enough to serve as an autopsy photo. He was shot through the mouth. Shot through the forehead.

He was finished.

A moment of dead stillness consumed the usually chaotic room. Nobody moved. The drone zoomed out, revealing Reed Montgomery stumbling against the trunk of a car. Leaning over and choking up blood. Looking ready to collapse.

Then came the Alligator, and Jordan Stratton exploded out of his chair, a sudden rush of cortisol flooding his body. He shouted a curse. Rockets filled the screen. The car vanished—Reed vanished with it. The street was on fire.

And a blink later, so was the Alligator helicopter. The sidewinder missile appeared out of nowhere, a streaking dart that smacked the chopper broadside and turned it to instant shrapnel.

More smoke. More flame. Stratton's heart hammered as the camera lens zoomed way out, a fifteen-thousand-foot picture displaying *dozens* of giant gray airplanes, each dispensing 82nd Airborne paratroopers like gumballs from broken dispensers. Parachutes flooded the screen—F-15E Strike Eagle escorts ripped by, still dumping missiles and guided bombs.

Blasting every Russian target from downtown to the river…and Stratton just stared, wide-eyed and open mouthed. For the first time in his career, totally lost for words.

A phone rang. General Yellin answered it, but didn't say much. He hung up and looked to Maggie.

"Our first wave has fully deployed, ma'am. Russian resistance is collapsing. We're launching another two brigades of airborne infantry into

Lithuania as planned, and mass air strikes are proceeding against targets in Estonia and Latvia. By nightfall we'll be ready to begin ground incursions through the Suwałki Gap."

Maggie nodded. Turned to Gorman.

"Lisa, we've prepared preliminary statements for both our allies and the Russian people. I don't have your gift with diplomacy, so you'll probably need to make adjustments. The gist for the Russian people is that we had nothing to do with Nikitin's death and have never been their enemy. The gist for everybody else is that NATO will be retaking every inch of illegally occupied soil seized by the Nikitin regime, while continuing our support of Israel and our operations against Iran. It's our intention that this war is concluded by the end of the year."

"You can't..." Gorman started, then stopped, seemingly at a loss for words. Finally, she managed: "You can't think the Russians will just roll over."

Stratton was having the same thought, but before he could interject, Director Aimes did.

"We know they will. We have an inside line to Nikitin's replacement—Prime Minister Maxim Romanov. He's disabling Nikitin's entire regime as we speak, and will be withdrawing Russian ground troops from the Baltic ahead of our advance. So long as NATO does not encroach on previously established Russian territory, their fight with Europe is ended."

More blinking. Catatonic disbelief. Easterling was next to speak.

"And what about *China*?"

"We don't know what the Chinese will do," Yellin said. "Maybe they'll invade Taiwan tomorrow. But with Russian folding and Iran on the retreat, my gut says they'll think twice."

The words were so calm, so matter-of-fact, that Stratton could barely process what he was hearing. Could barely believe any of it.

It just wouldn't compute.

"So this..." Stratton started. "This is it? This is your grand plan to stay in power?"

He looked to Maggie, and the president met his gaze. A soft smile, half sad and half exhausted, hung on her thin lips. Slowly, she rose from her chair. She brushed hair behind one ear and turned the corner of the table.

She approached to within a foot of the VP, forced to tilt her head back to make eye contact. Slowly, she reached into her pocket and produced a single white envelope, unsealed, and stamped with the presidential emblem.

"No," she said. "This was my grand plan to save America."

She extended the envelope, and for a long moment Stratton only stared. Then, slowly, he accepted it.

"Good luck, Jordan," Maggie said. "I'll be rooting for you."

Without another word, Maggie Trousdale turned for the door. She exited on silent feet, simply fading away into the dark. Leaving Stratton, still stunned, to lift the envelope's top and shake the contents out.

It was thick white paper—White House stationary. Maggie's letterhead was printed at the top, with a short, handwritten note recorded below.

To: Vice President Jordan Stratton, the Congress, and the American People—

Effective immediately, I hereby resign the presidency of the United States.

Very respectfully,

—Muddy Maggie

110

Kybartai, Lithuania

Lucy ran.

Through smoke so thick she could barely breathe. Through dust so heavy on the air it turned her skin chalk gray, a constant shower of exploded concrete and collapsing homes flooding the streets of a once peaceful Lithuanian town like the breath of the devil.

She was bleeding from cuts on her palms, arms, and face—products of a frantic scramble to extract both herself and Turk from a bullet-riddled house, even as it crumbled under helicopter fire.

She'd only just finished packing Turk's neck wound with hemostatic gauze when the helicopter arrived. At the first sound of rotor blade thunder, Lucy had shrank over his body while maintaining pressure on the dressing, holding her breath and praying that the airborne monster wouldn't open fire...

But it did. The rockets screamed in, and within a split second Lucy knew the house was coming down. She launched herself off the steps where Turk still lay and hooked her left hand beneath the shoulder strap of his plate carrier while maintaining pressure on the wound with her right. Another rocket flew, and Lucy launched herself off the steps, shoving out with everything she had in bunched thigh muscles.

Turk was huge—the largest member of the PF by a considerable margin. Two hundred sixty pounds of lean muscle tumbled down the steps but then stalled over a hardwood floor torn by bullets. Lucy choked. She shouted. Overhead, the next rocket detonated and the roof collapsed. Wood splinters and sheetrock, both infested with nails, rained over her body. The ground floor of the house was consumed by dust and darkness with only a narrow panel of light marking the front door, just five feet away.

Lucy prayed. She heaved. She asked for strength she knew she didn't possess.

Somehow, she got Turk's semi-conscious body through that door. She made it to the concrete patio outside just as the house collapsed into a heap of smashed timbers and twisted walls. Lucy hit the ground choking and turned her face away. The helicopter was just moving off, the downwash of its rotor blades blowing the dust away.

Three seconds later, the storm was gone altogether. Lucy's head was spinning. She staggered to her knees, breathing so fast she thought she might hyperventilate.

Then she turned back to Turk. He lay on his back, eyes closed and his face the color of printer paper. The gauze she had packed into his neck was still in place, but starting to turn red. The carotid artery, still cut, was still leaking.

Turk was going to die. He was going to bleed out, right there in the street, and there would be nothing she could do about it if she couldn't find help.

Airways and blood flow. Do what you can!

Lucy rolled Turk's head upright and held her cheek beneath his nose to confirm that he was still breathing. She repacked the gauze deeper into the wound. She straightened his legs and fired off another prayer.

Then she was on her feet and turning into the debris. Scrambling over busted plywood and between shattered two-by-fours. Listening to distant gunfire growing steadily louder as the battle the Prosecution Force had triggered spilled rapidly out of control.

She didn't know where she was going. She only knew she needed to find help, somehow and somewhere. Lucy couldn't carry Turk by herself and she lacked the medical equipment and advanced expertise to perform a battlefield transfusion.

So she ran. She made it past the collapsed house and dropped into a dirty street just as another Russian helicopter roared overhead. It turned in place about a thousand yards northeast of her position, and then bore south, nose down and rocket pods igniting in flame. It wasn't firing at her—but it was firing at something.

Lucy turned a corner just as the helicopter's rockets detonated with an earthquake burst that ripped up her spine. Dirt and flame erupted into the air in a hellish column just a hundred yards ahead, then a scream twice as loud as those rockets ripped out of the open blue.

The helicopter exploded. Lucy stumbled backward toward a wall and covered her ears, crouching as the gunship blew into pieces and rained over the ground. She looked into the sky just in time to see a familiar silhouette slice directly overhead.

It was an American fighter jet, and it wasn't alone. Everywhere she looked she saw American planes, with American parachutes opening beneath them. *Thousands* of incoming troops, storming to Lithuania's rescue.

But what had that helicopter been firing at?

Lucy lunged back to her feet, choking on smoke as she fought toward the site of the rocket strike. She passed gardens surrounded by picket fences. Dusty carports and a burning doghouse. She kept running and kept coughing, exploding around a corner and rushing right into the blast crater.

A tangled mass of metal that might once have been a car rested in the bottom of the shallow depression, with huge chunks of asphalt blown out of the earth and landing at random on every side. There was more smoke, more haze and...a rifle. An American-issue M4 carbine, torn free of its sling, just lying right there in the middle of the road.

"Reed!" Lucy shouted.

No answer. All she heard was distant gunfire, snapping like popcorn in a microwave, and the persistent ringing of her own ears.

Lucy sprinted through the smog and crashed into the crater. She leaned low and inhaled pure war fumes. They turned her head light and left her starved for air. It almost didn't *feel* like she was really running at all, but floating. Like all of this was just a nightmare.

But it was real. The road, the smell, the din of battle. And so was the pile of rubble massed just beyond the blast crater. She recognized the wheel of a car, lying on top. There was dirt and more asphalt also. Shreds of vehicle insulation and warped body panels, all cloaked in more inky black smoke.

And near the bottom of it all, protruding from the mound of dirt and twisted to one side, was a boot—black, leather, nondescript. But Lucy knew it had been supplied by the CIA.

"Reed!" Lucy shouted.

Then she was on her knees. Leaned close to the fire and scooping with her bare hands. Tearing earth and rubble away, burning her skin. Her vision was tunneled, but the boot was still connected to a leg, and that leg, although twisted, ran deeper beneath the pile.

She was digging past torn cargo pants. Past an empty pistol holster and the bottom of a bloody chest rig. Her hands came back sticky, and she clawed faster. His face was *buried*.

"Contact! We've got the body!"

The voice boomed from behind Lucy, barely audible to her ringing ears. Boots pounded closer. Lucy gasped, gagged, and nearly fell. She was pulling on Reed's leg but couldn't dislodge his body.

Then members of the United States Army 82nd Airborne arrived. Fifteen soldiers in relatively clean uniforms, surging the street with rifles sweeping every passing window. Lucy finally looked back to see a knot of American troops swarming a second body that she hadn't even noticed... but now recognized in an instant as the author of this entire catastrophe.

"Confirmed," one soldier called into his radio. "We have jackpot. Target is deceased. Collecting the body!"

"H-h-*help!*" Lucy choked.

Most of them didn't hear her. Probably, they couldn't even see her. The smoke was too thick.

But one did—and he slapped a second on the arm. A moment later a trio of muscled airborne infantry swarmed Lucy's position. They pulled her out even as she clawed at Reed's leg. Fabric slipped through her fingers and she shouted.

Then they went back in. Boots shifted rubble, and an entrenching tool sank into torn earth. Somebody radioed for a medic. Somebody else said they thought it was a Marine.

Lucy staggered, nearly falling before a tall Army specialist scooped her up, holding her off the ground. She gasped, her throat suddenly so dry and dirty that she could barely breathe. The specialist tried to calm her, but Lucy forced a single, rasping word.

"*Another*." Lucy lifted her arm toward Turk.

"I got you," the specialist promised. "We'll get him. You just breathe easy, now. You're safe!"

Slowly, he lowered Lucy to the ground, still supporting her back. With bloody hands shaking, she ignored the canteen he offered, and stared through burning eyes to watch the recovery crew gathered around Reed.

They pulled him out of the rubble. They stretched his body on smooth asphalt clear of the smoke and stripped the chest rig away. A chorus of curses rose from the group, and then one man shouted into his radio.

"He's still got a pulse. *Rush that medevac!*"

111

Moscow, Russia

"What the hell happened to you?"

Natasha Kirov sparked up a cigarette as she strolled past Ivan, never making eye contact and taking a seat at a picnic table with her back turned to him.

Sokolniki Park was quiet in early evening. With a fading sun casting its final glow over a nearby duck pond and a cool wind brushing Ivan's cheek, the overt peace of the place defied the chaos that Ivan knew to be exploding across the Kremlin. Rippling through the corridors of power in every military complex and government office across the city. Shaking the very identity of the sitting regime to its core—leaking as whispers to an increasingly attentive press.

Yes, the park was calm. For now. In another five hours, that peace would be shattered for months, perhaps years. Nobody really knew what would happen when Maxim Romanov assumed control of the Federation—certainly not Ivan. It was anybody's guess just how deeply Nikitin's power structure had been entrenched amid Moscow streets, or how many of his surviving lieutenants would make plays to seize his position atop the pyramid.

Romanov was not an overly clever man, and a large part of Ivan wondered if he was up to the task of managing the fallout of Nikitin's demise—if he was up to the task of truly leading Russia at all.

Time would tell. For the moment, Ivan was gunshot. He was aching so badly it hurt to sit up. He needed a surgeon, he needed a whole bottle of Green Mark and a place to sleep without concern of being shot in the back of the head.

But before any of that, he needed a picture.

"I ran into a door," Ivan muttered, his voice reflecting none of the humor his words conveyed.

Kirov didn't look over her shoulder, or so much as twitch. She just snorted in a way that told Ivan she had a good look at him on her way to the picnic table, and she knew that no door was involved in his present physical condition.

A haze of cigarette smoke drifted over the spy's shoulders. She thumped ash onto the pavement, her body perfectly relaxed, her gaze drifting over the duck pond. For all the world, she looked like an office drone freshly clocked out, enjoying a little R&R on her way home.

It was excellent tradecraft, but Ivan was growing impatient. The pain, so long ignored and defied, was finally getting the best of him.

"Well?" Ivan demanded.

"Mission accomplished," Kirov said, no hint of joy or delight or even satisfaction in her tone.

"Are you *sure*?" Ivan pressed.

By way of answer, Kirov reached into her pocket and produced an envelope. She slipped it onto the seat next to her, but didn't get up. Didn't make any body language acknowledgment of Ivan's question.

"Washington wants to insure that there will be no misunderstandings," Kirov said. "Romanov should withdraw all Russian forces from the Baltic by the end of next week. We'll give him a month on the Caucasus, but he's leaving those also. Russian naval assets should stand down. All public rhetoric should be selected with care."

"That's a hefty list of demands for a country that nearly had its teeth kicked in," Ivan said.

Kirov didn't immediately respond to that. She lifted the cigarette and inhaled deep. She held the breath and exhaled slowly, still watching the duck pond. She flexed her neck until the vertebrae crackled.

Finally, she said: "Yes. But we didn't have our teeth kicked in—and now we're back on top. Send the message, Ivan. I'll be in touch."

Kirov stood and stamped out the smoke before pocketing her hands. She departed the picnic table and turned the corner on the walking trail without ever looking at Ivan once.

The envelope remained behind. Ivan gave it five minutes before rising from his bench and collecting it. He proceeded a few hundred meters down the trail in the opposite direction as Kirov, passing into a grove of birch trees before he finally stepped into the shadows. He sliced the seal open with a trembling thumbnail. Bit back the misery in his shoulder as he parted the manilla shell and peeked inside.

It was one photograph. No inscription. Shot from a surveillance drone, Ivan thought, but with amazing clarity. Absolute detail.

It was Makar Nikitin, and he was as dead as a stone.

Without so much as a flinch, Ivan slid the envelope into his pocket. He withdrew a flask and gulped down one deep swig of Green Mark—the pretaste of a victory celebration that would drive him into merciful unconsciousness.

Then he drew a burner cell phone. He walked as he dialed. Maxim Romanov picked up immediately.

"Yes?"

The PM's voice was a little shaky. In the background Ivan could hear men shouting. Phones ringing. Feet pounding.

It was full chaos at the Russian White House...and it would grow from there.

"It's confirmed," Ivan said. "He's finished."

Pause. An audible swallow. "You're sure?"

"Positive."

Another hesitation, then: "Okay. I'll proceed."

Romanov hung up, and Ivan exited the park. He crossed the street into a mixed residential and retail district with a nearby hotel that promised a warm room and a soft bed. Not quite a surgeon, but that would still need to wait. At least a day or so.

On the way, Ivan would collect that bottle of Green Mark.

112

Nashville, Tennessee

Banks knew.

She would never know how or why—whether it was a divine whisper or simply marital intuition. The sensation didn't come as a voice in her head, or even a conscious thought, but merely as a *feeling*. A twist in her gut. A sudden conviction that *something* had just happened.

She stood at the granite countertop of her Gulch apartment when she first felt it, slicing strawberries for baby Liberty. Turk's wife, Sinju, lay on the couch, her midsection bulging with an eight-week baby bump, her face a little pale with morning sickness, even though it was midday.

Davy played on the floor—toy cars and trucks animated via the growls and gurgles of his two-year-old throat. On the flat-screen TV mounted to the wall, a child's television program displayed dancing stuffed animals and building blocks shaped like alphabet letters.

The music was turned down low so Sinju could rest. Liberty sat in her highchair, her face already smeared with bits of smashed blueberries, her wide eyes fixated on the flashing screen.

It was a quiet morning—the first quiet morning Banks had enjoyed at home in weeks. She was so tired herself she would have loved to flop out on the floor amid all Davy's toys and pass out, but Sinju had been covering for her with Davy between babysitters and the nanny, and it wasn't like she felt very well herself. Banks was content to slice the strawberries, listen to the baby music from the TV, and try not to think about war. About her husband.

Until the feeling rushed in, and her face snapped up. She dropped the knife on the cutting board and for a moment she couldn't move. She was frozen in place, unsure why.

But she knew that it was *something*, and she knew that it mattered.

"Sinju," Banks said. "Turn on the news."

"Huh?" Sinju groaned, turning her head but not opening her eyes.

Banks didn't bother to repeat herself. She circled the countertop and found the remote instead. She cycled off the kids' show and onto the cable TV network provided by her apartment. Banks didn't really know how to navigate it—she never had time for TV.

She only knew that she wanted a news station, and she found one after clicking through two dozen other channels.

Smoke. That was the first thing she saw—a camera feed displaying a column of inky black rising over a distant, unfamiliar town. The headline displayed beneath read: "Battle in Kybartai: President Nikitin Dead?"

Banks blinked. Her heart lurched. She flipped the channel again, landing on another news network. This one displayed a similar picture as the last, that of a distant burning town but this time with a reporter standing in front of it, speaking into a mic. Banks ramped up the volume.

"...just now confirming that President Nikitin is, indeed, believed to be dead."

The English was accentuated with an Eastern European accent, but Banks understood every word. She put her hand to her mouth as the reporter continued to speak, the camera angle switching to display *hundreds* of parachutes decorating a thick gray sky, with matching dark planes zipping overhead.

"While the belligerents of this conflict are not yet known, and five NATO countries have already denied any participation in the attack, the response of NATO forces to the conflict in Kybartai seems indicative of some pre-planned operation. We are told that as many as seven thousand American troops now occupy the town, driving Russian soldiers back across the river and into Kaliningrad. For a nation who stood, only hours ago, on the brink of surrender to Russia, this shocking turn of events may change the entire future of Lithuania."

Behind Banks, the couch creaked. Sinju groaned again, sitting up and blinking at the screen. Baby Liberty began to cry at the noise, and even Davy looked up from his toy racecar, wide eyes transfixed by the unfolding carnage on the TV screen.

But Banks didn't say anything. She didn't change the channel. She just descended into a seat at the end of the couch, still watching as the video feed displayed parachuting American soldiers and jet fighters streaking in on attack runs.

Chaos of the battlefield...but the battle, quite clearly, was over.

"Those videos come to us from our war reporters stationed in Lithuania," an anchor said, the picture abruptly changing to that of a newsroom. "We're now switching gears to bring you a word from the White House, where our network has just received notification that President Trousdale is about to deliver a national address...Here she is now, and it looks like...wow. Yes, Vice President Stratton is with her. My goodness, she...doesn't look good."

The anchor's candor was the understatement of the year. As Maggie Trousdale stepped behind the podium, she appeared as little better than skin and bones, pale with stringy hair.

But she wore a clean suit. She wore some makeup. She carried herself tall and proud while her vice president stood next to her. When she spoke, her voice rasped a little but still sounded like swamps and gumbo from way down south.

"Good afternoon. Thank you for joining me."

Nobody answered. The camera didn't move, and Maggie took a moment, as though collecting her thoughts.

Then she breathed deep—and resumed. "My remarks today will be brief, and I won't be taking any questions. I'm here because the United States intelligence sector has just received positive confirmation that Russian President Makar Nikitin...is dead."

That brought a momentary gasp from the press pool. A murmur. But no questions. Maggie gave the audience a moment before resuming.

"While the circumstances of President Nikitin's death remain a mystery, I can confidently state that the American military had nothing whatsoever to do with this act of violence. This administration, and this nation, would not dare to shortchange the Russian people on their claim of justice against the despot who has dragged their country into a pit of war."

The words were somehow both blunt and polished, spoken with confidence, and yet Banks couldn't help but think that they sounded more rehearsed than convicted.

She leaned a little closer and kept listening.

"Having said that," Maggie continued, "let me be clear when I say that this war, from its inception, has never been a war between the American people and the Russian people, but between the world and a regime of evil led by a man bent on collecting as much power as humanly possible...and steamrolling anyone standing in his path. That regime, I believe, was a fraud—a false face of Moscow and a seeping poison that has just been confronted with a withering antidote...*thank God*."

Maggie's voice changed as the speech progressed, a transition from production to natural ease. The developing tone reminded Banks of the early Muddy Maggie, a woman that Banks had learned to support, and even vote for.

"In context of these shocking developments," Maggie went on, "I know many around the world may be alarmed, and even afraid. Uncertainty in Moscow is no friend of peace, which is why my administration has already made contact with Russian Prime Minister Maxim Romanov who, per the Russian constitution, will be assuming the authorities of the presidency. Acting President Romanov and myself enjoyed a brief but highly productive conversation, during which he expressed his disinterest in pursuing further armed conflict in Europe, and his desire to broker a peace. As such, Acting President Romanov and myself have agreed to a cease-fire effective at midnight tonight, Zulu time, to be followed by a withdrawal of Russian troops from the Baltic."

This time the gasp in the media room was louder, and it was mirrored by a gasp in Banks's own living room. She sat with her hand still pressed to her mouth, just staring, as Maggie ran through a short list of technical details regarding American troop deployments and participation from NATO allies.

The president was peppered with questions. She ignored them all. She reached the end of her list and breathed deep before looking up.

When she did, her face had changed. Gone was the stern confidence of moments before—the iron facade. In its place Banks saw a softness that she had maybe never seen before. A gentleness. A halting vulnerability.

"It's been the honor of my life to serve as your president. I haven't done it perfectly. I've fallen short in a lot of ways and made my share of mistakes. Some might say...more than my share. But when I assumed this office after President Brandt's death, it was my sincerest objective to give my very life in the service of this country. To conclude my presidency leaving America better than I found her. Safer...stronger...more herself."

Maggie paused. Swallowed. Banks lowered her hand and leaned forward, squinting at the screen. She thought...Was the president crying?

"They say a wise leader begins with the end in mind," Maggie resumed. "I'm not sure exactly what that means, but from my first day of public service, I always promised myself that I would never allow my love of service to compromise my responsibility to those I serve. That I would remember who put me in office, why they put me in office, and be smart and humble enough to admit if the day ever came when I was no longer the best advocate of their best interests. If by time, or age, or lack of capacity, I ever reached a place where I had given everything I could...then I would be content. I would be grateful...and I would step aside."

A shudder ripped up Banks's spine. She sat upright. Her body tensed. She listened to the murmurings from the press corps. She watched Maggie stand tall and lift her chin.

"Effective immediately, I am resigning my position as president of the United States, and leaving this nation I love in the strong and steady hands of a man who has faithfully served by my side through so many fires. A man of wisdom, of passion, of patriotism. The *right* leader for America's next chapter—because it isn't and never has been about me...it's about you, and may God bless you all."

Maggie smiled. Ducked her head. And then she turned and left the podium without answering any of the storm of questions that peppered her like artillery fire. The reporters shouted, the cameras pivoted—but she was already gone. Stratton was gone with her. The press room was blank and the news feed returned to a split screen of burning Lithuania and a stunned, speechless news anchor.

"I, uh..." the anchor started. Stopped. Swallowed. "Well, I really don't know what to say...I think we're going to take a break now."

The anchor's voice faded as that picture of the battlefield in Lithuania resumed full screen, a chain of headlines churning across the bottom in an endless, unbelievable stream.

Pres. Nikitin dead. Pres. Trousdale resigned. Russian Act. Pres. announces cease-fire. Russian troops to withdraw. NATO forces to secure the Baltic.

Banks watched and her eyes watered. She blinked but the blur didn't leave. She wasn't crying at the headlines, or even reading them anymore. She was just staring at that burning town and connecting the dots in her head. Finally making sense of it all.

Davy, rising with race car in one hand, toddled to her and put his hands up. Banks lifted him, wiping her face with one thumb, and glanced right at Sinju.

Turk's wife was also crying, a blanket lifted to her face as she locked onto the screen, transfixed by the moment and what it meant.

Davy snuggled close to Banks, ducking his head in the way he did when he was afraid. She wiped Fig Newton crumbs from his face and forced a smile.

"Do you see that, Davy? Do you know what it means?"

Davy didn't answer. Banks looked up again and kept the smile going—even as she wanted to embrace the tears.

"It means your daddy just saved the world."

113

Landstuhl Regional Medical Center
Near Ramstein Air Base, Germany

The world wasn't black—it was just dark. Clothed in impenetrable shadow, like a fog too thick even to walk through. There were illusions of light, sometimes. Even visions of shapes.

But they were only a mirage. Only a phantom generation of a mind shaken by battle and pushed to the very brink of total collapse. They were, in a word, a fantasy.

Because Reed Montgomery was blind.

He first heard whispers of the problem while lying on medical cots in a field hospital in Poland, moments when he thought he was actually still unconscious or maybe dreaming. Footsteps and the clink of medical equipment matched the smells and tactile touch of a rough hospital bed, but Reed couldn't *see* anything, so he assumed it wasn't real. That he was trapped in an endless dream, cycling in and out of awareness of an imaginary surrounding.

It wasn't until they put him on a plane bound for Germany, and the sensation of the thundering engines was too visceral to dismiss as an illusion, that Reed first began to wonder if he really was awake. He didn't feel any pain—his body seemed to float, his mind seemed to buzz. He couldn't remember anything either.

He just took the flight. He faded into emptiness again. And when he next awoke...he knew. It wasn't a dream. He could put his hand to his face and feel the rough bandages. The ache of wounds in his body was too real. The pound of a headache not quite muted by the slow drip of whatever medications seeped into his arm.

It was darkness. Real, and absolute.

"You're going to live, Mr. Montgomery."

The doctor's voice was calm, seasoned with a German accent. Maybe he meant the words to be comforting, but the panic building in Reed's chest was nearly overwhelming. He clung to his own bedrails, sitting up. Trying to speak but finding his jaw wired closed. His face packed tight with bandages. Suddenly he felt like he was suffocating.

"Please stay calm, sir. I only have a few minutes, and I want to explain what you're experiencing so that you won't be confused. The damage to your mouth, jaw, and broken ribs is all healing. We've stitched your lacerations and treated the burns on your arms and legs. You'll be able to walk again—you'll be able to talk. But your vision..."

Pause. Reed's heart thumped harder. The panic was resuming.

What about my vision? What are you saying? Why can't I see?

"I'm afraid you suffered severe thermal burns to your face—likely from the initial blast of the detonating rockets. Your corneas were badly seared, and your retinas severely damaged...even your optic nerves were charred. Much of your face can be repaired with skin grafts but..."

That *but* again. That trailing off, refusing to finish. Long seconds of desperation and madness.

Then the kill shot.

"The blindness will be permanent, Mr. Montgomery. I'm very sorry."

Reed cycled in and out of fitful sleep for days—aided, no doubt, by heavy medication. Whenever consciousness returned long enough for him to sit up in bed, grunting and agonized, the panic would return with it. The sensation of being trapped, of being swallowed up. Of being helpless.

He would thrash. Attempt to shout. Claw at his face.

Then the medical staff would rush in, orders in German were exchanged...and very quickly, Reed didn't feel like fighting anymore. He didn't feel like doing anything.

He just faded into blackness.

On the fifth day—a German nurse told him it was the fifth day—the wire was finally removed from his jaw. Reed could open and close his mouth independently, although with a lot of pain, for the first time since the world had turned hot and bright and everything else had faded from memory.

The feeding tube was removed. Reed was asked if he would like to try eating something. His mouth still hurt so badly, swollen by stitches and staples, that the last thing he was interested in was food.

But then the voice asked again, and this time the tone was familiar. A gentle hand touched his arm.

"LB?" Reed hissed.

"It's me, Reed. I'm right here."

From that moment forward, Reed measured the difference between consciousness and sleep by whether or not Lucy was there. Seated close to his bed, spoon-feeding him Jell-O and pudding, she convinced him not to talk but failed to convince him to relax. As another two days slipped by, the memories returned in a flood—everything from the moment Reed drove a golf cart off an airplane in Lithuania to the moment that Alligator helicopter swiveled on his position. The psychiatrists were impressed that he remembered.

Reed couldn't forget.

"Who else?" he finally asked, his voice barely above a hiss.

Lucy, lost somewhere beyond that inky void, didn't immediately answer. A plastic spoon scraped a plastic pudding cup, and Reed's head ached so badly it felt like it might split open. He reached a shaking hand out from the bed and found Lucy's arm. He squeezed.

"LB," he whispered. "*Who else?*"

By way of answer, Lucy took Reed's left hand and guided it across an open space next to his bed. Something shifted alongside him, and then a matching hand landed in his. It squeezed—tight, confident, powerful.

Hope flooded Reed's chest. He managed another rasping word.

"Turk?"

"It's him," Lucy said. "He can't talk right now. They had to do surgery on his neck…it's just temporary."

Reed squeezed his burned and trembling fingers harder around Turk's. The grip he received in return felt like life itself. Like a miracle. Lucy's hand was still on his arm also. It was a three-pointed triangle.

And they were still missing a point.

"Wolf?" Reed said.

Silence again. Reed's heart began to pound. His mouth went dry—he tried to sit up.

Then, soft and rasping, a voice to his right.

"I'm here, Reed."

Reed twisted. He reached out. Lucy caught his right hand and guided it as before. He touched metal—a wheel. No, a *wheelchair*. He swept left, expecting to find Wolfgang's prosthetic leg…and found nothing.

Just the edge of the chair. The soft touch of cloth. Then a hand grabbed his, fingers gripping almost as tight as Turk's.

"Wolf?" Reed hissed. "Your legs?"

A pause. Wolfgang's hand shook. Then he managed something he might have intended to be a laugh.

"Who needs those?"

Reed blinked. His eyes burned and he fell back against the bed. Still clutching Wolfgang's hand with his right, Turk's hand with his left, and with Lucy gripping his arm, he clung to everything that was left in that broken room like it was his last hold on earth.

Because it was—and the blackness returned in a rush.

114

The Capitol
Washington, DC

Senator William Roper couldn't believe the world he was living in.

Changed in a second, reinvented in the blink of an eye, it was so far removed from the global reality of only a week prior that it was all he could do just to keep up—let alone figure out how to benefit.

First there was Makar Nikitin's death, a shocking turn of events Roper could have never imagined. While the nations held their breath to see who would seize the reins of power in Moscow and how they would respond to Nikitin's assassination, Roper only wanted to know the truth behind who had pulled the trigger.

The Lithuanians claimed ignorance, and their new president wasn't interested in investigating the question. NATO nations from Turkey to Germany to the United Kingdom all maintained their innocence. America, of course, toed the same line. It was the billion-dollar question that nobody would answer...and yet, swimming just beneath the surface of the sculpted political addresses and calibrated public statements, a whisper of common understanding underpinned it all. A sort of accepted reality that nobody would voice, nobody would question.

But everybody *knew* was there.

For his part, Roper had no doubts. He believed in his very bones that Maggie Trousdale had killed Nikitin—somehow, some way. It was the only thing that made sense, and with every fiber of his being he wanted to prove it...yet knew he never would.

Maggie Trousdale was no longer president, and following her exit from office, public opinion about the swamp girl had skyrocketed to an all-time high. Bigger than fame and stronger than glory, this public adoration burned Roper to his very soul even as he couldn't deny that it felt warranted.

The war in Europe was over. As quickly as it had begun, it was now in full collapse. Russian troops were withdrawing in orderly masses. NATO forces deployed across the Baltic, and Belorussia petitioned for peace.

In the Middle East victory seemed all but certain. Iran's Navy was destroyed, her forces reeling from combined onslaughts of United States Marines and Israeli Defense Forces. With the United Kingdom, Germany, and France pledging to enter the war in support of the existing US-Israeli coalition, it seemed only a matter of time before Iran answered calls for surrender...or else risked total destruction.

They were simply too weak without Russia to distract the West. Simply too outgunned. It was a lesson Tehran learned months too late...but Beijing was a lot smarter. The great sleeping dragon, withdrawing its naval forces back into Chinese ports and entering negotiations with the West to resolve outstanding political disputes, seemed content to sleep a while longer. To find a diplomatic route, or at least bide her time.

Whatever the case, nobody cared about Maggie Trousdale's numerous failures. Her rumored, hidden crimes. Her possible direct association with men like James O'Dell, who had already admitted to murdering on her behalf. All those sins, real or imagined, were forgiven—already forgotten.

The swamp girl was America's heroine, and by surrendering her office at the height of her golden hour, that legacy was all but certain to be written in stone.

Where did that leave Roper? he wondered as he sat slumped in a chair, watching his muted office TV play headlines on repeat, silent anchors pontificating about the as yet unanswered questions in this brave new world that Maggie had left. Issues such as a shaky economy, rampant inflation, skyrocketing oil prices and compromised international trade were all petty details that talking heads were happy to punt to another day.

Really, who cared? America had her fighting spirit back. Every battle was a battle destined to be won—if not now, then soon.

"Senator? I have a call for you."

Roper's intercom buzzed and he swore, slapping the answer key. "I told you not to—"

"Senator, it's the president."

Roper sat frozen in place, his unwashed shirt sticking to an unwashed body that must smell nearly as bad as that of his chief of staff. For the moment, White wasn't around. The office was empty save for Roper and the voice of his secretary.

"Sir? Should I put him through?"

Roper still didn't know what to say. He swallowed, snatched up the receiver, and managed a grunt.

Long pause. Seconds dripped by. Then a clear, crisp voice from just down the street on Pennsylvania Avenue filled Roper's ear.

"Hello, Matt."

Stratton's tone was neither friendly nor aggressive. Roper's mind snagged on that neutrality as his thoughts ping-ponged between the two options—whether this was a conciliatory call or an ambush.

Truth be told, Roper had never had much of an issue with Maggie's VP. Sure, Stratton was a historic Republican and Roper was a Democrat, but that hardly mattered. This was a game of power, not pretended policy. Roper's beef had always been with Maggie...

And yet Stratton was loyal to Maggie, or at least appeared to be. So maybe—

Stratton cut Roper's thoughts short.

"Maybe you're wondering whether I'm calling to extend an olive branch or slice your throat."

Roper swallowed. He couldn't help it. He leaned back and considered —then was angry with himself for the uncertainty.

What was he doing? This wasn't his style.

"Yeah, actually," he said. "I am."

"Well, as it turns out, it's neither. I haven't decided what to do with you yet."

There was an easy confidence to Stratton's tone that cut deep—a lethal warning that sank like a knife through Roper's armor. The new president didn't sound afraid. He didn't project bravado.

He sounded like he meant exactly what he said.

"So why are you calling?" Roper said, sudden venom fighting to poison his tone.

"To deliver a little piece of news—and orders to go with it."

"Orders? So you're my boss now?"

A short laugh. It was ice cold.

"No, Matt. I'm not your boss. I'm your *master*."

Roper's face flushed red. He sat forward. Before he could snap back, Stratton was speaking again.

"Just before signing her resignation letter, President Trousdale signed another document. Do you know what it was?"

Roper could guess, but he decided to let Stratton do the work.

"It was a full and unconditional pardon for Mr. James O'Dell," Stratton said. "A get-out-of-jail-free card...quite literally."

Roper's chest tightened. It was exactly what he feared. For three days in a row he'd tried to reach his contacts at the Justice Department, and everyone had either avoided him or claimed to know nothing about the James O'Dell investigation. It was a bad sign.

Now here was the proof in the pudding.

"Honestly, I wouldn't have done it," Stratton said. "Too much political liability. Between you and I, we still don't know exactly what he did or how *much* he did. At this point, I guess we never will. But you know what, Matt?"

The president was silent a long time—too long for Roper to ignore. Before he could stop himself, he was answering.

"*What?*"

"I was just thinking, it's actually better this way. For the whole messy, convoluted thing to just...fade away. Disappear from public view while other, more pressing business takes center stage. Stuff like negotiating with the new Russian regime. Securing liberation for the Caucasus. Keeping

China in her place. Rebuilding the economy. Heck, I'll say it. *Running for my next term.*"

Roper swallowed. His heart thumped faster. He was feeling the heat now. The rage. He wanted to reach through the phone and throttle Stratton—jamb his thumbs deep into both of those snotty, rich eyes. It was all he could think about.

But then, once more, Stratton was speaking.

"I guess what I'm saying, Matt, is this. Your little puppet game is *over*. Permanently. James O'Dell is off the hook, and there's not a thing you can do about it. Your whole operation falls apart without him, and if you're as smart as I think you are, you'll let it. You'll go back to sponsoring crummy legislation and grandstanding in front of every camera lens you can find. Actually, I hear that Governor Smith is retiring. Perhaps you could run to fill his seat? Make a nuisance out of yourself in Des Moines, for a change."

A pause. Roper heard the phone shift to Stratton's other ear. A seat creaked as the president sat up.

"Honestly, Matt, I don't care *what* you do. I just want you to know—to truly believe in your very soul—that I am going to lead this country out of the ashes. I am going to put her back on her feet, put money back in her pocket, put soldiers at her door and make sure she never loses another night's sleep. That her children are safe in school, her seniors secure in their retirement. I'm going to build America into the best possible version of herself. And if you get in my way, Matt—if I so much as *suspect* that you're conniving behind my back...*I will destroy you.*"

Stratton's voice turned granite hard and ice cold with the last four words. A frigid chill shot down Roper's back as the threat crackled into his ear.

He sat up. He almost dropped the phone. He fumbled for something to say in return.

But it didn't matter. President Jordan Stratton had already hung up.

115

Moscow, Russia

Maxim Romanov was on top of the world.

It was a smoking, shaking, bloody world. The ground beneath his feet seemed eggshell thin, ready to collapse at any moment. Every face he passed in the corridors of power across Moscow seemed caught someplace between terror and anger.

Some were Nikitin loyalists. Others were reacting, perhaps, out of vulnerability. The commands raining out of the Kremlin like machine gun bullets were unequivocally clear and reflected a 180-degree turn from pretty much every policy of the Nikitin regime.

Russian troops were ordered to withdraw from Europe. Russian naval and Air Force assets were directed into strictly defensive postures. Funds allocated for military expenses were diverted to stimulating a choking economy, pending the relaxation of Western sanctions. State police forces were deployed into every major Russian city, alongside executive orders issued for the immediate arrest of any "agitators."

And, yes, Romanov launched an "immediate investigation into the murder of the former president, Makar Nikitin."

That was just for show. Maybe most of the world knew it was for show.

Romanov wasn't a warrior and he lacked the killer instinct that had driven Nikitin to the very pinnacle of Russian power...but he understood a thing or two about political calculous.

He didn't *need* to bring the Russian people a head on a stake. He just needed to promise them the investigation was a top priority, let the details fade into the background...and then supply what they really wanted.

A better economy. Greater opportunities for their children. Security and peace. And no more conscriptions for a madman's war.

It was still a long shot, the craziest thing Romanov had ever attempted in his entire political career. The constant nausea rolling through his gut, and the tension in his chest, warned him that he was pushing his body to the limit, and he might not survive his own political coup.

But he had to *try*, because in this stormy world of opportunity, Romanov tasted something he had never experienced before. Something he'd never even considered if he wanted, or could obtain. A rich and intoxicating flavor that rolled smoother over his tongue than the finest red wine, and warmed his blood better than a hot fire on a cold winter night.

Power. True power.

Nikitin had built the stage...Now Maxim Romanov was stepping to the middle of it. And he liked it.

Exhausted after a long day of press conferences and meetings with the federal assembly, Romanov marched down marble hallways once occupied by Nikitin's regime, bypassing offices recently vacated by Nikitin loyalists whom Romanov had fired. In fact, the building was far quieter than it had been in some weeks, which was ironic given the turmoil sweeping the nation.

Romanov didn't mind the quiet. He was actually quite excited about it. A courier had just delivered a fresh meal of prime rib and fried potatoes from one of his favorite restaurants, and alone in the office that used to belong to Makar Nikitin, Romanov planned to hold a celebratory dinner.

It was his first opportunity since assuming office, and his political instincts informed him that it wasn't a stunt he should attempt in public view.

Again, Romanov didn't mind. Nikitin's old office was comfortable. There was a fireplace with gas logs. Plenty of good red wine on hand.

Romanov helped himself to a hefty glass and settled behind the desk. He tore into the prime rib, not even minding that it was lukewarm, and lost himself in the delight of a great meal in a great room at the end of a *great* week.

When the cigarette lighter sparked, Romanov almost came out of his skin.

Heart hammering, he spun in the chair to find a familiar face illuminated by the dancing flame, a dark form standing in the shadows barely six feet away. Ivan Sidorov's right arm was held in a sling, his right shoulder bandaged, but he managed the cigarette and the lighter with ease, inhaling a deep lungful of Russian smoke before breathing out...

Long. Slow. Soft. And the whole time, never taking his eyes off of Romanov.

"*Ivan!* What's wrong with you? How did you get in here?"

Ivan didn't answer either question. He dragged on the smoke again, then slowly removed it from his lips. He was still staring at Romanov, still unblinking.

Even as the wash of cortisol faded from Romanov's body, that unblinking stare birthed a new feeling in his stomach. Something a lot less sharp, but every bit as uncomfortable.

"What are you doing?" Romanov snapped. "You shouldn't be in here. This is a secured space! I could have you arrested."

"By who?" Ivan said, finally, tapping ash from his smoke straight onto the hardwood floor. "Your state police?"

Romanov frowned, momentarily confused. "What are you talking about?"

"*By order of the president, no assembly designed to agitate the public in opposition to the interests of peace shall be considered lawful until further notice.*"

Romanov recognized those words. They were taken straight from the executive order he had signed, authorizing national police to manage "agitators"...which was code, of course, for citizens of any creed who opposed the rapid change in national direction. He shook his head and cursed at the quote, sipping wine and turning back to his desk.

"Really, Ivan? Is that what you've come to harass me about? I'm managing a nation on ice! The people are terrified—they don't know who to trust. I'm protecting the peace."

Romanov stabbed a potato and chewed, that pit in his stomach still churning as Ivan remained behind him. Romanov refused to turn and look —he wouldn't validate Ivan in that way.

He kept chewing until, eventually, footsteps tapped. A tingle ran up Romanov's spine. Ivan circled in front of the desk, lifting the cigarette, inhaled...and then blew straight across Romanov's plate.

The acting president swore. Coughed. Waved his hand.

"Are you insane? Put that out!"

"What's wrong, Maxim. Are cigarettes an *agitation*?"

It was too much. Romanov burst from his chair, yanking the cloth napkin from his neck and throwing it to the table. He glared in the flickering firelight. Ivan stared right back.

"I am doing what I *must*," Romanov said. "It is not my desire to abridge anyone's liberty. As soon as the crisis has abated and stability is restored, the regulations will be lifted. Protests may resume—wherever, whatever. I don't care. You must believe that."

Romanov lifted his chin, standing his ground. Defying Ivan to say more, to challenge him further. Resting in the confidence that *he* was now in charge.

But what Ivan did next reopened the pit in Romanov's stomach and turned it into a black hole. Not a facial expression, not a word, just a slow lift of Ivan's bare finger. It reached Romanov's neck and traced upward.

It found the shallow wound, now scabbed over, where Ivan's switchblade had broken the skin in that restaurant bathroom.

No, not a switchblade, according to Ivan. That mark had been left by *the Russian people*.

Ivan touched the flabby skin. Pressed until Romanov trembled, then withdrew his hand and smiled.

"I do believe you, Maxim. And I anticipate you delivering on your promises...*as do the Russian people*. Enjoy your meal."

Then, without another word, Ivan Sidorov turned on the hardwood, lifted the cigarette to his lips, and vanished from the room in a cloud of silent gray.

116

Pope Army Airfield
Fort Bragg, North Carolina

The Air Force C-17 hit the tarmac with all the grace and majesty of an eagle gliding to rest on a mountain perch.

Landing gear down, kissing the tarmac. A puff of smoke and a soft squeal of brakes. The engines pounded so loud that the crowd of civilians waiting at the edge of the airfield were confined inside a utility building until the cargo jet had reached the end of the airstrip and turned slowly back around, rolling to a taxi before finally winding down its engines.

Surrounded by a crowd of eighty-four mothers, fathers, wives, and girlfriends, many of them waving the ten-inch American flags supplied by the Army, Banks clutched Davy close to her hip and fought with everything in her to not cry.

Eight weeks. It had been eight long weeks since she'd last seen Reed. During that time he had traveled around the world—she still wasn't exactly sure where. He'd charged into combat. He'd communicated in only broken, irregular phone calls, many of which were so one-sided that Banks might as well have been talking to a wall.

It had almost killed her. It was *still* killing her. With every moment that ground past that she didn't hear from Europe, the sleepless nights and burning anxiety developed closer and closer to meltdown status. She felt as though she was clinging to her very sanity by a thread, that she might have a nervous breakdown and be hospitalized in a psych ward.

Davy was the only thing that kept her going—just like Liberty was the only thing that kept Sinju going. Because breaking wasn't an option while their children depended on them. They had to be strong. They had to hang on.

And then the call came. Early in the morning, the number was unrecognized, but Banks's phone labeled it as originating in Germany. She answered to hear a familiar voice.

Lucy Byrne never identified herself. She wouldn't—maybe couldn't—go into specifics about where she was calling from or what the situation with Reed, Turk, and the rest of the team was. She merely advised Banks to get on a plane to North Carolina. To acquire a civilian pass from Fort Bragg. To be standing on the tarmac when this particular plane, apparently loaded with wounded members of the 82nd Airborne, returned to US soil.

So Banks did. She got up and called her manager and arranged for a private jet from Nashville to Fayetteville, North Carolina. She brought Sinju, Liberty, and Davy with her. They got a hotel and Banks worked the phone and eventually she found somebody in some department on Fort Bragg who was willing to talk to her.

Banks gave the name Reed Montgomery, and the officer informed her that no such person was listed on the manifest of the incoming flight. Banks's heart nearly exploded at that, but she held herself together long enough to ask about the names Rufus Turman, Lucy Byrne, and Wolfgang Pierce.

Also no record.

Okay, she thought. *Probably just a security measure.*

The next hurdle was acquiring a base pass. Banks was initially refused, as the officer insisted that the only way she could be present at the tarmac was if a member of her family was flying in. At that point Banks hung up the phone and called her manager back.

She got blunt. She cashed in a lot of accumulated political capital. The manager went to work calling friends of friends who were fans of the *Not Afraid* tour, and eventually, somebody knew an Army colonel.

Banks got her passes. She arrived at Polk Airfield two hours before the flight and politely secluded herself from the growing crowd of teary-eyed lovers and family members who assembled for the same purpose. A few of them recognized her—nobody was intrusive. The minutes crept by in slow motion while Davy ate animal crackers and Liberty crammed Cheerios.

Then the C-17 appeared. It touched down. The engines quit and the Army—finally—let everyone assemble outside. They were ordered to stand behind a white line while the Globemaster's ramp was lowered and lines of airborne heroes stepped off.

In wheelchairs. On crutches. Some with arms in slings. Some not visibly wounded at all. Four dozen soldiers in total, all with their heads held high and broad smiles directed at their cheering loved ones.

But no Reed. No Turk. Nobody Banks recognized.

Banks felt the tears bubbling up again and wasn't sure she could hold them back. She swallowed and glanced to Sinju. Turk's wife held her chin up, looking as iron as a statue. The last of the airborne troops met their families and began to move away from the tarmac. The C-17 was quiet...but the ramp was still down.

Then another wheelchair appeared—this one pushed by a woman so petite she almost appeared to be a child. Red hair, held back in a ponytail, was tousled by the wind as she guided the chair to the end of the ramp and turned it. Banks saw both faces and gasped before she could stop herself. Her hand snapped to her mouth.

It was Lucy Byrne pushing Wolfgang Pierce...and Wolfgang's legs were gone. Missing so close to the hip that fully half the chair's seat was visible despite the blanket covering his lap. He sat up with an IV line running from his arm to a medicine bag. His face was twisted with pain.

But he saw Banks, he saw Sinju...and he nodded. Just once. He patted Lucy's arm, and she stopped halfway between the plane and the crowd. She turned the chair, and they both looked back to the C-17. Banks held her breath.

Then Rufus Turkman appeared, a thick bandage wrapped around his neck, a crutch under his left arm. He limped down the ramp one half step at a time, reaching the tarmac and turning in the sun. Straightening and squinting toward the crowd—raising his free hand to shield his eyes.

Sinju broke. She screamed. She ran with baby Liberty right past the white line, defiant of a shouting Army MP. She threw herself at Turk, and long before she arrived, Turk was crying also. He opened his arms, dropping the crutch and not seeming to notice. He hugged his wife. Swept her up, swung his daughter into his arms and kissed her and cried.

Banks just...stood. Mouth half open. Watching and feeling suddenly dead inside. Empty.

Where was he?

Lucy started forward again, pushing Wolfgang. She moved with difficulty, her legs stiff and her body a little bent. With every rattle of the chair, Wolfgang winced, his jaw locked so tight against the pain that veins bulged in his temple. As they drew near, Banks noticed scars on his arms and skull—stitch marks and staples and horrible black bruises. Wolfgang was a bit glassy-eyed by the drugs, but he looked right at her as Lucy stopped the chair. They both did.

Banks swallowed. The cavern in her stomach opened a little wider. She was afraid to ask.

Wolfgang broke the silence, his voice so hoarse she barely recognized it.

"He's alive, Banks. He's on the plane."

Banks's heart leapt. Something between euphoria and raw adrenaline surged her veins. She started forward.

Lucy caught her. "Banks."

Banks stopped. Looked down and frowned in confusion—sudden fear.

"He..." Lucy hesitated. "He didn't want you to be here."

"What?" The word left her mouth like a bullet.

"He was injured, Banks. Badly. His face is messed up, and he can't see. He'll...never be able to see."

The cavern returned—momentary dread. Uncertainty. Fear.

And then absolute disregard. Banks jerked free and ran. The MP shouted, and she kept going. Davy slammed against her hip and started to cry and she didn't stop. She ran all the way to the base of the ramp, the tears leaking out as she scraped to a halt.

She looked into the shadows of the hulking aircraft, a bay only illuminated by soft LED lights. The floor was blank, the jump seats empty...

All except for the lone wheel chair halfway down the length of the aircraft.

Slowly, Banks squatted. Her arms trembled as she set Davy down, his little tennis shoes squishing on the asphalt.

"Mommy?"

"Stay here, baby."

Her voice was dry as Banks said it. From her peripheral she saw the MPs coming, but they were only coming at half speed. Not *really* trying to stop her.

She released Davy and stood again. She started up the ramp. Shadows closed over her. Her feet tapped against metal, her dress swishing against her knees. She edged closer to the middle of the plane and found a lone figure seated in the wheelchair. Bent over. His face turned away.

Banks stopped ten feet away. "Reed?"

No answer. Her stomach quaked, agitated by fresh anxiety. She started forward again. She made it only one step.

"Please don't, Banks."

She stopped. Her jaw trembled. The airplane was so quiet she could hear her own breath—and hear his. Rushing. Hissing. Not sounding right.

"Reed, I'm here."

She said it and she meant it. Banks started forward again. She reached the chair and circled around, hit her knees. She touched Reed's arms, and she saw his face.

It was bandaged, all over. His eyes were wrapped and only his lips and nose were visible. The skin of both was cherry red and mottled—burn scars, she knew. Just the sight of them unleashed a fresh wave of pain, but not for herself. Reed was shaking, his hands quivering. He tried to pull away from her.

Banks grabbed his arms. Sank her fingers in. She was crying, but her voice never wavered.

"Reed. *Stop.*"

Silence inside the airplane. Banks swallowed back the emotion.

She looked into her husband's face, knowing she could never again look into his eyes...and all she could think was: *He's home.*

"I am *so glad* you're back," she whispered. "Welcome home."

Then Banks wrapped Reed in a hug. She cried, and he shook.

117

Livingston Parrish
Louisiana

It wasn't Air Force One—not anymore—but the Boeing jet that carried Maggie out of Washington, DC, ten days after her resignation as president was actually the same aircraft that she'd flown all over the nation and across the world in. Now it just wasn't hers—it was on loan from Jordan Stratton.

It took ten days for Maggie to be ready to leave. As it turned out, departing the White House was a lot more complicated than just signing a resignation. Stratton needed support in the transition, which she felt that she owed him. Also, in truth, Maggie wasn't in the physical *condition* to travel. She actually spent three nights at Walter Reed, where she finally confessed to her doctors, on record, about her opioid problem.

Nobody was surprised. Nobody was unkind. The adoration spilling from every TV and news room in the country seemed to infect even Maggie's private staff. They cared for her with a dedication that somehow felt unmatched even by their previous three years of remarkable service.

The doctors spoke to her about a realistic treatment plan for the addiction—a slow and gradual removal of the drugs which would lead to sobriety without sending her body into shock. They recommended a rehab program as soon as Maggie returned home—and when she touched down in New Orleans to a crowd of seven thousand flag-waving supporters, Maggie already had her reservation in hand.

Eight months in a secluded facility in northern Louisiana. Guided medical care, great food, lots of rest...it sounded like paradise. But first Maggie had some people to meet.

A Secret Service Tahoe sat ready to collect her as she exited the plane, lifting a hand to the cheering crowd but not stopping to deliver a speech. The truth was, it was difficult to stand and wasn't easy to talk. It was as though all the exhaustion she had denied for so many months was finally catching up with her, released through floodgates by her resignation.

She didn't know if she would *ever* be ready for the public eye again. She didn't know if she wanted to be. She only knew that she wanted to reserve all her strength for the one difficult conversation ahead. A moment alone in the woods at the cabin by Lake Maurepas, in the minutes before her loving family arrived to gather her up and welcome her home.

The Secret Service provided both drivers and a secondary vehicle loaded with additional security personnel. It was a hefty crew, but by direction of President Stratton, Maggie's post-administration detail was to remain at elevated staff levels until further notice.

America loved their swamp girl, and America couldn't afford any more tragedies.

Up the bumping swamp roads, between the draping trees that Maggie loved so much. Even before she opened her door, the scent of the water and the mud and all that damp vegetation filtered into her lungs and brought a life to her blood that she hadn't felt in...*so long*. When the Tahoe stopped and her driver opened the door, Maggie dropped her feet onto the gravel but didn't immediately stand.

She just surveyed the trees. Inhaled the dead grass. Listened to the distant chirp of birds. Watched a squirrel dance between bushes.

And she smiled. Not for the cameras, or the nation, or for anybody watching. Just for herself.

An agent helped her out of the car and guided her around the nose of the Tahoe toward the front porch of the cabin. Maggie ignored the rental car she passed, keeping her eyes on the distant lake until she reached the steps and leveraged the handrail to guide herself up.

When she reached the top, the agents withdrew—but they didn't depart. Maggie looked left to her grandfather's empty rocker, worn and stained. She noted the carvings in the floorboards left by her cousins and their Swiss Army knives.

Finally, she looked right, toward her grandmother's swing...and the tall, broad Cajun standing in front of it.

"Would you give us a minute?" Maggie asked.

She was looking at O'Dell, but the Secret Service knew who she was addressing.

"Ma'am...we would prefer—"

"Please," Maggie said.

The agents lingered a moment longer, then they acquiesced and withdrew to their vehicles. Maggie started across the deck and stopped a few feet from O'Dell. She looked into his strong face, his deep eyes. She noted the tears shimmering there, and felt some of the same in her own.

But she denied them.

"Hello, James."

O'Dell extended a hand. Maggie didn't accept it. She sat in another rocking chair near the swing. She wrapped her White House hoodie tighter around her body and looked out over the water. She didn't say anything until O'Dell eventually took his seat.

"I...I wanted to thank you," O'Dell said. "For the pardon. I never expected it. I would have completely understood if it was better for you to..."

He trailed off, and Maggie closed her eyes. Fought back more tears. Swallowed a lump in her throat and tried not to be sucked in to all the memories, the late nights. The confusion and the longing and that connection born out of so many suppressed desires.

Was it love? Had it ever been?

She didn't know. Maybe it was only the lust of the moment. Maybe it didn't matter, either way. All that was behind them. Only one question hung in the air.

"James," Maggie said. "I have to know."

The quiver in O'Dell's lip told her that it was the last thing he wanted to hear. He looked away, closed his eyes, breathed a curse. But he didn't get up and he didn't run. Maggie waited.

Finally, he nodded.

"I killed him."

"For the liver?"

"Yes."

"And…O'Brien?"

O'Dell's eyes opened. A heavy tear slipped out. He locked gazes with her, but this time he didn't answer.

He didn't need to.

Maggie looked back to the lake, and the crushing sadness in her gut eased a little as confusion took its place. Confliction, maybe. A storm of uncertainty.

And guilt, too. Real guilt. How had it ever come to this? How had somebody she trusted, somebody she might have even loved…

"It was my choice," O'Dell said. "They both were. You had nothing to do with it. I did what I did and…"

He stopped. Maybe he realized the monologue was going nowhere. He rested both palms on his knees and rubbed them as though he was wiping sweat away. He breathed deep.

Then he asked his own question.

"I also have to know."

Fair is fair.

Maggie reviewed her thoughts one more time. Her emotional and moral logic, if that was a thing. She probed and questioned it, but really there was nothing to second-guess. She knew how she felt.

She knew who she was.

"I want you to know why I pardoned you," Maggie said. "You have to know that it wasn't because of anything between us, or even to save my own skin. I pardoned you for the simple reason that this country can't handle any more internal division. It's going to be all Jordan can do to put us back on the rails—to restore the economy, to stabilize the globe. We can't afford any more distractions."

Maggie stopped. James said nothing. He was still waiting...and she knew why.

"We've both spent the last three years making choices that we'll live with the rest of our lives," Maggie said. "Maybe you're thinking that you're not the only one who got too pragmatic—who crossed a line and even lived on the other side of it. Maybe...you're right. All I know is, I have to draw a line somewhere. And whether it's just or logical or pure hypocrisy... I'm drawing it here, James. I'm...I'm drawing it with you."

O'Dell said nothing. He sat still for a long time, and the lead anchor in Maggie's gut pressed her into the chair. It crushed her. It made it hard to breathe, but she never looked away.

She looked him right in the eye, without judgment or condescension or anything but honesty.

He looked back, just as raw and honest, and eventually, he nodded. He stood, the swing creaking as its springs retracted. He stepped across the deck and stopped at the steps and looked out over the lake. When he finally turned back, his eyes were sadder than those of any man Maggie had ever seen. And yet he smiled, just a little.

"For the record...if you'd said anything else, you wouldn't be the woman I want."

Maggie's eyes moistened. Her throat went dry, and her lips parted, but she didn't have anything to say.

James O'Dell broke the silence for her.

"Goodbye, Madam President."

"Goodbye, James," Maggie managed.

Without another word, O'Dell descended the steps and crossed over the gravel. His car door opened and shut. The engine purred and gradually grew distant.

Maggie sat on the porch all alone, her eyes closed as she shrank into her hoodie and tasted the flavor of the swamps and for the first time in so very long...accepted the moment for exactly what it was.

Not for what it would bring. Not for what she needed to make out of it.

Just a moment with the mud that gave birth to everything she ever loved.

It was good to be home.

118

Nashville, Tennessee
Three Months Later

The apartment in the Gulch was never actually quiet.

Even on afternoons like this, when Reed sat alone on the edge of the bed in his and Banks's bedroom, the AC turned off and the TV silenced and the laundry machines not running, there was still the traffic. The laughter of bachelorettes on pedal taverns and party buses. The bark of dogs. The hammer of endless construction.

Maybe they were sounds Reed wouldn't have noticed before. Maybe it was only here, in the absolute dark, that he could truly appreciate all the little noises that now served as his most tangible connection to surroundings out of reach.

The tick of a clock. The hum of a computer fan. The gentle creek of joists as an upstairs neighbor padded across a carpeted floor.

Such subtle sounds. Such trivial things. And yet suddenly...they were all that was left.

That, and the pistol in Reed's hand.

The SIG P226 Legion was his favorite gun. This specific model, purchased in a gun shop in Franklin not long after he and Banks moved to

Nashville, felt like an extension of his arm. Every part, every polished piece, so familiar to his touch that he could disassemble, reassemble, load, and fire it all blindfolded. He'd done so before—all except the firing part —as a training exercise, maybe just in case he needed to manipulate the weapon in the dark.

Now the world was always dark—empty despite the random obstacles that Reed stumbled into a hundred times a day. Like a metaphor for his entire existence, every horrible moment since his father disappeared and his mother ran off the rails and the killing—*so much killing*—took their place...it was all a pitch-black pit. An endless valley.

And yet the P226 Legion was as familiar as ever, an old friend, cold and hard. Alone on the edge of the bed with Banks and Davy gone across the street to the grocery store...Reed found the weapon. He withdrew it from its box. He disassembled it on the bed, reassembled, and loaded it. He tested the trigger with one finger.

He sat perfectly still and embraced the still-pulsating pain of the burn wounds that covered his face and arms, and closed his eyes just to sink a little deeper into the gloom. To bathe himself in the pain, the emptiness, the absolute solitude.

And to face it, like a man, once and for all. Stand right at the edge and accept a truth he'd run from for years.

You deserve this—you always have. You danced with death—now death has come to you.

The computer fan hummed. A party bus rolled by. Reed breathed deep and held the gun with his finger on the trigger. He sat staring into that abyss in his mind and wondered if it was finally time to surrender. To forget everything. To just let go...

"I found a way out of the darkness. I found the light."

Out of nowhere Lucy's voice echoed in his mind. It was that thing she said in Poland, right before the mission launched. He remembered and hot fire entered his veins. Pure rage, maddening and shaking.

Light? Really? Was this a sick joke?

Reed's jaw closed. His fingers tightened and he lifted the pistol. He placed the cold muzzle beneath this chin—he gritted his teeth.

And he made a deal. With himself, with the darkness. With anything or any*body* who dared to listen.

If there was something, he wanted to see it. *Right now.*

And if not...he was out.

Ten seconds—blackness. Reed's finger curled a little tighter around the trigger.

Twenty seconds—a void. He began to sweat, his tongue darting across his lips.

Thirty seconds—vacancy and shadow. Just that same miserable *nothing*. Exactly what he expected, exactly what he always *told* fools like Lucy. Reed's body turned rigid. He lifted his chin and defied the abyss, at the same time ready to throw himself into it.

If this was all—*fine*.

He began to squeeze.

Then...something.

Distant and vague, like the first hint of dawn in the eastern sky. It began as only a pinprick, at first so faint he thought he imagined it...but then it danced. It drew closer, and larger, and Reed began to shake. He didn't know why, but he wanted to look away. He blinked behind the blindfold, and his heart accelerated.

He *couldn't* look away.

Then it was on him. All at once, a crushing wave as bright as the midday sun in an open field. It blazed from overhead and from every side. It beat down on him, not hot but overwhelmingly warm. It burst out of the void and Reed felt it in his very blood, pulsating through his chest. His trembles turned to shakes, the pain in his face and his arms growing sharper.

Then he saw Banks. Just like that, as clear as a picture. She spun in a summer dress with her head thrown back, laughing. He saw Turk pushing Liberty on a swing. Sinju holding a belly swollen with their unborn son. Wolfgang, still riding a wheelchair, pushing himself around a bumpy backyard and throwing a football with Davy. Reed's son laughed and called Wolfgang "uncle"—he tackled him in the chair, and Wolfgang nearly went over, laughing also.

They were Reed's people—all of them that remained. *Still there.*

And then, out of nowhere, a hand. It reached straight from the dark. It pierced the black sky and touched him. The moment Reed felt it, the pain in his arms and face simply vanished—disappeared. Overwhelming calm took their place.

Then, a booming call. It was something else Lucy had said, but it wasn't her voice.

"Even in the valley of the shadow."

Reed's eyes snapped open. The light and the warmth and the hand vanished. It was all just irregular murk again—but still that voice pounded through his mind, the strongest and somehow most comforting thing he'd ever heard.

Even in the valley of the shadow.

Reed swallowed. He found his heart thumping. He relaxed his finger off the trigger, and suddenly the gun felt heavy. It felt very, *very* heavy. Like a backpack full of bricks he'd been carrying his whole life, and never really thought about, but all of a sudden it was too much. More than he could take. More than he wanted to ever carry again.

He dropped it. It clattered to the hardwood floor.

And Banks gasped.

Reed's head snapped toward the sound. He hadn't heard her enter—he didn't know how he could have missed her. Now that his mind returned to the present, he realized there were lots of sounds he had missed. He heard Davy making truck noises from the living room. The TV playing a children's show. The HVAC running.

And Banks, crying.

"Reed?"

Reed got off the bed. He rushed past it. His foot hit a baseboard and he smashed his toes but he didn't care. He reached Banks and he threw both arms around her and pulled her close. He buried his face, ugly and burned and blind, into her shoulder. He held her like he hadn't held her in years—like he needed her. Like she was the best thing in his life. He kissed her neck. Stroked her hair. Pulled her in until she stopped crying. Squeezed and shook.

When he finally withdrew, he was crying himself, the tears stinging his sensitive skin, but he didn't care. He lifted a hand, trembling, and laid it on her face. Touched her nose, her chin. Traced her cheekbones.

And then smiled. Breathed a short little gasp.

He saw her—he saw the light again. It was there in his mind. It was the best thing he could remember feeling in years.

And that voice—it was still there. Calling to him. Promising *the light*.

"I see you," he whispered.

"Yeah?" Banks's voice was wet. Soft.

"I do," Reed said. "And I want the light, Banks. I'm going to find the light."

Line of Fire
Ian Hale Book 1

Betrayed. Hunted. Driven by duty.

Born into a legacy of heroes, Ian Hale ascended from the 75th Ranger Regiment to Delta Force, dedicating his life to the cause of freedom. But when a Black Hawk crash ends his military career, he is left searching for purpose—until Sentinel offers him a fresh start. A private military firm known for its high-stakes operations, Sentinel promises danger and noble causes, the perfect match for his skillset. Or so it seems.

Hale's latest mission is simple: rescue a kidnapped business executive from South Sudan. But when his team is ambushed and slaughtered, leaving Hale as the sole survivor, he's forced to confront the truth—he's been set up. Someone wants his team dead, and they'll stop at nothing to finish the job.

Now, Hale is a man on the run, hunted by enemies who underestimate his resolve. With only his loyal handler, Laney Shaw, to trust, he launches a one-man war for the truth, uncovering a conspiracy that traces back to the very heart of the nation he so loves.

But Ian Hale was born for this fight, and surrender isn't an option. It never was.

ABOUT THE AUTHOR

Logan Ryles was born in small town USA and knew from an early age he wanted to be a writer. After working as a pizza delivery driver, sawmill operator, and banker, he finally embraced the dream and has been writing ever since. With a passion for action-packed and mystery-laced stories, Logan's work has ranged from global-scale political thrillers to small town vigilante hero fiction.

Beyond writing, Logan enjoys saltwater fishing, road trips, sports, and fast cars. He lives with his wife and three fun-loving dogs in Alabama.

Sign up for Logan Ryles's reader list at
severnriverbooks.com